The CORNCRAKE

Charles Moberly

Tancava
PRESS

The Corncrake

by Charles Moberly

ISBN

978-1-7398800-2-6 Paperback

978-1-7398800-3-3 e-book

Published by Tancava Press

https://charlesmoberlyauthor.blogspot.com/

part one

1909

part one

. . .

1909

22nd May 1909

Tristram is coming home tonight, after four months in Germany. How I have missed him. It was Helga who wanted him to stay in Leipzig with her Uncle Gerd. She has always insisted that both our children should learn about their German heritage, ever since they were small. I do not like it, but I have to accept it, being married to a foreigner. And it has been a good opportunity for Tristram to visit another country between school and Oxford.

I have chosen *The Return of the Prodigal Son* as the text for my sermon tomorrow. Not that Tristram has been extravagant in any way, but I cannot resist the jest. More excusably, the parable bears the simple messages of Our Lord: forgiveness and love.

I find myself pacing my study, pausing at the window to see how far the sun has dropped towards Lyme Bay. I cannot wait to tell Tristram what has happened on the farm since he went away. Adela has missed him too, I know she has. I am a bit worried about my daughter. That youth Thomas Knowles has been paying rather too much attention to her. There is nothing wrong with him in his limited way, but she is far too young to be contemplating romantic attachments. When I was courting Helga I was, Heavens, already halfway to being ordained. I had taken very little interest in young ladies before I met Helga, and Adela is only sixteen.

I don't think I'm going to get much sleep tonight. Papa says I can stay up late to meet Tristram's train at Lyme Regis. I wonder if he's changed. How I envy him; to have travelled, and above all to Germany, the land of Schumann, Bach, and our dear Mama.

Mama encourages us to explore our German roots. Papa says it's all to do with cricket. He says Mama's sent Tristram to a country where they don't do anything as English as play cricket. He's joking of course. Papa says Tristram's so good that he'll go straight into the University Eleven in his first year. He was captain of cricket at school, and rugby; and he's won a scholarship, so Papa won't have to pay a penny of his fees.

Thomas Knowles tried spooning with me today. He's a bit awkward, but kind and quite good looking. Not as good looking as Tristram, of course. No one is. I've told myself that I mustn't compare them. Thomas isn't captain of anything, and I don't mind that. But I can't help comparing him to

Tristram as a… as a… I can't say it. Go on, say it. A man.

23rd May 1909

My husband *ist so frech*. As the text for his sermon, Richard chose *The Return of the Prodigal Son*. Tut, tut; it was not at all appropriate, but I do not think that Tristram was minding. Adela was smiling and looking down, as she always is doing when she is uncertain of something.

After we had returned from Church and had finished our lunch, we assembled in the drawing room, as usual. Tristram announced that he had small gifts for each of us.

'For you, Mother, this small trinket.'

It was true that it was small, but trinket it was not. He has bought me the most exquisite brooch made of pearls and amethysts. I shall wear it with my green gown of *mousseline de soie* tonight.

Richard was receiving a shepherd's crook with a head carved in boxwood, made in Austria actually, but purchased in *Katharinenstraße*. For Adela, it was a book of poems by Nietzsche, in German. I froze, then darted a glance at Richard. Nietzsche, the author of *Ecce Homo* and *Der Antichrist*; the German philosopher who some claim has made atheism respectable. Richard was smiling, and I was concluding that he must be knowing nothing of Nietzsche.

'Not love poems, I trust? We must remember our daughter's age.'

'No, Father,' Tristram replied, 'they are about life.'

Adela frowned. 'I don't think that learning about life will do me harm.'

She is devout. For her Confirmation she was studying with diligence. But we must not deny her the opportunity of seeing the frailties of the world and of understanding its temptations. Whatever Richard may be saying, she is no longer innocent. When I hear her playing Liszt's *Mephisto Waltzes*, I can tell that she is understanding the passions of humanity. As for Tristram, a young man should be seeing all perspectives before he is forming his opinions. And there is more to Nietzsche than the hard-minded philosopher. I know; *Also Sprach Zarathustra* I have read.

The day thou gavest Lord is ended... My sister sings divinely. Her voice rises above the other members of the choir with effortless ease. I can't help watching her. Her face is full of devotion, which I find both fascinating and disturbing.

I feel the beauty of the liturgy too, but I know it's fickle. I'm seduced by the ritual, the sacrament, the unity of purpose. Isn't this a form of collective hysteria? The candles flicker, the beams high above us lurch and quiver in their light, and the church is full of gratitude and peace. We escape the world in here, but the world goes on outside, with its greed and pettiness and the grim realities of the hovels not half a mile away. We're beguiled into imagining we're sharing love, yet will Abel Hopkins and Noah Sunter hate each other any less when they meet in the fields tomorrow?

This achieves nothing, except to salve the consciences of those who should be doing something to improve the world. Nietzsche is right. People crave religion as a sanctuary from facing up to the challenges of life.

But it is beautiful.

My wife Helga has trained the choir to a state where they and those who hear them believe that perfection is attainable. And above them, the voice of my daughter soars like an angel.

Outside, the world's troubles continue. But in here there is Peace, the Peace of our Lord God Almighty. The doors are open to all who would come at this evening hour to take refuge, to praise, to renew their Faith and Trust in their Maker, and to feel His Divine Love. And look, so many have done so. Most of the village is here.

I am proud, proud of my wife and daughter, and proud of my flock. I am delighted that my Church can provide succour to so many. Forgive me, Lord; I should be humble, but may I not be thankful for all thy manifold blessings?

I am privileged to enjoy two vocations: the Church and my farm. One is the path that I have chosen; the other I inherited from my father. I love them both. I am vicar and gentleman farmer or, as my friend William Sawbridge once put it, pastor and pastoralist. I can move from one to the other in a matter of minutes. Just now, I walked from Church down through Hodges' fields to inspect my own land in the last of the evening light. Rain clouds were soon massing in the west, so I had to scuttle back before I got drenched. Back here in my study, surrounded by my favourite authors, Milton, Whitfield, and Bunyan, I find my mind wandering back to the farm.

I try to govern my life according to the teachings of our Saviour, but when it comes to agriculture, it is my own son and his inheritance that I think of. I cannot claim to be like Tristram, nor to possess his talents. He has a questioning energy which comes from his mother. This gives him a restlessness which I sometimes admire and sometimes fear. But one thing we share in common is a love of the countryside and of the farm. He is wise. No, that is not quite right; he is insightful. Left to himself, he does outrageous things, devoid of common sense, like when he corrected his headmaster on a point of history in front of the whole school on speech day. I admire his intellect more than his judgement, and do not always take his advice.

I do not know whether he will like what I have done. Once more, I find that I am on my feet, pacing in anticipation of showing him how we have progressed in his absence. I do hope he will be impressed.

24th May 1909

I had offered a brief prayer for a fine day, so that Tristram might see the land at its best. Perhaps a light drizzle was the most I could hope for from this wretched summer. Oh well.

I was about to harness Polly to the gig, when Tristram asked if we might ride. I was delighted. On most days I drive on my rural round of parish visits and, although I often walk the farm on foot, it is impossible to cover the whole area in one morning, so I sometimes ask for my cob Samuel to be saddled.

Tristram's bay gelding, Leander, had not been ridden for several weeks, so I was a bit worried at how he might behave. The tall thoroughbred was certainly on his toes, but Tristram sat him magnificently and soon had him relaxed, if eager.

We rode down past Gore's Clump and into Coney Piece. It is the best grazing on the farm, and I wanted to show this field to Tristram first. My new fatstock cattle, all Red Devons, were there and they looked splendid.

'So you do believe in beasts other than Shorthorns and Galloways after all?'

'I thought that you would like them,' I replied, pleased that he approved, and ignoring his good-natured jibe.

I decided that it was the right moment to break a less pleasant piece of news.

'We have lost Luscombe. He has left the farm.'

Tristram wheeled Leander round to face me, so that I had to pull up sharply on Samuel.

'No, Father, why?'

'It is all part of the drift away from the land. Now that the railway has come to Lyme Regis, there are factories springing up this side of Axminster. He has taken a job as chief engineer at Tubman's.'

Luscombe had been toolmaker, saddler, wheelwright, cooper, harness maker, and carpenter. His workshop had been the hub of the farm. A twenty-year-old plough would have been repaired so many times by Luscombe that few of the original parts remained. He would replace broken and bent mouldboards, coulters and axletrees. Tools were made bespoke for each worker. If a man was left-handed, short of stature, or was experiencing problems with his back, Luscombe would fashion the implement according to the need. If a hedger came to him complaining that his billhook chafed, Luscombe would replace the handle and reset the shaft. When gamekeeper stalked poacher who in turn stalked pheasant in Longside Wood at night, both would have been equipped by the hand of Luscombe. He made the simplest of implements: wooden rakes, four-tined forks and sickles. But he just as readily embraced the new technologies, such as the Hornsby self-binding reaper and the Lister petrol engine, as though he had invented them himself. Now who will maintain them? Who will I find to love them?

'Why did you let him go?'

The question stung me. 'Can you imagine the wage of the chief engineer at Tubman's?' I nudged Samuel on. 'We cannot compete on pay.'

'Then we must find some other way.'

'If you can think of one, I assure you that I will listen carefully.' I was trying not to sound peevish.

'Leave it to me, Father. I'll come up with something.' I did not care for the implication that I had failed to do anything about it.

The rain was coming down harder. The horses were twisting to reduce their profiles to the wind. Leander was cantering sideways at the pace of a walk and fighting the bit, so I suggested that they take a gallop up Topgallant Tump to shed some energy. They returned in no time, Leander still tittuping and tossing his head. We crossed the stream by Whiteman's Bridge, Leander's hooves setting up a clattering on the planks, and rode into the fields of young corn.

'It is coming on far too slowly,' I said. 'The decision to grow more oats this year may yet be proved right, but it will only be a matter of Divine Providence. Even if we have two full months of sun, we will do well to get twenty bushels to the acre, and I cannot see that we will harvest before Lammas.'

'And I suppose the hay crop's going to be poor this year?'

'The hay,' I replied neutrally. 'We will come to that.'

Tristram looked at me sharply, but said nothing. We hadn't far to go before he would see my surprise. I squeezed Samuel and we jogged down past Reed Pond and then cantered up the short rise past Turner's Piece, where I caught a glimpse of Ned, the shepherd boy, tending our flock of Hampshire Downs. We descended again to where wide fields stretched away to the river. Normally, these were grazed in spring and late summer, but left for hay in May and June.

Tristram reined in abruptly. 'Look there, over there, some cattle have got into the hayfields.'

'Relax,' I said. 'They are meant to be there.'

'But not now, surely? We're only a few weeks away from haymaking. They'll trample the crop to pieces.'

'Not this year,' I replied, enjoying my moment of surprise. 'The cattle will soon be gone. They are only in there briefly, and at a very low density; about one beast to every ten acres. This is going to be a hay meadow, a traditional one. It will not be cut until the end of July, and this year we are going to reap by hand.'

'By hand? You mean with horses rather than steam?'

'No, I do not mean that. I mean by hand, the old way, by men with scythes, working the fields like they did fifty years ago, then pulling the hay into ridges with wooden forks.'

'What's the point of that?'

'Do you not see, Tristram? Here is the purpose, to preserve this. A month ago, it was full of orchids and marsh marigolds. Now we have the pinks of campion and corncockle, the blue of bugle and speedwell, and white cuckooflower blushed with lilac. Next month it will be meadowsweet, poppies and oxeye daisies. I have been working quietly towards this for some time. I hope for snakeshead fritillaries. Hay meadows are dying out all over England, because they are cut too early and too rapidly. Reapers tearing through in June or early July give the wildflowers and ground nesting birds no chance. The corncrakes are back. There are at least a couple of nesting pairs in there; you can hear them every evening. You should come down here at dusk. Next year there will be many more, if we stick to my plan. See there, those grey feathery leaves, that is silverweed. In a month's time it will be covered in yellow flowers. The corncrakes love those. Yes, these are the corncrake fields.'

The wind had dropped. The sun, fitful between clouds drifting across the land, was hot on our faces. Here, even at the edge, we could hear the rising and fading hum of thousands of insects. Butterflies rose, fell and flitted above and through the forming heads of grass. A green and blue dragonfly darted, hovered and darted again.

My heart was beating faster. I could wait for his opinion no longer. 'Well, what do you think?'

'I think, Father, that this is your plaything.' And more than that he would not say.

We rode up the side of the meadow. Leander had calmed down. I kept glancing across at Tristram swaying beside me, but could detect no expression of feeling.

We entered the yard. Tristram leapt from his horse just as Malpiero ran up to take the bridle. I swung stiffly off Samuel, patted him, and led him towards his stable. Young Peter came tumbling out of the Great Barn, one hand holding his trousers and the other brushing across his face as he tried to disguise the fact that he was still chewing.

'I am sorry to disturb your lunchtime,' I said to

Malpiero, who had returned from seeing to Leander. 'I will untack Samuel myself. You two get back to your lunch break.' Of course, it was useless. Malpiero paid no heed. It was a matter of pride that his master need never attend to his horse while he was around.

'Come,' I said to Tristram, 'you must see the new layout of the cow-house and dairy before we go in.

'See,' I said proudly, 'we will soon conform to all the new hygiene regulations, and more. The cows will no longer face each other head-to-head. That reduces the risk of tuberculosis. I am throwing out all the old wooden utensils; only brass, steel, galvanised iron and glass from now on. I have ordered a totally new set of churns, and equipment for the dairy: hydrometers, coolers, sterilisers and cream separators; all new.'

'Father, you can be quite the essence of progress.'

'Thank you, but I must confess that milking will remain something of a headache. Fewer young men and women want to work with cows these days. It is especially difficult to get them to attend on Sundays, which is understandable, since it is the day when everyone takes their leisure. They want to be with their loved ones, and my conscience is not easy making them work on the Lord's Day. I wish I knew where the answer lay.

'Can I think about it, Father? I'd like to treat this as my project, if you'll let me. And the loss of labour to the factories.'

'I should be glad, my boy. I shall not have you for much longer, and any help you can give me before you go up to Oxford will be most welcome.'

Pleased, I absentmindedly walked across the yard and into the Great Barn, meaning to collect my new shepherd's crook, which I had left there earlier. Tristram followed. I was so preoccupied with the morning's events that I had completely forgotten that the men would be in the Barn having their lunch. Over half the farmhands were there, seated on crates, bales of straw, and upturned barrels. I had not thought to disturb them, but they put down their tin plates and clambered to their feet, one or two murmuring a greeting to Tristram, who had followed me. I apologised for the intrusion, but Jack Hearn responded that it was an honour to be visited, and there were quite a few 'hear, hears' to that. I instantly said Grace, and the enthusiasm of the 'Amens' put me at my ease. The men smile little, but they let one know when one's presence is accepted. I told them a joke about a farmer and a bull, which they seemed to like.

Back at my desk, I reflect that it has been a good day. I have both impressed Tristram and astonished him, which may mean more to him. It is foolish, I know. He was only in Leipzig a few months. He has been away at school many times for almost as long, and will be so again when he goes to Oxford in four months' time. But I could not help worrying that he might have lost his affection for this place by spending time in a German city. Yes, I admit it, I was frightened of losing him. If that is a sin, Lord, - covetousness? - then forgive me, you who know what it is to have sacrificed your only Son.

Tristram was badly thrown when I told him the news of Luscombe. He has said that he will give his attention to the problem of losing men to the towns. I hope that he does, because I have no solution. I believe that we treat the men well enough, but we cannot compete on pay.

My ride with Father this morning made me realise what I'd been missing. I hardly thought of Chaddingley when I was in Leipzig, except that when I saw something especially interesting, I wished I could share it with Adela. Leipzig was exciting, but this is where I really belong, with the rain and wind on my face and the light shifting and changing across the land. And Father. Who'd have thought he'd modernise the dairy like that? He, who so blindly and without question indulges in the rigmarole of church ritual. And the hay meadows. We shall suffer for his eccentricity. If this wet summer continues, and we have a bad winter, we'll regret the lack of sweetness in the hay. But I will help him. When it comes to wielding a scythe, quaint thought, I'll be there in line with the rest of them in my smock-frock and yokel's hat.

There can be no doubt that the affection shown by the men toward Father in the Great Barn was genuine. It may have been deference that made them put down their lunch plates and clamber to their feet. They don't smile much, but I could see their eyes widen in anticipation of what Father might say. Someone muttered 'Welcome back, Master Tristram' in my direction, but that was delivered with polite neutrality. But when Father said grace, I could tell they were grateful, even though their meal was half over. And I, for whom the act of blessing food is a sham, was glad for his sake that he'd done it. They call him "Squarson", a mixture of Squire and Parson. The title is pure affection.

They loved his joke, even if their laughter was muted. It went something like this:

A priest came down the road after Church and saw a man talking to the Devil.

'Now what do you think you're doing,' said the parson, 'communing with the Devil?'

'The Devil?' replies the man. (I can't do the accent; Father can.) 'Old Nick ain't bin nowhere round here.'

'There he is, I can see him,' says the parson. 'I can see his horns.'

'Ah-um, you see Gaffer, that's a bull, see; a gert fine bull he be too. All the best bull's got horns.'

'Then why has he got a forked tail?'

'Ah, that's because he's bin having trouble with the flies. I's bin magotting him, and neatly plaited his tail in two to make him look smart for Sunday. 'Tis looking like a fork, only looking, mind.'

'Then where is the ring in his nose?'

'Ah, you see, Vicar, 'tis like this. He wears it all through the week, but on Sunday, being a God-fearing man, I takes it off him to give him his day of rest.'

At this the bull starts laughing.

'That's no bull,' cries the parson. 'A bull would bellow; he would never start laughing.'

'I wouldn't normally,' said the bull, 'but when I saw you shackled in your dog collar and not even allowed to take it off after Church on a Sunday, I just couldn't help it.'

The men, who'd remained rapt but silent throughout Father's story, showed their appreciation with a deep rumble of approval, followed by a steady banging of mugs on their crates.

It's been a happy day, but I was saddened by the loss of Luscombe. Often, when I was a boy, I would stand by his lathe staring up at him, asking no doubt ridiculous questions, but drinking in his wisdom. Now he's gone. I never had the chance to say goodbye, nor wish him well. I'll help Father all I can to stem the drain of labour from the land. Already, I've got an idea.

25th May 1909

I cannot sleep. The air is so close, its thickness is oppressive. I am seeing Richard standing by the window of our bedroom, looking out over the orchard. He thinks that I am sleeping. I do not call out to him. My mind its own path is following.

With a mother's sensitivity, I rejoice at what I have and grieve at its passing. Tristram has changed. My boy has grown up. His features bear the heavy power of manhood. The prince is becoming the pretender, how is it said, waiting in the wings, knowing that he has the strength to challenge. His leisure time, before he goes to Oxford, is making him restless. I see dissent in his eyes. Or perhaps in

Leipzig he has seen new possibilities, on which he is brooding. This frightens me and, although I would not be expecting to control his life or restrict his freedom, I am praying that he will not throw away what we have taught him. So far, success in life has come so easily to him, too easily. Perhaps that is why he is questioning it.

From infancy he was precocious and so strong, always strong for his age. He still is, and I do not just mean physical strength. His starting point is to assume that over everything he will prevail. His extraordinary success at school, both academic and on the sports field, has not been coming through sweaty diligence, but from confidence and his natural gifts. Hardly anything he seems to practise. He does things, absorbs the experience, and moves on to the next. He was telling me that, once he has read something, he never forgets it, down to the smallest detail. His memory it is almost freakish.

Adela too is precocious, but in an entirely different way. She is gifted, but her curiosities run in narrow channels. Her music she is loving, and reading, but she cares nothing for sport, which is a characteristic she shares with me. Even when young, ducklings and piglets failed to amuse her, though of cats she has always been fond. She has some talent at drawing, but is not minding to exercise it, unless she wishes to be illustrating some musical point to me. Like Tristram, she is having a formidable memory. Often she smiles in a way which people find off-putting, as though she is indulging them. Of her parents I often think, though I never met them. Yes, it is so, Adela is not our blood daughter. She is adopted. In so many ways she is like me, yet when I am not her true mother, how can this be so?

The hour of Tristram's birth I will never be forgetting. It was in the darkness before dawn. He came so quickly in a burst of pain and was bawling at the world before the midwife had taken hold of him. And I was feeling this wet bundle of life that was mine but not me, and the surge of love, which I am still feeling now, is bringing tears to my eyes, even after nineteen years.

And then the fever and the operation were coming, and being told beneath a stark gas light that I could never be having another child, which made me love Tristram all the more. Richard, of course, was magnificent. Two years he waited, then placed before me as gently as an offering that we should be adopting a second child, a girl this time. And that is how Adela came into our lives, the daughter of poor factory workers in Zwickau. She is not knowing it, and Tristram is not knowing it; only Richard and I, and my elderly mother who is living in Hannover. To tell Adela it would not be right. We should not be bringing unnecessary turmoil into her life. But I must never forget it: whereas Tristram is having half my blood, Adela's is completely German, and none of it is mine.

My husband I am loving, and all his contradictions. He is an emotional man, and only I know how often he sheds tears.

He is still standing by the window. All this time he has been there. I call softly to him and he turns towards me. He is still dressed for the day. Slowly he is removing his clothes, pulling back the sheet and drawing me to his body. I, Helga von Thuren, Helga Hall, am a lucky woman.

26th May 1909

Tristram has come up with a bold plan on how to prevent the men from leaving the land. It is radical. Indeed, I would say that it is drastic. I believe that it might work, but at what cost?

'Father, a word, please. I've been thinking about the labour problem. I want to tell you something I saw in Leipzig.'

It seemed so improbable that a large German city could provide a solution to our rural English farm that I was at once curious and sceptical.

We walked down through the orchard and stayed leaning on the gate at the far end.

'Father, I think the key to our problem is that we don't make living here attractive enough for the men and their families. I'm not talking about pay. We need to give them some land for themselves.'

'You mean allotments?'

'I mean smallholdings.'

I tried to understand this. 'So the men would effectively become tenant farmers of our land? But we do not have sufficient acres to be able to earn enough from rent alone.'

'I mean something in between. About fifty years ago, a man called Schreber persuaded the authorities in Leipzig to allow the inhabitants to create their own gardens on wasteland. At first, the main purpose was to provide open spaces for poor children to play in but, later, after Schreber died, these *Schrebergarten,* as they became known, developed into areas where citizens could grow flowers, fruit and vegetables.'

'And this is what you propose for our farm?' I asked.

'Not exactly; I'd have something larger. A couple of acres of land per worker, or thereabouts. To start with, we could assist with drainage, laying down pasture and erecting sheds. I'd expect every man to keep at least a pig, and his wife to keep poultry. Pigs take up little land and are a source of both manure and meat.'

'There are sound Christian principles at work there,' I said, trying to think it through. 'But where is the land to come from? We have nearly twenty men working on the farm. At two acres per man, that would be a loss of forty acres, but that does not account for access tracks. I would think that fifty acres would be required. That is quite a proportion of our land. The loss of income would be considerable.'

'I think not, Father, not that much.'

'How can that be?'

'By greater productivity, not only per acre, but per labourer. We're behind the times in mechanisation, Father. The more we mechanise, the greater the yields and the fewer men we'll need to employ. The fewer men we employ, the less acreage we'll need to sacrifice for their wellbeing. So we'll turn the loss of labour to our advantage.

But the men we do employ will be more contented.'

I need to consider this. I will take it seriously. It is a neat plan, to turn a threat into an opportunity. When in doubt, I will do what I always do. I must ask myself what Our Lord would have done. I shall pray.

27th May 1909

Since one year, a secret about my daughter I am harbouring. Even though she is adopted, she shares a love of music with me, though her abilities far exceed mine. She has a musical talent the stature of which even she is not realising. She can take a new score, read it through once, and interpret it eloquently first time. The pianoforte she plays with compassion. I have no doubt that she could within a few years be making a name for herself nationally and internationally as a performer. She practises sufficiently, and her maturity at the keyboard is growing by the day. I am not talking here about the daughter of the house pleasing her neighbours. We are no longer living in Victorian times, with musical *soirées* where young ladies are expected to be displaying their talents, whether they have any or not.

Only I and her Maker know the extent of her gift. I have not told Richard this, and for now will not be doing so. He has no real musical sense, although he can deliver a passable baritone voice in the responses. To him, Adela is too young for the larger world, and in many ways he is right. The idea of her performing on stage or for money would appal him. She is only sixteen and, for the moment, further incentive she does not need. For now, my tutorship is sufficing. But the time will soon be coming when she will need a leading pianoforte teacher if her talents are not to be wasted.

Adela has been extending her interest beyond the piano. My Uncle Gerd has sent her his collection of orchestral and vocal scores of four of the operas of Richard Wagner. They are a generous gift. What she will make of them I cannot be guessing.

When I first looked at Great Uncle Gerd's Wagner scores, I didn't know what to think. They were so huge that they had to be divided. Not just long, though they seemed interminable; there was so much going on all at once.

At first, I just dabbled in them. I tried singing some of the vocal parts of *Lohengrin,* but they sounded sparse, with pauses and gaps which seemed unnatural. As for the male vocal lines, even when I sang them an octave higher, I sounded ridiculous and ended up in giggles. I then tried to pick out a suitable accompaniment on the piano from the sea of orchestration, but which instrumental line to choose? I learned from Mama that Wagner uses *Leitmotifs,* short musical phrases which identify a particular character or place. So I started to look for these and to identify where I could see them recurring. But that was like trying to find four-leafed clovers in Papa's meadow or individual hairs on Kitty's back. I needed to hear the sounds.

'Please, Mama, do. Do take me to the opera.'

Papa was against it, not because of the music, but because we'd have to spend a night in London. Dear Papa, he's so old-fashioned. But Mama won the day, so she and I have been to a performance of Wagner's *Die Walküre* at Covent Garden. I wanted to see all four operas of Wagner's *Ring* cycle, but Papa said no, and this time Mama gave in to him. The reason was that I'd be away from my studies with Miss Stone for too long. Papa also muttered about the unsuitability of his daughter seeing the "misbehavings of pagan gods", as he put it. Anyway, we went to see *Die Walküre,* and it was so exciting. The conductor, Herr Hans Richter, though he's really Hungarian, had a vast beard which covered his tie and the whole of the upper part of his chest. But we didn't see him much, as he was down in the pit. The love scene between Siegmund and Sieglinde made me shiver with delight, but my greatest memory was of Wotan, played by Clarence Whitehill, imprisoning his daughter Brünnhilde in a perpetual ring of fire. The music throbbed on and on, finally fading with an utter beauty which brought tears to my eyes, though I still don't know whether they were of sadness or ecstasy. Minnie Saltzman-Stevens, who played Brünnhilde, had her hair, or more likely a wig, plaited down to her waist in a great curly sausage, which swung when she moved, like a rubbery version of one of those harvest loaves. She carried a huge twisted cow's horn, which she pretended to blow now and then. At times she wore a warrior's helmet with huge feathered wings, each a foot long, sprouting from the top. But her singing! I realised how feeble and dull I must sound in Church, compared with such a range of expression and power. And when she was ill-treated by her father, you could sense the pity of the whole audience going out to her.

By the time I got home, I knew what I wanted to do. I would paraphrase the essence of some of the operas onto the piano, starting with *Tristan und Isolde*. Mama told me that it's been done before, by Liszt and others, but I didn't ask to see their music. I wanted the results to be my work and Wagner's alone, without further influence. It's taken longer than I'd have liked. I've barely started. But what has really astonished me has been the reactions of my parents.

Papa, when he heard me playing the pieces, made soothing, appreciative noises, and said how "pretty" they sounded. This would have annoyed me, except I knew he hadn't really taken them in and had produced a word to match his lack of understanding. Poor Papa, he's missing so much. Later, I heard him shouting in the library. I overheard the words 'Wagner is a contaminator'. I moved closer to the door. I could hear Mama in there, but could catch little of what she was saying. But I could hear every word of Papa's.

'I will not easily forgive you for this, nor Gerd. I will not have the young of this house corrupted by heathen influences and by licentiousness.' It sounded like she'd told him the story of *Tristan*. 'Now that you have explained it, it is quite clear. This opera clearly combines several sins at once. Suicide is an evil by itself, but when driven by lust and pooled with adultery, glorification of death, necrophilia... I could go on.' I had the impression that Papa had run out of words, but no. 'It is clearly a sordid corruption of the chivalrous tale of Sir Tristram and the fair Isolt, as recounted by Mallory. You have disappointed me, Helga. I had thought better of you. When we chose the name of our son, I thought it a noble concession that you should allow me to settle on the name of a knight of King Arthur's Round Table. I do not recall your bringing to my attention that some of your more degenerate countrymen had tainted the name with debauchery.'

Mama said something in reply, but I couldn't catch it and had to retreat quickly when I heard footsteps approaching the door.

Papa has rather frightened me, but I can't help giggling when I think of all those years during which he's had this courtly image of his son, Sir Tristram, when all along Mama has known that the name bears the torch of... debauchery! But although that thought amuses me, I mustn't forget that my parents' quarrel was really over me. Oh Wagner, what are you doing to my innocence? Can I remain a virgin of the keyboard? Hush, young Lady. Where is your sense of decorum?

Tristram has told me that Nietzsche and Wagner were close friends and mutual admirers. Then they fell out, because Wagner hated the Jews, which Nietzsche thought irrational.

I nearly forgot. When we were at the opera, Mama bumped into an old acquaintance of hers, a Mr Fielder-Grilsen. He's invited us back to London to attend a new work by a composer called Frederick Delius. I've never heard of him. It's called *A Mass of Life*. Tristram can come with us, but Papa isn't interested. He muttered something about Catholicism, but we all ignored him.

28th May 1909

As a mother, I am worrying about an incident at dinner this evening. A small thing, it seemed so, and in less than a minute it was over. But I am fearing that it may be the start of worse to come.

Hackett, having brought our soup, had retired from the room. Adela and I were sitting with bowed heads, looking up from the tops of our eyes at Richard, ready to lower them when he started to say Grace. I think that Tristram was staring up at the ceiling. There was a pause, then Richard straightened in his chair. He leaned back and, turning towards Tristram, said with a pleasant smile, 'You have not said Grace since you returned from Leipzig, Tristram. Will you oblige us now?'

Tristram's eyes jerked down from their upward gaze and flashed towards Richard in a manner which I was not liking. For a long while he said nothing. Adela from her bent position had slowly straightened and had turned towards her brother.

At last Tristram was speaking. 'We ought to be grateful for this food.'

And that was it. No one said 'Amen'. Adela was smiling, when in doubt she is always smiling, but it was Richard who was having my attention. His eyes were half-closing, and his nose and mouth, they were raised to one side with a look of pain and distaste. He grunted and picked up his soup spoon. The incident was over.

What has caused this I think I know. It is a small thing, as I have said, but I am fearing what may be growing from it. Tristram has taken a step. Seeing it unchallenged, he will be trying more.

29th May 1909

I know nothing of music, beyond our glorious English hymns. I must confess to being bemused by the classics. Symphonies and other orchestral pieces, even the piano music of Beethoven and Liszt so beloved by my daughter, seem to me to be always stopping and starting, unable to make up their mind whether to be loud or soft.

Yet it was an evening at a concert that changed my life. I had gone abroad, somewhat reluctantly, on a brief visit to Berlin with a fellow theology student. I felt uncomfortable there. Young men of my age swaggered through the streets, and even the ladies were arrogant. The country had only been unified by Bismarck some ten years before. Having defeated the French, Wilhelm of Prussia was crowned Kaiser of the Reich, not there in his capital Berlin, oh no, but at Versailles to emphasise the humiliation of his vanquished enemy. Christian principles seemed to have been trampled underfoot.

Anyhow, that is by the by. Here I was in Berlin, not sorry that we were returning in just a few days' time, when I was taken to a piano recital in a large room just off *Unter den Linden*. The music was mainly by Schubert, with a piece by someone or other thrown in. I was rather dreading having to sit through something I would neither understand nor appreciate.

We had been seated for some time when the pianist appeared, to neither announcement nor applause. She entered with a rather stooping walk for one so young, her eyes fixed on her stool, failing to make a bow towards her audience. When the buzz of conversation had died down, she sat looking rather crossly at the keyboard, as though she were about to chastise it.

But when she started, I found myself concentrating, not on the music, but on her. Her movements were not extravagant, any flourishes being confined only to those moments when the music appeared to demand them. Yet it seemed that here was a lovelier revelation of the feminine aspect than I could have thought possible. For the first time in my life, I became susceptible to that contradiction possessed by womanhood of being able to appear at the same time confident and vulnerable.

The concert, without an interval, seemed to last no time at all. The audience numbered no more than thirty and, at the end, after the applause, she simply became one of the roomful. The impression of her performance had started to fade already. My fellow student was attempting to converse with a middle-aged woman whose English was frankly appalling, a jumble of words which were mostly inappropriate and in the wrong order. Bored, I started to look around the room, and found that the pianist was staring at me and, in that look, all the ambiguities returned. It was so full of possibilities that I knew that I had to get to know her.

And that is how I met Helga von Thuren. We became engaged, and married six years later, when I had completed my studies. Her career as a musician, such as it was, died when she came to England. At first, I was apprehensive of how she would take to being a curate's and then a vicar's wife, but she has embraced the life with enthusiasm and energy. Her tireless work for the Church has brought me great joy. Her visits around the parish exceed even mine. She attends the sick, the bereaved and the down-at-heart. Foul weather will not put her off. Her sense of duty is boundless. When a baby is within a month or two of being due, Helga takes out the "confinement chest". This consists of a wooden trunk full of maternity smocks, napkins, bandages, swaddling clothes and bootees. There is also a small amount of food: a tin of tea, a packet of sugar, powdered egg and the ingredients for Helga's herbal infusions, together with the recipes translated from the German. If the family is especially poor, there is a small gift of money to tide them over the period when the mother-to-be ceases one sort of labour and enters another. I love her for this.

She has built up a fund of medical knowledge. The poor of the parish turn to her for their minor ailments: chilblains, colic and the like. They use Helga because they cannot afford Dr. Franklin's fees. But she is careful not to prescribe anything which is beyond her knowledge of physic. The gypsies who camp down by the river every few months are never left out. Helga fills her basket with little God Books and buns, but always makes payment for the curiosities which the ringed and braceleted Romanies have made themselves. She then redistributes these to the poor children of the parish.

The choir is Helga's too, and it is a triumph. So when Church is packed every Sunday, it is as much because of Helga as from anything I do. My sermons are, I think, appreciated. But it is due to my wife that the pews are filled. They love her for who she is and for what she does for them during the week. But it is when the choir leads the singing that the congregation aspires to higher thoughts. As William Sawbridge said to me the other day, 'Capital sermon, Padre. You told us what we ought to be doing on this earth, but your choir made us think of Heaven.' And is there anywhere in England where the rafters resonate to louder cheer than in my humble parish church?

Helga is a model vicar's wife, but she presumes to know nothing of the farm. She seldom walks around it for pleasure. She has no desire to keep poultry, nor to supervise in the growing of vegetables for the kitchen, although she does take a keen interest in medicinal herbs. Perhaps it is good for a marriage that it should be this way. We share our work for the Church and love of our children. She can retreat from me into her literature and music, and I from her onto the land. In that sense, she has Adela and I have Tristram. But am I being honest with myself here? I cannot escape a feeling of exclusion when the subject of conversation is music or anything Teutonic. My resentment is close to the sin of envy. Tristram and Adela are both fluent in German. They do not speak it around the dinner table; I will not allow it. Yet I cannot help feeling that it is because of my inadequacy that this is so. I have never troubled to learn the language. Why should I?

Adela disturbs me. That combination of confidence and vulnerability which I observed in Helga at the age of twenty-four, I now see in Adela at sixteen. She is too young for such womanly attributes. She loves her father, I know she does, but sometimes I think that she sees me as a quaint bucolic with few ideas beyond his pastures; a non-sophisticate who comes in from the fields on Sundays to preach, thinking that all the wisdom of the world originates from within his own hedgerows. If I catch her eye during the sermon, she always seems to be smiling. Sometimes I think it is encouragement, as though our ages had been reversed and she is a parent doting on her child as he strives to remember his lines in the school play. I am frequently pricked by a feeling of inferiority when I am with her, thinking that she is amused by my simple ways. Yet she is never anything other than affectionate towards me. She is shrewd, but she is only sixteen. I feel that knowledge of the world ought to be released to her selectively at this age. Tristram does not help. I have heard him telling her of carnal things which he has undoubtedly picked up in Leipzig. They talk of philosophy and art. Some of it, I feel, is precipitous. I know that I do not have the intellect of my wife and children, and why should I? Every scrap of knowledge is not necessarily beneficial. We do not all have to be bookworms, artists and musicians to follow the Truth.

Why am I saying this? We all share our Faith and our love of God, and in that we are united. We love each other. Is that not enough?

30th May 1909

I've reviewed Father's plans for the dairy, and have spoken to Edwin Blamey, the head dairyman. In some ways, I must congratulate Father. He's taken the trouble to understand not just the new hygiene laws, but the thinking behind them. His improvements will take us to the vanguard of dairy practice.

I wish I could say the same of the milking parlour. It's true that the new layout will reduce the risk of tuberculosis and other diseases. But our milking process, if allowed to continue the way it is, will remain rooted in the nineteenth century. Father has gone and ordered three foot-treadle milkers. I'm surprised they're still being sold. The manufacturer could present him with a medal for being the last person in history to buy one.

I've been looking at the new Thistle suction machines. I've calculated that they'd cut milking time from two and a half to one and a half hours. We could then reduce the number of people doing it from five to three, covering the whole week. And they can all go to Church. I've spoken to Mr Harrald, who says that we can change our order, but only if we do it quickly. Father mustn't sit on this one.

I can't get him to make up his mind over my plan for the *Schrebergarten*. He says that he's praying, as if that solves anything.

As I was passing through the cart shed after inspecting the new cow house, I happened to look up at the roof. I saw that one of the main crossbeams was sagging alarmingly. Water has got in, and the timber is in an advanced state of rot. A thick but crude prop has been wedged underneath the lowest point. It serves its purpose, but only until the first wagon is carelessly backed against it. When this happens, the smashed carts and fallen building may be repaired at great cost, but not anyone lying crushed underneath. No greedy, cost-cutting factory owner would tolerate the dilapidation I see around me here. I'll speak to Father. This is no time for procrastination and prayer.

31st May 1909

Father has agreed that the cart shed should be repaired immediately and properly. But when I mentioned the Thistle milking machines, he said he would think about it; by which he means seek guidance; by which he means pray.

As for the *Schrebergarten,* he thinks that the decision should wait for another year. Is that how long God takes to make up his mind?

4th June 1909

Tristram was in one of his elder brother moods. We'd walked down over Wester Ground and were sitting side-by-side on a wooden bench, looking out over the valley.

'Will you do something for me, Adela? Will you go back over all you've been taught and look at it afresh? Will you question everything you've learnt? I can help you.'

'I wish you would, but be gentle with your little sister. I haven't been hardened by jostling in the streets of Leipzig.'

Tristram smiled at that, then looked serious. 'When we were young, our parents and teachers had to say "no" to us. When we crawled towards the fire or strayed too close to the horse's hooves, we had to be restrained for our own safety. Hearing this word "no" so often built up a negative picture of life. "Better not to", and "Don't take risks", we subconsciously told ourselves. Feelings of negativity and guilt formed within us, as adults continually warned and chastised us. That was no one's fault. We had to be kept back from the fire, and we had to be pulled out with a scold from playing beneath the horse's belly.

'What was wrong was that this feeling of negativity was compounded by the additional loading of further, unnecessary guilt. "You are a sinner", "Christ died on the cross for your sins", "Jesus will love you only if you ask for forgiveness". These are frightening messages to a child; worse, they are confidence destroying. The Christian ideals of humility have made us miserable and weak. The concepts of sinning and having to pray for forgiveness chain us to a perpetual state of childhood. Children depend on adults; Christians remain in a childlike state by depending on God for forgiveness. Nietzsche taught that we should love ourselves and be strong and bold, to stride out and say 'Yes!' to the world.'

Ah, Nietzsche, I thought; it didn't take long for him to appear.

'The first cavemen believed that thunder was the wrathful breath of some monstrous dragon. We don't believe that now, so why should we believe the other?'

I had an answer to that. 'Papa would say that proves that Christ's life was so special. That is why superstitions have come and gone, whereas Christianity has lasted for nineteen hundred years.

But there's surely another reason. Christianity has survived because it teaches us to be good to one another. You can't deny the goodness of charity?'

'But it isn't what Christians practise!' Tristram cried out, making me jump. 'I see no evidence that Christianity is improving the world, even in the way you advocate. Christians pretend to follow Christ's rules, but they don't. Having joined the herd in slavishly signing up to rules fossilised in time nineteen hundred years ago, the Christian then proceeds to find ways of ignoring them. "It is easier for a camel to go through the eye of a needle than for a rich man to enter into the kingdom of Heaven". Those weren't the words of some obscure prophet; they were the words of Jesus Christ. Does Father really believe that? Do Lord and Lady Middleham, with their vast mansion and twenty servants? And if they do, why aren't they performing one tittle of an act to shed some of their wealth? Do we condemn them for not doing so? No, we honour them. The word "noble" has two meanings: "an aristocrat" and "virtuous". We abase ourselves before them, and we envy them the riches we would like to possess ourselves.'

I wanted to answer that, but Tristram didn't give me a chance.

'The beatitudes of Christ were written for a people already in slavery. If our ancestors had continued to obey them, we would still be slaves today. Our civilisation has progressed, not because we've obeyed the Christian code, but because we've found ways of dodging round it and, in many cases, totally ignoring it.'

John Hawkes came down the track behind two shire horses, talking to them gently, their harnesses jangling in reply.

Tristram was well away now. '"Thou shalt not kill." Not the words of some prophet, but of God himself, or so the Bible claims. Now that Colonel Sawbridge has ended his illustrious military career, does he think that his life has been a terrible mistake for which he should plead forgiveness? We preach the doctrine of passivity to the heathen, while conquering them with our armies. We expect them to show humility and servility, while we ourselves build huge dreadnoughts so that our navy may impose our will on the world by strength.

'One of the worst hypocrisies of all is that it's wrong to profit from the misfortunes of others. We do it all the time. We honour and revere statesmen, businessmen, soldiers, and sportsmen who've fought their way to the top by trampling their rivals underfoot. Exploitation is as natural to us as to the fox and the peregrine falcon. This is the natural law of evolution at work. This is how we've become strong, through competition and the forces of the marketplace. This is how we've become good.'

'Where's your Faith now, my darling brother? Like me, you've accepted Confirmation into the Church of England, and only two years ago.'

'I'm proud that I've cast it off. To rely on faith is to put on a blindfold. Theology is the art of justifying the myth, creating variations within it, inventing the detail to fit the assumption. The argument gets fierce and the debate's a learned one, but its premise is as false as any other legend and its objective as futile as alchemy. People talk about "a leap of faith". Religious faith isn't about taking a leap; it's a failure to take one. It's about clinging to what others have told you, without using your own ability to scrutinise. "*Sapere aude,*" wrote Kant, "Dare to taste, to discern. Have the courage to use your own intelligence." Don't just swallow the pre-digested food from your baby-spoon.'

'Don't let Papa hear of this.'

'Then don't say it to him. He preaches to the convinced, without debate. I only display the truth to those who can think for themselves.'

'Like me? D'you think you can influence me?'

'I hope not, my darling Adela; you're influenced too much already. I want you to reason for yourself. Did you hear little Georgie Palmer outside Church the other day? He asked where God was. "He was there," Father told him. "He was there in Church." "Well, I didn't see him," Georgie replied stoutly. Everyone laughed, no doubt pleased with his innocence, but they ignored the message that young Georgie is so far uncorrupted by fantastical notions.'

'Papa says that God allows miseries to take place in order to test us.'

'Without telling us that he's doing so? That's ridiculous. Would a class of students perform well if the teacher hadn't explained what they were meant to be doing? God is totally undefined, except by man, and so are his instructions. No god has ever spoken on any subject, but there's a convenient way round this. Their followers can elevate the sayings of prophets by declaring them to be the mouthpiece of God. Then their words may not be challenged or refuted, so they become permanent. The really clever religions go one better. The Christian idea was a stroke of genius. Take a real man, Jesus Christ, who claimed to be the Son of God. Wait until this man, who's never written anything down, is long dead, forty to sixty years afterwards in the case of the gospels, then elevate him to the right hand of God. Even better, make him one with God through the concept of the Trinity. Then no one can dispute that his reported words are the word of God, and that God has spoken, without denying the most basic truth on which Christianity relies, that Jesus was the Son of God. This conveniently explains why we haven't heard a single squeak from God since. He spoke via his only Son, what more do you want? Therefore anyone who denies the Word commits the ultimate blasphemy and is damned. That's why Christianity has survived nineteen hundred years, and that's why St Paul, who was the greatest genius behind all this, was the most successful corrupter in history.'

'My, you have been taught a lot in Leipzig.'

'I've been taught only to think for myself. I've knocked away nanny's spoon and have started to feed myself. It's time for you, my darling sister, to do the same.'

Dear Tristram, he does get worked up these days. He insists on freedom of thought, then presents Nietzsche's certainties as his own. But of course I didn't tell him that.

10th June 1909

Thank goodness Richard with us was not. Disgusted he would have been. The *Mass* is having nothing to do with the Catholic Church, or even Christianity. Its composer, Frederick Delius, is a non-believer. The words are from *Also Sprach Zarathustra*, by Nietzsche. Such poetry, but of course he too is opposed to God. We met a weird woman called Ethel Smyth, who parades a morality so outrageous that she is making Mr Oscar Wilde seem conventional. And Adela did not get to bed until after midnight.

On the positive side, we have been hearing music to move us to the depths of our souls; even Tristram was thinking so. And we met a man who, although I do not like him, drew out of Adela the revelation of a new musical talent, the extent of which I was failing to detect. When assailed with probing questions, she withstood the pressure unflinchingly with maturity and confidence. She was accounting for herself magnificently, and I am extremely proud of her.

We met Mr Fielder-Grilsen in the foyer at the appointed hour. His own description of himself he fitted perfectly, and it was not difficult for him to identify the three of us, for we were standing in a huddle discussing every man who entered the building, Adela giggling at Tristram's comments on the physical and sartorial appearance of each.

Mr Fielder-Grilsen must at first have been thinking my husband frightfully young, until I explained the substitution of Tristram for Richard. We were having little time for conversation before the concert, beyond Mr Fielder-Grilsen telling us about the conductor, Mr Thomas Beecham. He is the son of the Beecham's Pills tycoon, Mr Joseph Beecham, who has financed all of his son's lavish orchestral endeavours.

We took our seats and surveyed the scene. The paintwork was an unusual combination of light grey and terracotta, with mirrors surrounding the auditorium. There were medallions of famous composers on either side of the stage, and I was just beginning to enjoy identifying them through my opera glasses when Tristram let out an unseemly low whistle from my right.

'Well, how is that, Umpire? Will you look at this? Mother?'

I do wish he would not be speaking like that, especially in public. Adela and I leaned forward and saw that he was holding up the programme booklet and angling it towards us.

'Well, Mr Delius, we will look in vain for a *Kyrie* or an *Agnus Dei*. Guess who wrote the words to this particular Mass?'

I saw. It was Nietzsche, and the verses were from *Also Sprach Zarathustra,* with which I am familiar. A short period of animated whispering between Tristram and Adela followed, of which I was not approving. I was resolving to speak to them about it afterwards; although, as it happened, it later slipped my mind. When I looked again at Adela, she was sitting back in her seat with a smile which suggested anticipation, but which also was seeming dangerously close to smugness. For one wild moment I was wondering if she and Tristram had known of the Nietzsche connection all along, although later I was realising that this was unlikely.

The conductor, Mr Beecham, entered to wild applause. He is obviously popular. He mounted the podium and turned to face the audience. Just as we were expecting a bow, he tilted his head back so that his beard jutted forward, closed his eyes, then half opened them again and looked through his lashes as though critically assessing us. For several seconds he remained like that so that his bow, when it came, seemed loaded with irony. Then he smartly turned, held the orchestra with his baton and into the music charged.

Never have I heard a sound like that which burst through the hall, even from Wagner. For the next hour and a half, the most ecstatic music was gripping my senses. Time seemed to be flying or rather floating by, for I felt transported far from my seat, from the audience, from London, even from my earthly existence. At the end, the music swelled to a climax, then faded quickly to nothing. First there was total silence and nobody moved. Mr Beecham was standing with his back to us, head bowed. Slowly he straightened and turned to face the audience, raising his head until we could see that his eyes were still closed. He opened them, gave the slightest of nods, and the audience went wild.

I was looking at my children. Adela was bouncing in her seat and clapping enthusiastically. Tristram's right fist was clenched above his head and jerking towards the stage as though he were cracking a whip. My heart was knocking and I was short of breath. I seized Adela's hand, and when she turned towards me laughing, tears I could see splashing down her cheeks.

Out in the foyer, I started to give Mr Fielder-Grilsen our compliments in anticipation of bidding him good night. But he insisted that we should accompany him to a small room at the back of the auditorium.

Time passed slowly. Small talk was as difficult for my children as for me. Mr Fielder-Grilsen seemed uninterested in what Adela had to say about Uncle Gerd's Wagner scores. When we tried to comment on the performance we had just heard, Mr Fielder-Grisen did not respond. At last the reason became clear. We were about to meet Mr Beecham himself.

For a full half-hour Mr Beecham was keeping us waiting, and then the door swept open and he entered. He has piercing blue eyes, set in an oval face which ends in a neatly trimmed imperial beard. Although his bearing is upright, he appears less tall close by than when viewed on the podium. His brows are somewhat forbidding, but are being softened by his urbane manner.

He introduced himself and was receiving our compliments on the performance with a courteous inclination of the head. Tristram and he were taking their seats when the door opened again and a more striking figure than even Mr Beecham entered the room. At first I could not even determine whether it was male or female. Wearing tweeds and a necktie, and holding a large cigar, the creature was either a woman dressed as a man, or a man wearing lipstick.

'Ah, Ethel,' said Mr Beecham, straightening again, 'Please do meet…' and then he was reeling off our names, having remembered them perfectly. Ethel, it turned out, was the composer and writer Ethel Smyth. She advanced upon Adela, grasped her hands and said in a hearty voice, 'I have been dying to meet you. My, but you are pretty.'

I was surprised to see that Adela, although she was blushing, was not withering before this unexpected gush of ingratiation.

When we were all sitting, Mr Beecham took over. He speaks as though declaiming, his voice rising and falling within each sentence.

'You have sampled our fayre and drunk the wine of Frederick Delius. It is heady stuff. What did you think of his *Mass*?'

With great excitement, Tristram and Adela started to speak at the same time. Tristram yielded to Adela, who said, 'It has moved me to the depth of my heart. I love music, but I had no idea that it could produce such a vision.'

'Frederick will be pleased to hear it,' said Mr Beecham, 'and I would not disagree with one word. So much for the impression. What of the music itself?'

'The polyphonic scoring is remarkable. The music moves naturally between light and shade. Was I really meant to hear yearning, as well as peace and joy? And doubt and faith within night and day? I thought the baritone part near the end the most beautiful vocal writing I have ever heard, with the hushed entry of the choir before the great climax especially moving; although I did think that some of the female voices, earlier in the piece, were not entirely together.'

Mr Beecham gave an unpleasant twitch of his nose. 'The choir was perfect,' he said sourly.

This rudeness, stated baldly without any attempt at justification or elaboration, offended me. Adela is only a child of sixteen, and should not be spoken to like that. I could see that she was looking hurt. She had done nothing more than add a slight qualification to her lavish praise of both music and performance, and her opinion had been better reasoned than to use any word as extreme and unrealistic as "perfect".

But Mr Beecham was passing suavely on as though no insult on either side had been intended, turning instead to Tristram. 'And you, Sir?'

'I thought it a rapturous celebration of life.'

'Rapturous, yes, and celebration, yes, and life, yes. They are all there, but did you not also sense anguish?'

Having thought that she might be sulking, I was delighted that it was Adela who was responding promptly, 'I would rather say a longing, but the desire is made positive and is fulfilled, or so I believe.'

'Remarkable,' breathed Miss Smyth.

'This is interesting,' said Mr Beecham. 'Miss Hall, I understand that you have set some of *Tristan und Isolde* for the piano. Would you think that you could do the same for *A Mass of Life*?

'From what I've heard tonight, I don't think I

should. I believe that Mr Delius captures the spirit of nature marvellously, but there's also a strongly human element. This comes not just from the human voice – after all, the same could be said of *Tristan* – but also the rich harmonies of the instruments. I think the blending of soloists, choir and orchestra would be lost on the piano, and the spirit of the music.'

Mr Beecham gave a fearsome grunt. Amazed that Adela had said so much to such a testing question, I awaited his response with apprehension. No one was saying anything. Miss Smyth was gazing at Adela with a look of ardour.

Mr Beecham breathed in deeply. 'Miss Hall, you have clearly achieved a remarkably rapid understanding of Delius's music. Had you replied that a transcription to the piano would be profitable, I would not have gained such an opinion. I heartily concur with your judgement. I will give you this advice. Transcriptions of great choral and orchestral works for piano are futile, and that must include the operas of Wagner. Nevertheless, would you not agree with me that you might receive both enjoyment and inspiration from a perusal of the score of *A Mass of Life*?' Here he raised an eyebrow and his eyes twinkled.

Adela's eyes lit up with matching delight. 'Oh yes, I should like that. I've only recently entered the world of vocal and orchestral scores. There's no music which I should like to get to know better than that which I've heard this evening.'

'I will arrange it. You referred earlier, Miss Hall, to faith. Is it not a strange word to use regarding *A*

Mass of Life? After all, Frederick Delius, in setting to music the poetry of Nietzsche, joins him in celebrating life on this earth in denial of anything further. Delius puts forward his *Mass* in opposition to the ecclesiastical equivalent, with its emphasis on another life to come.'

Adela replied, 'Perhaps faith was the wrong word. Hope would have been better, but will you not allow spirituality? The poetry may not speak of God, but the feeling, surely, is of Man reaching out beyond himself? I felt that the music conveyed that, and I was greatly moved by it.'

Tristram said, 'Both my sister and I are familiar with the poetry of Nietzsche. Speaking for myself, I don't believe that spiritual feelings are confined only to dreaming of an afterlife.'

These words of Tristram's were not surprising me, but I was keen for the conversation not to be proceeding further down that line. I said, '*Also Sprach Zarathustra* I too have read. We are all three of us fluent in German, which is the language of my birth.' And Adela's, I thought, although of course I did not say it. We are far from Zwickau and its smoking factory here.

Mr Beecham preferred to return to the subject of music. 'Miss Hall, can you really hear the full sound, its harmonies, the chromatic shifts, its soul' – the last word was said with a long drawl – 'by looking through a score of such size?'

'I find that I can do so with Wagner's operas,' Adela replied simply.

'Provided you can overcome rampant prejudice against your sex,' said Miss Smyth hotly.

'It is a rare ability, although one I possess myself,' said Mr Beecham with no trace of modesty.

Too far this is going, I thought. What would Richard think? She still has her education to complete. Trying to turn the thrust of the conversation, I intervened, rashly as it turned out.

'I understand, Mr Beecham, that many productions for Covent Garden next season you are planning. May I ask whether they will be mainly Italian, or whether there will be some German opera as well?'

It seemed that quite the wrong thing I had said. Miss Smyth, I discovered later, has written several English operas championed by Mr Beecham, who is having strong views on the subject, as I was about to learn. His voice rose menacingly.

'Why should we trawl the slums of Milan and dredge the canals of Venice looking for hysterical melodramas of the third rate, when we have so much that is second rate in our own backyard?' He softened these cutting words by adding, 'And which operas would you like to see performed?'

Clearly not Italian, I thought. I told him about my love of Wagner and the fact that I had taken Adela to see *Die Walküre* at Covent Garden.

'Ah, Richter; he beats time very punctually.' It seems that Mr Beecham enjoys belittling his fellow conductors, for when I told him that I had also been to see Nikisch conducting Mozart and Beethoven he said, 'Nikisch is not without style. His neckties are fine and his cuffs are the smartest to be seen.' Later on, when prompted by Miss Smyth in a way which I think was set up deliberately, he said of

Koussevitsky, 'His interpretations are revealing, but he has one small defect.'

'What is that?' I asked naïvely.

'He can't conduct.'

Tristram was clearly enjoying these jokes, laughing so loudly that Mr Beecham turned to him and said, 'And where do your interests lie, Sir?'

Tristram briefly recounted his time in Leipzig, his love of sport and of the countryside, and the fact that he would be going to Oxford in four months' time. I could not help myself from adding that he had won a scholarship.

'Ah, Oxford,' said Mr Beecham. 'I hope that you are more successful in forming an attachment to the place than I achieved. I was always absenting myself without leave to attend the opera in Dresden and such places. I presented my divorce papers to my college just before they presented theirs to me. You too, my dear Ethel, have repeatedly shown your independence by walking away from your teachers.'

'It makes it more convincing when one claims that one's work is one's own,' said Miss Smyth with a wicked smile in the direction of Adela.

'As did Nietzsche,' said Tristram. 'He rejected academic life until he reached the stage where he rejected all formal education. He said that taking a degree was no more than a sign that the student had joined the herd. He said that the pupil's philosophy of life would become that of his teacher, together with his opinion of Napoleon.'

This seemed to be impressing everyone, although I was rather alarmed. Mr Beecham murmured, 'So I have heard, so I have heard.'

'My experiences exactly,' said Miss Smyth. 'I too spent time in Leipzig, Mr Hall. The Conservatorium there was packed with students who had come merely to qualify for certificates. The teachers showed a similar level of indifference to true learning. But the musical life, the concerts, the operas and the composers, they were nothing less than glorious.'

Mr Beecham said, 'Frederick Delius too studied at Leipzig. Like you, Ethel, he chose it because he regarded it as the most important musical and cultural city. Yet even he came to despise the Conservatoire there, and left. He is nothing if not his own man, and this shows in his music. Did you attend many performances while you were there, Mr Hall?'

'Only two, I'm afraid,' replied Tristram. 'My true understanding of what music can do only started with what I have heard here tonight.'

'Ah,' said Mr Beecham, rising to his feet, 'then we have achieved something worthwhile this evening.' It was clearly time to part. Mr Beecham took the hand of each of us, bowing. 'Please do let me have your impressions of the score I am lending you, Miss Hall.' And with that he strode from the room.

Miss Smyth got up to go. She turned to Adela. 'If ever you should want a friendly opinion regarding your assessment of musical scores, Miss Hall, I should be delighted to go through your work with you. We, who are the heirs of Sappho, must hold our torch up high.'

For some reason which I was not

comprehending, Tristram turned away in a poor attempt to cover a snigger.

Miss Smyth turned to me. I was not liking her smile, which seemed to be both mocking and triumphant. 'Goodnight to you all. I have been enchanted by our conversation.' Her eyes swept over Adela once more as she was leaving.

It will be many days for me to get over what has happened. Meanwhile, I must be deciding how much to tell Richard.

From the opening chorus to the rapidly fading coda, I was torn between wanting to analyse the music and abandon myself to its emotion. I know now what Tristram means when he says it's possible to feel in a spiritual way without thinking of God.

The forces Delius uses, four soloists, a chorus of up to eight parts, and an orchestra almost as large as Wagner's, produced an array of emotional effects, from hushed intensity to ecstatic joy. The opening of the work is vigorous, with the chorus and orchestra exploding immediately into an insistent, driving celebration. But the atmosphere of the later music excels even that. There's one moment near the end when the baritone voice of Zarathustra sings, *O Mensch, Gib Acht! Was spricht die tiefe Mitternacht? Ich schlief, ich schlief...* when I couldn't control the tears welling in my eyes. Yet it wasn't sadness. Longing, yes, but something positive which was fulfilled by the music moving faultlessly to a rapturous climax of joy, before fading away into peaceful silence. At the end, I turned to Tristram, and I could see his eyes burning with excitement. Before Mr Beecham turned towards the audience and the applause started, Tristram mouthed the word 'Yes' to me: 'Yes', the word which Nietzsche says that we should say to life. And, as the applause broke out, I was happy to shout it back, even as my body shook.

It was flattering to have all that attention afterwards, especially from Mr Beecham. To have founded one's own orchestra must be something to admire, but he's done it with his father's money from the sale of Beecham's Pills. And he's so vain! Tristram thought it hilarious when he lampooned the other conductors, but I didn't. It seems Mr Beecham can't take his own pills. Having received my praise of his performance of *A Mass of Life*, it seemed churlish that he should have resented the one small piece of adverse criticism which I did make. And the performance did contain several other defects which I didn't dare mention, although the music itself was sublime throughout.

Mr Beecham's rudeness to Mama was most unpleasant, and I can't forgive it. Anyone would think that she'd said she didn't want to hear English opera, from the uncouth reception her polite question received.

Still, I mustn't lose sight of the fact that my musical skills, such as they are, have been noted in high places.

When Miss Smyth first entered the room wearing masculine clothes and smoking a cigar, I merely thought of her as ambiguous. But when she spoke of

Sappho in such a leering tone, she left no doubt about where her inclinations lay. I'm not sure whether Mother understood, though she did ask some peculiar questions of Mr Fielder-Grilsen afterwards. Adela is completely innocent of the subject, and I won't upset her by mentioning it now. Although Miss Smyth has large hands and a parting down the middle of her head, which leaves two pats of hair looking as though they might have been laid by one of Father's cows, she's actually quite handsome for a woman of her age. But there's no doubting who in the room was the object of her interest. She was observing my sister with a predatory gaze which I didn't like at all.

It's uncanny what coincidences are shared between us. Like me and like Nietzsche, Miss Smyth has spent time in Leipzig, and so apparently has Frederick Delius. And all of us, it seems, have seen through the hypocrisies of Christianity. It's extraordinary how another thread ran through the evening. Nietzsche, Delius, Mr Beecham and Miss Smyth, all of them, have turned their backs on formal education, yet all have achieved success and an independence of mind. It's making me think.

I like Mr Beecham. He has style and panache. He's a showman, but it's also clear that he's a brilliant conductor, who's created an orchestra of his own and raised the standards of English music to great heights. He speaks his own mind, which I like, but above all he approves of Adela and thinks she's worthy of his valuable time and attention.

It's Adela who dominates my thoughts tonight. My sister's ability to interpret music astounded Mr

Beecham and Miss Smyth. But for me the greatest thrill was to hear her speak of spirituality freed from religion, a bold statement in front of Mother. It seems she's come to Nietzsche at last, and the fact that it's been through music rather than my own persuasion pleases me all the more. As for me, I now know that music can strike to the heart of my being. Adela's thoughts and mine are coming together at last.

17th July 1909

Colonel Sawbridge and his dear wife Alice to dinner this evening came, together with their daughter Elizabeth. They are our closest friends. Richard and the Colonel are having one of those relationships which most men never experience in their whole lives. When they are together, they become inspired. Each is skilled at prompting and goading the other to more and more outrageous banter. Some of their jokes are variations on old themes, but each meeting is increasing the range of their repertoire. Adela and Tristram look on in wonderment, both being sensible enough not to intervene when the sparks are flying.

It is fortunate that I am getting on so well with Mrs Sawbridge. She is a quiet lady, the perfect foil for her husband. She too is the butt for his tongue. 'Madam,' he bellows, 'where have you hidden the salt?' and this diminutive mouse of a creature pretends to cringe and be frightened, while twittering with pleasure.

With graceful ease Elizabeth bears herself. I think Adela is somewhat in awe of her. Afterwards, when we had left the men to themselves, an awkwardness came over Adela which she is not normally possessing. Elizabeth has been to Paris and Monte Carlo. She skis and is an accomplished rider to hounds. She is self-assured yet unassuming. For Tristram she would make the perfect match. I saw them glancing at one another, but could not be deciding whether their smiles were the result of Richard's and William's jokes or a communication of interest in each other.

William Sawbridge is my closest friend. It may seem odd that someone who has led such a different life from mine should inspire me so, but he does. He is a soldier of the old school. He began his military career as a young lieutenant with Roberts at Kandahar and ended it as a colonel with Kitchener at Dongola. "A few skirmishes in between" is how he describes such hair-raising campaigns as the Zulu and Matabele wars.

William was in topping form this evening, but after the ladies had retired, he told me some rather disturbing news. The isolation of Germany at the Algeciras Conference three years ago had, I assumed, reduced the risk of war. But William now tells me that ever since Russia, under direct threat from Germany, backed down from supporting Serbia's resistance to Austria's annexation of Bosnia and Herzegovina, all the major powers in Europe have been arming themselves at a frightening rate. Of this I had gained some clue from the newspapers, and I had also heard that Germany had embarked upon a huge programme of naval shipbuilding. *The Times* is constantly speculating along the lines of "What does Germany intend to do with such a vast navy?" and "Who else would she match it against, except that other great naval power, Britain?" The worst thing I had not realised, until William told me, is that in 1906 and 1907 we actually decreased our programme of building dreadnoughts. Because of my German connections through Helga, William considers it necessary to be uncharacteristically diplomatic. But he left me in no doubt that he believes that there will be war with Germany.

Elizabeth is so serene. I can't find fault with her. She's kind to me and doesn't flaunt her virtues directly, but she can't help revealing them. She makes me feel inadequate, though I know she doesn't mean to.

We were all of us, I think, stunned when she first entered the room, though Tristram, after a sharp intake of breath which I distinctly heard, feigned indifference. She was wearing an exquisite ivory-coloured evening dress of what Mama told me afterwards was shot silk *moirée*, buttoned high to the neck. A series of diminishing lace vees accentuated the startling decline from bosom to diminutive waist, below which the material hung off her hips straight to the floor. Her hair was drawn up and back, leaving a pair of ringlets bracketing her fawn-like eyes.

She was discreet in her attention to Tristram, but I wasn't fooled. She's enchanted by him, I can tell, and who can blame her? Their glances were like invisible threads, drawing gossamer meanings from each other's eyes.

How Papa and Colonel Sawbridge made us laugh. They're like a couple of swordsmen, thrusting and parrying with wicked smiles. I can't wait for us all to be together again. Although I'm subdued by Elizabeth's presence, fascination draws me into wanting to see her.

20th July 1909

I thank God. At last, three dry days in a row, the last two hot, so we have cut the hay. Many of the younger men had never lifted a scythe, so they had to be shown how by the old hands. I even put in an hour myself either side of lunch, before I had to leave on my rounds. I returned late in the afternoon, after completing my visits. But Tristram was at it all day, encouraging the men, consulting with Jarvis, leading from the front.

Helga and Adela brought a pin of cider in the governess cart for the men's lunch. We had a gay picnic beneath the oak tree, but Tristram was soon anxious to get going again. While many of the men were still drawing at their Woodbines and sucking on their pipes, Tristram was the first to take a whetstone to his scythe and the first to rise to his feet and turn towards the uncut hay. I had hoped against hope that we might complete the cut in one day, and thanks to Tristram we have done so. Tomorrow we will rake the swaths into windrows ready for the drying to begin.

I have left large strips uncut as cover for the corncrakes for the remainder of the summer, until they fly south on their autumn migration. I feel contented, and give thanks to the Lord that He has made me see the way forward. I know that this is right.

23rd July 1909

Is this what it feels to be nineteen, for life to be exploding inside my head? Out in these fields, the world expands as the daylight fades. Swallows no longer dive and swerve across the cut hay. The last of the sunset has turned from fire to layers of magenta and green. Corncrakes are rasping out their calls in the fields below. The smell of hay intoxicates, but not to drowsiness. I'm alert; sounds are sharp: squawks of blackbirds swooping to roost in the bushes; the barking of a distant dog. *Tief ist der Nacht.* Not yet. *Ich schlief, ich schlief.* Not yet.

I feel so strong. The world would overwhelm me, but I can ride it. This is me, I'm here, I can be anywhere tonight: the streets of Leipzig, the

Nachtsmarkt, the *Königshaus*, the *Nikolaikirche*. Time is precious, momentous, and it's mine. By dawn I'll have made my decision.

A barn owl is working its way up the headland of Turner's Piece. When perching by day, they seem to be all head, but now it floats on huge wings like a ghostly butterfly, silently jagging its way along the hedgerow. I'm in no hurry. The corncrakes are insistent, like nails being dragged across metal combs, on and on, drawing out the dusk. I feel no pressure. The minutes are slowing into seconds. There! All tension has gone; just a love of the present and a yearning for the future. Life.

It's no longer hot, but it's still oppressive. The air is like a warm sea folding onto my arms. There's thunder about somewhere. I may go to Oxford or I may not. It's as simple as that. Ancient History is my chosen subject, or is it? Who made the choice? I did, but who conditioned it? Nietzsche says that a student's philosophy would become that of his teacher, together with his opinion of Napoleon. "So I have heard," murmured Mr Beecham. I'm nineteen; I've become a man. I'm not a boy any more, to be guided and pushed by teachers and preachers. It's time for me to say 'Yes', not to Oxford but to life. I don't need to consider what Nietzsche would have done, nor Frederick Delius, nor Thomas Beecham, nor Ethel Smyth. Nietzsche's message is not like Christ's, that we should rise up and follow him, but that we should think, be ourselves, say 'Yes' and cast off from the shore.

The first stars are appearing. The Australians have been giving us a caning at cricket. Our men are no match for Ransford, Bardsley and Cotter. Mr Mason said there's no reason why I shouldn't be playing against them next time they come to England. Mr Mason also said that cricket's a preparation for life. "A mirror to life, my boy." Why should I want to approach life holding a mirror to it? I want life itself, directly. Preparation is for children. Yes, it would be wonderful to score a century against the Australians at Lords. But would it feel that much better than when the ball seared past cover point as I reached my hundred against the MCC a year ago? 126 not out. "Few of those who were there will live to see a better innings," wrote *The Times*, "and certainly not from a schoolboy." I did that, but it wasn't life; it was Mr Mason's preparation for it.

Father won't proceed with the *Schrebergarte*n, I can tell. He's hinted that his conscience and his status in the community won't allow him to reduce the labour force on the farm. This, in spite of the fact that the men who'd go would readily find higher paid work in the towns, and that those who stayed would be happier and better off. So everyone, including ourselves, will now be a loser. Such is the weakness which Christianity cultivates. Poor Father. It may seem that I despise him over many things, but that's not true. I love him dearly, not just as a son should, but for the man he is: principled, loving, a brilliant and witty speaker, and a friend. I only despise the system which was responsible for casting a net over him as a child, ensnaring him ever since. He hasn't had the good fortune that I've had, of being shown the door to freedom.

I don't believe in destiny. It's a curtain for the

feeble-minded to hide behind. I'll create my own life and take nothing but opportunities from nature. I have one before me now. My idea of smallholdings will revolutionise agriculture, which is why it'll meet with such opposition. If Father won't allow me to prove it here, I'll go elsewhere, perhaps to Germany. Once I've succeeded, clergymen will want me to open their fêtes, only to learn that the morality which achieved it comes from Darwin and Nietzsche, not their god.

The corncrakes are silent now. The stars are hidden by clouds. The last train of the day chuffed its comforting way down the valley and round the bend an hour ago. If I make my announcements in stages, I may yet succeed in forcing Father's hand.

How can someone who sits so still and says so little be so exciting? Elizabeth Sawbridge sends out an invisible energy even when she's motionless. She's always been quiet, ever since we were children. I've never found her awkward. I think that both of us have always accepted the other's presence, so it came as a shock the other night to find her appearing as she did, and looking at me in a new way. I've noticed young ladies and not so young gazing at me in the streets of Leipzig and London, and have found it easy to ignore them. But with Elizabeth over dinner, I kept wanting to stare at her, and when I did so, changes so subtle took place in her eyes that I don't think I could possibly describe what they were. Nor could I even be sure that the communication came only from her eyes. She transmitted a power over me which was totally at odds with her demure composure. It was as though she were asking silent questions which insisted on answers. But they were enigmatic, and the best I could do was to let her know that I'd received them.

After the gentlemen and ladies had separated at the end of the meal, there wasn't an opportunity to observe her further, except briefly at the end of the evening. As we gathered in the hall, I found myself wanting to move close to her and, when I did so, I felt an urge to touch her, which of course I did not. But I did breathe in her scent, and was almost frightened by the effect it had on me. I felt an immediate physical change, of which my surging heartbeat was the least alarming reaction. In my confusion, I actually wished that the Sawbridges, Elizabeth included, would leave at once. And when it was my turn to say goodnight, no sound came from my mouth. Since then, she's entered my thoughts every day. I can't wait to see her again, though I can't think of a way until the Sawbridges invite us back to dinner, and that may be a couple of months away, by which time Elizabeth and I may, either of us, be elsewhere. If I were to approach her before then, what would she think, and what would I say to her? I'm nowhere near being able to tell her that I admire her and want to know what she's thinking. All I know is that I won't find her amongst the spires of Oxford.

The silence since the corncrakes ceased has been broken by a tawny owl hooting up in Longside Wood. The clouds have parted and many stars are visible. The last traces of sunset vanished some while ago. It's fully night, but I can see a little by starlight. What's that? Something white is moving in the next field. A fear seizes me which someone of my age brought up in the countryside shouldn't feel. Whatever it is has moved behind the covert. I'm rigid, and realise I'm holding my breath. The form reappears. It's human, female. Wildly, I think of Elizabeth. She walks towards me. It's Adela. She takes my arm.

'You couldn't sleep?'

'No more than you, it seems,' I reply.

'I saw you leave a couple of hours ago. I was standing by my bedroom window. I waited for you to come back; then I thought I must have missed you, but you weren't in your room or downstairs, so I walked out here looking for you. What on earth are you doing down here?'

'This is purpose enough,' I say, not sure what I'm referring to, but realising that I've just echoed words which Father said to me a couple of months ago on this very spot.

We stand in silence. Normally, I would welcome my sister's presence, but she's broken the chain of my meditation. I've prepared myself for decision-making, but haven't finally made up my mind.

As if she reads my thoughts, she says, 'I can't accept that you really are going to be leaving me soon.'

'I've left you before.'

'I know, and it was hard.'

I'm determined not to give anything away until I'm certain.

'Sometimes I wish I'd been a boy and could go to

Oxford. Perhaps it's no longer boys you would like to play with?'

She's fishing, but I won't rise to the bait.

'And how did you find the *Frauleins* of Leipzig?'

'Oh, I just walked down the street and there they were.'

'Tristram!'

'Were there young ladies in Leipzig?' I pretend to be absentminded. 'I didn't notice.'

'You were thinking of Elizabeth Sawbridge all the time, that's why. She was asking after you this morning.'

My pulse quickens and I feel my cheeks burning, but I try to keep my voice even. 'Was she? I haven't given her the time of day since that dinner last week.' I'm not sure what that expression "giving someone the time of day" means, and hope it's as ambiguous to Adela as it is to me.

'Perhaps you should.'

'And how is Thomas Knowles? Mother says he's paying you much attention.'

'I know she said no such thing. You're a liar, Tristram Hall.' She nestles against my shoulder, looking up at me. 'I'm going to become a nun when you go to Oxford.'

'And pin a photograph of Thomas on the wall of your cell?'

She laughs, but there's sadness in her voice when she says, 'It's you I'll be missing.'

'If I go.'

'You're teasing me.'

'I'm being serious, dear sister.'

'But you're destined for Oxford; you always were.'

'Destined? You know my destiny? Do you know your own? Do you even believe in destiny or know what it means? There! You can't answer.'

'But what has brought this on? Is it Leipzig? Is it Nietzsche?'

'You make it sound like catching a chill.'

'Is it Elizabeth Sawbridge?'

'No, it's Thomas Knowles.' I pretend to be angry. 'I have to stay and keep an eye on you. Father says he can't control you by himself. You're too wayward. Come on, you'll catch a cold in this dew.'

We walk slowly back up the hill and across the orchard, arm in arm. I unlatch the door as quietly as I can, but I hear Adela catch her breath at the slightest noise. We tiptoe upstairs. She kisses me lightly on the cheek and returns to her room. I've made my decision.

26th July 1909

I thank God for another six days of dry weather. The hay has been tossed and raked into loose swaths, and turned again. The beige grass is flecked with faded colour from the dried wildflowers. It is time to bring it in.

The horses pace with measured tread, their rumps buried beneath the overhanging loads. The vast wagons lean and roll, their axles creaking under the strain. Each has a boy swaying on top, his knuckles clenched into the hay.

In the yard, Jarvis the rick builder is already singing out his orders. Ladders and pitchforks are being assembled and the new steam elevator hauled into place. The staddle stones are in position to make sure that the hay is clear of the ground.

Now it is mid-afternoon. The rick has risen and the ladders are coming into play. Tristram has taken a pitchfork. He sweeps down to take up a bolt and then pitches in one graceful movement, his arms firing to their full length above his head, so that the sheaf sails from his fork to land at the feet of Jarvis, who instantly stoops to pack where his expert eye dictates. By the time he straightens, another is at his feet, and the pace does not relent, on and on to a rhythm of sweeping and flinging, stooping and pressing.

Now the sun sinks low. The light will soon be fading. The rick has long out-reached the steam elevator, and it is all down to laborious loading up ladders, and the two remaining men capable of pitching to this height. Still Tristram does not tire. The more bolts he tosses, the greater the height of the rick and the further he has to pitch into gravity's teeth. The sweat flashes on his bare back and his muscles slide, yet he does not break, and still he pitches, until the last cart is empty and it is left to Folland the thatcher to top the rick.

Thomas came over this afternoon, just after Mama and I had returned from delivering cider in the governess cart. He asked me what I'd been doing, and I told him, but I didn't mention the Wagner and Delius scores. They are my secret, to be shared with Mama and Tristram in my own time. As for the Nietzsche poems, they're for Tristram and me alone.

I asked Thomas whether we might go and watch the men building the rick. He came reluctantly, I thought. I sensed he wanted to be alone with me, but since he seemed tongue-tied, I thought that the noise and activity might put him at ease.

The rick was rising rapidly. A steam elevator was puffing away, taking the hay steadily but slowly up to where the men were packing. But the rick soon outgrew its reach, and from that moment it was ladders or pitching. Only two of the men seemed capable of pitching beyond a certain height, and one of them was Tristram. I watched the muscles rippling across his back, the sweat washing down his skin. He moved with what seemed an effortless grace. The smell! There's nothing like fresh hay, but there were other scents in there too: sulphurous steam from the engine, sweat from the men, and some mysterious perfumes which I think may have been from the dried flowers.

I thought Thomas might want to join in, but he stood beside me awkwardly, with a fascination which somehow managed to seem strangely incurious. I can never tell what he wants. As for me, I don't know either.

13th August 1909

Our family, it has been tonight shaken. I am frightened, especially for Richard, who is hurt and bewildered. Yet, for all that, I should not be surprised at what has happened. Since his stay in Leipzig, Tristram has changed. His rebelliousness has been apparent for some time. Most young men show their independence by moving away from their parents. It seems that Tristram is intending to do the opposite.

He was making his announcement over dinner. Richard was praising him for his leadership and tenacity in getting the hay crop in.

'You are certainly in a fit state of health, and strong; excellent condition for the coming rugby season.'

'Perhaps not,' said Tristram.

'Come now, you have every chance of achieving a blue in your first season, with cricket to follow.'

'I'm not going to Oxford, Father.' These words were laid across the table with flat determination. Richard froze for a few seconds, then put down his knife and fork. He drew himself slowly upright in his chair, taking in a deep breath.

'You are not yet twenty-one,' he said, turning his gaze onto his son.

'I'm a year over eighteen. I intend to make my way in the world.'

I was aware of Adela leaning forward. She was smiling, as she is apt to do when there is tension, and staring at a point on the table two feet in front of her.

By Richard's next words I was surprised, because they seemed to be conceding the initiative to Tristram. 'Do you have a plan?'

'Yes, I intend to proceed with the *Schrebergarten*.'

Richard exhaled sharply. 'Do you, now.'

'Yes, Father. I know that certain aspects of my proposal disturb you, and I understand your concern. I don't want to impose myself against your wishes, dearly though I'd love to remain here. But if I can't proceed with it on this farm, then I'll do it elsewhere.'

I said, 'But think by not going to Oxford what you will be throwing away.'

'Yes, all right, Helga. I think that you had better leave this matter to me.'

I was not pleased. The lot of a wife and mother is so. All I had been trying to do was steer the conversation back to Oxford. It seemed a far more important subject than *Schrebergarten*. I was fearing that Richard was taking the wrong pitch, and so it proved.

'I cannot imagine who you would find to back your scheme, or where you would get the money from.'

'I have arranged a meeting with Mr Philipson at the bank.'

'How dare you.'

'Please Father.' Tristram held up his hand with calm authority. 'It isn't about Chaddingley. I've prepared my figures in general terms. We could even be talking about Germany.'

Richard let out an exasperated snort, at which Adela's head jerked up. She was still leaning forward, but now her gaze was darting around the table to each of us in turn. She had stopped smiling, poor child, and her lips were trembling. Tears were not far away. Only Tristram was returning to his food, although he seemed to be examining each mouthful with studied deliberation.

'I think that we should talk about this after dinner,' Richard said, more calmly than I was expecting.

'Yes, Father.'

In total silence was the meal concluded.

Much to my amazement, Richard asked me to join them in his study after dinner. Not many men would have done that. Most prefer to be making their own stews of their relationship with their sons. I was even allowed to speak; more remarkably still, I was encouraged to initiate and voice my own thoughts. Naturally, I concentrated on Oxford, telling Tristram of all the important contacts and friendships he could be making there for his future.

Richard, with considerable charm, pointed out that a degree would be greatly increasing the alternatives open to him. He tactfully pointed out that, although Tristram had been successful at school, such early achievements would count for little in the outside world. People would be asking why he had not been to university, and would shun him. 'You may not like it, but it is expected of a young gentleman. The world is full of presumptions.

People admire every kind of courage, except the courage of having turned their backs on society's prejudices.' These words might well have been spoken by Tristram himself, and I wondered greatly that they had come from Richard.

Tristram said, 'I've made up my mind. I'll be all the stronger for casting off in a new direction. If I go to Oxford and achieve my sporting blues, and get a degree in Ancient History, I'll simply be doing more of the same. I don't intend to make an academic career, nor a vocation of cricket. I understand what you both say about contacts and expectations. These may be valuable in the Foreign Office or the Indian Civil Service, where I'd be a rivet in some vast structure. As for reputation, I should like to be respected for what I achieve, and the time has come for me to strike out and create something of my own.'

'But your education, it is not complete,' I said.

'If I may say so, Mother, I've shown my academic ability. Modesty permitting, I've demonstrated success as a pupil to a greater extent than many who've completed a university course.'

'I think that will be all, Tristram, for now,' Richard said quietly.

When we were alone, Richard crumpled. 'Where have I gone wrong? I just do not understand it. Had he announced some great adventure in Antarctica or the Belgian Congo, I might have followed his reasoning. But all he wants to do, it seems, is stay at home and be a sort of foreman on the farm. And then he talks about making a reputation.'

'That is not quite being fair,' I said. 'He has a

scheme which, all right, you are not believing in, but let us say that it is a good one, yes? It is true that if it were successful, it could be revolutionising agriculture. And he is making it quite clear that he is prepared to implement it anywhere, not necessarily here.'

'Oh, yes, in Germany.'

'Anywhere,' I said firmly. 'Germany is just an example. He is speaking the language.'

Richard is taking this personally. He sees it as a criticism of himself, and as a mark of his own failure. With Tristram I am not pleased, but I am at least consoling myself that he is strong and intelligent and seems to succeed at what he does. I do not approve of his target any more than Richard but I am sure that, when he is aiming for it, he will be hitting it. Like that he is so.

At least Richard will not be vindictive, of that I am confident. I know some fathers who would be talking about cutting off their son's allowance, and of disinheritance. That Richard will not be doing. But I doubt that he will allow Tristram to remain here, and I am not sure that it would be good for either of them if he were to be doing so. Tristram talks of striking out; then he should do so. In any case, if Richard does not believe in the scheme, he should not be allowing it here. On that I will be supporting him. For now he is needing my comfort and affection. He is wounded, and I must heal him.

When Tristram said that he wasn't going to Oxford, I felt a tingle of delight. We would be together, after all. Then I realised that he'd be unlikely to stay here. I fought back the tears until after dinner, when I rushed up to my room and lay on my bed and sobbed. We've been such a happy family, and now it's all over. If Tristram leaves, we'll be sundered, but if he stays, there'll be unpleasantness, I can sense it. Poor Papa. He was so brave and dignified, but his pride has been hurt.

I'm angry with Tristram. It's Leipzig and that wretched Nietzsche. Why does he feel that he has to destroy things? He talks of casting out from the shore, regardless of the agony he leaves behind. He makes a virtue of rejection. Doesn't he realise that what we've been taught is good? It's our basis of loving each other and our… our… our civilisation. Oh, I'm so miserable.

19th August 1909

Father's asked if he can come with me on my visit to Mr Philipson, the bank manager. It's a conciliatory gesture. He told me that if he's got to make a decision on whether or not *Schrebergarten* would be appropriate for Chaddingley, he needs to educate himself more on the subject. That's a magnanimous thing to say. He's asked me to prepare a set of figures for Chaddingley, and has even told Mr Philipson to come here for the meeting.

I won't get excited by premature expectations. I welcome Father's presence, but I'm optimistic only in terms of the scheme itself, not whether he'll accept it.

23rd August 1909

Our meeting with Philipson is over. I had asked Tristram beforehand to prepare some figures on the financial effect of his *Schrebergarten* on Chaddingley. I wanted to see for myself how far Tristram had got with his plans, and whether there is a financial case for implementing the scheme here. Of course, I know full well that my decision should not be based upon money. Did not Our Lord cast the moneylenders out of the temple? But I was curious, nevertheless.

Tristram had prepared himself well and presented his case admirably. I could not dispute a fact or figure from within my domain, and Philipson made it clear that he was both satisfied and impressed. I realise that I have been a fool over the cow house. Of course we should go for the latest suction milkers. I have authorised Tristram to cancel the order for the foot-treadle machines. I hope it is not too late, otherwise I will be punished and exposed for the stick-in-the-mud that I sometimes am.

It was when Tristram started asking Philipson how he might raise finance for the *Schrebergarten* venture in Germany that my emotions suddenly took over. I felt a tightness in my throat and realised that there were tears forming in my eyes. A father must accept that his son has grown up and is moving on, but I just cannot help being alienated by the thought of losing him to Germany. There was no blackmail on his part. He had drawn up his original figures for England but, when I realised that Germany was a real possibility, I am afraid that my emotions began to get the better of me. It is the way I am.

The problem is this: Tristram's figures make sense, not because the case for providing a couple of acres to each worker is proven: it is not; but because the revolution in machinery is happening so fast, and the shortage of labour so acute, that a reduction in the workforce is inevitable. This is true on our farm, in the rest of England, and probably in most advanced countries in Europe, Germany included. It is technology which is driving this. Tristram's *Schrebergarten* scheme might allow us to retain the best and most skilled workers, without us having to resort to ridiculously high wages. Christian principles should always come first, but I cannot protect them against the march of the inevitable. An unprosperous farm functioning badly would do no one any good.

The reason why I am tormented tonight is that I cannot convince myself that the prospect of losing Tristram to Germany is not clouding my judgement. I cannot speak to him of this. To say that I would only allow him to remain here if the alternative would be for him to go to Germany but not, say, to Yorkshire, would be ridiculous. It would seem like blackmail, and I would forfeit his respect. I cannot consult Helga either. For obvious reasons, she does not share my antipathy towards Germany, and it is not fair to put her on the spot over the viability of the *Schrebergarten* for Chaddingley. She does not understand farm matters, and has no interest in them. It is a difficult decision, and it is mine to take. I must pray.

24th August 1909

So, it is over. Tristram will not be going to Oxford. Richard called me into his study and told me that all persuasions had failed. I have been excluded from the final negotiations. When I asked what Tristram was going to be doing instead, Richard replied without conviction, 'He will be running the farm.'

I think that Richard is making a big mistake. He was refusing to discuss the *Schrebergarten* idea with me. I am convinced that he is not believing in it, but it is easy for him to be keeping his true feelings from me when he is knowing that I am ignorant of the subject. When I asked him whether this meant that he himself would be relinquishing all control of the farm, he snapped back at me, 'Of course not.' So, the orchestra is to have two conductors. It will not work. He should have told Tristram to go and carry out his plans elsewhere.

Adela is ecstatic. She worships Tristram and cannot see beyond the fact that he is still going to be around. Of course, my mind I cannot speak to her either. I am feeling lonely and depressed. It is time for me to go on my visiting rounds, but I am doing so with a heavy heart. It is hard to believe that Mrs Shorter's carbuncles will be cheering me up.

4th September 1909

We plough the fields and scatter the good seed on the land; but it is fed and watered by God's almighty hand. Hm, well, he didn't make a very good job of it this year; he over-watered it. The harvest is in, but it's late, and quality and yields are down. Father's telling us we must give praise. I think he would say that even if we'd only had one bushel to the acre and foot and mouth disease in the cattle.

The church has been decorated with produce from all over the village and surrounding fields. Marrows, pumpkins and loaves of bread form the centrepieces, surrounded by all kinds of vegetables, garlanded and twined with whorls of honeysuckle, jasmine and wild hops. At least this year Nancy hasn't encased her cottage loaf in monkshood. A few years ago she'd have poisoned half the village if Mrs Clucas hadn't spotted it in time.

I think Father's pleasantly surprised that I haven't put forward any detailed proposals for *Schrebergarten* yet, but he knows I'm thorough in gathering my facts. For the past few weeks I've been documenting the tasks of each worker: his skills, the time he takes to carry out his duties, and my assessment of whether he could perform better. Farming is such a seasonal business, that it's no good watching a man for just a fortnight at harvest time, when he'll be potato picking in October, hedge laying in January, and planting mangels in the spring. But I can't wait a year before presenting my plan to Father. I'll compromise by taking my study through to December. By that time I'll have taken a sample covering both summer and winter months, and will draw my conclusions from that.

He only is the Maker of all things near and far; He paints the wayside flowers, He lights the evening star. In parallel, I'm exploring opportunities for improvements in working practices, especially mechanisation. But there's only so much I can do from reading journals. I need to travel, to visit shows and exhibitions, and attend demonstrations. I've persuaded Father to invest in a motor car. The Wolseley will arrive on the 19th. I'll take Adela for drives in it. She's never taken to riding, but I can picture her in her brown shawl and chinchilla muff, with her pancake hat pinned firmly against the wind. *God, our Maker, doth provide for our wants to be supplied.* And Elizabeth Sawbridge. No, I mustn't think of that now. But I can't help it. Elizabeth, I keep wanting to say her name. *Grant, oh Lord of life that we, Holy grain and pure may be.* I wonder where she is now. She isn't in Church, and hasn't been for the past two Sundays.

Come, with all Thine Angels come; bid us sing the Harvest-home.

Here in the Great Barn, Papa has everyone in stitches. The men and women of the village are howling with laughter, and I can feel tears streaming down my face. All through the day, we've been building up to this. First, the Harvest Festival service, with its cheery hymns, tempered by Papa admonishing us from the pulpit to be humble in our gratitude. Then the great Harvest Feast, when we could tuck into Mrs Hearn's mouth-watering ham and pickle. The few Methodists and Roman Catholics had been invited to join us. At the end of the meal, Papa rose to his feet and pounded the table with a wooden mallet, which promptly broke. Mama whispered that he'd partly sawn the shaft through beforehand. I nearly fell off my chair laughing. Papa clasped his hands together and looked upwards through the rafters in supplication, a smile of innocent radiance on his face, and the whole village went wild. And then his speech! It seemed he had something to say about everyone in the room individually. All through the year, he's been collecting anecdotes, and it seems that there isn't a single person who hasn't made a fool of themself at some time or other. But Papa tells each story with such affection that his victims emerge as heroes.

He's such a showman, but we'd seen nothing yet. After the meal, the tables were cleared away and the chairs arranged in theatre style, facing the stage. Mama's old upright piano was wheeled into place. It was so exciting. Then we had the concert, with performances by several of the village folk. I played a medley of country songs, which I thought suitably rustic and uncomplicated for my audience. They appeared to be well received, and I was pleased with the applause. Performing gives me such a thrill. I become absorbed in my playing, yet I feel that I'm communicating with the audience and they with me. I long for the day when I can engage with more discerning critics. I've been allowed to drink a little French wine, but only when I'd finished. Mama was right to restrain me, as it's made me rather giggly. Abel Hopkins and Martin Roper each sang songs, accompanied by Mama, and old Joseph Smith recited some poems which touched everyone deeply.

Now we're into the final performance. The Harvest Supper always ends like this. Papa and Colonel Sawbridge take the stage, with Mama seated to one side at the piano, ready to produce crunching chords when one of them does something really silly. You wouldn't believe the heights of buffoonery which the two men are scaling. The song they're singing now is about a farmer, a parson and a pig. They do this every year, but they improvise. Tears of laughter are running down my cheeks. Oh no, what is this? Now they've switched roles, each deliberately attempting to confuse the other. The aim is to get one's opponent to dissolve into laughter, but their resistance is high, and neither of them has cracked. Colonel Sawbridge daringly impersonates Papa in the pulpit, then suddenly Papa is galloping round the stage on an invisible horse, pretending to be Colonel Sawbridge at the charge on the dervishes. And now they're both pigs, attempting to out-grunt each other. Oh, I could die.

21st September 1909

I knew that troubles we would be seeing, ever since Richard was allowing Tristram to be remaining on the farm. But it still caught me by surprise when it came. As before, Tristram chose our evening meal as his moment to be laying down a challenge to Richard's authority.

It was typical of Tristram that he should have prepared himself so thoroughly and, having done so, inflicted the cut so clinically. He clinched the moral high ground, not because his argument was right and good, but because Richard could not respond to the detail of his knowledge. Tristram remained calm throughout, whereas Richard was floundering and being made to look weak. For this, I am not forgiving Tristram.

It started with Richard talking about St Matthew, whose feast day it is.

'Matthew wrote his gospel in Antioch. His story covers much of the same ground as Mark's, but he adds much that is new. He was a tax collector, you know.'

'That was Matthew the Apostle,' said Tristram, in the flat voice he uses when he is wishing to be assertive. 'Mark wrote his gospel around 65 AD, which is thirty-five years after the crucifixion of Jesus. Matthew and Luke wrote theirs much later, between fifty and seventy years after Christ's death.

Neither claims to have been an eyewitness to the life of Jesus. John's gospel came even later.'

'Some people believe that,' Richard replied carefully.

'It's true,' Tristram continued. 'St Paul wrote the earliest parts of the New Testament long after the crucifixion, and he certainly never met Jesus. The gospels came later still. Matthew plagiarised what Mark had written, some of it word for word, but added his own passages for a Jewish readership. Luke, on the other hand, wrote propaganda aimed at upper- and middle-class Romans. John, writing much later still, and again for the Jewish market, put greater emphasis on the alleged divinity of Christ, as opposed to his magic tricks: miracles and the transformation of bodies. But none of the gospel writers, or anyone else who wrote in the Bible, was an eyewitness to the life of Christ.'

Adela had been watching Tristram with a dumbfounded expression, but now she jerked her eyes downwards at the table and looked terrified. Plagiarism, propaganda, magic tricks, none of the New Testament's writers eyewitnesses: these were words to be igniting Richard. He had laid down his knife and fork and was staring at his son with a look of malevolence. But all he said was, 'I do not know where you have got these rumours from.'

Instead of informing him, Tristram ploughed on. 'Two hundred years after the death of Christ, there were scores of gospels. Constantine, the first Roman Emperor to be converted to Christianity, achieved order and cohesion by imposing political censorship. It was he who edited down the New Testament into what we have today.' He paused, looking Richard directly in the eye. Whether Richard was deciding not to respond to this deliberate challenge, or whether he was privately conceding Tristram's claim to be true, I am not knowing. A new and fearful heresy was to follow.

'Thirteen years ago, a German scholar walked into an Egyptian bookshop and purchased a previously unknown gospel written on papyrus. He took it back with him to Berlin. Further research revealed that it was a 5th-century copy of an even earlier 2nd-century account of the life of Jesus. What is interesting is that it was written in the name of Mary Magdalene, who said that women were as fit to be priests as men.'

I saw Adela's eyes dart up and then down again. Tristram continued, 'Now you can imagine why that particular gospel didn't get past Constantine's censors. But they didn't simply suppress it. To make sure that it never gained credibility, they branded Mary Magdalene a whore, which is how many in the Church described her, even though there wasn't a shred of evidence that she was.'

Richard was on his feet. 'That is enough,' he shouted. 'Your blasphemies are one thing, but I will not allow foul language in this house, especially in front of women and children. Get out.'

Tristram rose to his feet, and without a glance at any of us, walked calmly from the room. I was sitting there appalled. How could we have brought him up to be so destructive? Adela was shaking. Richard, bless him, was saying as steadily as he could, 'Eat up, my dears. We should not allow our food to be spoiled by that.'

The awful thing is that Tristram is excelling at Ancient History. It is the subject that he would have read at Oxford. He devours books avidly and nearly always gets his facts right. If what he says is true… but for now I will not think of it. His attack on Richard's beliefs, and for that matter Adela's and mine, was nothing short of murderous. One is not admiring an assassin for the sharpness of his blade, nor for the elegance of his thrust.

My poor, poor husband. He should not have to suffer this.

I pray for the soul of Tristram. It is natural for a young man to challenge his father. What has happened does not make him a bad person. I must accept that, but the feeling of rejection is for now too much to bear. Can you imagine what it would be like if your son were to tell you, not in a fit of pique but with considerable calmness, that everything you have ever done for him, every birthday present, every picnic treat, every lesson in how to hold a rod or fly a kite, has been wrong, has done him no good, and brought him no pleasure? I have failed. I have tried to bring him up by example and through love. He has observed my way of doing things and told me that it is false.

Dear Lord, whose infinite mercies are bestowed upon us, deliver us from heresy and from evil. Show Tristram the path to righteousness. It is I who have failed him, I who should be punished. Ever since he was a little boy, I have tried to teach him the path of thy Faith. This is merely a phase. He is testing, he is probing, that is all. Did not thine only Son go into the desert to be tried in the ways of temptation? Tristram is being tempted, that is what this means. It does not follow that he will succumb. He does not mean to deny Thee. Doth not the light of Truth shine most brightly when there is darkness? In his hour of bitterness, was not thine only begotten Son purged? I pray for the soul of Tristram. I pray as though he were dead. Oh Lord, comfort thy servant in his misery. Oh God.

Why does he do it? Tristram is beastly, beastly, beastly. I don't care if he is right and knows everything. He cannot do this to Papa and Mama. I will tell him what I think of him.

Adela stands in the doorway of my bedroom in her nightie. She's been crying. 'Why do you do it?' she asks.

'Because it's the truth,' I reply, as gently as I can. She's silent, looking at me in a pathetic way. I take a step towards her, but she shrinks back. I need a commitment from her, to show that she's still prepared to listen. 'Come with me to the corncrake fields. Come now, and I'll explain.'

'I will not.' To punish me, she adds, 'Elizabeth has gone to America for three years. She sailed on the *Mauretania* this morning.'

22nd September 1909

I've apologised to Father. It was wrong of me to use the word "whore", especially in front of Adela. Father has accepted my apology magnanimously, but he's also taken the opportunity to lay down his rules of engagement, as it were. He has every right to do so.

'You may hold your views sincerely, and I accept that they are different from mine. One day, you and I should sit down and debate them, but I do not think that the time for that is now.'

'Yes, Father.'

'What you must understand is that I will not tolerate challenges to be made to the established Faith in such a manner that they cause great offence. Further, you are unreasonable if you choose to undermine my authority by digging up some obscure pieces of historical conjecture and then challenge me to refute them in public without warning.'

None of the facts I put forward last night were conjecture, and yet Father is right. By choosing to make my attack in front of Mama and Adela, and by throwing little known facts into the ring, which put Father at a disadvantage, I have, in a sense, been cowardly. In future I'll be more circumspect. But I won't shrink from the truth, nor from putting it forward. The facts should be well known, even if they aren't. Lack of knowledge is perpetuating a falsehood.

25th September 1909

My sister took me by surprise after lunch today.

'Come with me down to the corncrake fields. Come after dinner.'

I smiled at this sudden change of attitude. 'But it'll be dark soon after dinner. The nights are drawing in.'

'It doesn't matter.' She had a kind of desperate intensity and was breathless. 'The moon is nearly full. It'll be fine tonight and bright soon after dusk, I can tell. Please, Tristram.'

'Very well, we'll go soon after the meal's over. Will you tell Mother and Father?'

She hesitated only briefly. 'No. I'm seventeen now.'

I laughed. She had a look of passion on her face.

We're there, and the moon has reared up over the eastern hill, huge and dark with the apricot richness of the harvest still in its bowl. The corncrakes are scraping away. Soon they'll be gone, flying south on their winter migration.

Adela's questions on the walk down sounded hollow. She takes little interest in nature or the farm. For the past few minutes she's been silent, but now that we've arrived she swings round to face me. 'Were the things you said the other night true?'

'About the gospels? Yes, though we can't be absolutely certain that Matthew the writer wasn't

Matthew the Apostle. It's very unlikely that they were the same person.'

'And that bit about the New Testament having been edited for political purposes?'

'All true. It's even more so in the case of the Old Testament.'

'Tell me about that. I'd like to know more about how the Bible was written.'

'Very well. Tradition has always had it that the first five books of the Old Testament, the Pentateuch or Torah, were written by Moses, as dictated by God. In 1753 a Frenchman called Austruc discovered that the book of Genesis had in reality been written by more than one author. Later research, up until very recently, has taken this much further. The Torah actually has four different sources. Not only that, they were written in the ninth, eighth, sixth and fifth centuries BC; so not only were they written in vastly different times to one another, but they were all written many, many centuries after Moses, who probably died in the middle of the fifteenth century BC; that's six hundred years before the earliest book he's supposed to have written. Mind you, people have been turning a blind eye to inconsistencies for millennia. In the book of Deuteronomy, Moses writes about his own death. Yes, really.'

Adela looks astounded. 'Are you saying that Moses didn't even exist?'

'Almost certainly Moses was a real man, and a leader, but there's no evidence that he wrote anything down. The existence of Abraham, Noah and other early biblical characters is far more questionable.'

'But does it really matter if the Old Testament was written by lots of different people who were not who we originally thought they were? Does it matter if the books got edited and rewritten many times? The hand of God could still have been guiding all these people.'

I'm disappointed with this. 'Yes, of course it matters. Either events happened, or they didn't. You can't say that God guided someone to write one truth, and then someone else to contradict it.'

'Weren't these things originally happening in days when very little was written down? This would explain why the stories of Abraham and Moses were written many centuries afterwards, and the gospels long after the death of Christ.'

'But in that case, why should we believe in ancient legends? We're told that St George slew a dragon. Do you therefore believe in dragons? But it doesn't end there. Most of the books of the Old Testament were edited and rewritten many times down the centuries, in order to comply with the political needs of the rulers of the day. Take King Hezekiah of Judah. Hezekiah was under constant pressure from the Assyrians in the north. He needed to strengthen his position with his own people, centred on Jerusalem. To do this he outlawed other cults and brought in monotheism, in other words one God and one temple at Jerusalem. You can understand the allegory: one God, here in Jerusalem, just as there should be one king, me, Hezekiah, in our capital. Hezekiah ruled that his people should pay taxes to the temple in order to be blessed by God. And although he was defeated by the

Assyrians and forced to pay tribute in order to buy them off, he used the Bible to assert that it was he who'd defeated them in a glorious victory.

'The so-called word of God has been changed time and time again, rewritten by unscrupulous men for political ends. This is no different to any other history. In his memoirs, Napoleon brushes aside his blunders at Waterloo, blaming everyone but himself. We know that what he wrote is untrue because there are other accounts of the battle which contradict him, and because Napoleon was exiled to St Helena, losing his power to manipulate history.

'The alteration of the books of the Torah continued right down until the fourth century BC. So although there were originally four different authors of the books purported to have been written by Moses, a far greater number of scribes had a hand in editing and revising the Torah until, at last, one last redactor, who may have been Ezra, pulled the whole thing together in a finally edited document around 450 BC.'

A train whistle blows far down the valley. Adela is motionless. I wonder what she's thinking, but she remains silent. I decide to tell her more about Moses.

'So who was this person Moses, who we're told was such a heroic figure, and who had a direct link to God as his spokesman? I'll tell you. First, he slaughtered people in their tens of thousands.'

'You mean in battle?'

'No, I don't mean in battle, though he was responsible for that too. I mean that he ordered his enemies to be massacred after the battles were over. I mean the ritual killing of men, women and children, not just by invoking the name of God, but by claiming that God himself had ordered it.'

'Surely that can't be right?'

'It wasn't right. It was cruel and vindictive; worse, it was justified by a claim of racial and religious superiority.'

'What I meant was that it can't be correct.'

'Oh yes, it's well documented. Moses committed both murder and genocide, which is peculiar for the bearer of the Ten Commandments, which include the words "Thou shalt not. kill."'

'Tristram!'

'Please listen, Adela. First, the murder, which was performed by his own hands, as recorded in the Book of Exodus. Moses saw an Egyptian smiting a Hebrew. After he'd looked this way and that and saw that no one was looking, Moses slew the Egyptian and hid his body under the sand. Later he ordered the stoning to death of a man who had merely been picking up sticks on the Sabbath. The description of what happened is devoid of any ambiguity. The genocide is far more serious.'

'Isn't genocide deliberately trying to destroy a whole race?'

'That's right, and I'm saying that Moses ordered it, claiming that he was carrying out the will of God. In the Book of Numbers, God speaks unto Moses, telling him to "avenge the children of Israel of the Midianites". As with the murder, the details are explicit. Under the supervision of Eleazor the priest, all the men and children of the Midianites were slaughtered. The women, however, were divided into two groups. Those who'd "known a man by lying with him" were killed, every one of them. But those women who hadn't known a man by lying with him, in other words virgins, Moses commanded "should be kept for yourselves". But listen to this, dear Adela. The Book of Numbers specifically states how many women were spared from death. It's thirty-two thousand. It's half the female population of the Midianites; that's stated too. So, taking into account the men and children who were also massacred, we can safely assume that the number of Midianites butchered by Moses was close to a hundred thousand. There can't have been many Midianites left, other than the thirty-two thousand virgins, who presumably didn't stay that way for long. Remember, this was mostly a sparsely inhabited desert country, then as now. Sand is frequently mentioned.'

'I see,' Adela breathes.

'Do you, my darling sister, or have you merely heard the words? People have been reading the Bible, and quoting from selected passages for centuries, while avoiding facts such as these. The case of the Midianites isn't the only one. When Joshua faced the Amalekites, it wasn't just victory in battle that Moses sought. God said he wanted to destroy even the memory of the Amalekites and said that he, God, would "have war with them from generation to generation". When the children of Belial had been seen "serving other gods", it wasn't punishment that Moses ordered, but permanent eradication, again in the name of the Lord. Later, in the Book of Joshua, Joshua destroyed the cities of Canaan, "neither left they any to breathe. As the

Lord commanded Moses his servant, so did Moses command Joshua, and so did Joshua; he left nothing undone that the Lord commanded Moses".

'In addition to murder and genocide, it's very likely that Moses sanctioned child sacrifice. Some scholars are certain of it. My own opinion is that the evidence isn't quite conclusive, but it's very strong. In the Book of Exodus, God commands that "the firstborn of thy sons shall be given unto me". It's been argued that this simply means that the eldest sons are to enter into the priesthood, but this seems highly unlikely, for the very next verse reads, "likewise shalt thou do with thine oxen and with thy sheep". Now, what would God be doing with oxen and sheep as priests? The only plausible explanation is that these animals were to be sacrificed to God, and that the word "likewise" implies that this was also the fate of the firstborn sons.

'Moses showed many of the classic characteristics of a tyrant. He enforced the law, dictated by God he said, that to marry a foreigner was a serious crime; yet he himself did exactly that, he married a foreigner. When Phinehas, Moses's great-nephew, saw an Israelite with a Midianite woman, he killed both of them with his spear. This so pleased God that "the plague was stayed from the children of Israel".

'Few tyrants in history can have been so terrible. Moses was ruthless towards his own people. In the Book of Leviticus, when an Israelite blasphemed, he ordered him to be stoned to death. This fate could be awarded for the most trivial of activities. I've told you about that man stoned to death on the orders of

Moses for picking up sticks on the Sabbath. In Deuteronomy, it's made clear that it's an offence punishable by death simply to "fail to hearken unto a priest."'

'You seem to have a lot against Moses.'

'There's a lot in the Bible against Moses. Don't you see why I'm telling you this? The Laws of Moses are the main foundations of Judaism and therefore of Christianity. Moses wasn't just the most frequently mentioned man in the Old Testament by a long way. He was the person who, more than any other, was believed to be the voice of God himself, and the man whom rulers like Hezekiah later decided would be their co-ordinating author and spokesman. Even though we now know this to have been a politically motivated lie, few people today are aware of the reality behind it. To them, the commandments of Moses are the word of God.'

The corncrakes have long since ceased. The only sound is of a late summer cricket chirruping in the hedgerow. I decide to tell her.

'If I tell you something, will you keep it secret?'

'That depends on what it is.'

'If you judge it reasonable that for the time being you shouldn't tell anyone, will you keep it secret between us?'

'If it's reasonable, then.'

'Very well. The greatest research into the Torah was performed by a German, Julius Wellhausen, forty years ago. When I was in Leipzig, Great Uncle Gerd introduced me to a brilliant archaeologist and scholar called Walter Grattin, who was a pupil of Wellhausen's at Göttingen. I was fortunate to spend quite a lot of time with him, and he seemed impressed by the fact that I'm fluent in English and German, have learnt Latin and Greek, and have some knowledge of Hebraic scriptures. He was also impressed by my ability to remember texts. Grattin told me that he's leading an expedition to Palestine next year and has invited me to join him as an assistant.'

Adela's eyes light up. 'Tristram, that's exciting, but you surely can't…' Her voice fades.

'Go? I think I will. Grattin's made two conditions: that I memorise eighteen of the early books of the Old Testament in English and German, and that I acquire a thorough knowledge of Aramaic.'

'Is that a language?'

'Yes. It was the language of Jesus. Parts of the Old Testament books of Ezra and Daniel are written in Aramaic.'

'Is that why you keep receiving parcels from the postman? I thought they must be books on farming.'

'Some are, but many of them are in preparation for my work with Grattin.'

'But what about the *Schrebergarten*? You can't force Papa into the scheme and then abandon him?' A frown crosses her face. 'Is this the real reason why you decided not to go to Oxford? Is the *Schrebergarten* idea just an excuse?'

'No, not at all. I believe passionately in revolutionising agriculture, and intend to do it. But I also want to help find out the truth about Judaism and Christianity.'

'So all these germs you've been feeding me with

for the past few weeks haven't all come from Nietzsche?'

'No, my darling sister, they have not.'

'And do you think that you've succeeded in demolishing my Faith?'

'That's for you to say.'

'I value my Faith. I'm sorry, Tristram; I still cherish it.'

'Du bist so leichtgläubig!'

'*Du Ungläubiger*!' She stares back at me, delighted that she's returned my thrust so promptly.

'So what will this expedition of Herr Grattin's set out to achieve? To prove that they were all worshippers of Satan?' She's teasing me, but I want to be serious for a little longer.

'Worse than that: human sacrifice. Worse still, child sacrifice. Everyone knows the story of how Abraham was willing to sacrifice his son Isaac to God. I've already told you that Moses probably sanctioned the practice. The Old Testament is littered with references to human sacrifice. King Mannasseh and King Ahaz had their sons immolated in the fire, and there's no doubt that child sacrifice continued in Jerusalem up until the seventh century BC. The place where the remains of the children have been found is called the Tophet, which lies just outside the walls of Jerusalem. The prophet Isaiah writes lyrically about the glories of the fires of the Tophet, though he does this in the context of burning and torturing enemies, such as the King of Assyria. This ritual burning is done in the name of God, Yahweh, at his shrine. What may be significant is that Isaiah, whose words form the longest book of the Old Testament after The Psalms, never criticises Kings Mannasseh or Ahaz. But once the practice ceased, it was utterly condemned. To their credit, those who refer to child sacrifice in the Books of Kings, Chronicles and Jeremiah describe it as an abomination.'

'So what's the purpose of your work with Herr Grattin?'

'The Hebrew words of the Old Testament don't contain vowels. The word "mlk" occurs frequently. It may mean "Moloch", a pagan god of that time; or "molek", a victim. It's always been assumed that children were ritually burned at the Tophet in sacrifice to the god Moloch. However, Isaiah and others link the ritual of the Tophet to Yahweh, in other words Jehovah. If one substitutes molek, the victim, for Moloch, the god, there is further evidence to link child sacrifice to Yahweh.'

'So is your aim to prove that the children of Israel sacrificed children to Jehovah?'

'No it is not. We don't set out to prove anything. We're historians seeking the truth. If Moloch and molek turn out to be different words, and all the child sacrifices at the Tophet were made to Moloch, then so be it.'

'So what will you actually be doing; and where does your learning Aramaic come in?'

'Walter Grattin is digging in the ruins of Carthage now. It's too complicated to explain it to you in detail here, and it's getting cold, but Carthage was the largest site of child sacrifice in the ancient world. There are many similarities between the Tophet in Jerusalem and the one in

Carthage. Grattin aims to find out what the connections were. When it gets too hot, in the summer months of next year, the research will switch to several libraries round Europe. The team has some renowned Hebrew scholars, but they're weak in Aramaic. That's where I come in. Also, Grattin was impressed by my ability to memorise things by reading them only once, which is why he's set me the task of learning those Old Testament books.'

I sense that she's impressed, or at least curious. I hope I've opened her mind at last. 'Come on, we should go back,' I tell her, and she smiles secretively. We walk slowly up the hill past Turner's Piece. She's silent, and I hope this is a sign that she's digesting everything I've told her.

Now we're halfway across the orchard. The moon is towering behind us, sharpening the shadows of the apple trees on the grass.

'If I give you all the references to the texts I've quoted this evening, will you promise to look them up in your Bible?'

'To make sure you haven't been lying? Certainly, Mr Hall.' She turns to me and laughs. Her eyes become intense. She moves without warning into my face and kisses me on the mouth. It's only brief, but its wetness takes me by surprise. Then she skips ahead of me towards the house, turning to laugh at me as she goes.

As we enter, I take out my watch and see that it's after eleven o'clock. My little sister is both a girl and a woman. The house is silent as we extinguish the lights and go upstairs. I turn to her on the landing and whisper, 'Don't forget, my secret must remain a secret until I say.'

She nods and whispers back, 'I promise. Goodnight.'

I am appalled, and cannot believe that I have really seen it; but I must not jump to conclusions. I noticed that the house was quiet when I came out of my study soon after nine. Helga was in the drawing room reading, but there was no sign of Tristram or Adela. I looked for them in the parlour and then went upstairs and called out on the landing to see if either of them was in their room. Nothing. I went down to Helga again, but she had not seen them since dinner. I even walked round the downstairs servants' quarters, including the kitchen, but they were not there either. I went back upstairs and looked out over the orchard to see if they had gone for a walk. Adela should not be out after dark without letting us know. The harvest moon was and still is bright, and I could see clearly beyond the orchard into the surrounding fields. There was no sign of them. I thought of taking a walk, but I am struggling with my sermon for Sunday and needed to put in another couple of hours before I retired.

I became absorbed in my work, and by the time I had finished, Helga had gone to bed. I had another quick look for Tristram and Adela, but there was no sign of them, so I assumed that they must have retired too, as it was nearing eleven o'clock. Helga seemed asleep, so I undressed quietly and stood, as I often do on light summer evenings and when the moon is full, looking out over the orchard. I saw instantly that Tristram and Adela were walking hand in hand towards the house. Greatly annoyed that Adela should be out at this time, I was about to go down and express my displeasure, when I saw them lean into each other in a most complicit way. I stood fascinated and transfixed. Imagine my horror when I saw their lips come together. Surely not? The kiss was brief, but the way Adela danced the remaining distance to the house, laughing as she went, compounded my suspicion. I thought of treading downstairs to apprehend them, but what would I say? My horror at their intimacy had overtaken my concern that Adela was up late and outside without permission.

I did, however, open our bedroom door a chink, so that I could be sure that they went to bed promptly. I heard them whispering on the landing soon after, and was relieved to be certain that they had gone to their separate rooms.

I am appalled, but uncertain whether I should be. I cannot mention this to Helga; it is too delicate a subject to discuss with her. What I will do is keep a close watch on them both. I fear Tristram's corrupting influence on Adela, in more ways than one. I will try to see what they are up to. A brother and sister are allowed to be tactile up to a certain degree. But I must never forget that, although they do not know it, they are not true siblings, not by blood. I am ignorant of such matters; for instance, I do not know whether it is propriety that discourages carnal feelings between members of the same family, or something that nature has created. I once heard a man talking about "sexual chemistry" between lovers. Perhaps the reverse can be true, a sort of natural repellent which mercifully discourages unhealthy feelings within a family. But, foul possibility, could this be lacking when the members concerned are of the opposite sex but not related by blood?

It may be nothing, but Adela is my ward, and I must seek to protect her from evil, whatever the source. It is better to err on the side of caution. I will seek guidance from Our Lord, and meanwhile I will listen and watch.

5th October 1909

Sie mischt sich in alles ein! We were having an unexpected visitor, today; unexpected, and unannounced. It was Miss Smyth. She arrived soon after lunch, when Richard had already departed on his rounds and I was about to leave the house myself. To appear without warning like that, it is extremely discourteous. The purpose of Miss Smyth's visit was to converse with Adela and to discuss Wagner and Delius. She was, she explained, returning from a hastily arranged appointment in the neighbourhood: a weak excuse, I was thinking. She arrived in a two-seater motor, a Delahaye Tristram told me later, alone and driving it herself. Of course, I could not be staying just because Miss Smyth had decided to appear. I had my commitments to Mrs Neeves and to the Sproat family, whose daughter Becky is very poorly.

When I was arriving back at the house late in the afternoon, I was grateful that Richard had not returned before me. Adela was sitting at the grand piano in the drawing room playing Brahms's *Variations on a theme of Handel*. Tristram was in his usual chair reading, while opposite him Miss Smyth lay sprawled across the ottoman with her head thrown back, eyes closed and lips parted in a look of sublime enjoyment. I stood watching the scene with some annoyance. When Adela had finished the piece, she paused for a few moments and turned eagerly towards Miss Smyth, who slowly opened her eyes and, seeing me, leapt to her feet, exclaiming, 'Mrs Hall, please forgive me. You must be familiar with your daughter's playing.' She then clasped my hands in a hearty squeeze, adding, 'For me it is a new experience, and it has made me forget myself.'

Indeed it has, I thought, lolling like that in someone else's house as though she were taking a bath, but I smiled back as pleasantly as I could, gratified by what at least seemed genuine enthusiasm for Adela's performance. I offered her tea, but they had already taken it. I was anxious that Miss Smyth should be going before Richard returned. If he formed the opinion that she represented musical society in the outside world, he would never be agreeing to my plans for Adela.

Miss Smyth asked me if we might speak in private. Not wishing to disturb Tristram, who seemed totally absorbed in his book, and because

Richard never allows anyone other than himself to use his private study, I led her through to the parlour.

'Mrs Hall, may I be frank with you?' I imagine that Miss Smyth knows of no other way but to speak her mind. 'I had come here principally to assess your daughter's ability for musical analysis. You know that Thomas and I' - she was referring to Mr Beecham - 'formed the opinion that Adela's ability to read and digest a complex score is truly remarkable? I now realise that she has an even greater talent: that of a concert pianist.'

I returned her gaze. 'Of that I am aware.'

'Then will you also concede that your daughter has the talent to be not merely a good pianist, but a great one?'

'You are impressed by hearing her play?'

'Impressed is not the only word I would use. I am delirious.' She had seized my hands again in that over-familiar way of hers. 'Don't you see? Thomas saw it. I have seen it. We saw it in her appreciation of complex scores. It is not her technique which will make her a great artist. It is her understanding of music!'

I feared the woman was going to throw her arms around me.

'Mrs Hall, we must not waste this talent.'

'We?'

'I can help you, Mrs Hall, help Adela.'

I gave her a look which I hoped would let her know that, although she could continue, I would need much convincing in a short space of time. The clock was chiming five.

'I cannot teach her myself,' she said. 'I have neither the time nor the inclination. Adela needs two things: a teacher who can broaden her artistic expression still further, and experience of the concert platform.'

'She has only just turned seventeen.'

'But she is so mature.'

'Even so, her wider education she has to complete.'

Miss Smyth shrugged her indifference to that. 'She could stay at my lodgings. There is plenty of space and the contacts which I could provide in musical circles would greatly enhance her career.'

'Have you been speaking of this to Adela, Miss Smyth?'

'No, and I would certainly not do so without your permission.'

For the first time, I was grateful to her. 'Of her talent you are convinced?' I asked, seeking confirmation of what she had already said.

'Completely. Her performances would very soon be attracting audiences of considerable numbers. She has a delicacy of touch which one might expect of her sex, but you have, I presume, heard the sense of power and structure she conveys when playing Liszt's *B minor Sonata*?'

Indeed I have, I thought to myself, and it almost frightens me. 'I will be thinking about it,' I said firmly. 'In a year or two perhaps she will be ready,' I added, knowing full well that in reality I was considering launching her career sooner. Miss Smyth's expression lingered between exasperation and contempt, but she said nothing.

'My husband will be home soon, and I must be preparing for his return.'

She accepted my hint, and soon after left. Richard passed her, but I did not introduce them.

'Who was that?

'Ethel Smyth, a composer of music.'

'Oh,' was all he said.

18th October 1909

Today is the feast of St Luke. He was a physician, though for all I know Tristram may have designated him a murderer or a thief. His feast day traditionally marks the time when the tups are put out to the ewes. "On St Luke's Day, let tups have play." This year we are a day or two behind, Jack Hearn tells me, as he has not quite finished dipping the ewes and clipping behind their tails. St Luke's Day was also known as Dog Whipping Day, when the boys were allowed to whip any dogs they could catch outside, a curious and unsavoury practice.

The smell of ivy blossom is like Molly Hearn's cake mixture: warm and sweet. It brings the bees out, even at this time of year.

We are about to make cider. I can see the men assembling their long ladders in the orchard. I will try to find the time later to go out and join in. I love this time of year. There is so much to be grateful for.

10th November 1909

I'm ahead of time with my research into trends in farming technology, but relating them to the activities of our workers is throwing up more problems than I'd anticipated.

A dilemma I haven't yet resolved is what to do about the working horses and the men who understand and look after them. It's definitely a skill, but for how much longer will we need it? Steam traction engines, which have replaced horses on many large farms, aren't suitable for most tasks on our land, with its small field sizes and steep slopes. Chaddingley isn't like the arable lands of the Midlands and East Anglia. We can't justify the purchase of the pair of Clayton & Shuttleworth machines which we contract in occasionally, not because they would cost more than the horses they'd replace, but because they'd lie idle for most of the time.

The men seem to accept my presence among them, and my enquiries. Fortunately, my memory's good, which means I don't have to take notes when I'm with them. Only Nancy has seen fit to pass rude comment. 'Woteree want, snoopin' around poking his nose in for?' She said it so that the men would know that I must have heard it. I didn't let it pass. I walked up to her and asked if she had anything to say to me. Her eyes darted around the men looking for support, but by that time I was towering over her with a solemn gaze, so she shook her head rapidly and said no. As she isn't one of the workers, her comments would be of little concern to me, except that she's the wife of Abel Hopkins, one of the best men on the farm.

I'll put my recommendations to Father in the first few days of January. I've received a letter from Walter Grattin saying that, subject to an interview in London sometime in December, he's inviting me to join him in Berlin in early April. I can't abandon Father without having put the plans in motion well before then. There isn't much time.

18th November 1909

I walked Adela home from Evensong.

'Tristram, why do you still come to Church, when you don't believe in it?'

'Because I'm fascinated. Like you, I'm seduced. The liturgy, the ritual, the flickering candles, your beautiful singing. Oh yes, I feel it too, the emotional pull. My senses are enraptured and my reason becomes paralysed under its spell. Christianity is the mistress of seduction.'

'Tristram!'

'What? Shall I go to hell for saying that?'

'No, though perhaps you deserve it. I only believe in heaven, and I shall find you there, in spite of your sins.'

'You believe in heaven but not in hell? Where's the logic in that?'

'You and your logic! I believe in charity and in a good God. Hell is an outmoded concept.'

'And heaven isn't? The Scriptures say there's a heaven and a hell. Are you sure it isn't that you believe in one because it's comforting, but not in the other because it's too horrible to contemplate? The notion that the spirit or whatever you choose to call it can rise up and go to heaven has been dreamt up because people can't face up to the finality of their death. "I simply cannot bear to think that there is nothing after death, that it all ends there," one hears people say. They mean for the individual, of course. Why not? No, it isn't a pleasant thought, but that doesn't mean that it isn't true. So they embrace the concept of heaven, which promises perpetual survival. The same people seem able to reconcile themselves to a god who allows appalling horrors to happen to thousands of the living, so why shouldn't they accept the lesser horror that it all ends in oblivion? I'll tell you why. It's because we're all such selfish individualists that the continuation of the species or the universe after our own individual death is inadequate comfort.

'We laugh at the mediaeval theologians who debated the size of angels' wings, because we now think that they started from a false premise. Yet we repeat their mistakes in new ways over and over again.'

'Such as?'

'The Resurrection, the Immaculate Conception, the story of Genesis; a thousand things for which there's no evidence.'

'Except the recollection of those who witnessed them.'

'Adela, Adela, have you learnt nothing? The evidence that anyone witnessed those events is as weak as the evidence itself.'

'Falscher Anklager!'

'Leicht beinflussbare, leichtgäubige Person! While it was perfectly acceptable to debate the size of angels' wings, looking through a telescope and proving that the earth went round the sun was blasphemy. Anyone who pointed out the fact that renaissance popes frequently indulged in acts of gross indecency was tortured by the Inquisition. Popes were infallible when they said the earth was flat one day, and they were infallible when they said it was round the next.'

'But these are examples from the Catholic Faith, and long ago.'

'We still have a law of blasphemy in England. The Church of England still protects itself from criticism and doubt. The law requires that Christianity be taught in schools to susceptible young minds. Why is it only the priest who speaks in Church, except for a few lines prescribed by Cranmer four hundred years ago, which we must all parrot in unison? If I were to stand up in Church and say politely to Father, "Excuse me, but I think that Christianity is a force against progress" or "Please will you explain why God doesn't personally make his intentions clear," there would be instant outrage, not merely at the simple questions being asked, but at the fact that I'd questioned at all.'

'I hope you'll do no such thing.'

'Because of Father? Ah yes, the priest. The shepherd and his flock: a well-chosen piece of imagery, for is there any less imaginative animal than the sheep? So long as we are conditioned to feel that we are incapable of thinking for ourselves, we'll need the clergy to intercede for us. How convenient. The priest must also be a physician. He comes with soothing ointments, but first he must create a need for them. He must inflict the wound…'

'Tristram! This time you go too far.'

'Do I? Do I offend you because I imply that Father is a torturer? He doesn't mean to be. There's no more affectionate man on earth, but don't you see, his conditioning, his blind acceptance, his calling, which is perhaps the word he'd use, all draw him like a sleepwalker to the encouragement of meekness, submission and guilt.'

'I see nothing of what you say. Papa offers cheer and glad tidings. We laugh with him. He's kind to everyone he meets. I won't have you talking of him inflicting wounds. What do you preach? That there's no life after death, that there's no heaven, that God isn't good. Yet you accuse Father of being the one who spreads misery. You've been swayed too much by textbooks. You're so absorbed in the words of Nietzsche that you ignore the evidence of your own eyes and the goodness of those you see around you every day.'

The word "preach" had stung me. I'd offended her. Worse, I feared I may have alienated her. She was right; I went too far. I was worried that my few careless words at the end have turned her against everything I've said. Wishing to convince her that I love Father as dearly as she does, and not wanting to deliver her home in an agitated state, I led her down the lane which would take us round the outskirts of the village and back the long way.

I said gently, 'You should recognise superstition for what it is. We mustn't govern our lives by studying the lie of the tea leaves or the entrails of a goat. A hundred years ago, tens of thousands of innocent Indian travellers were regularly murdered by ritual garrotting. Those who committed the crimes, Thugees they were called, believed that the goddess Kali would reward them.'

'You can hardly blame Christianity for that.'

'No, and it was Christians who rightly condemned the practice and stamped it out because it was barbaric. But no one can disprove that Kali had ordered it, and the Thugees clearly believed it, as they didn't rob the travellers and had no other motive for killing them. The act of faith behind it was no more ludicrous than any other.'

'It's dark. You're frightening me.'

'Then hold me close, and let me tell you another story. Long ago, late on a winter's afternoon, a man and his wife were returning home on foot in the depths of the mediaeval countryside. It started to snow, so the man said he would walk on ahead to light a fire to warm up the house. When he returned to his wife, he found her dying in the snow. She'd been savaged by a demon, she said, who'd first appeared to her in the form of a baby. The man distinctly saw cloven hoof prints in the snow by his wife's body. So what do you think was behind all this? The man clearly believed his wife's tale and had seen the evidence in the snow. Did demons exist all those years ago, but have vanished now? Or were the man and woman so steeped in superstition that they'd believed such things to the extent of hallucination? Why should the woman have invented such a story, to leave the man with this last impression of her, which he would have to live with for the rest of his life?'

'So what do you make of it?'

'That mankind is forever looking for ways to be impressed. The image of the child may be significant. Perhaps the woman was barren and had longed for a child. Or perhaps all her children had died. Whichever, the woman was leaving the man with one last cry about something tragic in their lives. Some real beast may have attacked her. Perhaps she scraped the footprints for effect.'

'Or perhaps he did, to divert attention from the fact that he'd murdered her himself. This is just a horror story. You're trying to frighten me.'

'It's all right, I've got you. We're nearly home. Look, there's the light by the gate. Can I say one more thing?'

'If you must.'

'You remember I told you that the Torah had several authors, and that a single redactor, possibly Ezra, pulled it all together?'

'Yes.'

'I've been thinking. It's like taking all our best loved fables and claiming to have written the authentic history of England. The tale of Robin Hood, Joseph of Arimathea, Saint George and the Dragon; what a rich tapestry we'd have, all motivated by honour, patriotism and political cohesion, just like that achieved by King Hezekiah and Emperor Constantine. But they'd still not be true; nor would they, in universal terms, be moral, especially since, like the Old Testament, they would be promoting a sense of racial superiority. We could throw in The Knights of the Round Table. We'd have a unifying history of Britain: improving, entertaining, but complete humbug.'

Arriving close to home had relaxed her. 'Oh Tristram! Perhaps we could speak in the language of *Morte d'Arthur*. Gentle knight, greatly I marvel that ye have delivered me unto mine abode safe from the perilous road that we have travelled. I am now yours to command.'

We walked through the hall, screwing up our eyes against the light and flinging off our coats. As we entered the drawing room, she turned to me laughing and said, 'Thou art ever courteous and chivalrous. Yet I am sore distressed that ye, a Christened man, hath born me from the chapel, yet art churlish toward the True Faith.'

Entering into the spirit of her play, I replied, 'Fair maiden, upon mine honour, I would do aught to please you. Suffer me to declare that I am indeed pledged to seek the Holy Grail.'

'Ah, Sir Tristram, then I have done you wrong. Pray forgive me for this slight. There is a nunnery hard by, and I must go there to pine away in grief at my false accusation.'

'Damsel, Fair Isolt, thou honourest me beyond my just deserts. Thou shouldst know that the Holy Grail is to me but an excuse for noble deeds and valour. I may forfeit my life for righteousness and truth, but it cannot be for the falsehoods of the Church of England.'

'Sire, I am sore perplexed. Right gladly would I proffer my heart to you, but not if ye would deny the One True Faith. Will ye not yield to my heart's desire?'

'Nay, Madam, that cannot be. Perchance I would love you, but if my terms are not requited, then I must bid you adieu and follow my quest.'

'Ere you do so, I will take this phial of poison.' Here Adela lifted a small vase from the window sill.

'Then fain let us die together,' I cried.

'I will rent my raiment asunder…'

'Adela!' We both jumped at the stern voice of Father in the doorway. Adela put down the vase so quickly that it was a miracle it didn't break. She stood with limp hands, trembling like a rabbit and staring pathetically at Father.

'Go to your room, child, and change. It will soon be time for dinner.' He strode through to his study, ignoring me. I wondered how much he'd heard; hopefully not so far back in our conversation as my reference to "the falsehoods of the Church of England". He knows my views to some degree, but I wouldn't wish to be insulting. I should be more careful. It was a piece of harmless fun to please Adela. I hope our silly language will at least have made that plain to him.

I'm so wretched. I don't know how much of our conversation Papa heard, and it doesn't really matter, because the last words of all were when I said I would rip my raiment asunder. He definitely heard that, which is terrible. I should never have said it. Poor Papa, poor me! He thinks his daughter a slut, and I deserve it. Oh, I must go down to dinner and face them all. Me, already a fallen woman at the age of seventeen. Poor Tristram. He'll get the blame, and it's my fault for uttering those awful words.

My worst fears have been confirmed. I distinctly heard it, yet I still cannot believe it. He said that he would love her. Definitely, those were his words; well, not exactly, but something like, 'perchance I would love you'. And he called her Isolt. Is that not the same as Isolde? And she definitely mentioned taking poison. I fear that the aberration has come from that appalling man Wagner.

There is now no doubt about the unhealthy nature of their relationship. I can no longer sit here pondering what to do about it. They must be parted. But how? Adela cannot be the one to go. She is too young, and her fault is the lesser. Besides, she needs my protection. It has to be Tristram.

I have made a bad mistake. I should have let him carry out his smallholding plan elsewhere, his *Schrebergarten*; yes, even if it meant losing him to Germany. Is it too late now? No, why should it be? He has not completed his analysis, still less set any plan into action. I must put it to him, and to Helga, but first I must think up a reason without causing a scandal. Before even that, I must speak to Adela. The child is being led astray and I must correct her. But first I must find out from her precisely how far this has gone.

19th November 1909

Papa summoned me to his private study this morning.

'Adela, I think that we should have a talk. You are growing up and will soon become a lady. Yet there are times when I still see you as a child, such as when I heard you talking to Tristram yesterday evening in that infantile way.'

I trembled to think what was coming.

'What exactly did you and Tristram mean?'

I was aware of blushing deeply, and a weight in my throat making it difficult to speak. 'It was, as you say, Papa, a childish game. We were acting out a story from the Tales of King Arthur. It was natural for us to choose Tristram and Isolt, because of Tristram's name.'

'And did I not hear you talk of taking your lives with poison?'

'No, no, Papa, well, I mean yes, I think I did laughingly talk of dying because my love could not be requited.'

'Is that not from Wagner's story?'

'Wagner? You mean *Tristan and Isolde*? No, yes, but not exactly. We were not playing Wagner's opera. It was Tristram and Isolt from the Knights of the Round Table.'

'I am well aware of the story of Tristram and Isolt. I could hardly not be, having chosen to call my own son Tristram. He is a noble knight who is killed out of jealousy. Shortly after, Isolt pines away. There is no mention of poison or suicide.'

'No, Papa. I'm afraid that, being familiar with Wagner's opera, which ends differently, I lapsed into mentioning the taking of poison. I shouldn't have done so, and I'm very sorry.'

'My child, thoughts of love are to be cherished, but you must be careful how you express them. Do you have such thoughts now?'

If I had blushed deeply before, that was nothing to the confusion I felt now. Was he thinking of Thomas Knowles?

'I, I, no, Papa, I don't think so.' There was a long silence which I wished would end. My mouth was dry. I could find nothing to say.

'You can tell me, Adela. It is not unknown for someone of your age to have feelings in a direction of which they are later ashamed.'

'Yes, Papa, really, indeed.' That wasn't what I'd meant to say. 'No such thoughts,' I added lamely.

He stared at me for a long time. 'How is your music coming along? I hear that the lady who visited you the other day, Miss Smyth, was most impressed by your playing.'

'Yes, Papa, so she said.'

'It is good to have a talent, and I am pleased that you are so devoted to it. But you must look to your wider education. You must realise that your life is ahead of you. You must not become obsessed only by the things around you, nor the people. Preserve yourself, and do not readily surrender that which is yours to give when the time is right. That is all. I will see you shortly at lunch.'

He gave me such an affectionate smile that I felt fortunate to have escaped so lightly. Yet he still seemed troubled, and I really didn't know what he was talking about near the end. He's rebuked me in his dear, gentle way, and I accept his chastisement. But I'm not clear what he meant at the end by preserving myself. I could ask Mama or even Tristram, but the trouble is, I was so flustered, that already I can't remember Papa's exact words, and I'd get them wrong if I tried to repeat them. Oh well. At least the encouragement about my piano playing was clear. I'll have to leave it at that. And there was no mention of my having said I'd tear my raiment asunder.

What can I make of that? She only gave one sign that she is in love with Tristram, when she said that her love could not be requited. But she said it in the context of playing a game. I wonder. Is it just a coincidence? Was the love not being requited Isolt's or Adela's? If Adela's, should I be concerned that she loves him at all, or relieved that she recognises that it cannot be fulfilled? I will sleep on it for a day or two and pray, hoping that things may become clearer.

20th November 1909

I cannot help thinking of Adela. My thoughts keep returning to the interview in my study. She sat there, demure and blushing, her hands clasped neatly on her lap, shifting and kneading them when she displayed anguish. What was she thinking? What did she think of me? I cannot say why, but I have a feeling of guilt towards her. I was making her squirm, both metaphorically and physically. Did I have the right? I am her father; well no, her guardian. I have a duty to protect her, and to find out the truth. Should I speak to her again? I keep thinking that I must look for opportunities, but then again, why should I? Nothing new has occurred. Tristram has been out for such a large proportion of the past forty-eight hours that she can hardly have seen him, except at meal times. Should I now speak to Tristram? I do have justification for that, yet I feel ill-prepared. But I must do so soon. I shall wait for one more piece of evidence.

22nd November 1909

Richard is behaving strangely. He frequently is asking where Tristram and Adela are, even though most of the time he full well is knowing. We are in bed, and it is late. Just now he embraced me with a passion which I should have enjoyed, but there was something unaffectionate about it. He did not start to attend to my desires gently or soothingly as he normally does, but quickly began to handle me roughly. He cried out in ecstasy, something he rarely is doing, but immediately rejected me as though I could not be the cause of his pleasure. Perhaps it is just the time of year. He is working hard, with Advent upon us and Christmas just around the corner. The shortness of the days is not helping. There is so much to cram in. Still, when Christmas comes he will no doubt be merry and full of fun. He always is, and then he will be planning for the New Year. 1910; how this century seems to be flying by. I have an urge to turn over and put my arms around him again. Somehow I know that he is not sleeping. But a still more subtle sense is warning me not to. I am frustrated, but I must try to sleep.

28th November 1909

Rejoice! Rejoice! Emmanuel shall come to thee, O Israel. Harry Bunby the slaughterman is braying out this hymn with such a fierce expression that it looks as though he's jetting abuse at some political protest rally. *Rod of Jesse, key of David, Sinai's height.* Has Harry any clue what the words refer to or why he should be singing about Emmanuel coming to Israel? I've no objection to the Jews doing it. They have a reason to celebrate their heritage, but it's got nothing to do with these villagers, and why should it? They're a blend of Celts, Angles, Saxons, Jutes, Vikings and Normans with perhaps a bit of Roman thrown in. As for their own noble culture and freedom, it was inspired mostly by the Greeks and gained by struggles within these shores. Has Harry any idea what he owes to the Greeks? Democracy, the jury system, physics, geometry, engineering, medicine, sport, the theatre, the musical scale, the organ, and above all ethics. Not a bad list. Harry should be singing about Pericles, Pythagoras and Socrates, not Israel.

Colonel Sawbridge read a lesson earlier about the Fear of God, saying "He will strike the wicked". Little wonder people use the phrase "Act of God" to describe something unpleasant like a flood or a famine. Yet Adela would have it that there's only a comfortable heaven, with nothing unpleasant like hell.

Now we're having the Pharisees and Sadducees. It'll be Cherubim and Seraphim next. Perhaps we should measure their wings.

1st December 1909

Father called me into his study this morning. He'd asked me yesterday evening whether we might at last debate Christianity together. Of course, I told him I'd been wanting to do it for ages.

We sat on either side of his blue leather-topped rosewood desk, bare except for his appointments diary, ink well, prayer book and Bible. He likes to be orderly.

'Before we start our discussion, Tristram, I should like you to know that I wish you to be totally frank with me. If I have shown anger at your views in the past, it has been because you have expressed them in front of Adela without warning.'

'I understand, Father'.

'Where should we start, then? You are studying the Bible assiduously, it seems. Do you find what you are reading to your liking?'

'In part.'

'Only in part?'

'There's a lot I find disturbing.'

'Then let us lead in with that.'

I told him what I'd told Adela that night down by the corncrake fields, about the atrocities committed by Moses and others in the Old Testament. Father listened patiently until I'd finished.

'You must remember that those were distant times. Standards of conduct were different in those days. Things which were normal then are no longer acceptable today.'

'So why should we hold the Bible up as a model for our behaviour in the twentieth century?'

'Because it is the word of God.'

'And God stopped speaking in the fifth century BC?'

'No, God continued speaking through his Son, Jesus Christ, which is the message of the New Testament. It tells of charity and forgiveness and love. For Christians, the Old Testament is a background, to explain the circumstances behind God sending his only Son into the world. This is the reason why I see no objection to something which clearly bothers you, that we may use the Old Testament with discretion, selectively if you like.'

'But you don't tell the people that. Ask Folland, Blamey, Jarvis, Harry Bunby, Mrs Hearn, Nancy: ask them the question, "Is the Bible the word of God, and is it all true?" And they'll reply, "Of course it is."'

'Then perhaps I am at fault for not explaining the difference between literal truth and implied truth. But I cannot confuse them by making the message too complicated for them to understand.'

'But wouldn't you agree that misconceptions ought to be corrected? People tend to believe what they're taught at the outset. Father, you kindly said that I might speak freely, and I will do so now. I believe that much of the evil in the world today stems from what to me is the absurd notion that the Bible is the word of God. This improbable and unsubstantiated claim has been indoctrinated into each generation for hundreds of years. So almost everyone in Christendom believes in the Bible as the absolute truth, and everyone in Arabia has a similar attitude towards the Koran. Yet they can't both be right. Would you agree that the Creed is at the heart of the Christian Faith?'

'It is our statement of Christian values and belief.'

'Then you must accept that the creed of a Muslim is fundamentally different from that of a Christian. People are Christians because their parents were, and their parents' parents before them. In Arabia, people are Mohammedans for the same reason. In India, Hindus. In Siam, Buddhists. They start life from a position of received belief and are then taught how to justify it. How I would respect an Arabian who had become a Christian, or a Briton who had become a Muslim. But everyone simply dons the coat they're given.'

'Africans have taken to Christianity.'

'Some have, and some to Mohammedanism. It depends on who conquered them.'

'Perhaps the difference is not as great as you assume. All religions, Buddhists apart, believe in God and they all, Buddhists included, believe in an afterlife.'

'But the differences between them are still fundamental. Ninety-nine percent of religious education covers what I would call unnecessary, unsubstantiated and unlikely detail. I can accept the argument that it's possible, probable even, that we've been placed on this earth for a purpose. If you choose to call the force behind that God, then I have no objection. But if just this one reasonable premise were taught, Church services would only last a few minutes, and the Bible would contain a mere sentence or two. But they don't, and all that comes thereafter leads to persecution and war resulting from the various religions having speculated in different directions. So each treats the followers of the other religions as damned, and they all condemn the people who have no religion, heathens they call them, even when they've never been given a chance to hear the messages. As for those who have, it's as though one group of people claims that a distant star is made of blancmange, another of lemon tart, and yet another of apple pie. But they're all puddings, so that's all right.'

Father beamed at me, but said nothing, so I pressed on. 'Even the differences within individual faiths have caused persecution, hatred and fear. Why are you a Protestant vicar and not a Catholic priest? Because of an unexpected turn of history four hundred years ago, when a selfish and arrogant King Henry VIII broke with Rome and divorced Catherine of Aragon so he could marry Anne Boleyn.'

'Perhaps that was God's way of directing history for the best in the long run.'

'Is it God's way that Italians and French should have one version of the truth, and Britons another?' I hadn't finished with pressing home my emphasis on the conflicts between the various faiths, because Father hadn't admitted that it mattered. I continued, 'Would you say that God has revealed himself in the Scriptures?'

'Certainly.'

'And which scriptures are those?'

'Why, the Bible, of course.'

'And the Koran? And the Vedas?'

'Perhaps they too are versions of God's truth.'

'But they can't all be true. They contradict one another.'

'Perhaps they do not. A cow is different from a sheep; summer is different from winter. Yet both exist. They are both real, both true. God reveals himself in many ways. You should not expect there to be just one side to Him. Perhaps he gives us a choice. Perhaps that is God's way.'

'Or perhaps it is simply that a Muslim has drunk from a well in the desert and a Christian from a fountain in the city.'

'I must use that in one of my sermons'. We both laughed.

'And preach in Church about Mohammedanism and the laws of Charles Darwin?'

'That would be going a bit too far,' he chuckled, reaching for the bell. When Hackett appeared, he ordered coffee and brandy snaps for two.

'I think that you are a child of your time, Tristram. You see an explosion of scientific discovery and think that it explains everything.'

'No, Father, not everything, but the scientific mind questions and tests objectively. To that extent, science is opposed to faith, which says something is so because it is said to be so. Comte looked back over the history of Man's thinking and found that it went through three stages. First, man ascribed everything in the world to the act of a deity. During the second phase, he tried to analyse this deity's motives; why life existed and what was the meaning of death. Of course, this analysis was futile and got him nowhere. So he turned to *how* things happened, and so to science, which proved highly informative. He should have concentrated on improving his life on earth and abandoned any attempt to speculate about the motives of gods and an afterlife. I hear people talk of Man as the crown of God's creation, the only animal worthy of redemption and a place in heaven, yet the same people cast him as a miserable sinner. He can't be both, and I say that he's neither. He's an animal who's attained a greater degree of consciousness and mental sophistication, no more and no less. I've heard it claimed that Christianity isn't affected by the revelations of Charles Darwin. I say they're in direct conflict. Christianity, and all other ethical codes based around self-sacrifice and submission to God's will, is opposed to the law of natural selection, which seeks to make the human race stronger. Fortunately, most people are instinctively aware of this and aren't so dependent, otherwise the human race would wither. The man who thinks that tuberculosis is to be cured by prayer is more likely to die than the man who seeks medical assistance. The former dies and the latter, who is more intelligent and less gullible, survives. That's natural selection.'

'That is neither true nor fair. The Church of England would never discourage the sick from seeing a medical doctor. As for me, I see no conflict between science and faith. The Bible tells us that God created the earth and all that it contains. Scientific theories, such as Mr Darwin's on evolution, tell us how he did it. Discussing whether God is responsible for the universe is not a scientific question. Scientists such as Newton, Faraday, Mendel and Pasteur have recognised this. All were Christians. I have heard the argument before that it is only the fittest who survive, and therefore we should be ruthless in not giving succour to the weak. I utterly condemn this line of thinking. If it were so, by protecting the weak and treating the sick, the human race should be dying out. But instead it is getting stronger, living longer, running faster, improving its morality and inventing new ways to improve itself. I have heard it said that conflict should be encouraged, because it allows the strongest to prevail. That is a dubious argument. The brave tend to die in battle, while the cowards avoid it and survive. In any case, not all the winners will be the strongest, because of the chaotic nature of conflict. Further, I cannot accept your implication that Christianity preaches dependence and is opposed to self-reliance. Yes, the Church welcomes sinners, the sick and failures. But that is not the same as saying that it encourages people to sin, become sick or fail. You are fortunate, Tristram, in being fit and strong. Think of God as a doctor. It is the sick who need the doctor most. Forgive me, but you are arrogant if, just because you are healthy, you despise those who need help and seek it. No, I see no conflict between religion and science. Faith is like love; it cannot be overturned by scientific analysis. Nor will changing knowledge and new discoveries alter its basic truth.'

He paused for a moment, looking intently at me. Not since childhood had I found him so impressive. He continued, 'You consider that science confirms everything, Tristram. It might if we knew everything there is to know, but we do not. Think back a hundred years. There were no railways, motor cars, electricity, photography, or telephones. If we were to look forward another hundred years, do you not think that we would be astounded by the things which we cannot even dream about today?' He leaned forward and looked intently into my eyes. 'It is my contention that science has so far revealed only the tiniest proportion of what exists in nature or physics or whatever you wish to call it.'

'God?'

He leaned back and smiled with such love that I could only shake my head in wonderment.

'You disagree?'

I shook my head again. 'No, Father, no.' No more words were necessary. He could see my admiration.

There was a long pause. Sunlight was pouring through the window. I followed his gaze out over the orchard. He said, 'Would I be right in thinking that for you the beautiful things in the world provide no evidence of a divine purpose?'

'The wonders of nature, and charitable acts, therefore God exists?'

'That sort of thing.'

'No, Father. We appreciate the beauty of our surroundings because it's the environment in which we've been nurtured and have prospered, just as a frog appreciates its pond and an eagle its windswept cliffs. I look at a rainbow and see a rainbow. It's beautiful for what it is. Its beauty is here and now, sunlight on rain, and its colours. Looking for anything more diminishes the thing itself. As with the rainbow, so with life. Life to me is beautiful, this life, this one life that I have.'

'I am glad to hear it, Tristram. It brings me great comfort that you are content with your lot.'

'Nor do I fear death. I don't subscribe to the argument that the finality of death is so unpleasant that there must be another life to come. No, I find that simply wishful thinking. It's also inconsistent. If life is so good that therefore there must be a God, how can it be so wretched that you should need to look for a better one beyond?'

'Then perhaps I can convince you that you may be wrong. For me, the good things in life *are* evidence of a divine creation. Think of what virtuous people of Christian persuasion have achieved in the past hundred years. Think of William Wilberforce, Lord Shaftesbury, Elizabeth Fry and Doctor Barnardo. How can you say that Christianity has not had a beneficial influence, when it has provided refuge for the oppressed and hospitals for the sick?'

'No, Father, you were right when you said that I would be unlikely to accept this line of argument. Healing the sick and other works of charity have been practised for centuries in non-Christian countries. Many of the scientific advances which have made our hospitals the best in the world have had to struggle against implacable opposition from the Church down the ages. When Richard I fought Saladin in the Crusades, it was Richard who behaved like a cruel barbarian, and Saladin who showed nobility and magnanimity. Christianity may have motivated some people to do good, but history is littered with cases of it promoting evil. I can't accept the implication that Christianity has driven forward morality overall.'

'Then we are indeed far apart.'

'I'm sorry, Father. I wouldn't choose it.'

Hackett returned with the coffee and brandy snaps. I glanced up at Father's bookshelves, heavy with religious dogma. There was a whole world encapsulated there, a tomb of restrictive conclusions, prescribed and sealed; to be examined, pored over, but never added to or replaced.

Father waited until Hackett had closed the door. He leaned forward. 'But can you not acknowledge that the criteria for examining and discussing scientific truths are different from those required for faith?'

'No, but you could try to convince me.'

'I will try, then. Tristram, do you acknowledge that the plays of Shakespeare can convey great meanings which could be described as truths?'

'I can accept that they illustrate truths, yes.'

'And that Shakespeare's works are fiction, except for his historical plays?'

'Of course.'

Father smiled. 'Then can you accept the Bible on the same basis?'

'As a string of parables?'

'Yes, if you like.'

'But it isn't presented like that. We're told that Moses did this and Jesus did that.'

'And that Macbeth did this and Hamlet did that.'

'I take your point.' I meant it. Father had put his case well. Now he pressed on with his advantage.

'Then let me tell you a parable of my own. Once upon a time, a family of squirrels lived near a church. They used to sit high up in their oak tree listening to a glorious sound coming from the tower. They did not know that it was bells, but they thought the music very beautiful. They wondered what caused it. Was it a sound of nature, or was someone behind it? The younger squirrels were sceptical. "What nonsense," said the squirrel who was the son. "There is bound to be an explanation, just as there is for the wind rustling in this tree." But his father said, "Something as beautiful as that does not just happen by chance." "Poppycock," said his insolent son. "There is a scientific explanation for everything. If one of us were to climb that yew tree over there and leap across to the tower, we would know for certain whether there was some higher being behind it all." "Go on, you're the fittest," said the others. "You do it. Go on, son." So the young squirrel waited until he next heard the sound coming from the tower. He dashed across the churchyard, climbed the yew tree, took a great leap and landed clutching onto some wooden bars near the top of the tower. He peered through the slats; then, finding the noise deafening at close quarters, he leapt back into the yew tree, ran down to the ground and scampered back across the grass to rejoin his family in the oak tree. "What did you see?" they clamoured. "I looked into the tower and saw huge metal cups hanging upside down. They were swinging from side to side so that hammers were striking their sides. That is how the noise is made. There is no one making the sound." The young squirrel was delighted with himself. Not only had he made the journey, but he had shown that the idea that some superior being might be responsible for the sound was a myth, an act of unfounded faith. The scientific explanation had prevailed. Metal was hitting metal; that was all. There was no purpose behind it, any more than the wind and the rain.

'Father, what a wonderful story. You must use it in one of your sermons.'

'Do you think so?'

'Yes, I do, seriously. It illustrates one of the points you've been making very well. I'll sit in my pew feeling utterly humiliated.' We both laughed.

'Well, of course, I did not make it up just then. I have been thinking about it for weeks. It sums up my philosophy that nothing is one-sided, and nothing is what it seems. It is all a matter of balance. We must weigh the evidence. The sceptic will point to all the suffering in the world, its wars, to the divisions and conflicts between religious faiths, and the lack of scientific proof of the existence of God. The man of faith will recognise these objections, but will also take into account the beauties of nature, love, kindness, goodness and the fact that God sent his only Son Jesus Christ into the world. Now you may not believe that He rose from the dead, nor that He died for our sins, but you must agree that He preached love and forgiveness. And one more thing: Jesus never claimed to be God, but He did say that He was the Son of God and could speak for God. Now either that is true, or Jesus was indulging in a hideous blasphemy. One has to choose between the two. There can be no middle ground.'

'I'm sorry, Father, but there are several possibilities which would qualify for the middle ground, as you put it. One is that Jesus thought he was on a mission from God, but he wasn't, either because God doesn't exist or, as the Jews believe, Jesus was not the Messiah. This wouldn't make Jesus evil; simply deluded. Another possibility is that Jesus aimed to do good in the world, and used the image of God as a parable, as the symbolic truth, as a fiction illustrating a truth, as you yourself described Shakespeare's plays, when you likened them to the Old Testament. A third explanation is that Jesus never claimed to be the Son of God, but that his later followers, writing decades after his death, put such claims into his mouth. A fourth and final explanation is that Jesus never existed, except as a minor rabble-rouser, and that most of the facts about his life as we know them were invented for political and cultural reasons long after his death. I'm sorry to put forward these theories to you, Father, but my extensive studies have led me to conclude that any one of these alternatives could be true. I agree with you that the *possibility* of a faith being correct should be taken into consideration as a counterweight to science. But in considering the right balance, I can't admit the fact – and you did use that word fact, Father - that God sent His only Son into the world is evidence of the very thing we are trying to prove. That begs the question. There is no such evidence, and only a relatively small minority of people in the world believes it.'

That was the end of our debate. I could see that I'd shocked Father greatly with my assertions, though it wasn't my purpose to do so. But I couldn't allow his sloppy logic to prevail: that Christ's divinity is proof of Christ's divinity. Until the last few minutes, he'd acquitted himself well. Although mine were the more persuasive arguments, he has given me much to think about. He is right. Science does not explain everything. Our knowledge only scratches its surface. He has convinced me only partly, but more than he knows.

In the end he picked up some papers, glanced at them, put them down and looking out of the window said that there might be snow. He looked so discomfited that I put him out of his misery by leaving his study immediately.

I have been humiliated. Like Our Lord on the Cross, I feel abandoned. But like Him, I must come to realise that this was a test, and I will come through it. My Faith has been badly shaken, but I will not let it topple.

It is a terrible feeling, to fear one's own son and to resent the satisfaction he seemed to gain from asserting himself. He was polite; he always is. But when he is like that, he seeks only one thing: domination.

Up until near the end, I felt that I had countered most of his objections, if not quite all to his satisfaction, then certainly to mine. I thought that up to then he had been impressed by my arguments, and that I had supplied him with sufficient reasoning to make him reconsider some of his wilder views. But then I slipped up, just once, and he pounced, and by that time it was too late. He was right. I did assert God's sending His only Son into the world as evidence, and it is not, not in the scientific sense. But that does not mean that it is not true. I might have retrieved the situation by returning to my point that not all truths are scientific, but before I could qualify my statement in order to recover from my blunder, the hammer blows fell, one after another. They are the real reason why I feel so depressed tonight. Jesus's life is well-documented. Better still, the evidence is complementary, by which I mean that there are very few contradictions and many, many consistencies. But the more I have looked into the writing of the New Testament since Tristram's first attack on it a few months ago, the more I realise that there is one inescapable fact: the texts all date from a considerable time after Christ's death. Does that make them invalid? Of course not. Why should so many people in widely spread places all make up the same story and, remember, there were a large number of Christians right across the southern and eastern Mediterranean by the end of the first century AD. And the normal method of communication was verbal, not in writing. That would explain why no one committed the life of Christ to parchment until long after his death. See, I am already comforted. Now, Tristram argues that there was a huge purge of all the different stories in the second century by the Emperor Constantine, and that a vast number of conflicting versions were suppressed. But this does not explain how such a large number of people could all have invented the same story, does it? I must pray.

I had completely forgotten. I meant to question Tristram about Adela. I am furious with myself for not having done so. It slipped my mind because of the traumas I went through at the end. Dear Lord…

3rd December 1909

Tristram never interrupts when I'm playing the piano, and he didn't actually do so this evening. But the moment I'd finished playing *Mozart's Rondo in C* he burst out, 'Adela, listen to this.' He was holding *The Times* up with both hands over his head, shaking it.

'This is Judge Rentoul. He says three quarters of the cases tried before him have involved the lowest type of alien: the Russian burglar, the Polish thief, the Italian stabber and the German swindler.'

'I thought it was the duty of a judge to be sober and impartial. He sounds a prejudiced fellow to me.'

'The German swindler. Do you think I fall into that category?'

'You are only half-German. Anyhow, with a name like Tristram Hall, you're nothing but an upright Englishman.'

Tristram looked thoughtful. 'I think perhaps the sentiment is as much anti-Jewish as anti-German. What he's trying to say is that Jews are swindlers and Germans are Jews. But there *is* anti-German sentiment about. Have you heard of a man called William Le Queux? No? He and others churn out lurid novels about the Hidden Hand and other nonsense claiming German spies are everywhere. They have titles like *While England Sleeps* and *Spies of the Kaiser*. We Germans are supposed to go snooping around with our thick Teutonic necks, peering through our monocles into every toy boat on the pond, noting down the number of sails and passing the information back to the Kaiser. There's a lot of prejudice in this country. Each Russian, Pole, Italian and German is expected to have stepped into the neat frame allotted to his race and nationality. It's simpler that way, and easier for the simple to understand.'

'Oh, Tristram, you do exaggerate. I've never heard Mama complain about being called a swindler or anything else for that matter. What goes on in the East End of London is hardly going to affect us at Chaddingley. Can you really imagine Abel Hopkins or Edwin Blamey thinking of us as spies?'

'I think I'll read one of those novels,' said Tristram.

6th December 1909

Christmas here is so very traditional and very English. As a German I enjoy it, but it is the only time of the year when I am feeling homesick. We always have the same service, but this year I have persuaded Richard to allow a new carol, just one. I have been *so wagemutig*, not just because I have chosen a Catholic hymn, but because it will be in German. Not the whole of it, but Adela will be singing the opening verse in our native tongue as a solo.

The carol is *Stille Nacht*, which is German for *Silent Night*. The story behind it is touching. It was Christmas Eve in 1818. The church organ at

Obendorf bei Salzburg in Austria had just broken down. The assistant priest, Joseph Mohr, took a poem which he had written two years before and walked through the snow to a neighbouring town. He was calling on his friend Franz Gruber, and what he was asking him to do was what, here in England, would be called "a tall order". Could Gruber set his poem to music, so that he, Joseph Mohr, could provide the accompaniment on his guitar? Oh, and could he please have it ready in time for Midnight Mass this very evening? Gruber sat down and quickly wrote a simple and very beautiful tune. Backed by the choir, they performed it together just a few hours later in the tiny church at Obendorf bei Salzburg. Is it not a lovely story?

25th December 1909

Stille nacht, heilige nacht, alles schläft, einsam wacht. Now what's this? No *Once in Royal David's City*? And my sister singing… in German? It's beautiful. What's Father thinking? He seems as spellbound as I am. And look at the congregation, peering at their sheets of paper as though searching for some watermark. But most seem to like it. Several have stopped looking down and are gazing at the choir with visions of rapture. Well done, Mother. Your little secret, kept from all of us.

I've had an interview in London, including a short exam in Aramaic. It's a foregone conclusion that I've passed, so all being well I'll be joining Walter Grattin and his team in Berlin on 4th April. Adela asks if I'm still going, and I ask if she'll keep quiet. The answer to both is yes

Now this is more like Chaddingley: good solid tradition. God is speaking to sinful Adam. What's he done wrong? He's eaten a fruit, allegorical of course. *And unto Adam he said, because thou hast harkened unto the voice of thy wife, cursed is the ground for thy sake; in sorrow shalt thou eat of it all the days of thy life; thorns also and thistles shall it bring forth to thee.* Do you know, I've heard those words so many times, yet it's only today I've realised how repressive they are. Adam's great sin: harkening unto the voice of his wife. I asked Father the other day why Adela couldn't become a priest. He laughed and said, 'I do not think that Adela wishes to become a priest.'

'But say she does. She can't become one, can she? Why not?'

'I think that you know why not. Are you trying to trick me? You know that only men can become priests.'

'But why's that?'

'Because Jesus only chose male apostles.'

'But he had female disciples. Some of them were his most devoted followers. Mary his mother and Mary Magdalene were the main witnesses to his resurrection.'

'But they were not among the chosen twelve.'

'Why do you think that was?' I asked.

'Perhaps it was the custom of the time. Women had a more subservient role then.'

'And customs change?'

'Times move on, as they must.'

I didn't go on arguing with him. It's the same old quillet. Times move on, but religious laws may stand still for millennia. We may not use evolving customs, advancing morality, civilisation or logic to question, debate or change them.

It came upon a midnight clear, that glorious song of old, from angels bending near the earth to touch their harps of gold. The whole church is vibrating to Mother's diapason on the organ. I'm stirred, as it's intended I should be. I wish Elizabeth Sawbridge were here. The Colonel says she may come back late next year, but I'll be gone by then. I saw a lady at my hotel in London. I couldn't help looking at her. Her movements were so restrained. She caught my eye and smiled faintly before turning away. I saw her once more as she was about to pass through the revolving doors, and the thought of her haunted me for several hours after. I looked for her in the evening, but never saw her again.

The wolf also shall dwell with the lamb, and the leopard shall lie down with the kid; and the calf and the young lion and the fatling together; and a little child shall lead them. And the cow and the bear shall feed; their young ones shall lie down together: and the lion shall eat straw like the ox. And the sucking child shall play on the hole of the asp, and the weaned child shall put his hand in the cockatrice' den. They shall not hurt or destroy in all my holy mountain: for the earth shall be full in the knowledge of the Lord, as the waters cover the sea. Such exotic images, and very beautiful. Who would wish to destroy the illusion? But I wonder how accurate those wise men of King James were when they made their translation three hundred years ago? I can't wait until I'm amongst scholars who've returned to the original sources. Then we'll see what new paralogisms emerge.

Then Mary said unto the angel, how shall this be, seeing I know not a man? And the angel answered and said unto her, The Holy Ghost shall come upon thee, and the power of the Highest shall overshadow thee. I wonder what Elizabeth's doing now? Church is strong in Virginia, so Mrs Sawbridge says. Elizabeth's probably doing the same as… no, she can't be, they're many hours behind us in time. She'll still be in bed, sleeping, with white linen sheets, the blankets rising and falling to the rhythm of her breathing. I must get away from here or I'll go mad. To meet people, like that woman in London; to be drawn into another being, to feel their pleasure, and comfort their pain.

In the bleak midwinter, frosty wind made moan. Earth stood hard as iron, water like a stone. Do you know, Elizabeth, there are actually tears in my eyes? The hold of this is very strong, and soon I must leave it. I argue with Father and Adela about unnecessary speculation and invented detail, but it's hard to deny simplicity. *What can I give Him, poor as I am? If I were a shepherd, I would bring a lamb. If I were a Wise Man, I would do my part. Yet what I can I give Him: give my heart.*

Mama's new carol *Stille Nacht* went down a treat. Even Papa was impressed. Some of the congregation were confused about my opening solo. Mrs Barnes asked me suspiciously afterwards if I'd been singing in Latin, no doubt fearing a new Popish Plot. Harry Bunby thought that it must be "one of them ancient biblical tongues", while Nancy said it was "just foreign talk". But when I asked her whether she liked the tune, she said it "were like peace on earth" so I knew that she really liked it. Now I must try to extricate myself from my circle of well wishers and make my way back with the others to the house and the Yule Log and Cook's joint of beef.

29th December 1909

How to be telling Adela? How to be telling Richard? My daughter will be going for an examination to enter the Royal Academy of Music where, all being well, her piano teacher will be Mr Tobias Matthay. I am having to arrange this through Miss Smyth, Mr Fielder-Grilsen having proved quite useless for the purpose. The examination will not be taking place until sometime in the Spring. Entry to the school will be in September.

When to be telling Richard? On the subject of Adela's future he is inflexible. He is going on about Adela's general education, but he is not appreciating how restricted it is already, staying at home being taught by Miss Stone and me. To have Miss Stone we are very lucky. She is a good governess and is widely read, and between us we are managing to cover a broad syllabus. But that is not the same as having a variety of specialist teachers and intercourse with her peers.

When Adela goes to the Royal Academy of Music, she will be lodging with Miss Smyth. I did not want this, but we are depending on her recommendation for the Academy, and she is insisting. Also, she has been kind in making the arrangements, and will be bringing Adela into contact with a wide range of musicians and, more importantly, impresarios. Miss Smyth's reputation is growing. Her *Mass in D* is widely admired, and her opera *The Wreckers,* championed and performed recently by Mr Beecham, has been causing quite a stir.

For now, I need not be worrying unduly. I have a month or two before I need to announce anything, so I can be choosing my moment. But Adela will need time to prepare for her examination. I shall have to be telling her soon; February at the latest, I am thinking. As for Richard, I must be preparing the ground first.

30th December 1909

My head is aching and my mind churning. All my fears about Tristram and Adela have returned.

Yesterday dawned crisp and bright, with hoar-frost on the elm stump and ice on the pond. Then the snow came. It first appeared as a few nomadic flakes, which sauntered above the earth as though looking for a place to alight; then in thickly packed smudges pressing purposefully down, swirling in the wind and packing into drifts against hedges and buildings.

When the sun broke through this morning, it revealed a white world of tinselled trees and padded hills. I thanked God for the beauty of the sight as I stood by the gate looking out over Wester Ground, my boots almost hidden in the pristine powder which lay rounded over the fields, quilted in neatly by the leeward hedges, banked up on the windward side. Snow muffled the land, deadening distant sounds, sharpening those close by: the faintest flutter as a thrush took off, sending a cascade down into the elder, the scritching of some animal just up the hill, and a clear snap as ice cracked in the ditch below. A subdued argument drifted up from the rookery in the wood to my left. A pheasant stalked warily from the bank. Otherwise all was still in the clear light, pink with warmth, blue with cold.

Adela appeared in the orchard, her breath clouding in front of her face. She wore a white fur hat and black leather gloves, which she cupped to her mouth as though to capture the warmth of her breath. I watched, wondering what she would do next. Tristram arrived, striding up to her. He put an arm round her shoulders by way of greeting, and she leant into him. They stood surveying the scene for a while, and then she backed away laughing, while he retreated several paces in the opposite direction. For the first time I could hear them as they whooped and hurled their snowballs, she with inadequate force, he with an aim which I felt sure was deliberately wide. Gradually they closed, and at last her missiles struck, though not Tristram's, until he lobbed one gently onto her hat. Adela cried out and charged him, hitting him full on the chest, which he clutched theatrically as though struck by a shot. He crumpled to the ground and she fell on top of him. They lay there panting and laughing, their faces inches apart. I felt a tightness in my throat, appalled as each moment passed. After perhaps ten seconds, Tristram rolled her gently off, straightened his arms, stood, pulled Adela to her feet and began to dust her down felicitously. They groomed each other to their mutual satisfaction, shaking their heads with mock disapproval. Then he offered his arm and they walked out across the orchard, disappearing through the farthest gate. I thought of following them, but realised that I would soon be spotted in the sharp light.

She is so pure in her white fur hat and coat. I cannot have her defiled like this. I feel a dread, which manifests itself in a constricted chest. I fear I have a cold coming on. They must be parted. They must. But how? What reason can I give? Do I have the evidence? I am fairly certain that I do, but how can I use it?

It's good to be alive. The snow is so beautiful, and today we made the most of it. I suggested to Tristram that we should take a walk. He's very busy, but said he could spare me an hour. He had to clear up some papers, so I went out ahead of him to the orchard and stood there, taking in the silence and the wonder of nature. Then he came out and we had a spiffing snowball fight. Tristram, gentleman that he is, deliberately aimed to miss me, but pretended he didn't, while I had no compunction about getting in close and hitting him as squarely as I could.

After that, we went for a splendid walk, and he told me how he'd been for an interview in London with Walter Grattin's man. He's sure he'll be accepted, and is still planning to join the team in Berlin at the beginning of April. So once again I'll have to prepare myself for life without him, the rotter. Isn't life cruel, that on a day so beautiful, there should have to be thorns?

5th January 1910

I am now seriously worrying about Richard. This morning, just after breakfast, he was hovering around me so closely that I half expected him to start barring my way. When he at last gave me room, it was to summon me to his study, which he did by singing out over his shoulder, 'Come, Helga.'

When we were seated, his gaze prowled across his desk as though checking that nothing unseemly was visible. Then he leaned back in his chair and almost lost his balance. He is sorely upset about something, I thought.

'What is it, my love? You seem bothered. Have you something to be telling me?'

'No, certainly not.' Then, 'It is Adela. We have to discuss Adela.'

My immediate reaction was to wonder whether this might be an opportunity to reveal my plans for her. It would be some way ahead of my intended time. Carefully I need to choose my moment. The circumstances must be entirely propitious.

'Life here is narrow,' Richard said. 'I mean that we live in a constricted world, with the four of us in this house, in a village isolated in the countryside.'

I could not believe what I was hearing. He was echoing what I had been thinking and saying for years.

'Tristram has turned twenty and Adela seventeen. They have few friends. It is natural that they should look to each other. Not natural. Natural.'

This stammering contradiction I put down to his discomfort. I said, 'It is fortunate that they get on so well. They each are having their own intense interests, yet there is a bond between them. They say that opposites attract, do they not? It must be so, yes?'

'Attract?' Richard said sharply. 'You think that it is that?'

'Come, my dear, you must have been noticing. They laugh together and discuss endlessly. When they are not working, it is clear that they love being together.'

'So you have seen it too?' he asked sharply.

'Seen what?'

'Their intimacy.'

'Certainly, and for both of them I think it is good.

Each is having the company of someone of their own age who can give them, how shall we say, a youthful perspective on life. Adela has opened Tristram's eyes to the arts, especially music, and Tristram has introduced her to philosophy and social reality.'

Richard snorted. 'You mean one preaches Wagner and the other Nietzsche.'

I was feeling like telling him that if he bothered to find out about such things, he might be in a better position to criticise. Instead I said, 'Adela was in danger of becoming a little, how is it said, unworldly. Thanks to Tristram, she is now taking an interest in the workings of her gramophone and the motor car.'

'And where do they go in it?'

'The motor? How should I know? They go out. Does it matter where they are going? He drives her for pleasure. I am not the slightest bit worrying as long as Tristram is with her.'

Richard stared at me for such a long time that I started wondering what it was that I had just been saying. Then he began shuffling his papers around and talking about the weather like a typical Englishman. Whatever it was that had so agitated him earlier seemed no longer important. I asked if that was all, and he seemed relieved when I was getting up to go.

For one moment, I thought that Helga had understood. But I soon realised that her meaning of the word "intimacy" was different from mine. It was when she said that she was not bothered where Adela went in the motor car, so long as Tristram was with her, that I knew that she suspected nothing. Any further hints of mine would have been futile, and I was finding the conversation very trying.

So who can I turn to now? There is only one more person in whom I may confide, and that is my greatest friend. I can be frank with him, more than I could with Helga. William Sawbridge is a man of the world. Goodness knows, we mock each other ferociously, but when he realises that I am being serious on some matter, he is a worthy confidant, and the straightest speaking person on this planet.

6th January 1910

We know each other so well. Normally if I call on William unexpectedly, he will greet me with "Lost your sheep, Padre?" or "Fertile ground for sinners, this." But he knew the moment he saw me that it was not that sort of a visit.

'Your advice, William, if you please. The benefit of your worldly experience.' I unburdened myself to him. I told him of my fears about Tristram, supplying all the information that I could think of. My evidence would have been incomplete had I not been forced to disclose that Adela is adopted. He received the news with tactful sangfroid, but when I told him that her natural parents were poor folk in Zwickau, his face clouded.

'Her paperwork is in order, I trust?'

'Her adoption papers? Yes, all in order.'

'That is just as well. The mood in the country towards Germans is not good, as I'm sure you know. You must be aware of the Aliens Act of 1905?'

'Tristram has mentioned it. I have not given it much thought, myself.'

'Directly, you and your family have nothing to fear. Its main objective is to control undesirables adding to the riff-raff building up in such places as the East End of London. It's the hysteria behind it that worries me. Not just poor German immigrants taking jobs and driving out English folk, but things like ripping down notices in foreign languages because they might contain instructions on how to poison people; ridiculous stuff like that. A lot of the resentment is really against powerful Jews of German origin, and that doesn't affect you either. No, what worries me is this spy-fever thing, the enemy in our midst, fuelled by cheap novels and the ranting of the gutter press like *John Bull* and the *Daily Mail*. It's all this talk of invasion, ever since that Childers fellow wrote *The Riddle of the Sands*. And I have to say, forgive me Richard, that although all this spy nonsense is so much poppycock, I don't trust the Germans; never have, never will. Behind all this, there's a simple truth, and it is a truth. This Kaiser's as ruthless and ambitious as the last lot, Wilhelm the First, Moltke and Bismarck, but with one important difference. They brought France to her knees in 1870 and then backed off. This Kaiser hasn't got his grandfather's sense, and won't know when to stop.'

This was taking us further and further from the subject of what to do about Adela and Tristram, so I gently pulled him back.

'Want my advice? Let the lad see the world. Army would be the best thing for him. No good? Won't have it? Damned pity. How about India? He's got the brains for the ICS. Suggest he sits the exams. No, that won't do; hasn't been to university. Let's see. What are his interests? Ancient history, you said. Hm. What's that fellow Evans been uncovering in Crete? That sort of thing. Don't worry about him, Richard. From what you've told me, you'd see a damned sight more evidence if there really were any hanky-panky between them. How can I put this? He's probably had the odd hot rush for her simply because there isn't anywhere else he can set his cap. It's like some of those chaps you get at public schools. Buggers to a boy until they leave, then they fall for the first girl they meet. Bet you a guinea your lad's only interested in Adela because that's all he sees every day. Put him amongst a few maidens in London and he'll be getting engaged before the smoke from his train's blown away. Pity Elizabeth's not here; they'd make a fine pair. Oh well. So that's my advice, Richard. Get the boy out into the world; let him see what's on offer, and he'll come good, I know he will.'

7th January 1910

Tristram's presenting his *Schrebergarten* plans to Papa in the library. I've been told on no account am I to play any music or make any other sort of squeaks until they've finished. They've been in there for two and a half hours. Mama's gone out for a walk, which is unusual, but I couldn't join her, as I have an essay to write on Oliver Cromwell. Tristram told me yesterday he thought the chances of Papa's agreeing to his proposals to be ten to one against. At least if they're rejected, we'll be spared all this flourishing and teeth baring. It's driving all of us dotty.

9th January 1910

Richard something quite extraordinary has just been doing. He has been consulting us, yes all of us, the whole family together over dinner.

I was so proud of him, because he presented the *Schrebergarten* plan in such a way that even those of us who have little interest or knowledge of the farm could understand it. Tristram was interrupting him only once to correct a point of minor detail.

But that was not the most dramatic part of the meal. Richard also announced that Tristram will be leaving home in April. I was torn between the sadness which every mother must feel when her child is about to take wing, and a thrill at hearing what he is intending to do. He is to be joining a team of mainly German historians who are researching the origins of the Bible, starting in Berlin. Richard, with a heart-warming spirit of generosity, asked us to raise our glasses to Tristram and wish him well. This so moved Adela that she committed an indiscretion by blurting out, '*Grabe für das Vaterland!*' It is our custom that we are not speaking our native tongue in front of Richard. Luckily, he had so much wind in his sails that he either was not hearing her or else did not mind and, in any case, he would not have had a clue what it was that she was saying.

But back to *Schrebergarten*. Richard was explaining that, although he believed Tristram's reasoning to be sound, the risks are high. When I was asking what other choices we were having, he said that we could only keep skilled men on the farm by paying wages which we could not be affording.

I said that this was not sounding like an alternative at all. 'And if we do nothing?'

'Then we will continue in a spiral of fewer men doing more work, leading to more dissatisfaction and still more loss of labour. Also, if we fail to mechanise, the farm will be uncompetitive.'

'Could we give up farming altogether?' Adela asked tentatively.

'We could…' Richard responded slowly.

'No,' I said. 'It has been our way of life, and it should remain so. If we managed to do it fifteen years ago, when there was a deep depression in agriculture, we can be doing it now. It is your vocation, Richard, along with your Ministry.'

'That's right, Squarson,' said Tristram, and we were all laughing.

'I must point out the risks, nevertheless,' said Richard gravely. 'It is your money, all of you. You Adela, and Tristram: if we invest and fail, your inheritance will be greatly reduced. You Adela, especially, would be the loser to something that does not interest you. Are you prepared to accept that?'

'Yes, Papa. I was born into a family who are servants of the Church and landowners. I am proud of that.'

No you were not, you poor child, I thought bleakly. Into a family of poor factory workers you were born. It is as well that you are not knowing it.

Richard stared searchingly at his son before speaking. 'And you, Tristram? If we proceed and make a good fist of it, and prevail, would you see yourself making a career in agriculture or in historical research?'

'That's a hard question to answer, Father. Cast thy bread upon the waters: isn't that what it says in the Book of Ecclesiastes? If I should set a precedent in agriculture, and also make my name as a historian, then I should be spoilt for choice.'

'A fair answer,' said Richard. 'Helga?'

'There seems to be no alternative. Whatever else we do is no good, yes? But,' I said, turning to Tristram, and speaking as sternly as I could, 'you will not land your father in the pie?'

'I think you mean the soup, Mother.' Tristram was trying to keep a straight face.

'You know what I mean. I am giving this proposal my support under one condition: that you see it through yourself, Tristram. If you are to be leaving us in April, then I cannot see how this might be so.'

Tristram went through all that he would be achieving before he would leave. Richard added that, although he would have preferred Tristram to have stayed through a whole farming year, he accepted this compromise.

'Very well,' I said. 'But if the project is delaying?'

'Then I will not leave, Mother. I will not go until all the stages I've described are complete.'

'So good,' I said.

'Then we are agreed?' asked Richard, looking at each of us in turn. There were nods all round. He climbed to his feet. 'To *Schrebergarten*.' He raised his glass. My eyes met Adela's and she burst into a fit of giggles. '*Zu Schrebergarten*.'

I think that I must have surprised everyone else, and I certainly surprised myself. There was no one thing which tipped the balance: Tristram's excellent presentation yesterday, my satisfaction that Tristram and Adela would be parted, the realisation that the alternatives are unpalatable, and unexpected support from Helga and Adela. Yes, I am both pleased and relieved. At least we will proceed in the knowledge that there are no dissenters.

I watched Adela carefully. Attentive and eager, she was looking me straight in the eyes as I spoke, and her expression did not change when I broke the news of Tristram's departure. I therefore concluded that she already knew.

Now that Tristram and Adela are to be parted, I must deal with Adela's future. When Tristram goes, she will be more isolated than ever. That must not be. I have to think of some way for her to meet people of her own age. I will speak to Helga.

10th January 1910

I'm so excited. Mama has told me the most wonderful news today: that I'm going to the Royal Academy of Music in September, and that my tutor will be a famous piano teacher called Mr Tobias Matthay. So I won't be left all alone here for long after all, moping by myself, brooding over my envy of Tristram and his adventures. Mama said that Miss Smyth has agreed to take me into her house and look after me, and she'll introduce me to her musical friends and acquaintances. To think that I may actually meet some real bohemians. Do you know, when she was young, Miss Smyth was even befriended by Brahms? I'm so happy, but Mama's warned me she's still got to speak to Papa, and that I can't go to London without his approval. Just now I felt my eyes burning with excitement when I played Schumann's *Fantasia in C*, but I was also biting my lip.

21st January 1910

Faszinierend. Adela has been showing me a letter from Miss Smyth. She has been invited to London in three weeks' time, to stay with Miss Smyth and attend a performance of Delius's opera *A Village Romeo and Juliet.* This is putting me in a dilemma. Richard will say no, I am certain of it, and I have to confess that my own first reaction was not favourable. I was affronted that Miss Smyth was approaching Adela directly rather than through me. But was this rational of me? If Adela is to leave us and live with Miss Smyth in September, why should she not be making a brief visit in February? I cannot send Tristram with her. He is far too busy, and in any case has not been invited. I could impose myself on Miss Smyth, and it would be an opportunity to inspect her house, but that would be embarrassing for Adela, who is at an age when she should be wishing to assert her independence. I cannot be chaperoning her in September, so why should I be doing so now? There is no alternative. I shall have to be tackling Richard about the whole thing: the Royal Academy of Music, lodging with Miss Smyth, and the opera on 10th February.

24th January 1910

I was wrong, Richard has not said no. Adela will be

attending the Delius opera on 10th February. She will be staying with Miss Smyth, and she will be going to the Royal Academy in September.

It was Richard who approached me. He said that after Tristram leaves in April, Adela will be isolated here and will be lacking the stimulation she needs from her peers. The last time we were discussing Adela, he had been agitated, but now he seemed calm, expressing quiet delight when he realised that my proposals were matching his objectives. More surprising still, he seems keen that Adela should be spending part of her time in London, even before September. I will speak to Miss Smyth about the possibility.

Richard's change of heart astonishes me. I do not know what has caused it, but as the English love saying, one should not inspect a gift horse in the teeth. I am too happy to go worrying over reasons. Yes, the daily intimacy of our family life will soon be over. But our bonds will be strengthened by the knowledge that our children will be entering the wider world with confidence, and with our blessing.

25th January 1910

Ausgezeichnet! Our family has reached an understanding which is pleasing me. We all know and accept that Tristram will be leaving on his travels in April, and that Adela will be going to London soon and will be living there from

September. Richard seems much more relaxed than at Christmas. There is an openness between us all which is so right, now that the children have become adults. But Tristram, typically, tested our equilibrium this evening. He will be pushing at the boundaries.

'I admire Ethel Smyth,' he proclaimed. 'I've been reading about her. She sounds an admirable woman who knows what she wants and speaks her mind. She'll be good for you, Adela, but you'll have to be careful.' Adela smiled questioningly at him. Richard beamed, no doubt expecting some good-natured witticism.

'Her passions are strong,' continued my impudent son, 'and they're not confined to music.'

'I understand that she is also making her name as a writer, is it not so?' I said.

'And not just writing, Mother. She devours people, too.'

'Good Heavens,' said Richard, 'whatever do you mean?'

'I mean,' continued Tristram, 'that her relationships are unusually strong, and that her taste is broad.'

'Broad?'

'She is from Lesbos.'

'You mean she is a Greek? The name Smyth does not sound Greek. Has she married an Englishman? But then why is she not Mrs Smyth?'

'I mean that she is from the school of Sappho.'

'Sappho? She is a poet, then?'

'I mean, Father, that she loves women. She

dresses in rough tweeds. She smokes cigars. She wears a pork pie hat.'

'And our daughter is going to live with this woman?' Richard growled.

'Oh, don't worry, Father. As I said, her taste is broad. The greatest love of her life was an American writer called Harry Brewster. He died last year. Don't forget she is over fifty. I was only teasing when I said that Adela need be careful.'

'It was not in good taste,' I said coldly.

'I'm sorry, Mother. No, I meant what I said. Miss Smyth will be an excellent model for you, Adela.'

I need not have been worrying. Richard had subsided from boiling point to a mild simmer. Adela was looking calm and amused. There was a time, and a recent one, when Richard would have been telling Tristram to leave the room, and he would have been forbidding Adela to go to London. It is strange how quickly he has accepted that she must be facing the temptations of the world. Perhaps I have been too hard on Tristram. If his testing leaves us all the stronger, why should I be complaining?

12th February 1910

We were all keen to know how Adela had got on in London. My sister glowed over dinner, elated from her visit.

'Did you meet Mr Beecham?' Mother asked.

'Oh, Mr Beecham, yes, and he was as haughty as

ever about his fellow musicians. I not only attended his performance of *A Village Romeo and Juliet*, but was invited to his rehearsal of *The Barber of Seville*. "The high notes, by all means, Mademoiselle de Savoie, ma non troposphere." And talking about a violinist playing a concerto, he said, "He scrapes away quite passably, but I do wish he would fiddle with his violin and not the score."

Father laughed louder than any of us at these, but then came the real test.

'So this opera by Delius, what is it about?'

'It is based on Shakespeare's *Romeo and Juliet*. Two children take a liking to each other, even though their fathers have quarrelled. As they grow up, their love is doomed. They're rejected by their families and sneered at in the street. Eventually, they climb into a barge loaded with hay and pull out the bungs, drowning themselves in the river.'

'So Wagner is not the only one,' rumbled Father. 'I don't know. Can these people not find anything better to write about than making a virtue of the sin of taking one's own life?'

It is, of course, pure coincidence that the end of *A Village Romeo and Juliet* has a superficial resemblance to *Tristan and Isolde*. But I think that all of us, Mother included, were aware of the dangers of a detailed explanation.

'And how was Miss Smyth?' Father asked, unexpectedly changing the subject.

'She was very kind to me. She invited some of her musical friends around one evening, and I was asked to play some pieces of my own choosing. Everyone seemed delighted, and an Australian composer called Percy Grainger said that his playing was bound to disappoint after mine. It was actually very good, and two of the pieces, he said, were being heard for the first time. He gives his works funny names like *The Gum Suckers March* and *Sheep and Goat Walking to the Pastures.* Afterwards, he gave me copies of some of his scores and said he would be honoured if I studied them.

'There!' said Father even more unexpectedly, 'Sheep and goats. Much sounder subjects. Not to the slaughter, I hope?' he added wickedly, and we all laughed.

4th April 1910

Alles ist vorbei! Tristram has gone. He was leaving this morning for Southampton. By now he will have sailed to Cherbourg, from where he will be taking a train to Paris and another to Berlin.

He was leaving here two days later than intended. I am very, very proud of him. Some piece of machinery, a petrol motor pumper or something so, had been delayed from the company supplying it. But his word he kept. He had given me his serious promise that he would be completing every task before he left, and he stayed on for two more days to be fulfilling his pledge.

What a scene at the station! I could not help dabbing at the corners of my eyes with my handkerchief. Tristram, the centre of attention, was proud and tall and noble, spending time with each of us in turn, saying words of assurance and comfort as the train was drawing nearer. Richard was hearty, supporting me and embracing Tristram, looking deep into his eyes with love and gratitude. Adela was… not what I was expecting. Her eyes were moist, but she held her smile bravely. She had an intensity of expression which I am only describing as ethereal. When Tristram turned to her, she gazed long, but it seemed through him rather than at him. I sensed that she had already parted from him in her mind. She is excited for her future. Every day she is growing in confidence. She is ready to be seizing what life is holding out to her.

Tonight, as I am sitting by the window in the fading light, I am feeling a sadness that our family life together is over. But I know that it could not have ended better, and that the past has surrendered so willingly to the future.

26th April 1910

I am loving my husband when he is like this. It is as though he has been set free to give himself to me. Over the past few weeks, he has been administering to my most profound needs at night, devoting himself to my pleasure slowly, deliberately and with exquisite patience. And when his own ecstasy has passed, he silently indicates that he wishes to preserve the intimacy into the night.

Last night, when I had been sleeping for perhaps an hour, I had a dream that I was being led into a chamber of the deepest peace imaginable. The only other time that I have been experiencing such a feeling of well-being was when I had morphine treatment during my illness after the birth of Tristram. My mind was entering a state of perfect tranquillity. All my cares had melted away. Everything was still, and yet I had a growing sense of communion with a living presence. Considering that I must be in paradise, it was dawning on me that true bliss, if it is to provide the highest fulfilment, is not merely a beautiful setting, a vision of Elysium from afar, but a spiritual experiencing of a divine being. Suddenly pleasure was searing upon me with an intensity which was close to pain, and I cried out, and awoke, as Richard's voice said soothingly, 'It is all right', and I felt his hand and sobbed in ecstasy and melted wide and became inert. On and on it went until, sated at last, I was kissing him and caressing him and rejoicing in our pleasure because, you see, waking was not a disappointment, a departure from heaven; no, it was better than my dream, and the reality was exceeding it.

part two

Four Years Later

part two

. . .

Four Years Later

31st July 1914

Adam and Eve before the Fall, proud in their nakedness. The animals respectful; tolerance everywhere. I walk in the Garden, and it is good. Lying on my back and gazing up through the trees. Light-dappled leaves of intense green against luminous blue, and sound so beautiful that I cannot guess what it is.

And God the Father is speaking unto me, and I do not need to hear His words, for they are not words, but thoughts of infinite love and reassurance. 'This is your right, you are worthy of this, this is where I have decided that you should be.' And all the time the sound. Is it running water? Are those the chimes of tiny bells? The rustling of wind in the leaves?

What is this? A little creature with a human face. Smiling, but is it sincere? Who is it? Satan? It slithers; ah, the Serpent, of course. It hangs from a branch above me, examining me, smiling down in a knowing way. Like God, it addresses me without speaking, but I know what it is saying, 'I too am worthy; do you think that I would be here if He did not approve? I come to do His will. No, I do not say that it is pleasant or unpleasant. It simply is. No, do not hurry me. There is always time in the Garden'.

What was that? The Serpent no longer hangs above me. Something slides across my face. Ugh!

I do not know which of us was the more terrified, the cow or me. Her wide, shining muzzle filled my vision. I leapt up – as much as a man of my age can leap directly from a recumbent position – twisting my back in revulsion at the slobbering nostrils. If the cow was slower than me, it was infinitesimal. She swung her neck away like a scythe and bolted along the river bank.

I rubbed my face and realised instantly what had awoken me. A band of mucus clung to the edge of my mouth. I clawed at it, attempting to fling the disgusting thing away before I could taste it, only to bring my hand down sharply on a thistle. The way my luck was going, it might have been a cow pat. It had been such a lovely dream. Gone. Ah well, there must be something in all of this which I can use in a sermon. Let me get this foul slobber off my face.

I remember sitting down here and, yes, I did lie back. I must have become drowsy and then fallen asleep, lulled by the heat of the sun and this glorious summer, which just sails on and on. Behind me, the stooks have gone, gathered in a week ago, so why is there still the sound of a mighty industry as millions of insects tug and push at the hot, still air? The reason is my policy of always keeping a portion of these fields unharvested each year. In front of me the river pauses, swirls and drifts on, as though it too is torpified by the heat. Ah, there! I knew it would: a corncrake has started to rasp, out-grating the sound of all the grasshoppers deep in the meadow.

I have passed into the afternoon of my life and, if nothing could match the freshness of the morning dew which has long evaporated, I thank my Saviour for the great beauty which I still see around me. No sounds of men intrude on nature here; only the trains passing up and down the valley every hour or so. They are a comforting sound, yet they represent time, and I do not wish time to pass any more. I do not want it, yet I cannot hold it back.

Impending peril holds a dazzling fascination. This gloriously hot and brilliant summer cruises by, and with it peace, security, and contentment, are sliding away. The events we face are too stupefying to seem real. Their shimmering tempts us into believing that it is all a mirage, but it is not. William thinks that there will be war within a few days. First we had the assassination of the Archduke Franz Ferdinand by that mad Serb student a month ago. Then last week Austria issued an ultimatum to Serbia in terms which could never be accepted. All that achieved was to get the Serbians and Montenegrins mobilising. Russia threatens to come to the aid of her fellow Slavs, so Austria mobilises on her border too. So what do the Germans do? Instead of acting as peacemakers, or simply keeping out of it and biding their time, they publicly announce to the world that they are issuing a blank cheque to Austria to support her in her war against Serbia. Two days ago Russia announced that she too was mobilising, and now the Austrians have started to bombard Belgrade, so the game is on. Eastern Europe has started to ignite. It is hard to see how the line of bigger and bigger powder kegs will not blow up.

Germany. It always seems to be Germany. It is central, in every sense. It is the Germans who can prevent the explosion. The Germans. My darling wife. What is she thinking? How different is she from her fellow countrymen? Does she know what will happen better than I do? The subject distresses her, I know it does, so I will resist the temptation to interrogate her. These are trying times for her, and she needs all my love and support.

What will the French do? They have a binding treaty to come to the aid of Russia. They must either renege on it or enter the fray. Need we follow? We have no such treaty, but William has reminded me that we stood firm against the Germans in a much less serious crisis in Agadir three years ago, and faced them down in support of the French. But the words "facing down" are hardly appropriate when your opponent is already at war. Brinkmanship is one thing; hurling yourself after your enemy when he has already plunged into the abyss is quite another. We are not obliged to fight, but that does not mean that we should not be prepared to do so. There is the call of duty. When all the other nations of Europe had fallen under the boots of Napoleon's army, or cravenly joined him in cowardly alliances, we alone stood firm and turned the tide. Do we have a Nelson or a Wellington, as yet unidentified, to stride forward in the name of Freedom?

William is concerned that all the other European powers have large conscripted armies while ours, although professional, is puny by comparison. But surely our youth would rally to the cause in the hour of need? And we have the Royal Navy, our great and glorious fleet. I do not underestimate the Germans. The hordes who marched from Potsdam in 1870 showed ruthless efficiency. They will try to do the same again. We must be firm. Yet I do not wish for war. *Pax vobiscum.* If mankind does not want peace, we must trust in God. *Dona nobis pacem.* My own duty is to bring succour to my flock and lead them, guided by our Saviour who is Christ the Lord, through prayer.

Where is Tristram? Can it be that he is unaware of what is going on? We have not heard from him for months, and we last saw him in January. As far as we know, he is still in the Middle East somewhere. He is amongst Germans, foul thought, so he should know better than we what they are likely to do. But one never knows with Tristram. In view of what is happening, one would think that he would keep in touch.

Down here by the river, it is easy to believe none of it. What if boots do tramp the cornfields of the Continent and guns flatten the vineyards of Alsace? What is it to that darter there, zooming back and forth, working its azure course? It seems random, yet I know that it is not. I had better get back. Evensong calls. Time has me by the throat. These are momentous times. The cow, now grazing on the distant slope, is once more meandering in my direction. Adam, Eve, God, the Serpent, the cow. Can we ever understand their roles? Or our own?

2nd August 1914

I arrived home yesterday afternoon, half hoping that Tristram might be here. I still think of Chaddingley as home, even though I've lived in London for ages. It's amazing to think I've seen him only twice in the last four years. Mama says they haven't heard from him for over three months.

Everyone says there'll be war. I hope not, but the whole of London seems to be hopping from one leg to another in a sort of fearful elation. I can't say that most people actually want war; and yet it seems there would be anti-climax, disappointment even, especially for the men, if it doesn't happen.

I sense Mama is worried about Tristram, and I think I know why. He's been amongst Germans for the past four years, and it could just be that he'll go to Germany rather than here. Papa doesn't seem to suspect the possibility, and I hope he's right.

I have a concert booked for the last day of the month. It'll be my fourth and most important yet. I do hope this silly war nonsense doesn't mean that it'll have to be postponed. It seems nothing these days is allowed to be certain or stay the same. Even Ethel has become conventional and patriotic. She says that if there's war, all demonstrations and direct action for women's suffrage will cease. She told me Mrs Pankhurst has decreed that it'll be no good fighting for votes for women if there's no country left in which to hold elections. In any case, Ethel thinks she's done enough for that particular cause. After all, she did go to gaol for throwing a brick through a cabinet minister's window. Thomas Beecham claims he saw her conducting her *March of the Women* through the bars of Holloway Prison with a toothbrush, though I never quite believe his stories. Anyhow, Ethel told me she'd promised Mrs Pankhurst that she'd commit herself to the cause for two years and no more. As for Beecham, he disdains all political opinions, even something as important as war. He enjoys being aloof.

I feel well prepared for the thirty-first. All the pieces I shall be playing, by Schubert, Brahms and Mendelssohn, are well within my grasp. I don't believe in over-rehearsing. Once I've mastered a work technically, the biggest danger is to become stale through over-familiarity. An interpretive review every two or three days is all that's required. It's more important to relax, though I never neglect my daily exercises at the piano.

Darling Papa. I think he epitomises the mood of the country. He's excited about the prospect of war, and his Christian sense of duty is rising up like a lion to wrestle with the charitable principles of his unicorn. Onward Christian Soldiers. I think he too would be deflated if they had to be called off.

7th August 1914

Verrückter! I am German by birth. My mother, God bless her, is living in Germany. Some of the greatest people who ever contributed to the advancement of humanity were German. The composers I most revere are either German or Austrian. But now I am ashamed of my heritage. That incompetent fool the Kaiser has squandered his inheritance. He has defied all the knowledge and wisdom passed down to him by Otto von Bismarck. As for the Austrians, they have become petty and spiteful in their decline. They are *decadent bis ins Innerste,* and would putrefy all those around them. From now on I will be regarding myself as British and nothing else. I will be proud to be called this. The act of a lunatic in the Balkans has been used as an excuse for a frenzy of snarling dogs to start tearing at each others' throats. And now this country too is at war.

Thank God Tristram is safe. He sent a telegram last night from Liverpool to say that he will be coming down by train today. I cannot say how relieved I am. I had actually begun to think that he might have gone instead to Germany. Now I am ashamed of the thought. Yet I fear with a mother's anguish what may lie ahead. We are the only large country in Europe, so Richard says, which does not have a conscripted army. But then who will fight for Great Britain against the German conscripts, if not young men like Tristram? They say that recruits in their tens of thousands are coming forward. Will Tristram be one of them? He does have a sense of adventure, but he is not one to be stampeded. Elizabeth Sawbridge's husband is already in the army. She returned from America two years ago and has married an army captain.

I am frightened for my son, my only boy. I must keep my new anti-German sentiment to myself. If Tristram is thinking that he will be fighting against my Fatherland, and that I love it, he is less likely to be volunteering.

8th August 1914

William invited me into his garden room. He has built a beautiful model of the battlefields, laid across two trestle tables. It covers Belgium and north-eastern France, and has a plywood base, with plaster of Paris to show where the land is of a higher elevation. On it are painted towns, rivers, railways and major roads. Little blocks of wood with coloured bands representing the national flags of Germany, France and Belgium, one for each army, show the deployment of forces. I asked where the divisions of the British Army were. He gave me a funny look and showed me an egg cup containing a single block painted with the Union Jack. In my ignorance I had not realised that the British Expeditionary Force was so small, and has only just started landing at the Channel ports.

'This is impressive work, William. You have crafted a masterpiece in only four days.'

'You mean since we declared war? No, as I told you long ago, Richard, I knew that this would come.'

He is in his element. He will not just track the war from his garden room; he will fight it. He moves his pieces back and forth in anticipation, weighing up the possibilities.

'Now see here, what if the French deploy to the north of Charleroi? They could end up winning the Battle of Waterloo after all, eh? Well, what do you think?'

'William, with you controlling the pieces, I think that we shall win this war.'

I share his excitement, but feel guilty that I do. It cannot be right for a servant of God to be entertained by acts of hatred and killing. Yet I know this to be a just cause. Surely the prosecution of it must allow for satisfaction, if not pleasure? Did the Archangels Michael and Gabriel not feel a sense of triumph when they thrust their swords at Satan and drove him out of Paradise? I will pray.

9th August 1914

They mean well, but I'm finding it hard to be civil.

'You must be tired, Tristram, after your long journey?'

'A little, Mother, but I am weary more because of what is happening in Europe.'

'See it as a challenge,' said Father. 'These are

stern times, but we must face them with fortitude. Good may yet come of it.'

If it weren't for Adela, I couldn't have taken it. I see all the petty meanness of the world encapsulated in this house. I'm grieving, following my parting from Walter, Fritz, Gerhard, Francois and the others, yet all I hear when I get home is what their countries are doing. Their countries! My comrades did not blame me for Asquith's and Grey's blunders. Did I look on them as petty Kaisers? Hans, it is true, will enlist as soon as he gets home, but he's a fool with principles instead of a brain.

I must have appeared very sullen this evening. Father started attacking the Germans as though they were nothing but rows of jackbooted *uhlans* in the image of Kronprinz Willi. It was insulting to Mother, though strangely she didn't seem offended. How would he like it if he had to sit listening to a German pronouncing all Englishmen to be a race of Jack the Rippers? What angered and frustrated me is that I had to prevaricate when Father started talking about duty and the sacrifice which Britain's manhood must make. Sacrifice! Isn't everything I stand for in contempt of that word and its implications of futility and waste? What I wanted to say was that I've no intention of contributing further to stupidity and destruction. Yes, I despise the German government for what it's doing, and the Austrians still more so. He didn't ask me when I'd enlist, nor even whether I'd do so, but there was a presumption there. The hints were so strong that ignoring them was painful and humiliating. I couldn't abuse Germany, for fear of offending Mother. Nor would I find fault with

Great Britain, who hasn't created this situation. So I sat there, a coward to myself in my silence, and no doubt cowardly in Father's eyes for not leaping to my feet and crying 'Tally Ho!'

Adela's my lifeline. How grown up she's become. I was able to deflect Father's admonishments from the pulpit by asking her about her life in London. Her eyes conveyed that she wouldn't tell me everything, not at dinner. Her voice has become deeper, more self-assured, and she no longer spends time gazing at the table in front of her when others are speaking. I could sense her pride, directed at me, when Mother talked about the success of her concerts.

'You must be reading the reviews of Adela's performances, Tristram. I am compiling a scrapbook. The critics are being most complimentary.'

But when I asked Adela about the people she'd met, she competently deflected my questions. Having been forced to give veiled answers myself only minutes previously, I sympathetically withdrew, knowing she would confide in me when we were alone together.

Tomorrow, Father and I are to ride the farm. It'll be just like old times. I've refrained from asking him about *Schrebergarten* so far. My reticence has been due to a numbness and a sense of loss. I mourn my colleagues, my work and the sanity of the world. And I feel a deeper loss, which I'll disclose to Adela later when we're alone. Then I'll try to be more positive after a night's sleep.

I forgot. There is one thing that Father and I do agree on. Britain would never have entered the war to defend Serbia. The mood was not for it. But when Germany issued an ultimatum to Belgium a week ago, this act of thuggery against an innocent and neutral nation outraged the British people. The Germans may be about to execute a brilliant military strategy, but they have stirred a sleeping lion, whose sense of injustice has been aroused.

I am thinking how Tristram over dinner was subdued, and uncharacteristically defensive. I could tell that he was being embarrassed by Richard's prodding. It was as trying a reunion for him as it was for me. Although thrilled to see him, and for all of us to be together again at last, my act of pretence I am not enjoying. I was longing to let Tristram know how much I despise the Kaiser and am ashamed of what Germany is doing. But I could not be saying this thing.

As for Richard, he may have taken my lack of support for his patriotism as disloyalty to him; worse, he may even be suspecting that my sympathies are with Germany. But what can I do? My first duty as a mother is to be discouraging Tristram from enlisting in Kitchener's army. What better way to stop him than to make him think that he would be betraying me by fighting the country of my birth, and the land where my mother still lives? This is what this wretched war is doing to us. It is making us deceivers of our own family.

I think I love my brother even more. Though neither

of us could be open at dinner, we held nothing back from each other once we were alone. I have surprised Tristram by telling him that it hasn't been easy in London; nor have I been an unqualified success. Tristram for his part feels a deep sense of longing, and that he has lost everything on which he has been building his life.

I said, 'Look at Mama's scrap book, by all means, but I'm afraid it isn't all like that. Not every review has been so complimentary; the ones she doesn't like she simply throws away.'

'But you're still getting bookings?'

'Yes, and my concert next week has already sold out. There's a rumour that George Bernard Shaw will be there.'

'So your star must be on the rise.'

'Perhaps, but there's a considerable body of opinion against women musicians. One critic wrote about my performance of Liszt's *B minor Sonata*, "With a work of such virile potency, which requires penetration to its core, it seems perverse to have left it to a mere butterfly to flutter across the surface."'

'Oh dear.'

I nestled against him. 'Yes, and that was particularly cruel as several other critics said how strong my interpretation was. "Like staring up into the girders of the Forth Bridge and marvelling at the strength of the structure." That was another review. You will be there on the thirty-first?'

'Of course I will. You don't think I'd miss it, do you? Point out the first critic, and I'll sit next to him with my cane at the ready. I'll give him penetration to the core.' He held my shoulders gently between his hands. 'And what was the Royal Academy like? Have you met lots of interesting people in London?'

'I loved it. Tobias Matthey's an inspired teacher, though a demanding one. He's brilliant at conveying new insights and techniques, but he insists that his pupils play music which they don't like. And the tasks he sets can be daunting.'

'And what about Ethel Smyth? Is she the wild rebel I thought too subversive to be looking after my little sister?'

'Not really. She cultivates interesting and unusual friendships, but in some ways she's quite conventional. She speaks her mind with utter fearlessness, and that's what upsets many people. She's writing more and more books now; in fact she writes more than she composes. She's been very generous to me.'

'And have you formed any deep attachments?'

'I've made several close friends. Some are musicians, one or two are composers, others...'

'I mean really close.' I could tell what he meant.

'You mean men? There is one who's very special to me. His name's Edgar Simpson. He's a painter, or is trying to be. I'd like you to meet him.'

The pleasure in Tristram's eyes meant the world to me. He took hold of my hands. 'Adela.'

'And you,' I said, 'tell me all that you've been doing.'

He sighed, something Tristram rarely does. 'It's a sad story, and I feel bitter about what's happened. I still don't know whether I've done the right thing or, rather, I do really, but I can't come to terms with it. Walter Grattin is writing a book on Babylon in the sixth century BC. I'm his co-author, an enormous privilege. He's writing most of it, but I'm going to be writing several chapters, in German, of course. Then I'll be translating the whole thing into English. Or would have been.'

'The war.'

'This bloody, bloody war. Walter's in Berlin, I'm here, and I don't even know whether we're going to be allowed to communicate.'

'I don't think you are. I've heard that they've started censoring the post. But correspondence with an enemy country is strictly forbidden. Were you tempted to go to Germany rather than here?'

He looked at me sharply. I was quite frightened by this look.

'Yes, but I have taken the decision not to.' He said it stolidly, obstinately, like a child who is trying to convince a parent, but isn't convinced himself. This was so unlike Tristram.

'I haven't told you all. I'm in love, Adela. Last year, I was introduced to Fritz Lehnart's sister in Damascus. Then six weeks ago we were together again in Cairo. Her name is Ingrid. In September, in only a few weeks' time, I was to go to Berlin to work with Walter on the book. Ingrid lives in Nürnberg, and we agreed that we would spend as much time together as possible. She loves me, Adela, and I love her. When I'm with her, even if there are others present, I feel I've stepped outside my life into something so wonderful that I can't believe it really exists.'

I think I must have forgotten to breathe, because

when I asked, 'So what made you choose England?' my voice sounded hushed and fearful.

'Because, for all… what I mean is, both countries are closing their minds to reality, but I think Germany is the worse of the two. You know what I'm like; I won't run with the herd. I may not like what Britain's doing, but I like Germany even less. If I went there, I would feel bound to speak out against it and, being the son of an Englishman, showing even the slightest disloyalty would lead to internment.'

'And presumably you might get conscripted? I'm glad there's none of that here. They say that Kitchener's recruitment campaign has been so successful that conscription may not be necessary.'

'Yes, but it's torture to think in those terms. Can you imagine what it's like for a man to weigh the alternatives in terms of his own personal danger? I feel a coward.'

'You are not a coward,' I said hotly.

'This is what war does to people. They feel bound to show loyalty, to be patriotic, not to appear cowards. So the war is fuelled by people who wouldn't otherwise fight. I hate it.'

'It's courageous to hold to one's own beliefs. At this time, it may be the greatest form of bravery.'

'Thank you for that,' said Tristram. 'You're more of a comfort to me than you could possibly realise. I know now that I've made the right decision.'

How things have changed. All our lives he's protected me. He's always been so strong, and I so timid. That he should be the one in need of comfort, and that I should be the one to give it. And I do, brother, with all my heart.

10th August 1914

I was riding back with Tristram up the track past Coney Piece. The sun baked down onto the crusted earth between lines of golden stubble. I was keen to get back, as the horses were sweating in the heat, but I was elated. Tristram, who had seemed so subdued last night, was obviously delighting in everything he saw, not least in the *Schrebergarten*. And I, with pride and gratitude, had been able to tell him that it had all been a success. We have lost only one farm worker in the past four years, and the men's contentment in being able to cultivate their own land is plain to see.

We passed Gore's Clump and were approaching the main farm buildings, when Peter ran out from the stables. He was clearly agitated.

'Squarson, sir, sir! 'Ave you 'eard the news?'

He was clapping his hands and hopping from one leg to the other as though he needed the lavatory. But somehow I could tell that he was excited rather than frightened. I was about to say, 'Get on with it, then' or some such thing when Tristram said quietly, 'What news, Peter?'

'Tis Mr Westaway, Sir, and Mr Folland, Sir. They've joined up, both of 'em. And they's more in the village.'

'Good heavens, when did you learn this?'

'From Ned, Sir, just now, Sir.'

Before I had time to be shocked or annoyed that I should have received the news in this manner, Malpiero and Westaway walked towards us from the stables, Malpiero to take my horse, and Westaway to ask if he might speak to me. It was then that I knew that it must be true.

I saw the implications immediately. I'm not sure Father does. There are fools who think that this war will be over within weeks. *Schrebergarten's* success, it seems, has been short-lived. We are starting to lose men again, and there may be more to come. The greatest loss will be Paul Westaway, the farm manager. He has a quiet authority, and the men respect him. I cannot see who could replace him from the ranks of our existing workforce. Jack Hearn, Edwin Blamey, Abel Hopkins, Franco Malpiero, John Jarvis: they're all competent and skilled, but they're specialists. Each lacks the ability to organise the others. Father won't be able to find anyone from outside the farm. The war's creating a shortage of manpower everywhere. There is an answer, but it won't occur to Father. Step forward Tristram Hall. It would solve one problem: I can't any longer endure this shadow boxing with Father as to whether I'm going to enlist. By putting myself forward as farm manager, I'll be signalling to him that I've no intention of marching to Belgium or France. Whether he'll accept it is another matter.

Adela to London has returned. The next time we are seeing my daughter, she will be on the concert platform. Tristram too is in London. He will be returning here at the end of the week.

Colonel Sawbridge has unsettled me this evening. I still cannot be deciding whether he is being kind, or whether he is taking some delight in frightening me.

Thank goodness that I am married to an Englishman. We were nearing the end of the evening, which had been full of the usual banter between the Colonel and Richard. But then it all was turning serious when Colonel Sawbridge started telling us about some horrid new legislations, passed in the first few days of the war. They have hateful names, like the Aliens Restriction Act and the Defence of the Realm Act. I was feeling insulted when he started talking about them. The implication seemed to be that they might be concerning me, because I could be classed as an Alien. He said that these Acts had been drafted in deliberately broad terms.

Richard responded, 'Well, if they are vague, I do not see how they can have any teeth.'

'I did not say vague,' Colonel Sawbridge replied, 'I said broad, in order to provide flexibility for future amendment without having to go back to Parliament each time. The Alien Restriction Order, for instance, empowers the Home Secretary to deport any Alien whenever in his judgement it is deemed advisable.'

'The Courts would never back him without good reason,' Richard said.

'He isn't required to justify his reasons in the Courts.' The Colonel is, how do you say it, a stickler for detail, but I did not like the way he seemed to be enjoying the display of his knowledge.

'Anyhow, Helga and I have been married for nearly thirty years, and as far as we are concerned, she is an Englishwoman. Is that not right, my dear?'

'It is so,' I said firmly.

'Let us hope so,' persisted the Colonel, 'but the Defence of the Realm Act does use the term "of hostile origin"'.

I glared at the Colonel. 'Those who are calling people hostile will find that they become so.'

Richard beamed at me approvingly. The Colonel was looking taken aback, but he was not to be diverted.

'If you were living in a prohibited area, Helga, these Acts might affect you more than you think.'

'What is this thing, a prohibited area?' I asked.

'It is the whole of the east coast, parts of the south coast and anywhere near a port, military base, training camp, ammunition store, that sort of thing.'

'Parts of the south coast?'

'Not Chaddingley; I've checked. But if you were another fifteen miles closer to Portland Naval Base, then I'm afraid that you would come under the restriction.'

'And what happens if Enemy Aliens… of hostile origin… are living in these areas?' The men laughed, as though I was making a witty joke, but the reason why I was saying it in this funny way was that the words were sticking in my throat.

'Then amongst other things they have to get a special permit to travel more than five miles,' replied Colonel Sawbridge.

'Well, we are not living in a prohibited area,' said Richard with some exasperation, 'so there is no problem.'

Bless him, he is as loyal to me as I could be wishing. William Sawbridge is a closer friend than most men experience in a lifetime, but when it is coming to a choice between his friend and his wife, it is I who will always be coming first. I love him.

16th August 1914

My funny husband is climbing the steps up to the pulpit. He is leaning forward and searching the congregation, as though assessing his audience, giving them the impression that what he is about to say is depending on what he is finding before him. Then he straightens, throws back his head and, just as he seems about to speak, leans forward again as though checking something. It is a device he uses to create anticipation, and to give the impression of spontaneity, although I know that he has rehearsed it all meticulously.

'A fortnight ago, with the sun hot on my back, I was strolling along the riverbank, delighting in

God's beauty all around me. So contented was I that at one particular spot I sat down. The murmuring sounds of a summer's afternoon must have made me drowsy, for I lay on my back and fell fast asleep.'

Richard is pausing. The congregation is stiff with anticipation. They know what his sermons are like. Not a muscle is moving in the whole church.

'I had a dream. I was in the Garden of Eden. Adam and Eve were there, and the Serpent, and God the Father, who spoke to me. His words were full of love and comfort. There was a beautiful sound. I could not tell what it was. The tinkling of a tiny bell? A trickle of water? Leaves in the trees? I had passed from what Shakespeare called this demi-paradise, down by the riverbank, to a true paradise, a foretaste of Heaven.'

There is an even longer pause. Richard gazes round the church, looking admiringly at the flowers.

'I was awoken in a most unpleasant manner.' He says this so abruptly, jerking his head down from staring into the rafters, that the whole congregation jumps. 'It was a *cow*.' His voice is loaded with bathos. 'You know what cows are like; always curious. They have to inspect everything unusual at close quarters, and what could be more unusual than a parson lying on his back, probably snoring? And you all know what else cows do: they like to lick things. And this one, a member of my own herd I am ashamed to say, had slobbered over my face, waking me up. I jumped, she jumped, and there I was, back in the world as it is now. And do you know? It was still beautiful. Not as beautiful as the

Garden of Eden, but still worthy of delight in God's creation.

'I have chosen two texts today. The first is taken from 1 Corinthians, Chapter 1, Verse 10. *Now I beseech you, brethren, by the name of our Lord Jesus Christ, that ye all speak the same things, and that there be no divisions among you; but that ye be perfectly joined together in the same mind and in the same judgement.* What St Paul is saying here in effect is that we must all pull together. My second text is from St Paul's Epistle to the Ephesians, Chapter 4, Verses 4 to 6. *There is one body, and one Spirit, even as ye are called in one hope of your calling; one Lord, one Faith, one baptism, one God and Father of all, who is above all, and through all and in you all.*

Now I should like to add a few words of my own to what St Paul has written. I should like to add *one King and one Country*. The early Church, at the time when St Paul was writing, was under great stress, and great threat. Its very survival was uncertain. So St Paul was saying, this is not a time for disunity, not a time for people to contradict one another. Again, we must all pull together. So how is this relevant to us today? We too are under threat; we too face a peril. Mighty forces are arrayed against us. We too must pull together, in the name of one Lord, one faith, one God and Father, one King and Country.

'We wish Godspeed to Paul Westaway, John Folland, and Bootsy Barnes. They have answered the call. In our hour of need, they have stepped forward. We salute them. May they be protected by the grace of God, and we pray for their speedy and safe return.'

There was another long pause as Richard searched the eyes of the congregation.

'Some of you may be thinking of following them, those amongst you who are men of the right age. You may have your doubts, your fears.' Richard's voice is full of trepidation. 'Should you be ashamed of your doubts, your fears?' He straightens. The young men must be fearful of what he will be saying next. 'Before I answer that, let me tell you about the sufferings, mental as well as physical, of our Lord Jesus. *He took with him Peter and the two sons of Zebedee, and began to be sorrowful and very heavy*. This was at the time of His greatest challenge, as the hour of His crucifixion approached, for He knew exactly what was coming. *And he went a little further, and fell on his face, and prayed, saying, O my Father, if it be possible, let this cup pass from me: nevertheless, not as I will, but as thou wilt.* And after that, He faced His persecutors, and His agonies, and died for our sins.

'So I say to you young men who may be wavering, and to your loved ones who may be restraining you: it is all right. Being afraid is nothing to be ashamed of. Perhaps *you* have been sorrowful and heavy in your hearts? Perhaps you too wished that the cup could be passed from you? And perhaps you too are ready now to say with Jesus, Thy will be done, and to face your enemies, not alone as Jesus had to do, but with your comrades and pals at your side. And perhaps you are able to say with St Paul: one Lord, one Faith, one Baptism, one God and Father, to which we add, one King and Country.

'For this is indeed a beautiful country. When the

cow started to lick my face and I awoke with such a jolt, I hated leaving the Garden of Eden, which I had visited in my dream. But then I heard birds in the trees above the river and the vast humming of insects behind me in the meadow. And I knew that Shakespeare had been right when he had referred to England as a demi-paradise; something which we should all rise up and pull together to defend and preserve, in unity. And just as God ordered the Archangels Michael and Gabriel to cast out Satan with their swords, so does He command us now to stand firm against Evil. So, with prayer and the love of God, we will prevail.'

17th August 1914

I asked Father what plans he had to replace Paul Westaway as farm manager.

'It has been a tiresome week while you have been in London, Tristram. I had asked Mr Buckle if he would kindly make a few enquiries with his fellow estate agents, but he reported back that he had been unable to generate any interest in the post. I also approached a few neighbouring farmers, to see if they might spare anyone suitable on a part-time basis. None of them could. I am at the rope's end.'

'So what will you do?'

Father looked hesitant. 'Jack Hearn is the oldest and wisest of the men. As you know, he is a shepherd through-and-through. He is well-liked…' he tailed off.

I completed the picture for him. 'He knows little of anything other than shepherding and is not a leader. Have you approached him?'

'Not yet.'

'Good. If he were to manage the farm, he would go from one dither to the next. All that would happen is that you would lose an excellent shepherd.'

Father put on a hangdog face. Now was the time to present my proposal.

'I could be your farm manager. My work in the Middle East has been cut off for the duration of the war. I know the farm, I can command the men, who I believe respect me, and I know how to reallocate tasks with a shifting workforce.'

For a second or two, Father's eyes lit up; then quickly clouded again.

'I'm not going to enlist.' At last, I'd said it.

'Ah.' He looked like someone whose last ticket in a prize draw has failed to win. 'I had wondered.'

'Father, may I make one thing clear? I do not support Germany; not in any way.'

'My dear boy…'

'Don't worry, Father. I'm as angry with Germany for what she's done as you are. Where we might perhaps differ is over our response to it.'

'But if we let the Germans trample all over the Continent, there's no telling where it might end.'

'In 1870 it ended with the defeat of the French. It was not a disaster for Britain.'

We didn't continue the debate. Neither of us had

the stomach for it. We'd both gained a small victory and were content to leave it at that. He has a farm manager, and I have employment which I enjoy. Though it's little consolation, it'll take my mind off the pain of losing Walter. And Ingrid.

While in London, I found out that Adela's right: I'm forbidden to communicate with Germany. I can't send a letter to Ingrid telling her I love her, I can't send further chapters to Walter, and Mother can't write to Grandmother in Hannover. She won't know whether she's ill, or even dead. The decency of the world has taken a vast step backwards. Culture and civility have been destroyed by politicians and generals.

22nd August 1914

I was returning Leander's saddle to the tack room, when I saw a piece of paper pierced by the bridle hook. In capital letters, it read, "LOOK IN YOUR OLD SADDLE BAG." Inside I found a newspaper folded inside out, revealing one of the middle pages. An article had been highlighted in red ink. It was the leader of yesterday's *Daily Mail*. It read, "The Germans who are staying here may be serving their country more effectively than by shouldering a rifle."

I leafed through the newspaper and came across another article which had been singled out. It referred to the Aliens Restriction Act, Defence of the

Realm Act and British Nationality and Status of Aliens Act. All of these cover restrictions on the activities of foreigners in this country or, as the *Daily Mail* would have it, the inadequacy of them. In the margin, my Mercury had written, "Spies not wanted here."

My first instinct was to scrumple the newspaper and hurl it to the floor, conveying my contempt to its bearer. But then I thought that if I took it with me, it might act as an incentive. That way I could tempt my informant into repeating the act, and I might even catch him at it. Mercury of the Tack Room might be a fanatic or simply spiteful, but he had bothered to read about three Acts of Parliament, so was no simpleton. Both he and the *Daily Mail* may let me know what the common man is thinking, or being led to think.

When I got home, I looked through the remainder of the newspaper. A letter to the editor had been highlighted too. It's from an unnamed person calling himself "A Travelling American". It claims that "thirty thousand Germans remain free in your country to stab you in the back. Some of the thirty thousand have signed their names at the police office. But does signing his name take the malice out of the man?"

Hm. I thought Germans were meant to be swindlers. Wasn't it some other nationality who were classed as backstabbers? Italians? Russians? It's hard to take this seriously, but there it is, personal and highlighted, just for me.

26th August 1914

William led me to his garden room and gave me a detailed review of progress of the war so far. It is looking grim. While the French invaded Alsace, the Germans struck at Belgium. How typical of the bullies to attack the child rather than the adult. It seems that the French, wearing blue trousers and red jackets, hurled themselves forward and were fodder for the German machine guns, suffering heavy casualties. With only the tiny army of Belgium to confront them, the Germans made quick progress in the north. Brave little Belgium! But the tide has been too much for her. On the 16th Liège fell, and four days later the Germans entered Brussels. The Belgian government has set up office in Antwerp.

Meanwhile, the French too have been in retreat, ceding both Charleroi and Namur, the latter falling in a single day. Now there has been a great battle at Mons, this time with the British Army fighting shoulder to shoulder with the French, but that has not gone well either. Two days ago Lille fell. Already, in only twelve days since serious fighting began, the Germans are halfway from their borders to Paris. The heart of France lies before them, ready to be pierced from the north-east.

The war could well be over in weeks. And it will be lost.

My Mercury of the Tack Room has returned. I'd hoped he might. What have we here? Riots. Anti-German riots. Listen to this: "An Irishman called Kelly entered a pork butcher's shop in Keighley owned by one Andrassy. He demanded to be served a pork pie without poison in it. A fierce argument ensued, and Kelly was ordered to leave the shop. Claiming that Andrassy had struck him in the face, Kelly returned with a crowd, mainly Irishmen, who pelted the shop with bottles and stones. Their aim being wayward, damage was inflicted on the adjoining property. Andrassy was taken, together with his family, to the nearby police station for protection. Meanwhile, mounted police and the fire brigade confronted the crowd, who were eventually calmed by the local Catholic priest."

Here is another: "Rioting occurred at a baker's shop after his wife, a German woman, had delivered a provocative remark to a drunken man." This says more about the drinking habits of the English and the Irish, than it does about the Germans.

Here again: "Another shopkeeper whose premises were attacked is said to have spoken contemptuously of the British Army, while his wife danced in the street on hearing of British casualties." I wonder.

Back at the house, I've now read what *The Times* has to say about these events. According to its reporter, the riots in Keighley, which are still going on, are the product of a long-running strike of moulders and engineers. When several of the strikers were facing arrest, they turned on the German community.

Thank you, Mercury. This has been educational. More, please.

31st August 1914

Oh my darling girl, far you can now be going. I was hearing it in the applause, I was seeing it in the confidence of your poise, and above all I was hearing it in the music. You knew when to be slowing the pulse. The *andante* in Schubert's *B Flat Sonata* was making me catch my breath. And you knew when to be strong and secure each crescendo. You were making a few mistakes, but they were small and did not interrupt the flow, or your unerring grasp of what the composer was saying. I am so proud of you, and the audience loved you, loved you, and what you delivered to them. The applause is saying so much, but it is the noise when everyone leaves the auditorium which is the best indication of the success of a concert. An audience which has not been satisfied will talk loudly as it leaves, proclaiming where the nearest taxi or best restaurant may be found. If they have been moved, both mentally and emotionally, there is a low buzzing sound as they speak their first impressions in hushed syllables. That is what I was hearing tonight, and I am so excited and happy.

Tristram was telling me that there was some disturbance at the back of the hall during Mendelssohn's *Rondo Capriccioso,* but I was not hearing it.

My brilliant sister has triumphed. She sparkled, she commanded, she conveyed humility and compassion, she withdrew into herself, and then suddenly exploded with bursts of virtuosity. The audience went wild after each piece, and at the end the applause lasted for several minutes. She kept returning to the stage to receive the adulation she so deserved.

There was an incident at the back of the hall during the Mendelssohn. A man shouted out "Traitor!" followed by what sounded like "Unmusic", though I now realise it may have been "Hun music." There was a scuffle and what sounded more like grunting than shouting. I turned round to see a man being led in an arm-lock up the top steps and through the curtain. Adela didn't hesitate. She'd just entered a quieter passage. Bent low over the keyboard, she seemed to be listening to the sound as much as making it. Then she gradually straightened and the gorgeous melody poured forth like an opening flower.

I had hoped to meet her boyfriend, Edgar. Adela said he was there in the audience somewhere, but was too shy to approach us.

I think it went well. I made a few careless mistakes, mostly in the Brahms, but I'm pleased that I didn't let them disrupt either my concentration or the flow. My listeners were very enthusiastic. In this performance, more than any other, I felt totally drawn into the music, yet I felt too that I was interacting with the audience. I can't explain that contradiction. All I can say is that it's the most wonderful feeling imaginable.

There was some kind of disturbance during my recapitulation of Mendelssohn's *Rondo Capriccioso*. It didn't seem to last, and I ignored it. I asked Tristram afterwards if he knew what it'd been, and he dismissed it as some kind of drunken scuffle. Mama didn't even hear it.

When it was all over, I was feted in a way which hasn't happened before. Acquaintances and strangers alike surrounded me backstage and heaped praise on my performance. Even Mr Fielder-Grilsen, whom I hadn't seen for ages, shook me warmly by the hand and actually managed to smile.

I can relax now. I think I've earned it.

2nd September 1914

I've tried to get the men to think for themselves since Father won't do it. Without wishing to appear unpatriotic, I've told them that it's their own decision, individually, as to whether to enlist or not. It's had little effect. They eye their neighbours expectantly like so many contestants before a race. If one twitches, they all twitch. Now we've lost John Hawkes and his brother Ned to the regiment. Head stockman Abel Hopkins has been particularly unhelpful. Even though he's lost a good cattleman in John Hawkes, to him Kitchener is a god, not just a talented soldier. Hopkins himself fought in the Boer War, surviving both Graspan and the Modder River, where he was wounded. Too old to enlist, he's young enough to be able to strut around like the sergeant he once was, drilling the younger men as though they were on a parade ground. I'm glad Father didn't even consider making him farm manager. He shouts a lot, but achieves through others next to nothing, although when he's with the cattle he's quietly impressive.

He's quite open about his perceived duty to prepare the younger men for what they have to face elsewhere. I can't get rid of him; Father would never allow it, and he's too valuable a stockman. When he passes me, he stiffens, which is hard for someone who's already as rigid as a gatepost. He'd love to yell at me too, and prepare me for the war. He doesn't dare, but his eyes follow me to the corners of their sockets, and I can see the contempt in them, which has nothing to do with our respective positions on the farm.

'Look at this,' said William, stabbing a burly finger at his model. 'Amiens fell five days ago, and now Paris has been placed in a state of siege. The French government is transferring to Bordeaux.'

'So it will soon be over,' I said.

'It may be,' he replied. 'The Russians have been routed at Tannenberg in the east.' He waved a hand in the direction of his shrubbery. His model only covers Belgium and north-eastern France. 'But Paris! It isn't just a capital city; it's a vast fortress, the greatest of all, the hub of the whole country's communications. Troops may be deployed from there in any direction at short notice. As for taking it, it will require a mighty siege. Look at this.' His hand swept up to Antwerp. 'Those Belgians amaze me. While the French and British armies have been rolled to the south-west, the Belgians still resist. It's only a month since the war began. The Germans have progressed so far into France in such a short time that their heavy artillery is far behind them, much of it in place to bombard Antwerp. The Germans can sweep further into France, their objective being the destruction of the French field armies. France will then fall. But it's my contention that the capital itself cannot be taken quickly, not without a premature surrender.'

'Are you hopeful?' I asked.

'No.' He gave a bleak smile. 'If the German armies halt before Paris, they will prepare for a long siege, waiting first for the necessary resources to be trundled up. But if they turn south now, they may obliterate the French Army quite quickly. And the British. We are facing the steamroller.'

6th September 1914

I am back in William's garden room.

'It is as I suspected,' he says solemnly. The Germans are executing a left-wheel. So it's to be the destruction of the French armies, not the siege of Paris. The end may be in sight.'

7th September 1914

'They've blundered!' I had never seen William so excited. 'They've wheeled to the south all right, but look. Look, Richard! Look what they've done. His finger zigzagged over his little wooden blocks to the east of Paris. This is von Kluck's First Army; and this is Bülow's Second. Here, in the outskirts of the city, is Maunoury's Army, the French Sixth, and to the south the British, with D'Espérey and Foch to their right, to the east. Notice anything?'

'No', I said.

'Here. Maunoury's Army. It's there for the defence of Paris. But Paris is not being attacked! Look where von Kluck is. They say he passed within sight of the Eiffel Tower. That's the blunder. General Galliéni, the Governor of Paris, has risen to the occasion. He's released troops so that they can allow Maunoury to attack, and von Kluck has felt cold steel piercing his underbelly.

8th September 1914

William is ecstatic. 'See this, Richard. It's all going to plan, as I'd hoped. This is one of the most important battles the world has ever seen. Look, they're tottering like ninepins. Von Kluck has been forced to turn about. He's back across the Marne, and has retreated 60 miles in 48 hours. That's left the next in line, Bülow here, with his tummy laid bare. So he too has been forced to pivot and retreat. Not only has that exposed him to attack by the British and the French Fifth Army, but even worse for the Germans, a hideous gap has opened up between von Kluck and Bülow. We have them routed, Richard, and it's the British Army which is punching its way into the gap. We've re-crossed the Marne. To the east, all these German armies, look, Hausen's Third, Wurthemberg's Fourth, Crown Prince Willi's Fifth, and the Sixth under Crown Prince Ruprecht: they've all had to turn about. We're on top of them at last. We're at the charge, Richard. We have them at the point of the lance.' And when he turned from his tables to face me, I could swear that his eyes were moist.

9th September 1914

This evening, before dinner, my impudent son was reading to me from *The Times*. It was making most unpleasant listening.

'Didn't you once meet Lord Haldane, Mother? He's the Lord Chancellor now.'

'I did so. He was charming. We were conversing in German, which he was speaking quite fluently.'

'It would be better if he didn't,' Tristram said. 'This is what *The Times* says: "We have opposed his becoming War Secretary, because of his predilection for Germany. He was partly educated in that country, he has frequently spent his leisure time there, his mind is coloured by his unremitting study of German literature and philosophy, and he cherishes close German friendships."' Tristram looked up from his newspaper. 'He has even named his dog Kaiser. Should we have this man in charge of our judiciary, when he may be heard calling, "Come, Kaiser!"?'

'It says that in *The Times*?'

'No, Mother, I read it somewhere else.'

I tutted at him. Really, Tristram can be quite impertinent.

I wish I hadn't done that. I thought Mother might be interested, but instead I've distressed her. That bit about the dog Kaiser came from the *Daily Mail*. Yes, Mercury of the Tack Room has left another deposit for me to read. Luckily, I managed to keep this secret from Mother.

I also refrained from reading out something else which really was in *The Times*, which would have upset her even more. This is Lord Charles Beresford: "The German who has become a naturalised Englishman is really a far more dangerous person here than the one who is not naturalised. He is able to get into a number of places in society where, owing to his position, his ability, his education and very likely his wealth, he can get to know things. Germans who become naturalised must be, to put it perfectly straight, either a traitor to their own country or ours." Poor Mother. Lord Charles Beresford has spoken. She must be a traitor, but to which country? It was a good thing that I didn't ask. That really would have angered her.

25th September 1914

Tristram Hall, you must be getting old. When I heard that Peter, the stable boy, had signed up, I felt quite fatherly towards him. He is so innocent.

He said to me, 'I don't really want to kill no-one, Master Tristram, but I don't like to think that they'm a-hurting Ned, Sir, not without I's being there.' Somehow I was moved by the phrase "a-hurting Ned". Peter can talk about doing the killing, but when it comes to Ned, they're only going to be "a-hurting" him, as though they might bend his fingers a bit or strike him with a bunch of nettles. When I wished him good luck, and watched him walk away, I knew that what I was really doing was praying for him.

Another one gone, but I've had an idea to help with the shortage of manpower. Father has agreed. We're taking on a new worker, starting next week. His name is Josef Reker. He's German, and has been interned since the first fortnight of the war. He doesn't have to work, indeed can't be forced to, but he wants to, in order to support his family. Release from boredom may also be a motive. He comes with no experience of farming. The closest he's been to animals has been serving them on a plate. He was a waiter in Bromley.

My biggest concern is how the other men will take to him. If I were being kind, I'd say they're a conservative and patriotic lot. Reactionary and tribal might be nearer the truth. We shall see.

Father and I had a good laugh today. He'd returned from Dorchester, where he'd seen a poster featuring the Kaiser and a flock of pigeons, one of which had alighted on the Kaiser's arm. The caption read, "Don't let him get the message". The purpose of the poster, Father said, was to inform the public that under the Defence of the Realm Act it's now forbidden to possess homing or racing pigeons.

'Do you think that we ought to take down the dovecote?' Father asked with a twinkle in his eye.

'Certainly not. The only racing our birds do is round and round the farmyard.'

'Ah, but soon we will have a German here. He might start sending messages and receiving them.'

'On his head, probably,' I replied, and with that we mocked this absurdity into touch.

Thanks to Mercury, I've been following the story of Nurse Grace Hume. According to the *Daily Mail*, Nurse Hume was working at a hospital in Vilvorde in Belgium, when it was overrun by Germans, who killed the wounded men. They then cut off Nurse Hume's breast, leaving her to die in agony. Her sister, living in Dumfries, received a scribbled note which read, "Dear Kate, this is to say goodbye. Have not long to live. Hospital set on fire. Germans cruel. A man here has had his head cut off. My right breast has been taken away. Goodbye. Grace."

That was a fortnight ago. But now Mercury has left a different paper, *The Star*, which reports that a Nurse Mullard, who was with Nurse Hume when she died, had also sent a letter saying how Nurse Hume had bravely shot a German who was attacking a wounded soldier, and stating that her left breast had been cut off.

Left breast, right breast. You'd think they'd know.

1st October 1914

It's all been explained in *The Times*. The whole story's a fabrication. Nurse Hume has been in Huddersfield all along, and nowhere near Belgium.

There is no Nurse Mullard. It's all been made up by Nurse Hume's seventeen-year-old sister Kate. It's likely that Mercury doesn't know the truth. Neither the *Daily Mail* nor *The Star* print corrections to their errors, let alone apologies. In such ways are we being led into hatred.

The Prime Minister has made a speech in Cardiff. He spoke of the "wanton invasion of Belgium and France by hordes who leave behind them at every stage of their progress a dismal trail of savagery, of devastation and of desecration worthy of the blackest annals of the history of barbarism." Really, Mr Asquith? "The blackest annals of the history of barbarism"? Worthy of comparison with the sacking of Magdeburg in the Thirty Years' War, when over 20,000 inhabitants were slaughtered? With Genghis Khan, who disposed of millions in cold blood? With the Hamidian massacres twenty years ago, when over 100,000 Armenians were slaughtered? Or when our own British colonists exterminated the Tasman population, with British officers pursuing natives on horseback, running them through with spears for sport?

Where's your evidence, Sir? It'd better improve upon that provided by Miss Kate Hume.

12th October 1914

Das ist wunderbar! Our lives, they are being brightened by a new arrival. His name is Josef Reker.

He is from Ulm in Bavaria, but for the past four years has been living in this country. He arrived clutching two little drawings, made in his internment camp. One is of Ulm Cathedral. He said it was not so good, because it was drawn from memory. The other is a view from his camp. He is no artist, but by the gesture I was touched. I have taken them to Lyme Regis to be framed, and will be hanging the cathedral in our bedroom and the landscape in the dining room.

He is a delightful companion. I was wanting to invite him into the house, but Tristram said, quite crossly I thought, that he would not permit it. He was saying something about the effect it would have on the other farm workers. I was about to say that it was up to me whom I invited into my own home, when Richard, to my surprise, supported him. So if Josef cannot come to me, I go to Josef. I have taken to walking round the farmyard when I know that he is likely to be there. Tristram disapproves, and has warned me that I must not be delaying him in his duties. But he must see the good that it is doing him, allowing him to speak in his native tongue. The moment he is seeing me, his eyes light up and he says in his Bavarian accent, '*Guten Tag*, Frau Hall,' so quietly that I can only just hear him. Tristram says he has addressed the men and told them how to treat Josef.

When I told the men about Reker the day before he was due to arrive, I was met with vacant expressions and total silence.

'With the loss of so many men to the war, he should be able to relieve the pressure on you, if only in a small way. He has no experience of farming, so I intend to give him several different tasks in the first few weeks, all of them in support of you. That way he will learn our methods, and we will be able to see where he best fits in. I am counting on your support to get the best out of him.' Blank faces. 'He has to pull his weight. If he does not perform adequately, I want to know. He will be on probation, which means that if he does not become a useful member of the team within a month, then back he goes.'

I tried to play on their humanity. 'It is no fault of his that he's been interned. He made no effort to return to Germany in the weeks before the war started. He has a family to support, and badly needs a wage. I hope that you will make him feel welcome and show that you are keen for him to succeed. Only then may he provide the valuable assistance which I know you all need. Finally, remember this: he will be working for the British War Effort. We are an island, and food is as important to our survival as guns. Are there any questions?'

None. I searched their eyes for disapproval, anticipation, anything at all. They're slow to react, always. I just hope that they'll be as slow and patient with him, and will give him a chance.

That was a week ago. My first reaction when he arrived was how slim he was, not exactly thin, but too refined for farm work. But he has a quiet charm and a steady eye. I put him with Jack Hearn first, to learn the ways of sheep, but most of all to give him to someone who I thought would have the patience to teach him. First reports have been that he is diligent and keen to learn, but that he lacks dexterity, for instance in catching and upending a ewe and applying the knife to her hooves. Hearn says that he's good with the dogs and that they are already starting to respond to some of his commands.

My greatest worry has come from an unexpected quarter: Mother. I wouldn't mind her greeting Reker in German if she happened to be passing him. But she's taken to touring the farm and chatting to him once she's found him. This is acutely conspicuous, due to the fact that she's rarely been seen around the farm in the past.

She actually wanted to invite him into the house. Thank goodness she talked about it before she tried to do it. I instantly forbade it, and Father supported me. He knows that we can't favour any one worker in this way. He may even be aware of the greater problem, that to grant a privilege to a German at this time would provoke all sorts of imaginings.

13th October 1914

William is in a rolling boil. His precious model can no longer track the progress of the war.

'You mean these trenches I have been hearing about?' I said. 'Nothing moves, is that it?'

'That too,' he growled. 'The war's been reduced to a crawling match, to see who can creep the lowest under the barbed wire. But that's not what I was referring to. It's censorship, British censorship,' he roared, as though it were more despicable than anything the Germans were doing.

He tweaked one of his wooden blocks angrily with a finger, and it scudded off the table. 'Useless,' he bellowed. 'It might be the Swiss Guard or the Emperor of Japan's kitchen staff for all I know. They won't tell us.'

'I suppose secrecy is important,' I ventured,

'S'pose so,' he muttered.

'But was it not like that before?'

'It was Mons that did it. All those newspaper correspondents trumpeting that it was the greatest clash of arms in history, which it may well have been. So when they started reporting that we were in full retreat, the War Office didn't like it, even though we could hardly have got from Mons to the outskirts of Paris in a fortnight without it having been a rout.'

'But what about The Marne? You seemed to know exactly where each army was then?'

'That's because we won it. They were happy to give us the full details of the victory. But it was all fed to us by the War Office through the Press Bureau, once it was clear that the Huns were on the run. Journalists aren't allowed anywhere near the front any more. The armies are at a standstill. A thin line wiggles from the Alps to the sea. Oh yes, it's all perfectly reasonable. One can see why they don't want to advertise to the enemy which troops are facing them, and in what force. But it isn't fun any more. Where are the cavalry? I'll tell you, Richard, they're finished. It's all lumps of metal now. I can't picture it any more. We've spent hundreds of years trying to find new ways of outflanking the enemy, only to sit down a hundred yards in front of him for weeks on end. Is that progress?'

Poor William. He is like a cricketer who has hung up his pads, looking forward to watching the game in his retirement, only to be turned away at the gate. Is there material for a sermon here?

14th October 1914

Sehr grausam. I have been weeping. I cannot believe how this is so. They have, oh dear, I still am, there, I am dabbing my eyes with a handkerchief. The pitiless cruelty of it. I have had my letters returned. I was sending them, two of them, one to my darling mother and one to Gerd. I posted them a few days after war broke out. And now I am sitting on my bed, clutching my letters, shaking and sobbing. How could they? Those hateful words, stamped boldly across each envelope as though they were proud of them. "UNDELIVERABLE (ENEMY COUNTRY) RETURN TO SENDER."

They are inhuman. They have not even bothered to open them, to see that they are entirely innocent. Just love and good wishes, something which these barbarians are not possessing; something which they do not understand.

I am not wanting your stupid war. I am not wanting to be a part of it. Oh, my poor darling mother. I may never see you again. I may never be at your side when you are ill. And now I may never be able to be sending you words of comfort and love and faith when you are dying. I may never even be knowing of it.

And everywhere I see Lord Kitchener, with his fierce unbalanced eyes, poking his finger at me, calling me a Briton and saying that he needs me. *Er ist so aufdringlich.*

15th October 1914

'Where is the evidence?' I want to shout. 'Give us the evidence!' Now the priests are at it. "Children have been found by the roadside decapitated," noted an Essex clergyman, adding that "it's been ascertained that at a convent in Bocking there really *is* a young Belgian girl with both hands hacked off." What does, "it has been ascertained that there really *is*" mean? Ah, but of course. In a game of Chinese whispers, the last to pass the message is a priest, so it must be true. Careful, priest, or your role of feeding the gullible may be usurped by the *Daily Mail* and *John Bull.*

Adela is coming down tomorrow, resting before her next concert. She'll bring some sanity to this rotting world.

My Saviour, help them in their hour of need. Philip Clucas has been killed at Arras. So the war has penetrated the village, and my flock. He was a greengrocer's assistant by trade. He leaves a wife and three daughters, all under six.

Nora solemnly held the letter, which she pulled out of its buff envelope with a steady hand. Nellie, fingers clutching at her mother's skirt, gazed up at me. "It is my painful duty to inform you that a report has been received from the War Office notifying the death of Private Philip Clucas." She then handed me another from his commanding officer. "He was of the best. He perished gallantly on a night patrol, dying instantly. He cannot have felt any pain. He will be sorely missed by his officers and fellow men, with whom he was extremely popular."

'I'm proud of him, Vicar, really proud.'

Tears came to my eyes at her fortitude, but I held them back. 'So you should be, Nora. He died doing what was right. You are not alone. You are not the only one to be proud. Is there anything I can do for you now? We shall of course be saying prayers for his soul on Sunday.'

'There is one thing,' she said, not hesitantly, but firmly and with determination. 'I should like to put up a small memorial outside the gate, on the grass facing the road. Do you think I might do that?'

'Of course, Nora. It is the least we can do. Are you all right for money? You will get a widow's pension, you know. What kind of memorial have you in mind?'

'One saying what a good man he was.'

'And he was. I will see what I can do in the way of a contribution towards it. I will speak to my wife. She is keen to visit you in any case.'

'Thank you, Vicar. You have been a great help. I loved him,' she added wanly. There were no tears.

'I know. And now he is comforted by the Love of God.'

How can we fail to win the war with people like this?

20th October 1914

It's in all the papers, not just Mercury's. Serious anti-German rioting has been going on in London and elsewhere. The worst is in Deptford. Some of the people are so ignorant that all foreigners have become targets, even though some of them come from countries who are our allies. With violent crowds up to five thousand strong, the police have been unable to cope. Soldiers have been brought in, but even they've had difficulty quelling the fires and looting.

I can get all I need from *The Times*, but Mercury has taken the opportunity to mull a full punch of it. His *Daily Mail* contains even more red ink than usual.

Bill Munday came up to me, devoid of breath and good sense.

'Have you heard about the angel at Mons, Squarson?' he panted.

'Yes, I have heard.'

'So God is on our side!' the stupid boy grinned.

'God is on our side, but not because a few retreating soldiers, in their panic, have wished that they might see an angel defending them with a sword.'

'So you don't believe the truth of it, Squarson?'

'No I do not, and neither should you. If there has indeed been a miracle, then the Church will investigate it and pronounce in due course. But I hardly think that our Lord would send an angel to Mons, for him to be left standing there while our poor troops retreat to the west. Come,' I said more gently, 'we must pray for our brave soldiers. They will not prevail by spreading rumours. I am sorry that I was sharp with you just now, Bill. You are not alone in mentioning it. Given time, I am sure that the Church will come to some conclusion on the matter.'

21st October 1914

That's perfect. He's doing just what I wanted. Mercury has broadened his fire, from highlighting newspaper articles to writing his own comments. So, for the first time, he's revealed his handwriting. He'd made only brief comments in the margins in capital letters before. But now he's written in longhand, 'I see that you have planted a real enemy in our midst. A German waiter, no less. Have a look on page 5.' I could see nothing relevant in the *Daily Mail*, but Mercury had also given me his copy of this week's *John Bull*. There, on page 5, is a typical rant from its editor, Horatio Bottomley, calling for reprisals against Germans. All their property should be confiscated and they themselves should be locked up. Naturalised Germans should be made to wear a distinctive badge. Their children should not be allowed to attend schools. Ah, here it is: "If by chance you should discover one day in a restaurant that you are being served by a German waiter, you will throw the soup in his foul face." I couldn't help laughing, but I wonder whether Mercury shares my humour or is deadly serious.

By revealing his handwriting, he's presented me with an opportunity. It's reasonably neat, though not particularly cultured, but there are no spelling mistakes. That narrows the field right down, assuming that he's a farm worker, although I suppose it's just possible that someone in the village has got hold of a key to the tack room and comes in early, before anyone else is about. So far, I've resisted the temptation to get up before dawn and waylay him. My main reason for not doing so has been that I don't want to put him off.

Now I have another way of finding out. I could ask the most likely culprits to send me an unrelated message – I could think of something – so that I could compare the handwriting.

Franco Malpiero is the most obvious candidate,

and the least. He's the only man who has regular access to the tack room, now that Peter's gone to the front. He's probably well-educated enough, but – and it is a huge but – his English is far from perfect. He's an excellent worker, courteous and respectful. Italians too have had their houses looted by the hooligans. It doesn't have to be Malpiero. He knows my saddlebag is private territory, and if another person is putting things into it, Malpiero might not know, unless he were to catch him at it. Still, he'd be my first target for the handwriting test.

As for the rioting, they're still at it.

22nd October 1914

I've thought long and hard about my quest and have decided to abandon it. Unless Mercury shows any tendency toward violence, or encourages it, I'll leave him alone, ignorant of who he might be. He's so far made no threats. True, he has referred to Josef Reker as "the enemy in our midst", but nothing more. Also, I have a certain image of him, which would be spoilt if he turned out to be someone known to me. And I do now believe that he has a sense of humour. I can imagine him chuckling over "you will throw soup in his foul face", noting the irony that Reker was a waiter. If I were to find out that Mercury is one of my men, I might be forced to take action which I'd regret. So long as he behaves himself, and keeps me both informed and amused, I'll be happy to remain ignorant of his identity, which he himself has chosen not to reveal.

Still rioting.

28th October 1914

It was horrible. I'm still shaking from it. I'd have continued playing, really I would, but Mr Plaister told me I must leave the stage for my own safety.

The first time it happened, I tried to ignore it. I think the shout was, "Traitor! Play some Allied music!" I did pause, who wouldn't after that, and it did come at a tricky moment in the *Bunte Blätter*. But I managed to recover and began to lose myself in the music again. Then came the chanting, "Belgium, Belgium", and after that I couldn't keep the flow. I heard some clapping, which Mama told me later was sympathetic applause, but all that did was confuse me more. By that time the hubbub was so great that I began playing with far too much *forte*, and the performance became bombastic and gross. Soon after, Mr Plaister told me there was fighting and that I had to stop.

Edgar has been comforting me. He says the critics will give me nothing but sympathy, and that the publicity will do me good. I doubt it. I want to be known for my playing, not for being the pianist who attracted a group of boorish drunks to her concert. It happened to Stravinsky last year in Paris, when there was a riot during the première of his *Le*

Sacre du Printemps. But that was because of the music. Here it wasn't my playing which caused a riot. It was because dear Robert Schumann, the most gentle and loving of souls, happened to be German.

Mein Gott, it will be taking me a long time to be getting over this evening. At one stage it was looking as though Tristram was going to be spending the night in gaol. Adela, thank God, is recovering. Her young man has been comforting her because, *ach,* I could not be with her.

The mood of this country is ugly. The superintendent of police was saying that behaviour of that kind is excusable, "under the circumstances". He means the war. It is so that Tristram struck a man, and hard at that; I saw him fall. But such provocation. The man was braying like *ein Esel*. He was the one who was causing a public disorder, not Tristram. Our saving angel, bless her, was Ethel Smyth. How I have misjudged her in the past. While I was going with Tristram to the police station, she was taking a cab immediately to the home of Sir Henry Wood, the conductor, who drove straight to the police station and secured Tristram's release. And now, look at the time, we are at last reunited.

'What is it, Mother?' Tristram rouses me from my trance.

I force a smile. 'It is nothing. I am tired, that is all.' I do not tell him that I have been thinking about something which he is not knowing. What might have happened if the louts had found out that the performer was not only playing German music, but that she herself was a full-blooded German? And that Robert Schumann, the composer, and Miss Adela Hall, the pianist, both come from the same town in Germany, Zwickau?

The banality of the champing repetition drove me wild. One particular oaf, upper lip curled forward like a donkey, turned to me and without ceasing his chanting, grinned his toothy grin. It was too much. I hit him as Mr Foreman my old boxing instructor once told me to hit a man; not with a raking swing, but with a hard straight jab aimed two feet beyond his head. He corkscrewed down between the seats. His companions, cowards to a man, held back, none daring to approach me. But when two policemen appeared, they pointed to me and to my goofy victim, who was just trying to raise himself from the floor.

I was taken to the police station, where I was charged with causing an affray and actual bodily harm. The second charge I could accept, but I became angry when I realised that I alone was being charged with causing an affray. Mother's pleas were in vain, and she was just preparing to leave when Ethel Smyth appeared, accompanied by a middle-aged man with receding hair and a greying beard. He turned out to be the conductor, Sir Henry Wood. I don't know what powers he has, but within half an hour I was told that both charges had been dropped and that I could be on my way.

When I got back to the hotel, Adela was there with Edgar Simpson. She leapt to her feet and hugged me, tears and smiles splashing across her face.

Now, lying in bed, I realise an interesting fact. The audience included many men in uniform, yet I can't recall even one of them joining in the chanting. One man, an officer I think, was even restraining a group of loudmouths over to my left. I gained the impression that it was the foppish dandies of the West End who were causing the trouble. I have a new respect for our troops. I wish now that I could have talked to them, to ask them what they'd seen. How typical of this world that it is the players doing the doing who show respect, while the ignorant mob whinny from the terraces. Didn't someone once say that Jingoism is the passion of the spectator, not the participant?

I forgot. First impressions of Edgar Simpson: I like him. He's slim and handsome in a Mediterranean way. Come to think of it, his skin is too pale for that. He's quietly spoken and rather shy. I must remember to tell Adela first thing in the morning that I approve, and that I should like to get to know him better.

A comfortable bed, the onset of drowsiness and an only slightly sore hand. I've been lucky.

29th October 1914

I'm at Waterloo Station with Mother and Adela, waiting for our train. Doors slam, porters shout, whistles blow, steam hisses, and fumes of sulphur fill our nostrils. My collar, fresh on only three hours ago, will be blackened at the rim with soot.

Adela was pleased when I told her at breakfast that I like Edgar, but now she's subdued. A railway terminus is a depressing place when the train one is about to board will take one further away from one's love. I should know; I will never forget the *Gare du Nord* three months ago.

Mother is silent. I suspect she may be wondering how to tell Father that her son was taken to a police cell. I honestly don't think he'll mind. After all, I was upholding the honour of his daughter, and he wants me to fight.

To humour Adela, I read out some of the posters which I thought might amuse her.

"To the women of Britain. You have read what the Germans have done in Belgium. Have you thought what they would do if they invaded this country? Do you realise that the safety of your home and children depends on our getting more men NOW? Do you realise that the word GO from you may send another man to fight for our King and Country? When the War is over and someone asks your husband or your son what he did in the Great War, is he to hang his head because you would not let him go? WON'T YOU HELP AND SEND A MAN TO JOIN THE ARMY TODAY?"

Adela doesn't smile. I look around. Half the people milling about the station are soldiers with kit bags, some thumping them down, others heaving them onto their backs. Everyone is about to be somewhere else. I spy another poster.

"Is your Best Boy wearing khaki? If not, don't YOU THINK he should be? If he does not think that you and your country are worth fighting for – do you think he is *worthy* of you? Don't pity the girl who is alone – her young man is probably a soldier fighting for her and her country – and for YOU. If your young man neglects his duty to his King and Country, the time may come when he will NEGLECT YOU. Think it over – and then ask him to JOIN THE ARMY – TODAY."

I add, 'Well, sister, I think you've already done your bit by playing Schumann.'

'It is time to go,' Mother interrupts curtly. I look up to see that our platform number is on the board. Adela seems close to tears.

'Come on,' I say. 'Let's get you home.'

2nd November 1914

It's the bucketful of eyeballs, all over again. Thank you, Mercury, I know about this one. It's been dredged up from wars in the past. When I was in Damascus a couple of years ago, we were talking about the Crusades, and how European history had been slanted to give the impression that the

Christians were noble knights doing chivalrous deeds, in contrast to the Saracens, who were portrayed as cowardly and barbarous assassins. The truth was that Saladin was extraordinarily humane for a military leader of his time, and the Crusaders were cruel, even by the standards of theirs. Someone mentioned the eyeballs, an early case of the use of propaganda in history. And now they've dredged the story up again, claiming the Germans are so degenerate that they've extracted the eyeballs of their victims and displayed them in a bucket.

There's another old chestnut about a boy scout with a wooden gun being killed by *uhlans* for refusing to divulge information about the French Army. That one comes from the Franco-Prussian War. They could have written these stories, or rather copied them, on the day war broke out.

I can see why they do it. Most people are naturally averse to war. In order to lure men into the army, it's necessary to make them hate. Not just the men themselves, but the whole nation must indulge in collective loathing. There must be no ambiguities, no shades of grey, no mitigating circumstances to excuse the enemy's behaviour. Guilt must be of the most complete kind on the other side of the line, with not a trace of it on ours. Hence the eyeballs and the boy with the wooden gun. The problem is, no one will want peace, only total victory at any cost, the crushing of the enemy and revenge.

Mrs Bunby came up to Father after Church yesterday. 'I've been praying to God that He may strike the Kaiser dead.'

Father looked embarrassed. He said, 'He will be brought to account on the Day of Judgement.'

That doesn't solve the problem now. If God had wanted to strike the Kaiser dead, He would have done so without waiting for Mrs Bunby's prayer. But I don't think she wants Him to hold back until the Day of Judgement.

The Church is playing a dangerous game. By giving unqualified support to the war, it's gambling on it being a successful one. But if the war should become really ugly, the people will turn against the Church for its sponsorship of suffering.

The whole moral code of the Church is rotten. Adela, in her younger days, once said primly to me, 'I cannot be sure that God exists, but I think that it's safer to assume that He might.'

'Why's that?'

'Because if he He does exist, I'll have done the right thing, whereas if He doesn't exist, it won't matter either way.'

This muddled thinking had to be corrected. 'But if God is good, he will hardly punish you for failing to believe in Him. He may punish you for other things, being unkind or harming others, but not for lack of faith when He hasn't revealed himself and you're doubtful that He exists.'

If that's the effect of the Church's morality, it's no morality at all. It's selfish expediency arising from a fear of the unknown. It's doing the right thing merely to avoid punishment in hell, or to earn points for entry into heaven. True morality is to understand and respect the position of others, to imagine what it would be like to be the person whose life your deeds are affecting. Jesus understood that, and tried to preach it, but the humanity and compassion of his message has been lost by those who follow Him now.

6th November 1914

I'm worried and frightened. I've had a letter from Edgar. I couldn't make up my mind whether to write back or go to London. I decided to confide in Tristram.

'Edgar's so impressionable. He says he's ashamed of himself. Doesn't that sound like he isn't in control of his own thoughts?'

'What exactly has he written?'

'He says he was walking along Kingsway, when he saw a man ahead fall victim to The Order of the White Feather. At first he seems to have found it quite amusing. He writes that it was so theatrical. "This tall graceful young woman barred the way of the unfortunate, who stepped back, surprised. She held a white feather aloft, turning round to display it for all to see, then took the hand of her victim and pressed it into his palm." Edgar says he stopped barely twenty feet from them and could see the burning zeal in the woman's eyes. The man, he says, walked on ahead of him, but Edgar was so shocked that he immediately crossed the road to avoid the woman. He said he felt that he'd compounded his shame.'

'What shame? Of not enlisting? Of having successfully avoided one of those hysterical harpies? He shouldn't be ashamed of either.'

'I know, Tristram, but he is. The horrible thing is that he seems to think that he'd be doing the right thing by me if he were to sign up, even though I've said the exact opposite.'

'Then he's been reading too many posters. Ah, is that why you were so upset when I read them out to you at Waterloo?'

'It isn't nice.'

'No, I'm sorry, I didn't realise.'

'It's all right. You weren't to know.'

Instead of offering a solution, Tristram started telling me what I'd already gathered from the newspapers. 'A portion of the female population, and an educated one at that, seems determined to take on the male, and the game is to out-do each other in madness.' Tristram had launched into his rhetorical mode. 'That Baroness Orczy woman, the one who wrote *The Scarlet Pimpernel*, has formed some crack-skulled organisation called the Women of England's Active Service League. It sounds worthy, doesn't it? So what do you think they might be doing? Enlisting as nurses? Working in munitions? Helping on the land?'

'I know who they are,' I said, but Tristram continued as though he hadn't heard me.

'What these women do is sign a pledge never to be seen in public with any fit man who's failed to respond to the call of King and Country. Now the Mother's Union are at it. Not content with advising their members to urge their menfolk to go, they spout some nonsense about hearts beating high with thankfulness and pride when their hero returns. But if God should have another plan for him – quaint words – they will have an even greater cause for thankfulness, because he will be placed on the Roll of Honour and will enter the bosom of the King of Kings. They might as well spare themselves the wordiness, and say it simply: he'd be better off dead.'

'Tristram?'

'Yes?'

'I know all this. You don't have to tell me. You can't walk down a street in London without being aware of it. War is everywhere: soldiers, the wounded and the bereaved. There's a woman barely turned twenty – Edgar doesn't know this – who stands on the corner of Grafton Street. She's dressed in mourning black, and you might think that she's begging. But what she does is accost young men who aren't wearing uniform, stepping in front of them and staring into their consciences with baleful eyes. I don't know what she says to them; perhaps it's nothing. The reproachful gaze doesn't need supporting words.'

'And you can be sure,' Tristram said, 'that no one is bold enough to tell her to mind her own business and move on. This is the trouble with war. It stifles free comment and debate. Nobody dares criticise for fear of upsetting those who've succumbed. A mother or wife who has a loved one at the front has to be cosseted into feeling that her man has done the right thing; for the next day she might feel the agony of bereavement, and who would want to be the one to have told her the day before that he'd done something futile or, worse, harmful? The worst sentiment of all is that we should continue the struggle because otherwise they would have died in vain. We don't owe it to the dead to send more people after them.'

'Tristram, I know all this.'

'And Edgar doesn't?'

'Perhaps he does. But the pressure to conform is terrible, far worse in London than it is here. All the time there's the implication of cowardice.'

'So much so,' Tristram said, 'that it takes courage to resist and not to conform.'

'Yes, but few see it that way. Few recognise your kind of courage. Bravery is seen as stepping forward, not shrinking back.'

'I do not shrink back.'

'Tristram, Tristram. Your greatest fault is that you judge others by yourself. Sticking your neck out and being different come naturally to you. It's part of your creed. Edgar isn't like you. He's sensitive and vulnerable. He can't take criticism easily; perhaps it's the trait of the artist.'

'Would you like me to go to London and talk to him?'

'No. You're very kind, but I don't think it'd help. He'd feel yet another form of intimidation. He likes you, but he'd see your strength in terms of his own weakness. He'd contrast himself with you, not try to emulate you. It'd scare him even more, and might panic him into doing the wrong thing.'

'Would it help if I were to write a letter? I would of course agree the contents with you first.'

I stared into the fireplace. 'Yes. Yes, I think it might. Especially if it'd acknowledge his dilemma and sympathise with his fear.'

We had that conversation a couple of hours ago. Tristram has written the most beautiful letter, full of compassion. I didn't want to change a word. Tomorrow we're going to have dinner with the Sawbridges. I'll go to London the day after.

8th November 1914

Dinner at the Sawbridges by quarrels it was being contaminated. I do not know why the Colonel is being so irritating. Tonight he was vexing me so much that I was letting my anger show. I cannot help it. I will not be staying silent while he abuses me for being who I am.

We were having dinner at their house. It was the first time that all of us had been together – the Colonel and his wife, Richard and me, Tristram and Adela, and Elizabeth – since when? I realise that it must be as long ago as 1909, before Elizabeth went to America. Anyhow, the controversy was starting when the Colonel asked us what it was like, having a German working on the farm.

'He is wonderful,' I said. 'The other day I was hearing him whistling, so I asked him if he could sing. It turns out that he used to be a choirboy in Ulm Cathedral. We were singing a duet there and then, the hymn *Ein Feste Burg ist unsere Gott*. A lovely tenor voice, he is having. I have asked him to join the choir, where he will be a great asset.'

'How nice,' said Mrs Sawbridge, which seemed to provoke her husband, who snorted.

'He may wish to ingratiate himself into our society by any means. My dear Helga, you should be wary as to his motives.'

To this I was not replying. I was hoping that Tristram might be saying something about Josef's performance on the farm, which he did, but only when asked by me.

'It is early days.'

'And how have the men taken to him?' asked Mrs Sawbridge.

'All parties are feeling their way.'

'Well,' said the Colonel, 'it is the duty of everyone to watch him closely, and others of his ilk. As Lord Charles Beresford was saying the other day, you cannot change a man's nature. If the call of blood should come for just a few minutes, who knows what mischief he may do. Now that we have been declared a Prohibited Area…'

'What did you say?' asked Richard.

'Yesterday,' said the Colonel. 'Announced yesterday.'

'It's true, Father,' said Tristram. The new boundaries are in today's *Times*. They include the whole of Dorset within twenty miles of the sea.'

'Well, that does not have any bearing on us,' said Richard. 'Reker has already registered as an Alien. We checked his papers when he arrived from the internment camp, and we make sure that he reports regularly to the police.'

'It might, Father.'

'What?'

'It might have a bearing on us. I need to find out. The Aliens Restriction Act says that Enemy Aliens have to leave Prohibited Areas within four days. It may be possible to get him a permit to stay.'

'The law is acting in our interests,' said Colonel Sawbridge.

'Why is that?' I asked, unable to be keeping an edge out of my voice, which was sounding too much like a challenge.

'As I have told you before, Helga, the Defence of the Realm Act and the Aliens Restriction Act have sweeping powers. The Home Secretary can draw his definitions pretty well how and where he likes, not just of what Aliens must do, but who is defined as an Alien.'

This was really angering me, just as it was so when he raised the subject three months ago.

'Are you saying that I am an Alien?'

'No, of course William is not, my dear,' said Richard. 'You married me a over a quarter of a century ago. On that day you became an Englishwoman, and have been so ever since.'

To my utter amazement, Colonel Sawbridge was not leaving it alone.

'You have been naturalised, it is true. But you are still defined as Alien by birth. As I once told you, the phrase used by the law is "of hostile origin".'

That was bad enough, but then he proceeded to look at each of us in turn. 'We should all be asking ourselves who could fall within that definition.'

So appalled must have I been looking – indeed I

was speechless – that Mrs Sawbridge said hastily, 'I hear your concerts have been a great success, Adela.'

'All except the last one,' replied Adela simply.

'Ah yes, I am sure, how unfortunate,' said Mrs Sawbridge, all confused.

'It was disgraceful,' said Richard. 'It amazes me that people who have nothing better to do can be allowed to go around harassing people for doing things which have always been done.'

'Yes, wrong,' said the Colonel, 'but one can understand how they feel. After what has happened to Belgium, it's to be expected that folk are wary of the imposition of another culture, however long its pedigree.'

Fearful of an outburst from Tristram, and to spare Adela, whose feelings as a musician must have been as offended as mine, I turned to Elizabeth and said quickly, 'Have you heard from your husband recently?'

'He's in Flanders, Mrs Hall. He writes that he is well.'

'And has he seen action?' This was Richard. Was he oblivious to everything the Colonel had been saying, or was he as keen as I to see the subject changed?

'I believe so,' said Elizabeth demurely. Poor girl, she looks so wan. I cannot imagine what she is going through.

But we had still failed to divert the Colonel. 'Returning to your concert, Adela, most unfortunate. But I'm not sure that I can agree with you, Richard, that we should all be silent in the face of provocation, even in the arts. A number of eminent writers, including Thomas Hardy, H G Wells, Rudyard Kipling and Conan Doyle have spoken out in favour of the law-abiding ideals of Western Europe in the face of aggressive domination by a military caste. You, Vicar,' he said turning to Richard with a chuckle, 'must sympathise with the Fight for Right Movement, Hardy, Buchan, Newbolt, that lot. Their manifesto talks about Faith, the understanding that Right will only prevail through purification, the efforts and the sacrifices of men who make it prevail. We are facing an assault on our culture. Take the destruction of Rheims Cathedral. The thing was visible enough from miles away. The Germans could hardly miss it - no, that was not what I meant to say - they could hardly hit it by accident. It's been called the Kaiser's crowning infamy. I say that it was his crowning lunacy. It showed the world just what we're up against. Someone described it as the act of a madman piling up logs for his own pyre. If that's the German attitude towards cultural heritage, I can sympathise with those who want none of it.'

How Tristram was remaining silent I do not know. I can only be saying that I, who was as shocked by the shelling of Rheims Cathedral as anyone, could not haul myself away from the fact that the Colonel had once more insulted us by generalising wildly about our culture. He had even implied - no, I do believe he actually said it so - that by playing German music Adela was being provocative.

Torn between wanting to defend the poor girl and not wishing to be prolonging her pain, I was beaten to a response by Richard, who said very firmly, 'We will destroy ourselves if we turn in hatred on everything which we have previously admired just because it is German. Take poor Prince Louis. His forced resignation last week was unnecessary, unfair and unjust. It has done a great disservice both to him and to the British nation. He has been a distinguished and loyal First Sea Lord and member of the Royal Family. His brother Prince Maurice has not only fought for this country, but he has now died for it. Yet because a few fanatics have been given undue prominence by an even smaller group of unscrupulous newspaper editors, his Austrian name and ancestry have allowed some people to misuse the term Alien and hound him out of office.'

'Bravo!' I cried. There was a stunned silence. The Colonel was looking taken aback. His wife was fidgeting. But Richard, oh my dear, dear husband, what a speech, worthy of one of your best sermons. Our eyes met, and it was in pure love and mutual respect. I could have got up from my place at the dinner table and thrown my arms around him.

After quite a long silence, during which I must admit that I could not refrain from looking round the table with a triumphant smile, Elizabeth, of all people, rescued the situation by asking Tristram calmly, 'Do you still have Leander?' and the conversation was moving on.

I will never let the Colonel get away with it, and now I can be certain, as if I did not know it before, that Richard will always be backing me up.

Back home preparing for bed, Richard put a hand on my shoulder and said tenderly, 'You must realise that William is under considerable strain. He worries for Elizabeth's husband, and for Elizabeth herself. He is angry and frustrated that the war is dragging on and has sunk into a stalemate in the mud. Although a soldier himself, he has taken the naval defeat at Coronel and the loss of Admiral Cradock badly.

'William has always been direct in his speech, with a tendency to express himself bluntly. And, my dear, I am afraid that it is true that the views he was expressing are those of the majority of the population, whether we agree with them or not. And if one takes the view that we should all support each other in a time of crisis, then it is sometimes necessary to swim with the tide rather than to fight against it.'

Long after, lying in bed in the early hours, I cannot get the tensions of the evening out of my mind. I keep returning to the Colonel's obsession with the word "Alien". I will be giving him this: he is not an unkind man, yet he knows how offensive the term is to me. So why is he persisting? Is he warning me about something that I have failed to grasp? But what? I took the nationality of my husband in 1888.

Oh well, I suppose that some good has come out of the evening. Tristram was behaving impeccably, and Adela was not seeming too upset by the jibes about peddling an alien culture; there, that word again. And I must always count at the top of my blessings my darling Richard, who was supporting me magnificently. With his firm assertiveness, he was resisting the falsehoods and countering them, while preventing the evening from dissolving into acrimony.

Soon it will be dawn. I must try to sleep.

9th November 1914

For half the dinner last night, my mind was elsewhere and fearful, thinking of Edgar. He must not go. I'm counting the hours until I can be with him. Yet even I can see the weakness of what I'm thinking.

It was fascinating to see Elizabeth again. She was simply dressed, but as beautiful as ever. She's always been quiet, but now she seemed so sad. Her husband is in the trenches, and I can see what it's doing to her. If I can sympathise with Elizabeth for the agony she's going through, and respect the sacrifice she and her husband are making, what am I if I'm not prepared to do the same with Edgar? As Tristram says, this is what war's doing to us, tearing us apart. I can see why the most frequently used phrase, which one hears every day, is "pulling together". It solves the dilemma, closes the argument, soothes the inner turmoil with a certainty. It has been collectively decided: we all pull together.

The older generation built up a steam around the dinner table on all sorts of subjects: Josef Reker, Mama's German birth, the disruption of my concert, and various aspects of the war. I was glad Tristram kept out of it, and I had no inclination whatever to join in. To be honest, I wasn't listening much of the time.

Already, it feels as though I'm in London.

Once more, I've been made to feel a coward, this time in front of Elizabeth. There were so many times when I wanted to intervene that I spent the whole dinner feeling I was holding down a coiled spring. Rheims Cathedral, for all the propaganda claims, wasn't destroyed, only damaged. I felt I really couldn't let the matter rest when Colonel Sawbridge said that playing German music was provocative, but I held back just long enough for Father to intervene, and very effectively he did it.

Yet for all that, I know that I'm hiding behind the real reason: that I don't want to be the centre of controversy. It would have been easy for spiteful words, said in the heat of debate, to cascade towards my refusal to enlist. And I know that, if forced to defend myself by pouring forth my reasons, I'd end up saying things which would be hurtful to Father and all he believes in. With Elizabeth present, I'd have caused even greater offence had I gone down that line, and I had absolutely no desire to upset her further than she clearly is already. So although it was painful for me to remain silent, I had to do it. Elizabeth is as attractive as ever, and sadness adds to her beauty. Seeing her made me think of Ingrid, and I felt a bleak longing come over me, so that at times my mind drifted away from the conversation, which may have been just as well.

My distaste was not confined to what Colonel

Sawbridge was saying. I didn't know that Mother had sung a duet in German with Reker somewhere on the farm, nor that he'd joined the choir. The choir is her domain, but the farm is mine. She's being extraordinarily naïve. Reker's position is extremely precarious. I'll explain it to her privately. Someone, Mrs Sawbridge it was, asked me how the men were taking to him. The answer, though I didn't say it, is not well. I've moved him on from shepherding under the protection of Jack Hearn, to working for John Jarvis on general tasks.

There are many indications that he's being mistreated. When he first arrived, he smiled a lot; now he's serious. He doesn't take his breaks with the other men, but moves off somewhere else. This has nothing to do with language problems; his English is adequate. He's being shunned.

All this I've observed. But reports from others have indicated there are more unpleasant things being done to him. Jarvis told me that Reker's work on hedging is extremely slow. When I probed deeper, Jarvis said the reason was that he was frequently without his tools. I pressed him, and it was then that Jarvis admitted that the other men had been taking Reker's tools and hiding them. I decided to come down hard on Jarvis.

'I have put you in a responsible position of trust. I chose you because I thought that I could rely on you to ensure that Reker was taught our ways to the benefit of all. I asked you to report any problems to me as they occurred. Not only have you failed to do that, but you didn't volunteer the information when

I asked you just now. I had to prise it out of you. What do you have to say?'

'The men don't like him, Master Tristram. 'Tis not the man himself, 'tis who he be.'

'You mean he's a German.'

Jarvis looked uncomfortable. They all know my ancestry.

'Well?'

'Some of them feels they'm being spied upon.'

I paused. It's not as easy to refute this as it ought to be, when the sorts of places where they get their information from claim there are sixty to a hundred thousand spies in this country.

'Reker is not a spy,' I said, 'and there is nothing here for anyone to spy on. He is not allowed to travel more than five miles, and you know as well as I do that he doesn't even go that far.'

Jarvis said nothing to this.

'How is his hedging when he does have his tools?'

''Tis all right,' he replied grudgingly.

'Right,' I said. 'I want you to speak to your men. I want you to tell them that if any more of this goes on, I will suspend whoever does it immediately. I will follow that up myself with them in a week's time. And, Jarvis, listen well to this. Your position on the farm is dependent on my being able to trust you. When I say that I want you to report to me on a matter, I expect you to do so. Is that clear?'

'Yes, Master Tristram.'

I'm not optimistic. Jarvis will speak to the men, they will stop hiding Reker's tools, and they will think of other ways to harass him. Meanwhile, they will continue to ostracise him. Human beings communicate in all sorts of subtle ways. They cannot all be controlled and enforced by discipline and a code of conduct imposed by me.

25th November 1914

I was proud of my flock. Philip Clucas's memorial had all been arranged. People had been generous, even those for whom a small contribution was a hard sacrifice. Helga and I had put up the balance of the money, so that Nora did not have to pay a single penny. The wording was simple, "In loving memory of Philip Clucas, a good man, who died for the country he loved, 11th October 1914." The size, shape and type of stone had all been agreed, and the order placed.

And then we heard the news. Private monuments to those killed in the war are henceforth banned. Outlawed. From now on, all memorials will have to be communal. I could not believe it. The government claims that it has to control the number springing up everywhere. A leader in the *Times* has supported the move, on the grounds that all soldiers who sacrifice their lives should be commemorated equally, and that it is wrong to indulge in a competition to see who can erect the grandest monument. Then why not ban memorials over a certain size?

I took it upon myself to break the news to Nora.

'Oh,' she said.

'We will pay tribute to him in other ways.'

'Yes,' she said.

My words were as empty as her responses. This dreary, deadening, destructive war. Are we to abandon the dead and bereaved because the scale of the killing is overtaking our capacity to honour them?

9th December 1914

I am preparing for the Christmas service. Richard has told me that it would be unwise to be singing the first verse of *Stille Nacht* in German, as we normally are doing. I had thought of asking Josef to sing it, but Adela will be home, and she is always doing it so beautifully.

'I think not, dear,' Richard said. 'We have seen that the mood of the people is easily aroused. I do not think that it would be prudent to risk any anti-German sentiment, however irrational it might be.'

'You mean *provoke*?' I challenged.

'Helga! Be reasonable.'

'So good,' I sighed. 'We will be singing the whole carol in English.'

But Tristram would be having none of it. For all his disagreements with us in the past, he usually puts his views calmly. Now he was passionate.

'You don't understand what people are thinking out there. Lord Northcliffe and the gutter press have whipped up the common man into a frenzy. I see it every day with my own eyes.'

'See what?' asked Richard, surprised.

'The anti-German feeling!' Tristram seemed agitated.

'Oh, that,' I said. 'Well, here we are having an opportunity to be making a stand against this nonsense without causing too much offence.'

Tristram gaped at me. 'You think so? Do you really think so? Are you aware how cruel the men are being to Reker? Can you imagine what it is like for him every day, when no one will speak to him except to throw foul-mouthed insults? How he has to hide his lunch box because someone has spread chicken dung in his dripping? He's been spat upon, urinated upon… I'm sorry, Mother, I didn't want to tell you this. But you must realise that we cannot give anyone the slightest chance of thinking that we're defiantly pro-German.'

'But I *am* German,' I wailed. 'How can I not be pro-German?' All my vows at the start of the war that I would henceforth be nothing but an Englishwoman are vanishing in the face of bigotry and discrimination. It was only later in the day that I was reflecting that my outburst at least is having the merit that Tristram will not be wanting to enlist to fight the country of which I am "pro".

'My dear,' said Richard gently, 'I think that Tristram may be right. It will only be for this one year. Remember Lord Haldane and Prince Louis? The attacks on their characters were spiteful and irrational, but they did happen. It is not wrong to leave *Silent Night* out of the service this once. God will still appreciate our other carols. But if we make life miserable for Reker and ourselves, where is the Christian goodness in that? What will anyone have gained?'

I was giving in then. It is amazing me that these brainless simpletons should be allowed to get away with it, and I feel shame in yielding to them. But I will not be defying Richard, who is after all our vicar and in charge of the church overall.

We will not be singing *Stille Nacht*.

10th December 1914

I give thanks to Our Lord for this. We have got them. Admiral Cradock has been avenged. The *Scharnhorst* and *Gneisenau*, which blew our ships out of the water at Coronel last month, are at the bottom of the Atlantic.

The German fleet under Admiral von Spee sailed towards the Falkland Islands, thinking that they would grab our coal. Imagine their horror as they rounded the headland to see the masts and tripods of two mighty dreadnoughts, *Inflexible* and *Invincible*. A pursuit ensued, our cruisers after the lighter German ships, and the two battleships after the biggest. Only one German vessel escaped, the *Dresden*.

Sad thought, though, that of those thousands of brave young men who faced each other far from home off the coast of Chile six weeks ago, nine out of ten were to die: the British that night, and the Germans two days ago.

17th December 1914

The German nation should hang its head in shame before God. Have they no compassion? In those poor north-eastern towns of Hartlepool, Scarborough and Whitby, children are waking up in hospital to find that their fathers, mothers and siblings are dead, dying or horribly maimed.

Yesterday, German battle-cruisers, cruisers and destroyers bore down and shattered the peaceful life of these seaside towns. Over a hundred people of all ages are said to have been killed, and nearly six hundred wounded.

What has enabled Satan to enter the soul of Germany? What perversity is eating at its corrupted mind? What can have been the point of blasting little children with shellfire? I cannot conceive that there could be a motive beyond blind hatred. The thoughts of the German people must be as depraved as those of the Romans who sat in the Coliseum, laughing at Christians cowering before lions.

Father is right, and for once I agree with the *Daily Mail*. The bombardment of the eastern towns is a barbaric and foolish act. Most of those killed and wounded were civilians who were not even directly involved in the war effort; and most of the buildings destroyed were private homes. The Germans have been able to cock a snook behind the Royal Navy's back and have made the Admiralty look incompetent, even though the German ships were lucky to escape in ever-thickening fog. But what pouring shells into residential areas has done is make the Germans look cruel for the sake of it. It'll harden people's hearts; this kind of thing always does. As a nation, we'll become even less tolerant, still less desirous of peace, more keen on revenge. Through innocent people's suffering will innocent people suffer.

18th December 1914

Abel Hopkins strode past me like Zeus on a mission of vengeance, lightning in his eyes and thunder in his heart. I stared after him, unsure that he'd even noticed me.

Round the corner, I found Mother, shaking. It was just after one o'clock. The moment she saw me, she started speaking very fast in German, something she does when she's agitated. I seized her by the hand and half-led, half-dragged her to the house. It took a minute or two for her to begin to calm down and speak in English.

'Your men, they are monsters, torturers.'

'Mother, what have they done to you?'

'Done to me? Nothing to me.'

'Josef, then?'

'He was not there.'

'So what has upset you?'

'Your men. They were singing, so.'

'Singing?'

'Horrible songs. *Sehr abstoßend.*'

'What were they singing?'

'It was horrible.'

I thought that if I went on asking her, she would never tell me. So I waited for her to say it in her own time. Suddenly she flared up in anger. 'This!' She started tapping her hand on her knee to a rhythm.

"Huns at large
Eating pork
Bayoneted babies
On their fork."

They were singing it in the Great Barn.'

'Mother, I'm sorry that you heard this. The men are thoughtless and cruel.'

'You must punish them.'

'It's difficult, Mother. If I were to catch them doing it myself, I'd reprimand them. But since I didn't hear them myself, I know what they'd do. They'd look blankly at me and stay silent. If I had a witness, that might be different, but they'd close ranks and deny it. Even loyal workers like Jack Hearn won't tell on the others when only words are involved.'

'But I am your witness. Am I not reliable? No?'

'Of course, Mother, but you are not seriously suggesting that I lead you into the Barn to face the assembled men having their lunch?'

'Already I face them once.'

'When?'

'Just now. I stand before them, and I let them know what I think.'

'Mother…'

I remembered: Abel Hopkins. That was why he'd stormed past me like thunder. She'd gone in and confronted them. Very brave, but very foolish. Foolish for no other reason than she is German. How could I make her understand? Father does, at least partly. He would have to know about this.

We both stood in Father's study like naughty children accused of fighting in the playground. I repeated what Mother had told me, inviting her to correct me or add her own comments. She did neither.

'What a terrible experience,' said Father. 'Tristram, do you think that you can deal with this?'

'It's difficult. Without Mother present, the men would deny it or simply stay silent'.

He thought for a long time and said, 'This cannot go on. Do you have a suggestion?'

'Yes, Father.' This was the moment I'd been dreading. 'Mother, you can't deny that you went out there to see Reker. You hardly ever used to go out into the farmyard; now you go there regularly.'

'And why not? You have already said, Tristram, that the men will not be talking to him. It is only decent charity that I should be doing so.'

'It would be, Mother, except for one thing.'

'And what is that?'

'You are a German.'

I had expected an explosion, and I got it.

'You speak like Colonel Sawbridge. You are half-German, although you would seem to deny it like a Judas. Am I an Alien? Go on and say so.'

'Helga!' Father spoke sharply. 'You must listen to me, and to Tristram.' I breathed out with relief. I'd thought it highly likely that he'd side with her. Their loyalty to one another is absolute. More softly he added, 'For your own sake and ours. William has made me realise…'

'Pah,' Mother responded with a toss of her head.

Now Father rose up and spoke powerfully, the stern head of the family. 'We are all in greater danger than you seem to think. I am not prepared to go into details, but if any further communion is made between you and Reker, the hostility which he is bearing will fall heavily on you, and not just you. That is all.'

I have got over my tears. Richard can be strong and decisive, but he has never, ever, been speaking to me like that in front of Tristram. He was not losing his temper. I sensed no irritation that made him snap. He seemed to be in full control of his emotions. He did not linger over what he thought that I had done wrong. His main purpose did not seem to be to chastise me; merely to be stern enough to make sure that I would stop visiting the farm.

Poor Josef. I wanted to be helping him. Now Tristram says that I have not been helping him at all, and Richard says that I must stop trying to. I will obey. When it comes to it, I always obey.

That was astonishing. I hoped Father would support me, but I never thought that he'd be so imperious. He clearly endorses my view completely, but I'm sure there's something behind it which I don't understand. Why did he mention Colonel Sawbridge? He doesn't know much about what goes on at our farm.

I returned to Father and tried to ask him, but he rose up again and commanded me to leave.

Dear Lord, help me to see clearly. There are times when a thought is so oblique, so peripheral to the field of mental vision, that it is no more than a vaguely sensed flutter at the back of the mind. There, and it is gone, and one is hardly aware that it has been.

Thus it was with Adela. When William had been holding forth, perplexing and troubling us all about how Helga might be an Enemy Alien, it passed into my mind and out again in an instant that what he was saying might possibly apply to Adela. I suppose that the reason why I dismissed the thought immediately was that she was formally adopted long ago and is therefore as English for the purpose of nationality as Helga is through marriage. I could not possibly think that William had been referring to Adela, or hinting that he might be referring to her, because William does not know the circumstances of her birth in Zwickau. Helga and I vowed from the outset that we would never tell anyone: Tristram, Adela herself, or anyone else.

It came to me with a cold horror, just as I was about to get out of the bath, that I *had* told William. I had completely and utterly forgotten. Four or five years ago, before Tristram left for Berlin and Adela for London, I had spoken in confidence to William. Concerned at the time about the intimacy of Tristram's relationship with Adela, I had sought William's advice. I did not tell Helga, who seemed unaware that there might be a problem, and to this day she does not know that I confided in William. In speaking to him, it was necessary for me to disclose the circumstances of Adela's birth and adoption, which were pertinent to my hypothesis. I had clean forgotten that I had made this disclosure.

So when it became clear that Helga's flaunting – yes, I am afraid that the word is accurate – of her Germanity, particularly around the farm, but also in front of the Sawbridges, was causing unwanted scrutiny of my family's status, I pondered how I might intervene. Now Tristram has provided me with both the justification and the means. I knew that I might not get another chance, so I acted swiftly and firmly once Tristram had approached me. I have forbidden Helga to commune with Reker.

Back to William. It appeared that he had been dropping hints, and that the hints might pertain to Adela. The obvious course of action seemed to be to discuss it with William. But now I have thought again. Firstly, I cannot be sure that I am reading William correctly. His comments about Aliens were addressed to Helga, in front of us all. Yet I realise now that he could not raise the subject of Adela directly, as he is not supposed to know that she is German by birth. I cannot think of a more sensitive issue than Adela's nationality which, if he remembers what I told him at all, he will realise is both highly controversial and utterly secret. And if he does recall the conversation, he will surely remember the context in which it was held; again, very delicate.

All this would appear to lead to the desirability of my going to speak to William. But what could it lead to? I know all I need to know to be wary of Adela's Germanity. Drawing attention to it might put William in a difficult position, by making him an accomplice to the crime of not disclosing her alien identity. And anyhow, what could William advise further? Well, he could recommend that we have her registered as an Alien. We could not do it for her. She is an adult, not a minor, so there would be no question of her not learning the cause. There are a number of reasons which would make this action abhorrent. First, the shock to the girl herself, and the realisation that we are at war with her natural parents. Then there is the problem that the matter would be on public record, and the knowledge that not one, but two of my family are full-blooded Germans. And what if she did not need to register? We would have announced to everyone unnecessarily that Adela is a German. She would be German to the world in every sense except the legal one. No, it is better that the matter should rest. But Helga must be kept away from Reker.

Mercury has never written as much as this before.

"The call of blood has certainly come rushing. Your Germanic mother has graced us with a visit as welcome as the Kaiser's army in Belgium. How bravely she defended her pup. News of her intervention is rapidly spreading from farm to village to county. How does it feel to have an infamous mother? Your family does like putting its head above the parapet. If this goes on, we will soon be so well educated that we will be able to sing our songs in German."

This is both literate and nasty. I have to concede that it's skilfully done. The word "pup" implies that Mother deserves an epithet which I won't spell out, even to myself. "Germanic" is clearly a pun. "Your family does like putting its head above the parapet." That is threatening, but in a subtle and implied way. Does it reveal knowledge of events beyond the farm? Could it be referring to Adela's concert? Or is it merely my refusal to enlist?

What really worries me is the bit about the news spreading. I'm afraid Mother has done much damage on the farm, which will be irreparable. But I wouldn't want it to extend to the village and beyond. Mercury seems to delight in telling me that it will, or already has.

Today's highlighted articles from the press are linked in a clever, but supplementary and malevolent way. There is mention of the word "mongrelism", which is underlined in red ink.

Clearly this does not apply to Mother or Reker; only Adela and I are half-breeds.

Further on we have, "There can be no doubt that many of them are in cahoots with spies, back stabbers, turncoats, sedition mongers and posers of pacifism. In our efforts to appease them, we ignore what our brave men are fighting for in the trenches and on the high seas in defence of freedom." And further on still, "Craven weakness, a tendency to lie on cushions and enjoy the soft living at home, a rottenness at the core, these are what caused the Empire of Rome to fall. And now the British Empire faces a similar fate, and the victor now, as then, will be the Hun."

Although the articles are mostly absurd and extreme, what Mercury writes himself tends to be accurate. Any exaggerated statements are for satirical or sarcastic effect. In view of what he's written here, that's worrying.

Has the time come to waylay him? Every time I ask myself this question, I come back to the same answer. He's providing me with not just useful, but essential, information. If I'd caught him and snaffled him before today, I wouldn't have found out what a perilous situation we're in. I must be patient.

23rd December 1914

Drowsy from this stuffy compartment and the rhythm of the rails, I'm weary but relieved. Edgar has told me he won't be answering Kitchener's call. We had a tearful parting this morning. He'll spend Christmas with his parents, but will come down to Chaddingley for New Year.

I feel a mixture of anti-climax and contentment. Contentment to be returning to my dear family and being cocooned by traditional festivities, but a part of me will be elsewhere.

My presents are in a suitcase on the rack above. I'll wrap them properly when I get home, then I'll snuggle down in front of the fire and catch up with all the news.

I must have dropped off, because when I awoke, it wasn't to my darling Edgar far behind, nor to the comforts ahead. I can't help thinking of those poor men, huddled in their trenches, far from their families. It seems wrong to be looking forward to log fires and big meals. Guilt is becoming a duty, joy a sin.

25th December 1914

Poor Papa. At first it seemed as though something had gone wrong with the time. Why were so many people late for Church? I sat in the choir, craning my head forward, wondering why the pews were so empty. Papa, dressed in his white vestment, came out of the vestry and walked the length of the aisle. I could just see him standing outside the church, looking down the path towards the lych-gate.

Minutes passed: five, ten, fifteen beyond the time for the service to begin. No one else appeared. Papa came back into the church, walking slowly up the nave, a worried expression on his face. The service began, with only two thirds of the normal number present.

We sang well enough. The released German prisoner, Josef Reker, has a fine tenor voice. There was no *Silent Night* this year, which is understandable in view of the war with Germany and Austria.

Papa's sermon was all about reconciliation. I secretly thought it wasn't one of his best. He seemed to link two themes which didn't quite fit together: reconciliation and fighting the good fight; the wolf shall lie down with the lamb and pulling together to fight the foe. A little over halfway through the sermon, a man I didn't recognise got up from his pew and walked out of the church.

When the service was over, we stood talking in the churchyard as usual, but it wasn't like a normal Christmas. Several people had already left and were walking back down the road towards the village. Those who did stay seemed to be hanging back, looking as though they might suddenly bolt towards the gate. A few greeted us as warmly as ever, wishing us a Happy Christmas and praising the choir. And then it was all over after only a few minutes. Father is looking worried, Mother loury. Something is wrong. No doubt I'll soon be told. This is hardly the cheer of Christmas.

A boycott, that is what it is. I, the shepherd of my flock, have been slapped in the face, and it is smarting. I am trying to enjoy the festivities. My duty for the next few hours is to my family, to show them love and joy. Yet all the time I am counting faces: present faces. and absent faces; working out who was there and who was not, and whether it was principally those from the farm who stayed away. I have concluded that it was not. If anything, I would say that more villagers unconnected with the farm were absent than farm workers and their families. This may be because farm workers would be more scared to do so. I simply do not know.

Just now I completely failed to hear what Tristram had just said to me. Helga is glum, Adela worried and perplexed. We have discussed it a bit, but we cannot lose the whole of Christmas Day to a morbid post-mortem.

Nancy was one of the few who spoke to us in the churchyard. "The wolf shall lie down with the lamb, Vicar. Perhaps he already has." And then she walked off. What a peculiar thing to say.

Oh dear, I have spilt the gravy. Adela has left the room. What is happening?

4th January 1915

Adela's young man has been staying with us. We have taken to him gradually, Helga and I, the longer he has been with us. He is a good-looking boy, though his features are so refined that one's first impression is that he appears effeminate. He is quietly spoken, with considerate manners. At first he seemed pitifully shy, looking out of the corners of his eyes in a way which did not inspire confidence. On the first day, all his answers to our questions seemed unnerved and evasive. But the more he has got to know us, the more he has responded with a direct answer and a steady eye.

Like Tristram, he is disinclined to enlist. The reason he gives is that he believes that his best contribution would be as a war artist. He says that he considers himself to be capable with a brush, but knows that he is hopeless with a gun. Tristram behaved oddly when we were discussing this. He and I have a tacit agreement that we will respect each other's views and not clash over the subject of volunteering. But when it was being discussed with young Simpson, Tristram became heated, and gave a speech which bordered on outright pacifism. He even said something like, 'Both sides have created factories on the western front and what they are churning out is death; what they are not making is progress.'

Adela obviously adores the boy, and he her. I am pleased for both of them, and there is an additional reason why I should be gratified. The shameful thoughts which I once had concerning Adela and Tristram have been finally laid to rest. Now, observing her clearly in love with a young man of her own age, I have found it easy to forget the past, and as a result have experienced an inner peace. It is as though I had been performing a function of vigilance so long as it seemed that Tristram was the most important man in her life. Now that her Edgar has come along, I am able to step back, delighted that nature is taking its true course. And I thank God that it has come to this. I feel cleansed, and free.

The Bunby clan has returned to Church, but attendance is still far below what it should be. I have decided that I will allow a couple more weeks to pass, then I will visit each of the truant families in turn and confront them in a gentle, open manner, hearing what they have to say and responding peaceably.

18th January 1915

Father and Mother don't realise what the newspapers are doing to this war. The brothers Alfred and Harold Harmsworth are two of the richest men in the country. They've obtained their wealth by transforming journalism, bringing newspapers to a massive new audience. Their *Daily Mail* has over a million readers, but they also own *The Times*, *Evening News* and *Weekly Dispatch*. They've brought a direct interest in the affairs of the world to the literate, if not discerning, masses. These laudable achievements have been realised by appealing to some of the lowest instincts of mankind: voyeurism, tribalism, intolerance and the capacity to hate. Two of their techniques stand out above all others: sensationalism and the fostering of mob hysteria; in other words, galvanising the majority to think and act against minorities. In bringing pleasure to millions, the Harmsworths have inflicted degradation, suffering and fear on countless others. They've brought information to the people, but it's a perverse and twisted knowledge, often so far from the truth that it's the opposite of enlightenment. Unscrupulous, unelected and unaccountable, they are the two most powerful and dangerous men in the country.

Josef Reker has left us, hounded off the farm. It must have been a terrible decision: to return to the internment camp, knowing that he would be committing his wife and children to poverty, malnutrition and rags. I pleaded with him to stay. He looked at me with haunted eyes, making a horrible effort to smile.

'I have tried, Master Tristram. The insults, I take, even about my wife and mother. I can drink water which is urine. I can clean out my bag when the… how do you say it, of a dead calf, no smaller, *ja Fötus*, foetus, is inside. But I cannot live with the knowing of what I will do. There are two men here, I will kill them. And this hating, I cannot live with it.'

So Reker has gone. You, the Harmsworths, if you knew of this, you wouldn't care. For you there's a higher purpose, the bigger picture. The trouble is you've lied for so long that you've forgotten what that purpose once was. And so your destiny is not a noble ideal, but a base, selfish objective: to sell more newspapers, to gain power and influence, and wealth for yourselves.

23rd January 1915

I can't believe it; I've heard from Fritz. He's beaten me to it. And I've heard from Ingrid, and she loves me, loves me. Let me explain the background.

When I was in London in October, I did some research into censorship. I wanted to find out whether it might be possible to communicate with Walter, Fritz and Ingrid in Germany. I discovered that the only way of doing so was by totally evading the censor. It seemed it might still be possible to send post via Muscat, Persia or the United States of America. All three countries were excluded from the censorship warrant, and all have significant British and German populations. It'd be reasonable to assume that a few people in those places would be engaged in aiding communications between Britain and Germany. The problem was how to identify these people, and how to contact them.

For several weeks after I'd been to London, I scoured the personal columns of *The Times*, looking for coded messages. I saw some pretty weird stuff, but nothing which seemed to convey what I was looking for. But I did come across a short advertisement in the *Weekly Dispatch*, one of Mercury's occasional offerings, whose wording seemed unusual. It read, "Not frightened of danger, man/youth required to further England's war effort via new form of outlet, terms to be agreed. Box 5813."

I stared at it for a few seconds, and then I saw it. "Danger, man/youth" contained the word

"Germany", "England" was clearly "England", and "outlet, terms" contained the word "letter". It seemed possible that the advertiser was offering a new service to send letters between England and Germany, at terms to be agreed; possibly a hint that the service wouldn't come cheap.

I carefully penned a response which wouldn't incriminate me if I were mistaken, or if my letter fell into the wrong hands.

'Dear Sir, I am most interested in your advertisement. I'll wager man/youth means that you are looking for a young and strong male for the post you are seeking to fill in the service of England. I look forward to hearing from you. Yours faithfully, Ali Ashdown.' I submitted the correct address for Chaddingley.

As you can see, "Germany" is still there ("wager man/youth"), "England" is still "England", and "letter" has become "post". Finally, "male" is "mail". All I had to do now was wait for a response, try to get to the postman before the other members of the family, and to think up a reasonable explanation as to why I should receive a letter addressed to "Ali Ashdown", which, if you haven't already spotted it, contains the word "Alias". To cover this eventuality, I decided that I'd say to Father or Mother that I'd applied for a service under an assumed name, so that I could assess it without being pestered: more or less the truth.

In the event, I didn't have to say anything to my parents, not because I got to the reply before them, but because I hadn't received one. My letter to the advertiser was posted on 4th December. That was seven weeks ago, and although Christmas has intervened, it seems that my hopes were unfounded. My code could hardly have been clearer to someone looking for it, so there didn't seem any point in sending anything more in the same vein. I looked for the advertisement to be repeated or slightly altered, but this was near impossible, because Mercury rarely gives me the *Weekly Dispatch*. I buy it when I can, but it's not the sort of newspaper I'd want to be seen delivered to Chaddingley.

I'd returned to looking through all the personal columns and advertisements in those publications which did come my way, when much to my surprise and delight, this letter came today from Fritz via America. Here is what it says, translated into English:

'My Dear Tristram, I send you the warmest greetings, and those of your friends, especially Ingrid, who is more than a friend. You will always be in our hearts, even though our countries are at war.

'We are well, and I sincerely hope that you and your family are too. If you do get this letter, it will have been on a long journey. It is best that I do not write down the route, but it involves five countries.

'Of those whom you know, Michael, Hans and Max went to war. I am sorry to have to tell you that Max was badly wounded on the Sambre in August. He was hit in the face and will always be blind.

'Walter is well, but I am afraid that I cannot send greetings from him. I tried to tell him that I had found a way of writing to you, and asked him if he wanted to use it, but he clearly does not approve.

Nevertheless, he talks about you, and his words are very warm. But in the end, he does not know that I have sent this letter.

'Ingrid misses you so badly. She loves you, Tristram, and I am happy and proud to say it. She wanted to send her own letter with this one, but I would not allow it. If anything should go wrong, I would not want her to be in trouble. I hope that you agree with this. But she sends a message, which must be personal between you. Remember the cedar at Latakia, she says, and do not forget. Never forget. You will know what she means.'

I felt such an overwhelming passion at this that I let out a howl. I felt partly thrilled that she still loves me, and partly despairing that we're apart. These emotions built up to such a sense of longing, that it was several minutes before I could finish Fritz's letter.

'If you wish to reply, write to the following address in Cleveland. There will be no cost, but you may be told later how to make a donation. Place the envelope addressed to me here inside the one to the United States, which you will, of course, stamp. Do not put your own address anywhere. When the time comes, the right people will know how to contact you.

'I do not recommend that you try to communicate with Walter. I am sure that he would not disclose it to anyone else, but I think, my dear Tristram, that we should respect that he has chosen not to be part of this process.

'That is all for now. May our next contact be when we throw our arms around each other in a tearful embrace. But when will that be? Your ever-devoted friend, Fritz.'

I shall, of course, reply. It's such wonderful, wonderful news, tempered by the fact that I can't advance my work with Walter. Not until this squalid war's over, and it seems as bogged down as ever.

25th January 1915

I have been rounding up my flock, visiting those parishioners who have strayed. What a mixed bag. In some homes, I have been made to feel welcome, and in others not. Some make it clear that they blame me, by which they mean Helga. Others are evasive and make excuses, some plausible, others absurd.

I have persuaded the Roper family to return to Church. Mrs Roper said that she had made her point, about "them spies, like", and her husband Martin, the village wheelwright, grunted his approval. The wife of Bootsy Barnes, who is away at the front, pretended that she had been ill, but I was not deceived. Having responded to the pressure of others, she has now responded to mine. She says that she will return, and I believe that she will.

The Smith clan, which includes Billy the gas lighter and part-time slaughterman, Doughy the baker, and Joseph the hurdle-maker, were all assembled when I called, which was quite intimidating. But they made me feel welcome, and I was soon telling them jokes. I did not feel it necessary to raise the subject directly. My tactic paid off, because when Billy showed me to the door, his last words were, 'See you on Sunday, Vicar.'

I had a shock when I knocked on the door of the Swains. Stanley has gone to the war, but no one had told me. His wife Patricia was guarded. I am not sure whether she will return to Church.

I also called on Nora Clucas, not because she had failed to attend, but because I wanted to find out how she was coping. She shocked me by ushering me to the mantelpiece, where she proudly displays Philip's blood-stained purse. At first I recoiled from this ghoulish souvenir, but then I remembered the denial of the memorial outside her gate, and let her know that I understood.

There has been a terrific sea battle off the Dogger Bank, where Beatty's battle-cruisers have clashed with their opposite numbers under Admiral von Hipper. We should have annihilated them, but early on in the engagement Beatty's flagship, *HMS Lion*, was crippled and her signal halyards shot away, so that control of the battle was lost at the vital moment. As it was, the *Blücher* was sunk, but the enemy as a whole once more wriggled from our clutches and fled before we could finish them off.

8th February 1915

I have had a message from Gerd, saying that my mother is ill. My tears have flowed and flowed, bitterness adding to pain.

A Red Cross form, a form, would Gerd be sending me a form? That is all these brutish people will allow, blinded as they are by hatred and their own selfish ends.

My poor, poor mother, whom I love and may never be seeing again. Gerd says that she has a malignant growth on her leg, and the doctors can do nothing about it. She may be living for six months or two years. His letter is only facts. He would never be writing to me like that. It is so cold, it is not like Gerd at all. Where is human kindness, where is sympathy, where is love? Carried off by boots, on the point of a bayonet.

Richard has been comforting me. Tristram could not prevent a few tears of his own as he put his arms around me, but I could feel his anger; above all, he is feeling anger. Adela is still in London, but will be home for the weekend.

Now I have to make a reply. A cold, cold reply. A message, no more. I know that Gerd will not be reading it out to my mother. It would be hurtful to do so. His own words he will be making, and saying them from me, better words, conveying my love and comfort, which I cannot be sending myself. I know he will. Please, Gerd, please.

11th February 1915

I was sixteen when I was given Leander. In those days he used to rear, and once went over backwards, pinning me underneath. He has all the fire of his thoroughbred race. Countless times he's bucked me off; but there's not a trace of malice in him. He loves me as deeply as I love him. We've galloped for miles along beaches and over heathland, forded rivers, hunted, raced, cantered by moonlight and fallen together. We've even - he in his horsy way - laughed together. If I've felt stressed, it's to Leander that I've turned, resting my hands on his glossy coat and letting my hurt flow into his muscled frame.

Tomorrow he'll be gone. Not to a quick and painless death, not to some caring owner who'll pasture him through his twilight years, but to those butchers in Flanders. He'll be shouted at, tugged at, hit, given work unsuited to him, and subjected to unimaginable terrors of noise and blood, which horses loathe. In the end, he will almost certainly suffer a fate as horrible as that which he'll have been forced to witness in others. And he'll feel betrayed, not understanding why I've let this happen.

An hour ago, I was convinced I was going to get my gun and shoot him. I'd have done it, but I thought of Mother. In these subverted days, obstructing the war effort is about the most serious crime that one can commit, and I'd almost certainly be gaoled for it.

Goodnight, my friend. I'll see you in the morning. I'll see you looking helplessly round as you realise I'm not coming with you. May the good times we've had together carry you through what lies ahead, and may your end be swift and painless.

12th February 1915

My cold, cold message to the Red Cross I have sent. Tristram, who is grieving for the loss of his horse, came to me this afternoon. I could see that he had been crying. My strong, strong boy, I understand your pain. This we share.

'Mother, I am in communication with Germany.'

I looked at him dumbfounded, thinking that he was telling me that he was becoming some sort of spy, or that this was his way of serving his country without going to the trenches. Wild thoughts, prompted by my distress.

'You can write to Great Uncle Gerd.'

'I cannot.'

'You can write to him, properly.'

'Tristram, what are you saying?'

'Yes, Mother, you can write what you want. I've had a letter from Germany, from a friend I worked with in the Middle East.'

'*Mein Gott*!' This news was like being told that it was possible to fly.

'Post to and from the United States isn't censored. I have an address in America. They'll forward it to other countries, places like Cuba and Argentina, and from there it'll be sent to somewhere like Spain, and on to Germany. I don't know exactly where, and it doesn't really matter. The point is that a letter arrived from Nürnberg a few days ago. I'm writing a reply. If you'd like, you could write to Great Uncle Gerd, and our two envelopes could go together via Cleveland.'

I will write, and I will be pouring out my true feelings to Gerd, and sending a real letter, not a cold message, to my darling mother. It is not enough. I should be able to be seeing her. I should be able to be going to her. But if I cannot be boarding the train and sailing the seas myself, at least my words can.

6th March 1915

Nancy Hopkins came to the house, the insolent woman.

'I hope you don't mind, Mrs Hall, but we're canvassing door to door for Great Britain.'

A bold claim, I thought. I was brusque with her, and was not inviting her in. I am not trusting the woman.

'I didn't think you'd want to be left out.'

'Well, what is it?'

'It's on behalf of the War Office.'

I looked at her coldly. She was holding out a bunch of leaflets. I took them quickly and closed the door before she could say anything further.

When I looked at them in the drawing room, I saw that there were three. One was familiar, a scaled down version of a poster which I had seen recently in Dorchester of a row of uniformed soldiers, one of whom was not a soldier, but a placard, which read, "This space is reserved for a fit man." The caption read, "There is still a place in the line for YOU. Will you fill it?"

I glanced at the other two leaflets. One was of a well-dressed couple: a middle-aged woman and a young man. The caption read, "Go! It is your duty lad. Join today." The last had only words. "There are three types of men. Those who hear the call and obey, those who delay, and The Others. To which do YOU belong?"

Angrily, I scrumpled them up and threw them in the fire.

14th March 1915

I give thanks to Our Lord. At last the war is showing signs of moving. Battleships have been pounding Turkish forts overlooking the Dardanelles. Once they are silenced, we will be able to pour through the narrows into the Sea of Marmara, at the end of which lies Constantinople. Here is an opportunity to open up a new front at last, with a thrust straight into the heart of the Ottoman Empire.

That is not all. For the first time since the deadlock on the western front following the Marne, we are on the attack in France. After a half-hour bombardment, during which more shells, they say, were fired than during the whole of the Boer War, our troops have captured the village of Neuve Chapelle in just four hours. Let us pray that we keep up the momentum.

27th March 1915

Mercury didn't highlight this one, I spotted it myself. It was a garbled mixture of news item and comment in *John Bull* under the headline, "We must all be vigilant."

"An attempted uprising may have been foiled in London. Police officers broke down a door in Tooley Street, where they had been tipped off that a number of Germans had armed themselves with rifles and bombs. Three men were arrested, but were later discharged. Although no ammunition was found this time, we must not underestimate these people. They are both well-organised and clever. The absence of arms and ammunition shows that they must have been tipped off in advance, which is why the police were unable to incriminate them. Let us hope that next time they will be caught red-handed. Meanwhile we must all be vigilant."

Really? No evidence was found, so in the bigoted and topsy-turvy world of *John Bull*, no evidence of guilt equals proof of it. *John Bull* is edited by Horatio Bottomley, and frequently includes contributions from J H Clarke, and the MPs Leo Maxse and Pemberton Billing, who between them are rabid nationalists, self-publicists and Jew-baiters. It's here you'll read such noble and statesmanlike pronouncements as, "Lucre is their Deity and Shylock their High Priest." You might think this refers to Jews, but actually it was part of an attack on Germans, making no distinction. This is the sort of publication where Jews might be labelled "pork butchers".

John Bull is where I read, in the context of another red herring, of the "plain, hard and indisputable facts of the case. Of course it would be totally wrong to divulge these facts." Of course it would, Mr Bottomley; the facts might reveal it all to be a figment of your imagination.

I nearly forgot. Mercury is not Malpiero, definitely not. I received a note from Malpiero, and careful comparison showed me that his handwriting is different from Mercury's. I never thought it was him, but if not, who is able to have such ready access to the tack room under Malpiero's nose? Naturally, I've made sure that my saddlebag remains there, in spite of the departure of Leander. And I do still visit the tack room daily.

Other gems from Mercury this week: "The Potty Potentate of Potsdam" and "The Berlin Butcher". The Kaiser is a versatile man.

8th April 1915

Stanley Swain has been killed. He joined up only

four months ago, and had been in the line for just five weeks. I called on his widow, Patricia, who no longer comes to Church. She was quite open with me.

'The words don't mean nothing to me no more, Mr Hall. I was hearing them, but they was just going round and round in my head without resting.'

'Can you not receive the comfort of Our Lord in your distress? It is through Him that you will be reunited, you know.'

'No, I don't think I can,' she replied. ''Tis the Church that supports this war, and the war has taken him.'

'What he died for was right. The whole parish joins you in feeling proud of him.'

'Does it?' she asked dreamily. 'All I know is that he's gone, and I won't see him no more.'

'Of course you will'

'When I heard that he'd died, there was nothing to be done. No funeral, no nothing. So I just gets on with my life. What more can I do?'

'But we have been saying prayers for him,' I cried, a little too vehemently.

'Well, that's fine, if that's what you want. Pray by all means. I don't want to sound ungrateful, but they won't bring him back, will they?'

I performed a quick blessing, which she received in neutral silence. After I'd left, I realised that I was shaking. If only there had been a funeral, a focus for her grief, perhaps it might be different. But the government made a decision a long time ago: no return of bodies.

No bodies, no funerals, no personal memorials. So, in Mrs Swain's words, she just gets on with it.

17th April 1915

I spoke too soon. The attack on Neuve Chapelle has produced a tiny result for thousands killed. William says that the aim was really to take the village of Aubers, and it failed.

Things have not gone right in the Dardanelles either. A few ships, mainly French, in trying to force the narrows, have struck mines. William is so furious that he is in danger of jumping out of his trousers.

'We've been losing men on the western front in their tens of thousands. But our aged and lesser ships turn back because of a few mines. They should crash through. Once in the open sea, the Marmara, nothing can stop them. Here's a chance to knock Turkey out of the war. If Constantinople falls, the whole rotten Ottoman Empire will fall like a house of cards in a few weeks, or at the most months.'

'What about the Turkish forts in the straits?' I asked. 'I read that some of them are still firing on us.'

'A few of them are. But why? Because we've sent no troops. If we'd put some men ashore, we could have cleared the lot of them. Here's a great opportunity being squandered because of a lack of coordination, and because we cannot contemplate a few casualties in one sphere, while we ratchet them up on a greater scale to no effect in another.'

I left him to his fuming.

22nd April 1915

Richard had already been seeing Patricia Swain. His visit was not successful, but I am feeling it my duty to persevere. Her failure to attend Church is no reason to abandon her. Christ taught us that charity should extend beyond those we call our own.

As I was approaching the house, I saw that the curtains had been drawn, in spite of it still being daylight. It was a warm evening, which may be why the front door was being left ajar.

Voices were coming from within. Just as I was about to knock, I heard what was sounding like an incantation, not singing, but monotonous words like those which one might be hearing in a monastery. I pushed the door a little, put my head in and looked round the corner. I could see down the short passageway to the room at the end, the one where the curtains had been drawn. The voices were coming from there.

'He's smoking. There's another man with him.' That sounded like Nancy Hopkins, but it was not her normal voice. 'He's called Arthur. Is it Arthur? Or Albert.'

'It must be Alf.' That was Mrs Swain. 'He's mentioned Alf in his letters. Alf's his pal.'

'He's smiling.'

'Who is?'

'Stanley. Stanley's smiling.'

'Did he get the socks, the thick black ones I sent?'

'Yes.' There was a pause. 'There's something yellow. It's a small tin. No, it's soft.'

'That'll be his tobacco pouch.' Mrs Swain was getting excited, but this had to stop.

I swept down the passageway and burst through the door, knowing what it was that I was witnessing. A séance!

Three faces were looking up at me. I recognised them all: Mrs Swain, Nancy, and Digby Shoreman. For a few seconds we were staring at one another. Then everyone was speaking at once.

'Oh no.'

'Mrs Hall!'

'What do you think you are doing?' That was me, but all this was overtaken by Nancy, who was shrieking, 'The Devil! Out! Out!' There was a shocked silence. I think Mrs Swain was weeping. Digby Shoreman was rising to his feet, saying quietly, 'Mrs Hall, we are having a private meeting.'

I was standing there appalled. I was wanting to assert the authority of the Church in the face of this pagan ritual. But now, outnumbered in someone else's house, which I had entered without knocking, I realised that it was not the time, and that this was a matter for Richard to be dealing with.

'The enemy,' screeched Nancy. 'This is what Stanley died for.'

A coward I am not. When attacked, as by Colonel

Sawbridge, I stand and fight. If retreat I must, it would not be in the face of those words. But by then Digby had come round the table and was taking me by the arm.

'Please, Mrs Hall. Patricia is very upset. We should all think of her, yes?'

Richard was receiving the news gravely. 'I cannot go to Mrs Swain now. She has already indicated that she does not wish to receive the comforts of the Church. But I will speak to Nancy and to Digby Shoreman. Both should know better. They were in Church last Sunday, were they not? Yes, they were, both of them. Leave it to me.'

I am thinking that society is breaking down. We are returning to the Dark Ages. In the face of superstition and paganism, we must be strong. I hope that Richard will be.

24th April 1915

I have tackled both Digby Shoreman and Nancy. I received two very different reactions. Digby was conciliatory. He said that Patricia Swain had been approached by Nancy, asking her if she would like to "contact" Stanley. Patricia had invited Digby herself, because she thought that she ought to have a man present.

'This is wrong,' I said. 'It builds up false hopes. If

God wanted us to speak directly with the dead, he would have arranged it.'

'I realise that now,' said Digby. 'I'm sorry, truly sorry. I shouldn't have gone along with it.'

'No, you should not. You did not seriously believe that Stanley would speak to her?'

'No, Vicar, not really, but Nancy said he would…' he trailed off glumly.

'And did he?'

'No, Vicar, not that I'd believe.'

Nancy responded very differently.

'He was speaking all right, but before I could get to the heart of it, I was interrupted.'

'You mean by my wife?'

'When I came to her door the other day, at least I knocked.'

'Nancy, I do not understand you. You come to Church every Sunday, and often on weekdays too, yet you indulge in this nonsense.'

'That's your opinion, Vicar.'

'And the opinion of the Church. You cannot accept the sacrament of God, and then go communing with the Devil.'

'I did not commune with the Devil,' she said defiantly, then added mischievously, 'The Devil came, but it weren't my doing.'

'What do you mean?'

'Oh, nothing, Vicar. I just thought you should know.'

I realised what she was hinting at. She was referring to Helga. Although I felt my anger rising, I did not wish to invite any more insults, so decided to end with a stern warning.

'You have been christened and confirmed into the Church of England in the name of the Lord, Nancy. You have made your vows and renewed them by regularly reciting the Creed in Church. Your allegiance is to your Maker and to the Lord Jesus Christ, who died for your sins. Do not stray, Nancy, do not stray. Come to evensong this evening. After the congregation has left, we will pray together.'

She came to evensong, and afterwards we prayed. She did everything I asked. There was only one thing which she did not do. She did not assume the mantle of humility.

That has not been the only defiance of the laws of decency this week. Once more, the Germans have shown themselves unfit to be a member of the community of nations. At Ypres they have used a weapon so foul that it brings a new dimension of horror to the poor troops. They call it poison gas. It drifts on the wind in clouds and chokes those who inhale it, leaving them in agony and permanently blind. They are saying that we will now use it in retaliation. So what has been the point? Is there no end to this frightfulness?

4th May 1915

Father's been telling me about the séance. I nearly responded that it reveals one of the great inconsistencies in what the Church teaches: that God should speak to us, but not the dead. God speaks to us, we're told, yet we can't actually hear his words. No one, except for a few self-elevated characters like Moses, St Paul and Joan of Arc, has claimed to hear the actual voice of God, so it would be risky for the Church to allow people to start listening to the voices of dead soldiers for, if they succeeded, it'd be all the more noticeable that they can't communicate directly with God whereas, if there's no response, that would show that there's no communication with the supernatural, including God.

A story is circulating that a Canadian soldier's been found crucified on a barn door in Belgium. Everyone's appalled. If the Germans took a dead body and attached it to the door, they're fools, but if they nailed a living man and let him bleed to death in agony, then that's a hideously cruel act. But no one seems to ask or care which it was. All that matters to them is that their sensibilities have been ruffled, and that they've been given an excuse to cackle in outrage.

The question of whether a man suffered means less than the desecration of a sacred image.

5th May 1915

To my letters to Gerd and my mother, I am not receiving a reply. Tristram says that I should be patient. I sent them nearly two months ago, but perhaps he is right. If they are having to go through all those different countries and back again, it will be taking time. I cannot do anything about the growth on her leg. I am just wanting her to know that I am thinking of her.

To be safe, I am sending another two letters, with more news for Gerd and comfort for my darling mother.

8th May 1915

Edgar and I are both in shock. Here in London, people are drifting up and down the streets, stunned by what has happened. We have never lost our horror of the memory of a vast liner disappearing beneath the waves. But when the *Titanic* went down three years ago, it was an accident. This time it has been done deliberately, within sight of the shores of Ireland. It's impossible to shake off the images of sloping decks, a rearing stern, sliding furniture and the wails of the dying.

A thousand dead. Huge numbers of children have gone down with the *Lusitania*. From the side, a few men in a black tube, who had condemned them to unimaginable terror, watched them die. The word "unbelievable" is so over-used, yet it's hard to understand the minds of those men in their submarine, and those who sent them. And it's very hard for me to believe that this has happened at all.

My next concert is only five days away. At the moment, I can't think that I'll be able to perform. Will anyone want to listen to me? I've chosen a completely non-German programme: Fauré, Bizet and Chopin. That may not be enough. This is so unreal.

The language of *The Times* is as strong as any of Mercury's rags. "The whole world is ringing with the stories of this crowning crime. The Germans and their pliant tools will wreck the fabric of civilisation unless every civilised person joins in branding with eternal infamy the renegade among nations."

It's hard to disagree. What amazes me is that apparently there were large numbers of Americans on board the *Lusitania*. I've long thought it: the Germans have no feeling for world opinion. It's a flaw which may eventually prove fatal to them. In the meantime, the backlash will be terrible, and it'll reach out to us here at Chaddingley. I can sense it coming.

9th May 1915

It's started. Serious rioting has broken out in Liverpool, and the emotive language of pain and retaliation is coming from far wider than before. A priest has written, "If popular fury results in the expulsion of all Germans from Britain, it will be a blessing in disguise."

This is Lord Derby: "This country calls no longer for men to fight an honourable foe. It calls for men to hunt down and crush once and for all the race of cold-blooded murderers."

Mercury's quickly in on the act. Here's an article penned by Robert Blatchford, under the headline, "The Branded Race. Why Are Any Germans Left Outside Gaols in Britain? Lesson of *Lusitania* Murders."

"The Germans who sank the *Lusitania* are the same scoundrels as the Germans who poisoned the wells, who shelled Scarborough, who dropped bombs on Paris, who used poison gas at Ypres. They belong to the same people who are frantic with desire to drop bombs on the crowded area of London: the same people who, women as well as men, would go mad with joy if their uniformed savages could get loose in an orgy of atrocity in some quiet English village. How many Germans are living in this country – and not in Gaol? What are they doing here? Why do we allow them to mix with decent people?"

And again, under the banner of "No Compromise with German Savagery. It is not the Kaiser, nor the Kaiser's generals who sank the *Lusitania*: it is the men and women of Germany; the German people. Those gross and loutish savages are mad with the exposure and the failure of their inglorious war. There is no crime too bad for them."

11th May 1915

I don't think my family realises how serious this is. Father's still explosive with outrage at the atrocity. He reads out articles from *The Times*, grunting his agreement, but fails to grasp the implications. Mother seems oblivious. She appears genuinely shocked and ashamed of what the Germans have done, and she's equally scathing of the excessive reactions. But she doesn't understand how they may affect her.

Adela is trying to stay calm in preparation for her concert. I daren't confide in her and tell her the real truth; it would be too shocking for her.

The riots are still continuing.

12th May 1915

Still rioting in Liverpool. All the shops owned by Germans have been destroyed there, and also pork butchers, whether owned by Germans or not. Other shops of Russians, Scandinavians and Italians have been smashed, burned and looted. They've attacked Chinese homes, and people with no more than foreign-sounding names have been beaten up, even a poor Scotsman.

The rioting's spread to other towns and cities, including London. Most of the East End is erupting. They say that very little work was done there yesterday, as groups of men took to the streets, some hunting down in packs anyone rumoured to be a German, others hacking at staircases, walls and ceilings with any weapon they could lay their hands on. "Every man seemed to have given up the day to the anti-German orgy," says *The Times*.

The correspondence pages are full of letters from well-to-do Germans, expressing their loyalty to Britain. They sound effusive and desperate. Those who've felt driven to write them are clearly frightened.

A procession of City businessmen has marched on Parliament, demanding the disabling of Germans in London from doing any harm, by interning them all for the duration of the war. I fear this kind of pressure more than the rioting mob, who can't distinguish between a German, a friendly ally, a Chinaman and a Scot.

13th May 1915

Even more rioting yesterday. Mercury, who I think must have bought all the newspapers he could find, has widened his range. This is from the *Daily Sketch*, under the headline, "Lock Them All Up!"

"If the government does not act promptly and vigorously on the enemy alien question, it may be confronted by a situation of the utmost gravity. It has taken a long series of outrages, increasing in savagery, to kindle the anger of the people, but the country now is in a most dangerous mood which must not be trifled with." Accompanying pictures of the rioting contain the banner, "Clear Out the Germans, Say the People."

Some of those arrested are starting to appear in the courts. It's interesting how many charges relate to assaults on the police, looting, theft and handling stolen property. *The Times* has reported, "At Poplar, in an area of a quarter of a mile, half a dozen houses were attacked simultaneously by different crowds. Before the constables were able to disperse the mob, horse-drawn carts, handcarts, and perambulators – besides the unaided arms of men, women and children – had taken everything away from the wrecked houses. One saw pianos, chests of drawers, dressers, and the heaviest types of household furniture being carted triumphantly through the streets. "Here is wealth for the taking," said one man who had possession of several spring mattresses, and was calmly driving his overloaded donkey-cart down Crisp Street."

A crowd in Bermondsey has attacked a baker's shop, despite the fact that the owner was displaying in his window a portrait of his two sons who are serving in the British Army.

Lord Charles Beresford, speaking in the House of Lords, has said, "If you have bad laws, or no laws at all, the people will take the law into their own hands. Intern these men as soon as possible, and before the people make you do it. Let the Government govern and not let the people indulge in outrageous performances because the Government has not done its work."

A petition signed by a quarter of a million women has been handed to the House of Commons, asking for internment of all alien enemies of military age, and by removing all alien enemies – men and women alike – to a distance of at least thirty miles from the sea coast. Chaddingley is less than ten. Ah, here it is, "The Prime Minister said that recent events have made it necessary to look beyond merely military considerations." What other considerations? Blind hatred? Revenge? Mob rule? Asquith's beginning to crack.

14th May 1915

I do wish Father and Mother would wake up. What I've been dreading is now about to happen. The Prime Minister has outlined his new policy towards "persons of hostile origin".

"There are at this moment 19,000 interned and there are some 40,000 (24,000 men and 16,000 women) at large. We propose that in existing circumstances, all adult males should, for their own safety and that of the community, be segregated and interned, or, if over military age, repatriated. This will not require fresh legislation. We recognise that there will be cases for exceptional treatment. The women and children in suitable cases will be repatriated, but there will, no doubt, be many instances in which justice and humanity will require that they should be allowed to remain." Repatriated!

Mother, you will have to start preparing your case on the grounds of justice and humanity.

Asquith has used that phrase "of hostile origin". Isn't that what Colonel Sawbridge has been saying all along? I have a new respect for him, but he can hardly have anticipated this. And yet look at the words, "This will not require fresh legislation". The Colonel had said too that the range of the Aliens Acts is broad, giving the Government huge discretionary powers. Again he has been proved right.

15th May 1915

Scheusslich! It is fortunate that I was the first to be seeing that piece of paper, on the floor by the front door. It had come through the letterbox.

"Is the Hunwife still here? You won't be much longer. Dorset will soon be cleansed of its alien scum."

I have taken it to the drawing room, sitting down heavily on the sofa. I am staring at it. My hands are shaking. Richard is out visiting. Tristram is somewhere on the farm. Adela is in London. They must protect me. It is me they are after.

Right, if it is to be so, yes, I will be strong. Come for me, you cowards, who cannot even say what you have to say to my face.

There, so; it is in the fire. I will not be telling anyone. Why should I allow my family to suffer this

Dreck? It has gone. It is burnt. I will be strong. Just give me time for my hands to stop shaking.

16th May 1915

The riots are at last starting to die down, but the vitriol is getting worse. This is Robert Blatchford, writing in the *Weekly Dispatch*:

"We are so sick of the Germans, of their treachery, their sneaking, their spying, their lying, their brutality, their arrogance, their loutish conceit, their cold-blooded dastardly cruelty, their murderous bitter hatred, that we never want to see or hear a German again, nor touch anything made by Germans.

"To every decent Briton, a German is an unclean, dangerous and bloody monster. Such is the fact. And the people are right to demand that every Hun should be put behind wire or bars. We loathe them. We feel they pollute the air. We see blood on their hands. We demand that the wretched creatures be removed. The thought that there are 20,000 of them walking our streets is enough to make all London sick."

Even worse than that is this, from Horatio Bottomley in *John Bull*: "I call for a Vendetta – a vendetta against every German in Britain, whether 'naturalised' or not. You cannot naturalise an unnatural beast – a human abortion – a hellish freak. But you *can* exterminate it. And now the time has come." This is incitement to violence of the most extreme kind. It goes on.

"Personally, I am prepared to avenge every German outrage in *kind*. And I should welcome the formation of a National Council of Righteous Retribution – a National Vendetta – pledged to exterminate every German-born man (God forgive the term!) in Britain – and to deport every German-born woman and child."

That is no less than an incitement to genocide.

Now, on top of all this, a new fire has been started and is raging. The Government has published the long-awaited Bryce Report into German atrocities in Belgium. It's a propaganda exercise and a sham. Over 1,200 Belgian refugees were interviewed, hardly a dispassionate group, yet they weren't made to testify under oath, and there's no list of sources or names. The committee members didn't even visit Belgium, and were themselves hardly involved in the process of interviewing.

It's not surprising that some lurid tales have emerged from under this spurious cloak of authenticity, which a credulous public will believe. This is what the Government wants. It's a juicy bone for the baying press to chew on, diverting them temporarily from flying at the Government's throat.

21st May 1915

There was a knock on the door. Tristram had already

left for the farm. I was in my study and Helga was preparing for a morning visit. It was William, sprightly as ever.

'Good morning,' he said, 'I'm glad that I've caught you both. I've had an idea.'

'Then you will find receptive ears,' I replied, for Helga's benefit as much as William's. Her attitude towards him has been cold of late.

'This anti-German hysteria: misplaced in my view. We should be attacking the enemy in the field and on the high seas, not in the home.'

'Quite,' I said.

'Most disagreeable, but there it is,' he continued. 'But its impact may be lessened by speaking out. I'm sure that you will have seen these loyalty letters in *The Times*?'

'Ah yes,' I said quickly, 'prominent people with German connections confirming their loyalty to Great Britain.'

'That's it. I've got one here.' He pulled out a piece of paper, clearly a newspaper cutting. "In view of recent events, we desire to express our unswerving loyalty to the country of our adoption, to which we feel bound not only by gratitude, family ties, and our solemn oath of allegiance, but also by a deep bond of common work and intimate knowledge of the nation's life and character." Now, if you, Helga, were to write some such letter, I am sure...'

The door opened and Tristram entered.

'But surely,' I said, 'they only print letters from well-known people?'

'Mostly,' William replied, 'but I've been thinking

about that. If you were to mention, Helga dear, that you are the mother of the concert pianist Miss Adela Hall, that might do the trick.'

'I will not,' Helga said quietly, but with a menace that parted the air. 'I am not needing to say these things. I will not be,' she turned to Tristram, '*servil*?'

'Obsequious.'

'Obsequious. *Nein, unterwürfig*.'

'Submissive.'

We do not speak German in this house when I am present. To use it at a time like this in front of William, no, I would not have it. I thought desperately how I might retrieve the situation. I did not wish to speak sharply to Helga in front of William and Tristram, but she is not one to back down unless I call for her obedience. I had just decided to start by asking Tristram to leave, when William took matters into his own hands.

'I must return,' he said. 'Clearly my advice has landed on stony ground.'

William is not a man to beat a retreat, hasty or otherwise. But it is no exaggeration to say that he fled the house.

Tristram followed him out. Trying to stay calm, I turned to Helga.

'My dear, you should realise that this is a time for nurturing friendships, not pouring poison onto them. William proffered his advice, and you threw it back into his face.'

'He was calling me an enemy. Is that worse than alien? I do not know.'

'What? He did not. I'm sure…'

'He was saying that we should be fighting the

enemy on the battlefield and the oceans, not the home. I do not think that you can be doubting his meaning: that Germans in this country, in their homes, minding their business, are the enemy. But of course I should be grateful. Colonel Sawbridge has kindly said that he is not going to be fighting me.'

'Helga!'

'I am sorry, Richard; those letters are ridiculous. Do they sound sincere?'

'Sincere or not,' I said sternly, 'and whether writing them does good or not, it is for you to be polite. Why did you have to speak those words with Tristram?'

'*Servil*? *Unterwürfig*? They are not so bad words.'

'But why in German?'

'I could not think of the English. When I am upset, I am turning to my native tongue. I am sorry that they offended you.'

'I thought that I had made you realise the wrong you had done by visiting the farm, singing songs with Reker and conversing with him in German. And now you have snubbed William, again using that language at a time like this. No more!'

In other times, I might admire her strength of character. Now, all I see is stubbornness, and the danger beyond it.

31st May 1915

Harry Neeves, the policeman bobby, came to my door, and my life is not being the same again.

'Mrs Hall, I very much regret to inform you that by Friday 4th June you will be required to register as an Enemy Alien. That's this coming Friday, Ma'am.'

'No. No! Why?'

'Well, Ma'am, it has to do with this being a Prohibited Area and you being, well, forgive me Ma'am, it says here, of German Origin.'

'What do you mean? What am I having to do, register?'

'Well, Ma'am, Sergeant Vickers, he'll explain it all to you at the Station, see. But as I understands it, you'll not be allowed to travel, not without permission. Five miles it is, Ma'am, not more than five miles.'

'So how will I be getting to the police station in Bridport, which is seven miles away?'

He gave me a peculiar look to see if I was joking. I was not. 'Well, Ma'am, now that's an interesting point you've got there. But seeing's how you won't be registering until you gets to the police station, I can't see that it minds you travelling more than five miles before then. To get there, I mean. An interesting point, though. Hm.' He looked at me again, to see if I gave him permission to see the funny side. I did not. 'Anyhow, Sergeant Vickers will explain it all to you. Here is a list of documents he says will you please bring with you, Ma'am.'

4th June 1915

Richard drove me into town in the motor. We were going first to our solicitor, Mr Oakley, who agreed to come with us to the police station.

We produced my birth and marriage certificates. 'But surely,' said Richard, 'my wife achieved complete British nationality when she married me all those years ago.'

'That's right, Sir, said Sergeant Vickers, 'but she is still of Enemy Origin. That is what it says here.'

'He's right, I'm afraid,' said Mr Oakley.

The Sergeant continued, 'Most Enemy Aliens must leave Prohibited Areas within four days. However, in your case, Mrs Hall, the Chief Constable is allowing you to remain on compassionate grounds, in order for you to continue living with your husband, who in turn has his duties to fulfil with his parish. It says here that in this particular case the humanitarian considerations outweigh the military necessity. Those are the words used.'

'So what does my wife have to do?' asked Richard.

'She must report here once a week.'

'Once a week?' I cried.

'Helga, dear, please. In person, Sergeant?'

'In person, Sir.'

'Anything else?'

'Mrs Hall cannot travel more than five miles from her place of residence; not without a special permit.'

I could not resist it. They had started to talk about me as though I was not being there. Summoning all my *Sarkasmus*, I asked, 'And do I have your permission to travel more than five miles each week to come here?'

The Sergeant did not blink. 'I have the necessary permit for you here, Ma'am.'

'Is that all?' asked Richard.

'There are certain things which Mrs Hall may not do, and items which she may not possess. You will have to fill in this form Ma'am, and either sign that you do not possess them, or surrender them on your next visit.'

Mr Oakley asked, 'May I establish that the items on the list, and the prohibited activities, do not apply to Mr Hall? For instance, where there are possessions of Mr Hall, such as his motor car, may I presume that they may remain so?'

'That is correct, Sir. Mr Hall may continue to possess them, but Mrs Hall may not. And, of course, she may not use anything on the prohibited list.'

'Thank you, Sergeant.'

Richard asked, 'Would it be ridiculous of me to ask why my wife is being made to do all these things now, but was not required to before?'

'Not at all, Sir. The Home Office and the War Office have been tightening up on their procedures recently. Several cases have been reopened which were not deemed necessary for action before.'

'And may we know the specific reasons in Mrs Hall's case?' asked Mr Oakley.

'That I may not disclose, Sir. You would have to apply directly to the Chief Constable in writing. But

I regret to inform you that all previous requests of this nature that I have seen have been turned down.'

I have succeeded in holding us together, and persuading Helga to keep a sense of proportion. It is an arduous chore, driving down to Bridport each week, and one that I could do without, but it is no more than that. As for the travel restrictions, we shall see. We may be able to get her a special permit if she wishes to attend one of Adela's concerts in London.

As for the rest of it, what does it matter? She does not drive a motor car; Tristram and I do. She does not fire a gun, and we have not been asked to surrender our twelve-bore. She may not and she does not run a business, or possess a camera, naval map, military chart, boat, motor or pedal bicycle, explosives or signalling apparatus.

We have all had a good laugh, even Helga, about the homing pigeons. Tristram asked whether it would be two or three crimes if she were to drive up to the dovecote in the motor and blow it up.

Mother's got off lightly, though she doesn't know it. Father thinks the authorities have been generous allowing her to stay within a Prohibited Area, but that's not the real issue. The subject of repatriation hasn't gone away. Advisory Committees have been set up, one for internment, and the other for repatriation. Cases are pouring through at dozens a week. I've studied the reasons for exemption carefully. They include pregnant women, those with dependent children, the elderly, and those involved in industry. Women who've lived in England for at least thirty-five years are allowed to stay. Mother's been here for twenty-eight. Only single women who've been in this country for less than five years are deported automatically. All other cases may potentially be brought before the Advisory Committee. Repatriation doesn't necessarily follow. It's early days, but it seems from *The Times* that extenuating circumstances may be taken into account, and many women are allowed to stay.

Be very, very careful, Mother. No more singing of German songs. No more outbursts against the Government or the war. You don't like it, but you must be *servil und unterwürfig*.

10th June 1915

Has Our Lord deserted us? Everything we do in this war becomes a bloody stalemate. After the failure to force the straits of the Dardanelles in March, we launched an invasion of the Gallipoli peninsula to the west. In April, Australian and New Zealand troops poured ashore and dug in, but failed to take the heights above the beaches from the Turks. Several desperate battles were fought hand to hand; and then, in early May, the Turks began a fierce counter-attack which left thousands of dead on both sides.

Now it is stalemate. Massive assaults lead to small gains and huge casualties, just like on the western front. And disease is taking its toll of our troops. No end is in sight, not even the glimmer of a light at the end of the tunnel. Carnage, carnage, for no strategic gain. Can it get any worse?

16th June 1915

Ned is back from the war. It's a heartrending sight. He's lost his left arm and suffers from bouts of shaking. They can be as mild as a continuous shiver or as severe as rapid spasms, when he's unable to speak.

He's asked for his old job back, and of course I've agreed. He was a competent assistant to Jack Hearn, capable of performing all the basics of shepherding and helping generally around the farm. Now he'll be able to tackle few of the tasks which he so easily undertook before, but he's welcome to try to contribute where he can.

I keep thinking of his brother John, who's still out there, and Peter, the stable boy. I remember Peter's reason for joining up. "I don't like to think they'm a-hurting Ned, Sir." They have, Peter, they have. Ned's a-hurting. Once more I find myself close to prayer.

28th June 1915

Poor Ned. He's suffering more than ever, and I believe Hearn when he says that his contributions are worthless.

I haven't heard from Mercury for several weeks. Nothing has appeared in my saddlebag; I don't know why. No one has left the village or gone to war, or even been ill, to my knowledge. It's a mystery.

I came across a sight which moved me to tears. Ned was sitting in a pen with a ewe, his one arm crooked around her neck, howling his eyes out. The old girl wasn't struggling, and didn't seem to mind. It was as though she, in her motherly way, knew of the comfort she could provide. Jack Hearn and placid sheep: they'll be as therapeutic as any medication.

9th July 1915

To her home has Adela come. She will not be going back, she says. There is no comforting her. Her young man, Edgar Simpson, has joined the army.

It was the outcry from the *Lusitania* that did it, she is saying. He wanted to be an official war artist, but they turned him down because he was not selling enough paintings, and they were not liking his style.

I cannot console her. I have never known her not to be practising at the piano. Since she got home, she has not been near it. She is spending most of her time in her room.

The last five years of my life have been wasted. I've been sent back to my childhood. My love and my career have both gone. Why did Edgar have to do it? I'm certain he doesn't believe in the war. He said he was outraged by the *Lusitania*. We all were, but it was disappointment and guilt that made him enlist, not conviction. By his own admission, he'll make a useless soldier.

He was bitter when they turned him down as a war artist. The reason they gave, that he hasn't sold enough paintings, preyed on his sense of failure. And they didn't like his style. Who are they to judge? Conform, conform, we must all conform. At a time when we need to be creative, to break out of the mould, we must all pull together, even if it's in the wrong direction. Tristram made an interesting comment yesterday: when everyone is saying the same thing, everyone is talking and no one is thinking.

My career's in tatters. I didn't play well a month ago, I know it. I didn't need the critics to tell me, but tell me and the world they did. "Superficial", "Perfunctory", "Error-prone"; I deserved them all. I have little feeling for French music, and even my Chopin was erratic, due to nerves. I was on the edge. Now I've fallen in.

I'm back in the cradle of my family, whose love is unquestioning. But it's a reminder that my attempt to step out into adulthood has ended in failure.

11th July 1915

Again, it was I who first was seeing it. Another piece of paper stuffed through the letterbox.

"Dear Frau, You and your fellow Hogs…"

I tore it into tiny pieces before I could read any more.

15th July 1915

A man from the Home Office came to see Helga today. He had a speech impediment, as though his mouth was full of bread. I insisted on being present throughout the interview.

'I understand that you had a German internee working here.'

'On the farm,' I said.

'It has been reported that you had meetings held in the German language with this man.'

'That was only natural. My wife is fluent in German, which was considerably better than Reker's English. So they spoke in the way that was best for both of them.'

'Mrs Hall to answer please, if you don't mind, Sir.'

'True,' snapped Helga, 'all true.'

'I see. It has been reported that you used unpatriotic language in front of a number of witnesses, it says here, in a barn.'

'What is that?' asked Helga. I had barely understood his slurping vowel-sodden drawl. Now he laboriously repeated what he had just said.

'All true,' responded Helga in a dismissive, sing-song voice.

'What do you mean?' I asked, appalled. I could not think what they were referring to.

'I was provoked. They were singing disgusting songs about bayoneted babies and pork. You must remember, Richard. Your men, in your barn, sometime before Christmas. So I told them that they were deserving to be made into mincemeat themselves. My language, it was mild compared with theirs.'

I remembered now. Tristram had brought it to my attention. I had had to be firm with Helga, telling her that she must stop seeing Reker.

'Look here,' I said sternly. 'I recall the incident. My wife had heard the men singing some offensive and obnoxious songs. She remonstrated with them. She should be praised for doing so, not have her actions questioned.'

'I see,' said the official, working his jaw. 'But I do not think that the words,' – he searched through his notes – "you should all go to the trenches and then we will see who is the best butcher" are mild. No, not mild at all.'

'For Heaven's sake, man, can you not grasp a sense of proportion?' Are we to sit here arguing about which is the worse out of "bayoneted babies" and "butchers in the trenches"? Have you got nothing better to do?'

He sat there, munching air. I strode to the door, held it open and glared at him across the room. He rose to his feet hesitantly, seemed about to speak, and then passed wordlessly through, fingers kneading at his hat, a spoffish quibbler who swallowed his consonants. The man was ridiculous, and together we had seen him off.

17th July 1915

The air around Helga is explosive. Only two days later, and we have had another visitor, this time from the War Office. A careworn, gaunt-looking man, retired army I should think, with a grave stoop. At least he had the courtesy to explain why he was here.

'I am sorry to intrude. We are in the process of reviewing security throughout the Prohibited Areas, and this has led to the necessity of interviewing anyone connected with points of risk.'

'Points of risk! We had all this two days ago,' Helga said, before I could stop her. 'It is small wonder that you are not winning the war.'

He looked puzzled and hurt. I sat frozen. It was the word "you" which had jarred. If she had made reference to "us" not winning the war, it would not have sounded so bad, but the "you" made it sound like the voice of the enemy.

'A man from the Home Office,' I explained. 'He came two days ago. He did not get very far.'

'The Home Office, no, that is not surprising. But I am sorry that you have been put to such inconvenience.' He made a note or two on his pad. 'Now, if you do not mind, I have one or two questions to ask Mrs Hall.'

'Questions, questions. Every week I am having to account for myself at the police station like a criminal. Now I must be doing it in my own home.'

'I am sorry, Mrs Hall. The war is making us have to do things which would be intolerable in peacetime. I ask for your indulgence, if you will permit me to continue.'

Helga remained silent. The man could not have been more courteous. His questioning was chiefly concerned with where Helga had been since the outbreak of war, concentrating on key military locations such as the naval dockyard at Portland and the army camp at Ragdown Heath. She had not been to either, although she had been shopping in Weymouth. Had she ever used a camera? No, none of us had. How many times had she visited the coast? Apart from brief visits to Bridport and Lyme Regis, only once, last summer, but no, that was before the war started. Had any persons of an enemy combatant nationality visited her here? Only Reker, and he had been working on the farm. Had she had any contact at all with anyone of enemy nationality? How could she? Was there anything which she felt that she ought to tell him? No, nothing.

I sensed that Helga was becoming more and more agitated towards the end of the questioning and feared an indiscretion. But rather her answers became briefer and more subdued. The man left, once again apologising for the inconvenience.

22nd July 1915

Paul Westaway, who used to be our farm manager, is home on leave. I asked him what it was like at the front.

'Everyone's asking me that question. With you, Tristram, I can speak plainly. Nothing I tell them, I promise, is a lie. I haven't fabricated a single word in answer to their questions. But I'm not telling them the truth. I have to spare the feelings of my parents and those who have husbands and sons fighting in the trenches. I've withheld from them the horrors and the degrading squalor. I don't tell them about the rats and stench and putrefied limbs and bloated bodies. I'm probably right not to mention these things. But I feel the shame of the moral coward who comforts their sensibilities with noble phrases, such as "the glory of sacrifice". To them, we all have to be heroes. No one has died screaming for his mother, or lain cowering in a shell hole, too terrified to go on, or been left strung up on barbed wire until death from thirst or a bloodthirsty sniper claims him.'

I'd suspected as much, but was still shocked. People at home must all be fed soothing words, lest they choke over their teacups and doubt if it's all worthwhile.

6th August 1915

I have let them down, betrayed them like Judas. The corncrakes flew back from the other end of the world in spring, trusting me, relieved no doubt after their long migration to find the fields unchanged. It was an illusion. They nested, thinking that this year would be the same as any other. But now their habitat has become a jungled mess, overgrown and brambled, with thorn saplings tangling and choking in fierce competition with the uncut grass.

Financial necessity and patriotic duty have reduced the tending of these fields to the lowest priority. The nation needs food, nutrition for the population in the fight against the U-boats, and it will not be found in silverweed and corncockle.

The corncrakes rebuke me with their silence. I have not heard one for several weeks. Whether they have gone entirely I do not know. One thing is certain: if they do return next year, and this miserable war is still writhing and churning, it will be in vain, for they will not be able to breed.

Worse things by far are happening in the world, yet I feel a wretchedness that even here there is no relief from the contamination seeping around the globe.

9th August 1915

I pray to God that we succeed this time. A vast new assault is taking place on the Gallipoli peninsula. Simultaneous attacks have been launched by the British at Cape Helles; by the Australians and New Zealanders from Anzac Cove, and from a massive new landing at Suvla Bay. Fighting is fierce, they say.

William says that the aims are to cut the Turks off from land communication with Constantinople and to gain artillery positions which will prevent their army being replenished by sea.

10th August 1915

A summons I have received, a notification that hunted I am getting. At first I was not understanding it. Then, when I understood the words, I did not know what they implied.

What is this Advisory Committee for Repatriation, and what has it to do with me? Advisory Committee: are they there to be helping me, to be giving me advice? Repatriation: what does that mean? Is it because certain people have been questioning my right to be here? That horrible phrase "Of Enemy Origin", is that it? These people are advising me on how to formalise my right to stay here as a married Englishwoman. Is it so?

Richard stared at the letter. '6th September,' he kept repeating. 'Just under four weeks.'

'Please, Father, may I see it?' Tristram read the letter through. When he had finished, he placed a hand gently on my shoulder and told me to be seated. Richard was still motionless, staring ahead.

'I know what this means,' said Tristram. 'You have to appear before the Advisory Committee in London, who will decide whether you will be allowed to remain in this country or be forced to return to Germany.'

I took in a great gasp of breath.

'Do not be afraid, Mother. This Committee has been sitting for several months. The majority of women appearing before it have not been repatriated. Those who have been sent back have either been in the country for a short time, with shallow roots, or else have done something wrong. Neither applies to you. Many people have been allowed to stay on humanitarian grounds. You will be safe, Mother, but we must prepare your case carefully.'

I started sobbing. I was hearing Tristram's words, but I could not be comforted. Richard had said almost nothing. Repatriation! So that is what it is meaning.

I have become a hunted animal. I have heard the call of the horn and the cry of the hounds. They are scenting my blood. Reassurance and sympathy from those around me will not be influencing them. When the moment comes, those whom I love will have to stand back. They are coming for me, only me. 6th September will begin to hurtle towards me, and there will be no place that I can be running to. It is me they are after. Only I must be facing them. I am alone. Oh Richard, Richard, say something.

I knew what it meant. William and Tristram had each discussed the possibility with me several weeks ago. Tristram is right. The majority of cases do not lead to compulsory repatriation. For someone who has been established in Britain for as long as Helga, there has to be some reason, something bad, for repatriation to be enforced. I read the other day in *The Times* that extenuating circumstances include having sons who are fighting in the war. Will that work the other way? Will Tristram's failure to enlist count against Helga? I fear so.

Then there is Adela. This is what terrifies me. What if we are asked to prove her identity? All her adoption papers are in order, but if Helga is a candidate for repatriation, how much more so Adela, who does not have the protection of an English marriage? But far, far worse than any of this is the fact that we have kept the nature of her origin secret. Have I sinned? Undoubtedly I have. I have not told a direct lie, but I have withheld the truth. Dear Lord, forgive me. But have I done the right thing for my family? Adela should have registered as an Alien. For her to have registered, she would have had to be told. Would that have been in her best interest? Or Helga's? Helga's, yes. But how could I have known? What if this Advisory Committee does find out? They will blame Helga. This will be the crime they are looking for, their excuse to deport her, for withholding Adela's true origin, for secretly harbouring an Enemy Alien. The words are too horrible.

But the chances are that they will not find out. So then will I have done the right thing? I have gambled, and I have not yet lost. Gambling is a sin, and I have staked the lives of my wife and daughter.

I must seek understanding, forgiveness and guidance through prayer. Then there is William. No, not William, not without careful thought. First my Saviour. I must pray.

My parents seem to be in a frightful funk. Apparently, Mama has been asked to appear before some tribunal in London in four weeks' time. Strictly, Tristram says, she could be made to leave home and go to Germany, but he says that would be most unlikely. He says it only happens to people who've done something wrong, and the worst thing Mama's done is to perform a duet in German with Josef Reker, and tell the farm workers off when they sang rude songs.

I can't imagine why Mama and Papa are pulling such long faces. I think they're just worried about all the preparation they have to go through to prove that Mama isn't one of the Kaiser's spies.

I'm not worried at all. I've just had a commission

from Lady Lewes to give three recitals in November: one in Chichester, one in Brighton and one in Guildford. My enthusiasm for playing is greater than ever, and I live to perform before an audience again. My Schubert flies and soars, though I won't be able to play him in public. I'm becoming more at ease with Chopin, and won't make the same mistakes again.

Best of all, I've heard from my darling Edgar. He's nearly finished his training, and will soon be going overseas. He doesn't say where; perhaps he's not allowed to or doesn't know. He's got three days' leave in three weeks' time and is coming down here. Mama and Papa will be in London for most of the time, so I expected them to say that Edgar couldn't come. But they've agreed to let him stay for three whole days with just Tristram in the house. Tristram will be my chaperone. Little do they know.

18th August 1915

I have received comfort and guidance through prayer. Our Lord Jesus Christ placed love of one's fellow human beings above the laws of the Pharisees and the Sadducees. I will be judged above all else on what I have done in the interests of Adela.

I know that I have done the right thing for her. I could not have predicted that Helga would become involved in this way. I have prayed that she will be saved, and have thrown the trust of my whole family on the mercy of our Saviour who is Christ the Lord.

Now I have two appointments to attend. The first is with Mr Oakley, our solicitor. And I will speak with William. Now that my moral dilemma has been solved, what I need is down to earth, practical common sense. And no one possesses more of that than the Colonel.

William had a welcome surprise for me. He has been summoned to testify at the hearing on the 6th, so we will have a friend on our side.

'Now, William, for a rather delicate matter. Do you recall that I once told you a few years ago that I was concerned about the closeness of the relationship between Adela and Tristram?'

'I have not forgotten.'

'I soon realised that it was all in my imagination. Nothing ever happened to confirm my fear. Adela has her own young man now, and Tristram has told me that he was in love with a young lady out in the Middle East.'

'None of that surprises me. I remember saying at the time that they just needed exposure to the outside world.'

'Exactly. You may also recall that, in order to seek your advice, I had to disclose certain facts to you by way of background information.'

'I do.' I sensed that he knew what I was about to say.

'Part of that background information was that I revealed, in confidence, that Adela had been born of

German parents, and that we had adopted her as a tiny infant.'

'I had not forgotten, and your confidence has been respected.'

'That I never doubted. Apart from Helga and myself, you are still the only person in this country who knows the circumstances of Adela's birth. And now to the heart of the matter. Adela does not know that she is wholly of German origin, and neither do the authorities. As the law stands, she should have registered as an Enemy Alien. How could she, when she does not know that she is one? But Helga knows and I know. Do you see what this is leading towards?'

'Perfectly, Richard, but I have known this all along. I am aware that Helga has taken great offence, understandably, by my sustained use of the terms "Enemy Alien" and "Of Enemy Origin". I was saddened when this upset her, as well it might, but you must realise, my dear Richard, that my motive was to make you both think of Adela.'

'I had suspected as much,' I replied, 'and do not think that I have not thought long and hard on what you have said. I concluded, rightly or wrongly, that it was best to say nothing on the subject, even to Helga. Forgive me, William, but it was a convenience, no, a mercy, to let Helga think that you were referring to her. Otherwise, she would have been terrified on behalf of Adela, needlessly. I am now worried that it may be revealed at this hearing in London.'

He thought for a moment. 'Not by me, on that you have my word.'

'William, I am so relieved to hear you say that. It has preyed on my mind for so long, and since Helga received that summons, it has been agony.

'There is, however,' said William slowly, 'one line which I will not cross. As a gentleman and man of the cloth, you will understand my position. As an army officer I cannot tell a lie. If asked a direct question, I must answer it directly and in truth, but I will not volunteer information which has been told to me in confidence, unless specifically asked.'

'That is unlikely to happen,' I said. 'Why should they ask you? I am more afraid that Helga might be asked to produce certain papers, and that these might include Adela's birth certificate.'

'And have they requested that?'

'Not so far; only Helga's own, and our marriage certificate.'

'Then it sounds like you have nothing to fear.' He stared me straight in the eye before speaking. 'Richard?'

I looked back at him eagerly, and I am sure my affection showed.

'I am deeply fond of Helga and all your family. I will do all I can to support you by speaking of her good character. It pains me that I have caused her offence recently. Germany has fine and noble traditions and has given much to the world. Nothing will disguise my contempt for what her leaders are doing now. I know that Helga has no sympathy with Germany's behaviour. I therefore have no hesitation in saying that her heritage need not be a source of embarrassment to either of us, nor disagreement.'

As I walked away, I had tears in my eyes. Yet for

all my love of my greatest and truest friend, they were primarily tears of relief.

28th August 1915

William, my dearest, dearest friend. I sit at my desk, my mind and my hand too disconnected to write. Poor Elizabeth, in her home far to the north. What will she do now?

Her husband has been killed leading a charge above Suvla Bay. In that dry, wind-blown grass, a bullet ended a brave young life.

My heart is clenched and cold. What can I write, I, whose profession is the giving of comfort?

Let us hope that he did not die in vain. Too negative. Hope? Is there hope?

So many, so many. Fierce hand to hand fighting, they say. So many sons, so many husbands, so many who only a few years ago were little boys laughing and pulling faces and chasing their hoops with sticks.

William is stoical, rigid. He, who has seen death so often, will not display his emotion, not in front of others. Strength is his calling and his training; it goes to the core of his existence. Poor Mrs Sawbridge. She looks lost, abandoned, her eyes staring from her tiny frame.

It is not important now, yet I know that it is. William's testimony in support of Helga at the Advisory Committee will be lost. I will not attempt to persuade him to attend, not with this burden. We shall just have to do without him. Soldier on. Are those words apt or ridiculous?

Elizabeth, quiet, quiet Elizabeth, bleeding internally, silently, deep within your great beauty. How I have looked up to you, with your grace and poise and your air of attainment. And now, your loss.

Edgar will be here in eleven days' time. I've been so excited, so looking forward to it, determined not to let three days become a long farewell. Now everything's changed. I won't be able to look at him without seeing the soldier and knowing what may happen to him.

I expect Elizabeth will come home. We can be widows together, and comfort each other in our old age, which has come to us in our twenties.

31st August 1915

Colonel Sawbridge with us on the 6th will be going, he is insisting. A brave and honourable man he is being. All our differences have been healed by sorrow. In his great grief, he is still managing to say kind words of encouragement to me about how he could not let anyone be casting doubts upon my character. He was making a little speech about how I should be proud of my Englishness, while never feeling ashamed that I was born part of another great nation.

He is being a man.

6th September 1915

My eyes are brimming with happiness. I laugh uncontrollably, and when I'm not laughing I'm still smiling. I'm as light as a leaf, and will soon be carried away on the breeze. I want to be swept away. I am being swept away.

Edgar has proposed to me. I'm dying to tell Tristram. He only has to look at me to know; perhaps he already does. But we must observe the formalities. First, Edgar must ask Papa for the hand of his daughter in marriage. That's me. Me.

The moment Mother and Father walked into the room, I could tell that it'd gone wrong. Mother, without once lifting her eyes from the floor, peeled off her gloves and flicked them onto a chair. Father stood blinking, as though disappointed to see us.

'Father, what's happened?'

He stared at me wearily. Edgar and Adela were standing close together, motionless.

'Is it… have you lost?'

There was silence. Assuming the worst, I moved closer to Mother, who was staring into the fireplace.

'No,' said Father slowly. 'No.' He looked towards

Mother, then across at Adela. 'Your Mother will not be repatriated. She is safe for now.'

Edgar stepped forward. 'Mr Hall, may I have the honour of asking for the hand of your daughter in marriage?'

Mother looked up sharply. Father let out a great sigh. 'Oh God, no.'

Adela froze and then stepped back. Letting out a sob, she turned towards Edgar, shook her head and fled from the room.

As soon as Helga and I had entered the wood-panelled chamber by Westminster Hall, we had to part. I squeezed her hand, and she was escorted to the front by an usher, accompanied by Mr Oakley. I, as a non-participant, had to sit at the back.

As I was led to my seat, I caught the eye of William, seated near the front. He smiled faintly with a slight inclination of the head. It would not do to appear chummy with a witness and, besides, he was in mourning. To my astonishment, I noticed Nancy from the village sitting next to him. What was she doing there? I do not like that woman, nor do I think that William has any time for her. Had she come all the way to London to gloat?

Mr Oakley had found out beforehand which members of the Committee were sitting today. The hearing was to be chaired by a High Court Judge, Sir Robert Younger, accompanied by a Colonel Lockwood, Mr J J Mooney, and two female members, Maude Lawrence and Meriel Talbot. Just before we were about to start, two men entered the room. I recognised them as our recent visitors, the round-faced man with the speech impediment from the Home Office, and the gaunt ex-army officer from the War Office.

There was a short, sharp tap and a man, presumably the Clerk to the Committee, rose to his feet.

'The case of Mrs Helga Anne Hall.'

Sir Robert Younger - it was clearly he - said, 'We try to keep these hearings as informal and as open as possible. This is not a court of law. There are no barristers present, and no adversarial procedures, although you may cross-examine witnesses if you wish, Mrs Hall, or your solicitor, Mr, er, Oakley, may do so on your behalf. The purpose of the hearing is for the Committee to hear all the evidence presented to it, and to make a formal recommendation to the Home Secretary as to whether you should be repatriated to your country of origin. Do you understand, Mrs Hall?'

'I do.'

The Clerk rose again. 'The birth certificate shows that Mrs Hall was born Helga Anne von Thuren in Münster in Germany, on 26th March 1867. She married Richard Christopher Hall, pastor, on 29th June 1888 at Hannover in Germany. Shortly after, in the same year, Mrs Hall started living with her husband in Godalming, Surrey. It would appear that Mrs Hall has lived continuously in the United Kingdom for a period of twenty-eight years up until the present time, apart from infrequent and brief visits to the country of her birth, Germany.'

Sir Robert asked, 'Is that correct, Mrs Hall?'

'It is.' Helga's voice was clear, firm and respectful. Both Mr Oakley and I had stressed the need to remain calm, speak clearly and not to show resentment of anything said.

The Clerk continued, 'In view of the fact that Mrs Hall has been resident in the United Kingdom for twenty-eight years, and the qualifying period of residence for a woman without English-born dependent children is thirty-five years, there is a *prima facie* case that Mrs Hall should be repatriated.'

'Thank you,' said Sir Robert. 'May we have the police statement, please.'

The statement was read out, giving details of Helga's registration as an Enemy Alien, her regular weekly attendance at Bridport Police Station, and her clean record regarding the obligations placed upon her by the law.

'The first witness, please.'

The bread chewer from the Home Office stood up.

'I visited Mrs Hall on 15th July of this year and interviewed her with her husband present. Before that, I had spoken to a number of workers on Mr Hall's farm. I had been told of Mrs Hall's fraternisation with a German,' he looked at his notes, 'one Josef Reker. A number of witnesses interviewed by me stated that Mrs Hall showed great favour towards this man Reker, laughing and singing songs in German with him. They always conversed in German, it was said, which made the workers nervous as to what they might be saying. I formed the impression that several of the workers had been frightened by this liaison. On one occasion it was alleged that they were intimidated by Mrs Hall, who screamed at them,' again he referred to his notes, 'telling them that they ought to be in the trenches, where they would learn to be butchered.'

Helga started whispering in Mr Oakley's ear.

'When I interviewed Mrs Hall, with her husband present, she did not deny this, but was sullen and uncooperative. I was escorted to the door by Mr Hall and forced to leave before I had concluded my interview.'

He sat down. After further consultation with Helga, Mr Oakley rose to his feet. 'Is it correct, Mr Saler, that Mrs Hall's remonstration with the farm workers followed their singing of abusive songs, which included the words "Hogs eating pork" and "Bayoneted babies"?'

The man rose to his feet again. 'I did hear that said, Sir.'

'And is it not also true that you were not in fact forced to leave Mr and Mrs Hall's home, but merely shown the door? Were you physically accosted in any way?'

'No, Sir, but I felt intimidated by Mr Hall.'

'But not by Mrs Hall?'

'Well, Sir, she was abusive.'

'Yet you said just now that she agreed with what you had said to her. What did she say, then, that was abusive?'

'About butchery in the trenches.'

'Did she say that to you?'

'No, to the farm workers.'

'But that was not aimed at you. Mrs Hall was not suggesting that you should be butchered?'

'No, Sir.'

Sir Robert intervened. 'I do not think that this is getting us anywhere. We have heard your evidence regarding this man Reker and certain incidents on the farm. Thank you, Mr Saler, that will be all. Next witness, please.'

The man from the War Office stood up. 'I visited Mrs Hall's home at Chaddingley on 17th July. I asked her about her movements since the outbreak of war, with a particular emphasis on the possibility of her having visited military or naval establishments. I was satisfied that she had not done so.'

'Could you be certain of this?' The question came from one of the other members of the Committee; I suspected it was Colonel Lockwood.

'One can never be certain, Sir, but there was nothing incriminating in Mrs Hall's replies to my questions.'

'Was she cooperative, then?'

'Certainly, although she did make one remark which shocked me at the start. She appeared angry that she had been interviewed twice in as many days, the other time being by the gentleman you have just heard. She said, "It is small wonder that you are not winning the war."'

There was a brief buzz around the chamber.

'Thank you.' Sir Robert looked at Mr Oakley, who shook his head.

'Next witness, please.'

To my amazement, Nancy stood up.

'You are Nancy Mabel Hopkins, from the village of Chaddingley?'

'I am.'

'Please continue.'

'I have known Mrs Hall for several years. She has never hid her loyalty to Germany. She got us singing German carols in the Christmas service, and she and that Josef Reker were as thick as thieves. We never knew what they were plotting. Her son has refused to serve his country, even though he's able-bodied. If you want my opinion, he's a pacifist. And her daughter's been caught playing German music in London and been kept off the stage for it. When I came to deliver some recruitment leaflets from Lord Kitchener, doing my bit for the war effort, Mrs Hall snatched them off me and slammed the door in my face. Then she came uninvited to the house of a poor woman whose husband had just been killed in the war, who we were trying to comfort, and started abusing us.' She suddenly dried up.

Helga and Mr Oakley conferred briefly. To my alarm, Helga stood up. 'Mrs Hopkins, is it so that the Christmas carol you referred to was *"Stille Nacht"*, a traditional Austrian hymn from the early nineteenth century, known in England as *Silent Night*? And would you agree that you were not in fact being asked to sing it in any language other than English?'

Nancy gaped at her. 'Your daughter!' she shouted. 'Yes, her, she sang it in that language.'

'The first verse, yes, only the first verse in German. One single verse, just once a year, and last Christmas not even that. Once the war was starting, we were not singing the carol at all, even in English.'

Nancy gave a sulky grimace towards the bench and fell silent.

'And is it so, Mrs Hopkins, that the incident you were referring to when I was entering the house of a recently widowed woman, Patricia Swain, was in fact a séance being conducted by you? And that before I was saying anything, you referred to me as the Devil?'

'You didn't knock!'

'The door was ajar. I was entering. I was on a mission on behalf of the Church to comfort the bereaved.' Helga turned to the bench. 'That is all I am asking this lady.'

My darling wife, you did everything that we asked of you. You stayed calm, you spoke clearly, you stuck to the facts, and you did not lose your temper when provoked. You made Nancy look ridiculous. Well done.

Nancy sat with her eyes bulging, flouncing her shoulders.

'Next witness, please.'

William stood up. 'I have known Helga Hall and her husband Richard for sixteen years since 1899. I have known Mrs Hall to be a patriotic, loyal and diligent servant of the neighbourhood in which she lives. She has worked tirelessly and selflessly for the Church and for her husband's parishioners, spending great parts of her time in charitable works, visiting the sick and bereaved, training the Church choir, and organising events for the benefit of the whole community. In my opinion, she is a thoroughly decent and honest Englishwoman. I have heard her in front of others condemn both Germany and the Kaiser as being responsible for this war. As far as I am concerned, her patriotism is not in question.'

Sir Robert glanced across at Helga and Mr Oakley, but it was clear that they were not going to challenge any of that. Oh William, thank you. That was a noble speech. The balance has now shifted wholly in our favour.

'If there are no more witnesses…yes, Mr Mooney?'

'Colonel Sawbridge, you clearly hold Mrs Hall in great esteem. We have heard from another witness earlier that Mrs Hall's son is of serviceable age and in good health. Do you not think it remarkable that he has not answered his country's call?'

William, who had remained standing, replied, 'Mrs Hall's son Tristram manages the family farm. I am aware of the sacrifice which many young men are making… have made,' he paused, then steadied himself, 'in the service of their country in the front line. Food production is, however, important for the war effort.'

He did not like saying that, I could tell. He does not approve of Tristram's failure to enlist; and he was clearly thinking of Elizabeth's husband as he spoke.

'The previous witness also mentioned a daughter,' said Mr Mooney. 'She referred to her being barred from the stage for having played German music.'

'An exaggeration,' William replied. 'The daughter, whose name is Adela, was booed by a handful of people for playing piano pieces by well-known German composers. Fighting broke out in the hall, and the recital had to be halted for reasons of public safety.'

'What do we know about these two children?' asked one of the lady members of the Committee.

Helga rose to her feet. 'Tristram is aged twenty-five and Adela twenty-one.'

Mr Mooney asked, 'This son, it has been said that he is a farm manager. On his father's farm? Has he always done that? Did he go to university?'

'No. Since leaving school he has either been working in farming or as an historical research assistant as part of a team working in the Middle East.'

'Turkey?'

'I am not thinking so. I have heard him mention Egypt, Palestine and Mesopotamia, but not Turkey.'

'Where is this team based?'

I held my breath. This was dangerous territory.

'It is not existing any more. It was disbanded at the start of the war.'

'Even so, where was it based?'

'In Berlin,' Helga replied calmly, but she must have known that this did not sound good.

'A German team?'

'They were mainly Germans. There was, I am understanding, a Frenchman. And Tristram.'

'Your son is fluent in German?'

'Yes, fluent.'

'And your daughter?'

'Also fluent.'

'Where were your children born, Mrs Hall?'

'Tristram was born in Guildford. Adela was born in Zwickau in Germany.'

There were murmurs around the room. I felt a cold chill grip me.

'You say that Adela is younger than Tristram, and that he was born in Guildford. Forgive me for expressing it so, Mrs Hall, but if your daughter is only twenty-one, she was clearly not born out of wedlock. Yet it was said earlier that you have only visited Germany infrequently and briefly since your wedding. Were you visiting Germany when you gave birth to your daughter?'

Helga paused only briefly. 'I was visiting Zwickau to collect her. She is adopted.'

'Adopted? You mean from German parents? Both of them?'

'Yes.'

Sir Robert intervened. 'Have we seen her adoption papers?'

The Clerk looked through his file and replied that adoption papers had not been submitted.

'And her birth certificate?'

Again the answer was negative.

Mr Mooney continued, 'Has this fact been reported to the police?'

'No, Sir,' replied Helga.

'So you have kept the matter secret?'

'No one knows, except for my husband and my mother in Germany, and of course her parents, if they are still alive.'

'The girl does not know herself?'

'We have always thought that it would be better not to be telling her.'

Sir Robert intervened again. 'Is there anyone else in this room who knew of this?'

There was a long silence. Slowly William climbed to his feet. 'I knew,' he said.

Helga spun round to stare at him, a look of incredulous horror on her face.

'I was told in confidence several years ago.'

'Who told you?'

'Mr Hall.'

'Do you know why he told you?'

For the first time, William's demeanour crumpled. He turned round and looked helplessly at me. Then he faced the front, slowly regaining his soldier's height.

'Mr Hall approached me about five years ago. He was concerned about a family matter which was troubling him at the time.'

'What was that?'

It was a long time before William replied. 'Mr Hall told me that he was concerned that the relationship between his two children was becoming rather too close. He felt that in order for me to understand the background to the problem, I needed to know that one of them had been adopted.'

'You used the phrase "too close". What precisely do you mean by that?'

'Mr Hall indicated that their behaviour toward one another might be more intimate than is normal between siblings.'

'Do you mean that their relationship might have been of a sexual nature?'

There were gasps in the room.

'I believe that that was what Mr Hall was referring to. However, I also believe and understand that Mr Hall now considers that there are in fact no grounds for his suspicion, nor have there ever been.'

Sir Robert said, 'I think that we are now getting rather far from the issue in hand. However,' he added sternly, 'two matters of great importance have been raised. The first is that Adela Hall, by reason of her birth, is of Enemy Origin. And the second is that you, Mrs Hall, and your husband, have been guilty of failing to disclose your daughter's true legal status as an Enemy Alien. Have you anything to say?'

Helga stood up. Remarkably, her voice remained steady. 'We were doing what was best for our child. We were taking the decision long ago, long before the war, that we would not be telling Adela, for her own sake. Without knowing the circumstances of her birth, she could not have been registering as an Enemy Alien. Our first duty was to our daughter. Had we been thinking that she might be posing a security risk to our country in any way, we would have acted differently. This was not arising. She is as loyal to her naturalised country as I am. Indeed, she is believing that Britain is her native country. How could she be thinking otherwise?'

Perfect, I thought. Factual, succinct, but playing the humanitarian card, and showing that she has been a good mother. As Helga turned to sit down, she cast a look of utter loathing at Nancy. And, as her eyes passed over William, I did not think that it lessened.

'Thank you, Mrs Hall. Are there any more questions from the members of the Committee? No? Is there anything final which you would like to say,

Mrs Hall? No, then will the room please be cleared so that the Committee may deliberate.'

Helga was shaking. She had held firm, she had stuck to the brief we had given her, and she had exceeded it magnificently. Now, with the pressure off, she cracked. Nancy was nowhere to be seen. William hovered uncomfortably some distance away. Helga was quietly sobbing.

After ten minutes or so, we were called back. Helga dabbed at her eyes with a handkerchief and struggled to regain her poise.

'Mrs Hall,' said Sir Robert, 'The duty of this Committee is to make clear cut recommendations to the Home Secretary, one way or the other. We have agreed unanimously that your case is exceptional. In your favour is the length of your marriage, your family ties and your service to your husband's parish and to your community. We have heard no conclusive evidence to make us doubt your patriotism. On the other hand, you and your husband have committed a serious offence by knowingly harbouring an Enemy Alien in the person of your daughter. Moreover, your son has had prolonged and close contact with Germans.

'We are therefore taking the following steps. We are informing the police that your daughter is an Enemy Alien, and that you have not disclosed the fact. It is for them to decide how to proceed regarding those matters. And we are recommending to the Home Secretary that the question of your repatriation be held in abeyance for ten weeks from today while further investigations are carried out, to include the history and activities of both your son and your adopted daughter. This hearing is now closed.'

Our train, it is flying through the countryside, carrying us home. I am too tired to be upset any more. Richard is sleeping, though every now and then he jerks awake.

I realise now that Colonel Sawbridge is not to blame. He did not want to be speaking about Adela or Tristram, or the two of them together. It was forced out of him by an unfortunate sequence of questions. He is somewhere on the train, but not in our compartment. Richard says that he took the decision to be travelling independently of us. I am respecting that.

Yes, I can forgive Colonel Sawbridge, and now I must try to forgive Richard. We swore that we would never be telling anyone about Adela's birth, and he broke that vow. Worse, he did so without informing me. Now we have to tell the poor girl all at once that we have deceived her; that we are fighting the country of her parents and her birth, and that she must be bearing the odious title of Enemy Alien, with the humiliation of having to register each week. The shock, it will be terrible.

At least she need not be knowing about that absurd fantasy of Richard's about his imagined relationship between her and Tristram. What was he thinking? A filthy stew he has cooked. I am not wanting to think about it.

That Nancy woman is unspeakable. But at least she was making a fool of herself, not me. She will be thinking twice before making false accusations again.

Ten weeks. I have ten weeks. Then what? I cannot believe that they will be deporting me. They were describing me as patriotic and selflessly hard-working for the Church and the community. And my long marriage, living in England, it is in my favour. What did Sir Robert say that was counting against me? Not disclosing the truth about Adela, yes, yes, but that is Richard's crime as much as mine. What was the other thing? I am so tired. It was Tristram. His failure to enlist. No, I am not thinking that Sir Robert was mentioning that in his summing up. No, it was Tristram's having had prolonged contact with Germans. He was meaning his work in the Middle East. But that was not my fault. And anyhow, the moment war broke out, Tristram came straight home to England.

Now I am happier for myself, but worried about Adela. She is not having the protection of marriage, nor is she committed to serving the Church and community. But she is innocent of anything which might be incriminating her.

'Richard?'

His eyes jump open. 'What? What is it? Oh. Yes, my dear?'

'I am very tired. Can we leave telling Adela until the morning?'

'Yes, I am sure, my dear. We should speak to her then.'

'Thank you.'

He seems weary and defeated. He is half falling asleep again. He is looking both guilty and innocent.

Soon we will be there, and I shall have to be waking him again. Perhaps he will be feeling better in the morning.

What I was completely forgetting was that Edgar Simpson was staying with us. We enter the house, needing peace and sleep, only wanting to tell Adela and Tristram that I was not about to be repatriated. Edgar is there, standing with Adela. I am only just starting to come to terms with him being there when he steps forward and asks Richard if he might be marrying Adela. Richard, confused and exhausted, his mind on other things, says, 'Oh God, no.'

Now Adela has left the room in tears.

It is all right, my darling. There, it is all right. We have been comforting her and explaining that we are delighted that she should be engaged to Edgar. They are having our full blessing. Richard has apologised for his first reaction, explaining that he was worn out and distracted. She has been reassured. Little does she know that we must be comforting her again tomorrow. I have told her that it is all right. But it is not all right.

7th September 1915

What else could Richard and I be doing? We could hardly be telling her while her Edgar was still here, especially as he was about to be leaving. Her emotions were in a brittle state, understandably so, caught between distress at his departure for the front, and joy that they will be marrying when he is next on leave. But our timing, waiting until we got home after seeing him off at the station, must have seemed like another act of deception. She has reproached us for it, not just with words, but with agonised looks, starting with disbelief, then realisation, and finally mistrust and anger.

Her obsession is, 'Do I have a brother? Edgar will be fighting my brother.' We do not know whether she is having a brother. We are not thinking that she had one before we adopted her. And a sister? We are not thinking so, but we cannot be sure, and anything might have happened since then.

'Why didn't you tell me?'

'We thought that it would be best for you.'

Tears, not of release, but a howling rejection of our compassion. She is not minding that she is an Enemy Alien. What does it matter what people are calling her? She can only think of her Edgar, fighting her brothers. Yes, they have become plural now.

When she is calmer, I will be reminding her that Zwickau was the home of Robert Schumann. She will like that, but for now she would only be seeing it as a trivial sop. She can feel only the pain, though other miseries may not have sunk in yet: that her parents chose to give her up, that she must be going to Bridport to register once a week, and that soon she will be having to face the Advisory Committee, with uncertain outcome. My darling girl, why should you have to be bearing all this when nothing wrong you have done?

It's five and a half hours since I said goodbye to Edgar. How brave we were, clinging to our tenuous happiness, holding the dread at bay. After he'd gone, and his train had slid round the bend, I was ashamed to be returning to comfort and safety, and the normality of life. Normality! What can be normal now? How can they do this to me? If they didn't want to tell me before, why now? Oh, they had their story, about how they had to tell the truth at Mama's trial. So what is it about a judge that makes them want to tell him, but not me? Hasn't every child a right to know who its parents are? All this time, I could have been visiting them in Zwickau, my real parents. Are they thinking about me? Do they ever? Or is it easier for them to pretend that I don't exist? They must, they must. Mother, Father, I'm thinking about you now. Across the sea, across the land, through the trenches and beyond, can you hear me, can you see me? Your tiny little baby, you knew me, I was part of you, I still am; think of me now. You're out there. I haven't lost you; I've lost Edgar, and Edgar is coming towards you. Oh God, no. Don't stop. Go on through, past the war and on to Zwickau. You're my ambassador, leading the way.

There's a knock at my door.

'Who is it?'

'Me.'

Tristram enters, his face full of concern. He sits down beside me on the bed. He doesn't speak. No words of comfort; so unlike him. Does this mean he shares my pain? Suddenly another horror breaks over me. It's taken all this time to dawn. He's not my brother. A choking feeling grips me. He isn't my brother, he isn't my fiancé, he is what? A strange man who's seen me naked. I realise my whole past life has been shattered. Oh Edgar, don't die, you're all I have, my new life, my strange new life, my future.

A fit of sobbing overwhelms me. Tristram puts his arm gently around my shoulders. I fling myself away and shiver my head into my pillow. He follows me down, placing his arm across me.

'No, Tristram, no; not now.' His is the life I've lost. I feel the pressure on the bed lighten. I hear every step as he walks to the door. He closes it quietly. I am alone again.

Never before in our whole lives has she refused my comfort and support. For me, it's heartrending. For her, it's devastating. She's lost so much, and what she's gained in its place she can't have: something strange and remote.

It's strange for me too. It's as though she died a few hours ago and has returned as a phantom. She's no longer my sister, even though she remains Adela. It's we who have changed; Mother, Father, me: we'll never be the same to her. Only Edgar remains from her life this morning, and he's mutated from a benign and sensitive artist into a blundering killer of men. I pray, yes I pray, that he'll return safely to her.

When she's ready to receive me, I'll go to her and

support her all I can. My next task after that will be to make her understand why Mother and Father have done what they've done, and ask her to forgive them. It'll take her some time to realise how much they're suffering too.

8th September 1915

Adela in her nightie hangs in the doorway, eyes puffed and hair confused. She didn't appear for any of our meals today. Mother and Father haven't seen her. As far as I know, this is the first time she's left her room.

I put down my book and walk to the sofa. I pat a cushion, inviting her to join me. Seated, she stares ahead. Mother went to bed early. Father followed soon after.

'He said I had my father's eyes.'

'Who did?'

'Mr Dixon, in the shop, when I was a child. I've never forgotten it.'

I'm no longer sure whether I ought to touch her. When I cup her chin, she turns a bleak and hesitant face towards me.

'You have. And his kindness, and his wisdom.'

'It's just coincidence.' She looks away, as though ashamed of her face.

'You're wrong. Your eyes are not exactly the same colour as Father's, but you've got a manner of looking which is completely his. You're the person you are because of the way you've been brought up, and it's a good way. If you reject your parents, you demean yourself. And because I love you, and admire you, if you run yourself down, you're also rejecting me.'

After a while, she rests her head against my shoulder. 'Tristram.'

I hope my breathing may soothe her.

'It was such a cruel thing to do.'

I stroke her forehead.

'The way they abandoned me. How could anyone give away a baby? What can they be like, to have done a thing like that?'

'They were decent people, poor, but honest.'

'How can you know?'

'I know they were poor.'

'You're making it up. You're trying to make it easy for me, but you can't possibly know, any more than I do.'

'Father told me.'

She jerks up and flings an outraged face into mine. 'So you did know. They told you, but not me, because you're a boy.'

'No, Adela. I only found out yesterday. I never knew you'd been adopted, any more than you did. They did what was best for you, both of them. They knew you were facing a wretched childhood, so they found you a loving home.'

She subsides. Her breathing slows to the ticking of the carriage clock.

'Will you come to Zwickau after the war? Will you help me find them?'

'Of course I will.'

'Promise me you'll never fight them.'

'I promise.' Stupidly, I add, 'There may be conscription one day.'

She grits her teeth. 'Promise. Whatever happens, promise.'

I've been wondering what I'll do if they make joining up compulsory. For now, I take the easy route. 'I promise.'

The chiming of the clock makes her jump. She looks round, shivering. She picks up a cushion, clutching it for comfort.

'Can you imagine what it's like to be at war with your own parents and brothers?'

'I can, I think.'

'So why did they have to tell me now, in the middle of this war?' She's becoming defiant again.

'You mustn't blame Mother and Father for that. They didn't want to.'

She looks at me pityingly. There's disdain in that look, and I feel I've lost her again.

'Mother was under oath. She had no alternative. When she was asked where you were born, she had to tell them. Once the Advisory Committee found out you'd been born in Zwickau, when Mother and Father were living in England, nothing could stop it coming out that you'd been adopted.'

For several seconds she stares at me. Then she crumples, lost in her own thoughts.

'You're entitled to be angry. Take your time. When you're ready, I hope you'll see that it isn't Mother and Father who've abused you, but the people responsible for this war. You've become a victim of it, like so many others.'

'I don't deserve them.'

I struggle to take in what she's just said.

'I've been so cruel.' She presses her fingers against her eyes.

'It's all right.'

'It isn't all right.' Her voice is muffled. 'I'm horrible.'

'No, you're not.' I regret letting out a sigh. 'Just human.' Weariness is catching up with me. With it comes despair, if I were to let it.

For a long time, we sit in silence. I ought to be building on what she's just said, comforting her, encouraging her to expand on her forgiveness. But I'm burdened by fear of the future, and what we haven't yet discussed. I wonder if she's taken in the prospect of her own repatriation. I doubt it, and I'm not going to load her with further worries until she's ready.

I see a movement in the doorway. Father has appeared. Adela notices me looking up. Seeing him, she starts. I fear she's going to scream. He moves towards her, looking benevolent and dependable in his dressing gown. She shrinks back into her cushion. Seeing this, he stops.

She uncurls herself and stands up, facing him. Each looks as though they might say something, but Adela has her back to me, so I can't see her expression. I hold my breath. Father is smiling. Now, Adela, now. Tell him you forgive him.

She dips past him and disappears through the doorway. He doesn't turn round to watch her go, but stands there pained, as though imagining her retreating figure. When all is silent, he turns his eyes on me, and I realise he may think it's my fault, that I've been setting her against him.

'She loves you, Father.' Was it a cowardly desire to defuse the situation that made me say that, or conviction that she really has started to come round? 'Please give her time.'

'Thank you, Tristram.' His voice is strained, but not unkind. 'You look tired.'

I feel it. 'How is Mother?'

'She is exhausted. We expected this reaction from Adela, but it has still upset her.' He walks up to me. He leans down and puts a hand on my shoulder. 'Try to get some sleep.' He nods, and in that gesture I know that he understands my pain, too. We abandon the room to its ticking clock and climb the stairs together.

In my room, I recall her words. "I don't deserve them. I've been so cruel." Surely that was a start? But I can't be sure, and now it seems that I never heard them.

9th September 1915

Her place, it has been laid for breakfast, but still she does not come. Richard and I are late enough, as it is. Tristram finished his meal and left for the farm long ago.

Sunlight is slanting through the window, brightening the yellow tablecloth. It ought to be a cheerful scene.

Richard is pretending to eat, but I know that he has no appetite. Neither do I. Adela slips into her seat before I realise that she has come down. I cannot stop myself from letting out a little cry, and I cannot prevent it from sounding like a protest, but it is not; it is surprise and delight.

When she was young, she used to stare at the table in front of her whenever there was tension. Now her gaze is fixed on the milk jug.

Richard quickly says Grace, even though it is not customary at breakfast. I am thinking that I see Adela's lips move to say 'Amen', but I cannot be sure. Still she is not moving or looking at either of us.

With eyes still lowered, she gets up and walks round to me. She leans down and kisses me on the cheek, as she has always done first thing in the morning. As she returns to her place, my sobs I cannot help.

'Helga, my dearest.'

Adela's face is full of compassion. 'I love you both so much.'

I hear Richard gasp.

'Papa, what can I do to let you know how much I love you?'

He turns the full generosity of his gaze onto her. 'You have just done all that you need. Oh my girl.' Now he too is silently crying. As for me, I am trying with a ferocious effort to control my breathing.

'There, Mama, don't cry.' And I don't. She smiles at me, and now her hands start to move freely across the table, pouring, slicing, spreading, and then she is eating.

'What would you like to do today, Adela?' Richard's eyes are damp, and he sounds bunged and rheumy.

'I think, Papa, that I should like to be with you and Mama. How about a walk? If you can both spare the time?'

'Well, I've work to do on my address to the Mothers' Union. Which can be postponed. Then I have to visit the Sproat family, which is hours away. And I thought I might read some texts by Thomas Aquinas. But I will not, not today. Helga?'

'It is a beautiful day. A clear day. Let us make it clear; so I say, we will walk.'

'Can we go to the seaside?' Adela is like a child again.

'The sea.' Richard is beaming. 'We will take the motor.'

Tut, tut, what a naughty Enemy Alien I am. We are walking arm in arm along Chesil Beach, all three of us, Adela between Richard and me. Our footsteps are crunching on the shingle. It is only now that I am realising that I have broken my curfew. I have travelled more than five miles in a Prohibited Area without permission. Richard must have forgotten too. I smile to myself, but I am saying nothing. It is all too ridiculous, and I will not have those evil men spoil this day for any of us.

I tried again with Patricia Swain today. Still she does not come to Church.

'I manages all right. I just gets on with my life. I don't ask for nothing from nobody. Stanley meant everything to me, but now he's gone; there's the end to it. He did what his country asked, and the Church, and he paid the price. Isn't that what you wanted?'

'Good Heavens, no. I mean, you're not suggesting that I think that his death was a good thing? I know that there are some people who talk of a glorious sacrifice. The Church approves of those who are prepared to lay down their lives for others, but it does not glorify death.'

'Doesn't it? I thought it did, that bit about sending his only son who gave his life for our sins. I thought that Jesus chose to die. Maybe I got it wrong. Well, anyhow, it makes no difference to Stanley now.'

'Is there nothing I can do?'

'You could send your son.'

The words cut like a knife. They were probably a reflection of her resentment that her Stanley had been killed while others stayed at home. But it felt like a statement of revenge. She had lost her Stanley. Satisfaction would only come if Tristram were sacrificed too.

I crept away like a poltroon cringing down an alleyway. Fear is the enemy of charity, but the friend of cowardice. I have made no impression on her, given no comfort. She, on the other hand, has wounded me with guilt.

20th September 1915

I've received a very strange letter, weirder than anything Mercury ever wrote.

"Dear Master Tristram,

Here's we thinking you're a coward, shirking your duty. You're a dark horse, make no mistake. We all thought you was as chaste as the driven snow, we did. All the skirts you ever saw were your mother's and your sister's. Now we know the truth. Your sister ain't your sister and haven't you been taking advantage of it. Why go all the way to France to face the Germans when you've got one here you can put your face into and more besides. We've got to hand it to you, Master Tristram. We've never known all this time that you was laying her. Make sure you don't get her in the family way. We don't want no more Germans round here.

Yours truly,

Your Admirers (for having fooled us so long)"

What an offensive accusation, that just because Adela isn't my sister, I must have been laying her, to use the same vulgar term.

Mother said Nancy Hopkins was at the Advisory Committee hearing. She hasn't waited long to spread the gossip about Adela being adopted. But it still seems strange that this person – I don't think it's Nancy, the writing's too masculine – should come to such a fanciful conclusion. By the way, it isn't Mercury either. I haven't heard from him for months. I kept some of his stuff, and a comparison of the handwriting shows that this is different.

It's remarkable how this war seems to spur so many people to do and say such spiteful things, especially those who aren't doing the fighting. If only they would show as much creative imagination when it comes to religion and politics, we wouldn't be locked together in the mud, with slaughter the only prospect.

26th September 1915

Mama asked me if she might hear some of Liszt's *Années de Pèlerinage*. She likes listening to me play in the evenings after dinner and, it being Sunday, Papa hadn't retired to his study, so I was able to perform with all my family present; my foster family.

I'd decided to play some of the *Petrarch Sonnets,* and had just begun the second when there was a crash to my right which seemed to be repeated on my left. I cowered over the piano, Papa roared, 'What?' and Mama started whimpering. Tristram was already up and out of the house like lightning.

A rock had smashed through the window and passed close behind me. Since it was still just light, the curtains hadn't been drawn, so its course was only impeded by the glass, which meant not at all. It ended up by the bookcase at the far side, having gouged out a notch in the floorboards.

I surveyed the damage. I discovered a small cut on the side of my neck. When I touched it, I felt not just blood, but acute pain. Clearly some glass was still there. Worse, the piano had been scratched in three places by flying shards.

By the time Tristram returned, Mama had removed the glass from my neck with tweezers. It hurt. And then I started shaking and sobbing. All the terrors of the past fortnight returned. Why are they doing this? What have I done? Why do they hate us? I want to get away, to get away from here. Oh Edgar, why can't you come back? I'm frightened for you.

Tristram is in a cold anger. He says they chose the window farthest from the doors so that by the time he'd got out and round the house, whoever it was had raced out of the garden and down any number of ways between the farm buildings. Because it's been so dry recently, there were no footmarks.

Papa led us in some prayers, but his voice was faltering. Then we set ourselves to clearing up the debris. I've got over the shock and the pain, but it's the feeling of violation which I can't get rid of. It's difficult to forget there are people out there who really loathe us. All the time, I know we're being watched, and any moment they may strike again. It's a horrible feeling.

6th October 1915

There was a knock at the door. Mama was in the kitchen.

'Can you see who it is, Adela? I am stirring a herbal ointment concoction for Mrs Roper's knee.'

I went to the door and found a uniformed policeman standing outside, and behind him another man in plain clothes. I didn't recognise them.

'Good morning, Miss,' asked the man in blue. 'Is Mrs Hall at home?'

'Yes, but she's busy with some medicament.'

'Who is it, dear?'

'The police, asking for you, Mama.'

'Tell them to be waiting two minutes, while I turn this off.'

After more like five minutes, Mama came to the door.

'Mrs Hall? Good morning, Madam. We are here to conduct a search of your property. Here is our warrant.'

Mama took the piece of paper, stared at it and handed it back. 'What is this for?'

'I cannot say, Madam, but our instructions are to search your possessions. Only yours, Madam.'

'But my husband, he is not here.'

'I am afraid that makes no difference, Madam.'

'Adela, take these men on a tour of the house. No, I will do so. Your father has gone visiting, where I do not know. Go and get Tristram, as quickly as you can. He will be out on the farm somewhere. I will be staying here.'

She seemed remarkably calm. Perhaps this was just preparation for the Advisory Committee hearing next month. But they didn't seem interested in searching through my things, only Mama's, they said.

I changed my shoes, seized a coat and ran down to the farm. I went to the dairy, and luckily Edwin Blamey was there. He said he'd go and get Tristram. He wasn't sure where he was, but he'd make sure he found him.

Now for Father. I must find Colonel Sawbridge. I ran back up past the house and on into the village, past the post office, down Back Lane, left again and up the Sawbridges' drive. Elizabeth answered the door. She said her father had gone to the village not fifteen minutes earlier.

Back I ran, panting now. I had a stitch, but kept going, determined to ignore the pain. I burst into the post office, the bell clanging angrily over the door. No, they hadn't seen him. Into the ironmonger's: yes, there he was at the counter.

'Colonel Sawbridge, Colonel Sawbridge!'

'Adela, what is it, my dear, what is the matter?'

I explained what was happening. He took over.

'Right, back to my house. I'll get the motor. I'll drop you at Chaddingley and then I'll go and look for your father. You don't know where he went, you say? Don't worry, I will find him. You stay and look after your mother.'

Back at the house, I found Mama weeping in the drawing room. I heard voices coming from the parlour. The men were searching Mama's desk, while Tristram stood over them, watching their every movement. He came over to me and said quietly, 'See to Mother. I'll keep watch here.'

'It is so humiliating. My personal possessions, fingered by dirty and accusing hands.'

'I expect it's just a routine, Mama, something they need to do to prepare for your next hearing.'

'I am not thinking so. Why were they not making an appointment? What is this search warrant? They are hunting me. They are baying on my trail.' The last words were barely audible as she broke out sobbing again.

Another twenty minutes or so passed. Then the two men came into the drawing room, followed by Tristram.

'Mrs Hall, are these letters yours?'

Mama glanced at them and looked quickly away. 'Yes.'

'I regret, Madam, that we must take them away for further examination. Will you please sign here. You will have them returned to you in due course.'

'What is this?' Mama asked suspiciously.

Tristram stepped forward and looked at the piece of paper on the clipboard. 'It lists the documents which they're taking, Mother. It is best if you sign.'

Mama took the pen and held it high over the document. For one moment I thought she was going to bring it stabbing down through the paper. She signed with a great sigh and looked away.

'Thank you, Mrs Hall. We are grateful for your co-operation, and yours, Mr Hall. Good day to you all.' He nodded at me. 'Miss.'

Ten minutes later, Papa burst into the room.

When William appeared at the cottage, I could tell that something was wrong. He excused himself to Mrs Bunby and said quietly to me, 'The police are at Chaddingley with a search warrant. Adela is there with Helga. I think you'd better go there straight away.'

By the time I got there, they had already left. I only found out later that it had taken William over an hour to track me down.

Adela looked shocked, Helga much worse, white and shaking. I went straight up to her. 'What is it, my dearest? Have they gone?'

'They took my letters.'

'Letters? What letters?'

'My correspondence.'

'To whom? From whom?'

'Gerd, and my mother.'

'You have been corresponding with Gerd? But I thought that the Censor would not allow it?'

'Father, may I have a word?'

'Just a minute, Tristram. What letters? When were they written?'

'Months ago, a year ago, I don't know.'

'But I do not understand. A year ago? Was that after the war had started?'

'I wrote two letters then. They were returned by the Censor.'

'Father, I can explain.'

'Well, then?' I said sharply.

'The letters which the police have just taken aren't the problem. They include correspondence from before the war and the two letters which Mother sent in 1914, which had been returned by the Censor. I'm afraid they must have other letters in their possession.'

'Why should they? What other letters?'

'May I, please, Mother?'

'Go on, if you must,' Helga said bitterly.

'Father, you should know that Mother has written a letter to Germany…'

'Four,' said Helga.

'Four letters to Germany. They were sent via America, via an address which I gave her.'

'You what?'

'Yes, Father. I too have been writing, to my ex-colleagues, the historians I worked with in the Middle East. One of them had written to me early in the year, saying that it was possible for us to correspond while avoiding the Censor. He gave me an address in Cleveland, in the United States of America. From there the letters get forwarded via a number of countries and eventually to Germany.'

'You fool. You utter fool.'

'Hear me, Father, please. When I received the letter from my friend Fritz, it was just after Mother had received a message from Great Uncle Gerd via the Red Cross, telling her that Grandmother had a malignant tumour on her leg which would eventually kill her.'

There was a sob from Helga. 'Go on,' I said.

'Mother was upset that only brief messages could be sent via the Red Cross. She wanted to send a proper letter, full of love and sympathy. So she wrote one...'

'Two. I wrote two letters: one to Gerd and one to my mother.'

'Two letters. She sealed them in her own envelope. I also wrote two letters, one to Fritz and the other to his sister, Ingrid, and sealed them in another envelope. Our two envelopes were sent together to Cleveland.'

'And you are telling me that they have been intercepted?' I was shaking with rage.

'No, Father, I think that is most unlikely. They were written a long time ago, seven months. The police have been searching Mother's possessions, not mine. Mother, how many times have you written again?'

'Once,' wailed Helga. 'I was not receiving any reply, so I was writing again. Still I have not heard. *Mein Gott!*

Tristram put a hand on her shoulder. 'There. When did you last write?'

'In May,' Helga snivelled. 'I was writing a long one to Gerd with all the news, and a loving, comforting letter to my mother. But they have not replied!'

'And you?' I asked, my eyes blazing at Tristram.

'I have written twice more, separately from Mother,

the last time a month ago. I too have never had a reply, not since that original letter from Fritz in February, and that was written by him some time before that.'

'What is going on here? You seem to think that you can take these appalling risks without caring a thought for what they might do to the rest of your family.' I struggled to stay calm. 'So what do you think has happened, then?'

'A letter must have been intercepted. It must have been one to or from Mother, or they would have searched me.'

Adela leaned forward. I had almost forgotten that she was there. 'Please may I ask something?'

We all looked at her. 'Tristram, you wrote to Ingrid, didn't you?'

Tristram nodded.

'Papa, I don't think you should be too hard on either Tristram or Mama. Tristram was in love, deeply in love; he told me at the start of the war. I know what it must have been like for him to be parted from Ingrid. When he received that letter from Fritz, giving him an opportunity to write to her, he knew how desperate Mama was to communicate properly with Great Uncle Gerd and Grandmama. Can you blame him for helping her do so?'

This moved me deeply. I was impressed even more by what she said next. 'Haven't we all been guilty of keeping secrets from each other? Tristram and Mama with their letters; you Papa and Mama with the truth about my birth. It's no good us blaming one another and dwelling on our past mistakes. I couldn't hope to be part of a more loving family. We must help each other now.'

I felt a great tide of emotion sweep over me. This was Adela's final affirmation that she loved us and had forgiven us. I took a deep breath and found my voice. 'Let us pray. Almighty Father, who has seen the error of our ways, whose only Son taught us the virtues of humility and forgiveness, help us to see the truth of what Adela has said. We pray that you may protect and preserve us in this hour of peril. Show us the path of love, and forgive us our sins.' Tristram said, 'Amen' as loudly as any of us.

'Come here, my boy.' We fell on each others' shoulders, weeping.

All four of us ended up in tears: Father, Mother, Adela, even me. Adela has been magnificent. She brought us together and modestly said that we'd all been guilty of keeping secrets from each other, when in fact she herself is entirely blameless.

This is serious, and Father knows it. I'm not sure what Mother thinks. She seems to oscillate between calm practicality, defiance and emotional collapse. I should never have gone along with Fritz's idea, but I was driven by a force too strong to resist. Now Mother has two frightening prospects: she has committed a crime which technically could lead to imprisonment, and it's just such a crime which is likely to tip the balance in favour of her being repatriated. Hopefully, the contents of the intercepted letter will reveal the innocence of the writer's motives, but if they're looking for an excuse to deport her, they'll now have one.

I must decide what to do myself. If I were to tell the police that I sent the letters, and that I'd duped Mother into thinking that what she was doing was perfectly legal, that may exonerate her in the eyes of both the police and the Advisory Committee. But first we need to find out which letters they were, and what they contained.

There, I've done it. I've destroyed the letter from Fritz. It's become ashes in the grate. I stared and stared at the beautiful words, "Ingrid misses you so badly. She loves you, Tristram, and I am happy and proud to say it. She wanted to send her own letter with this one, but I would not allow her. If anything should go wrong, I would not want her to be in trouble. I hope that you agree with this. But she sends a message, which must be personal between you. Remember the cedar at Latakia, she says, and do not forget. Never forget. You will know what she means."

These words are burned into my mind forever. Now, if they come to search me, and if they bother to use the services of a German translator, all they'll learn is the history of Babylon. They may incriminate Nebuchadnezzar, but they won't be able to inculpate me.

7th October 1915

Having an hour to spare, and needing a break from writing my sermon, I decided to walk around the nearer parts of the farm. Passing the door of the storeroom, I heard laughter and some words which made me stop and listen.

'Oi've called the new Suffolk ram Master Tristram. He'll soon be running with the Miss Adelas.'

'Aw, that's a good 'un, namin' 'e after the boss, and his sister who ain't his sister.'

That sounded like Bill Munday's voice.

'You heard what Nancy was saying. It all did come out in Court, true as God's word.'

I stood rooted to the ground.

'You'm not believing that, be ye?'

'Sure, 'tis true. 'Tis raddle to a ewe's arse he's tupped her by now.'

'Now there's an ideal. Tie a bag of raddle to his tumper, and you'll soon see where he's been.'

This was talk of a most repugnant nature. That they should mention raddle, strapped to the underside of a ram, to show when mating's occurred… it was disgusting.

'Ah, she'll soon be bagged up. That'll mean the lambs'll be cross-bred, she being German an' all.'

I burst into the room. Bill Munday and Josh – I should have recognised the voice – looked up, and then shrank back.

'Get out, you filthy boys.'

Josh scuttled past me through the door. I took a

swipe at Munday as he passed, catching him between the shoulder blades.

I returned to the house, shaking. I should have known that Nancy would repeat everything that she heard in London, and that she would embellish it, ignoring the fact that William had said there had been no unnatural relationship between Tristram and Adela.

I wonder if Tristram has heard any of this. We did not tell him every part of William's evidence, of course, nor Adela. Should I confide in him now? Better that he hears it from me than from Josh with his bawdy smut. On the other hand, if Tristram had been listening just now, he would have dismissed it as groundless fantasy, which it is. Better leave it at that.

I am sickened and frightened. I cannot stop shaking. I am disgusted for Adela, and terrified for Helga. I am unmanned by the fact that there is little I can do to help either. This year has become a nightmare. My hands shake, and I am losing weight. I can barely eat my meals. As for sleep, like my God it eludes me. And when at last it comes, I am soon awake again. And so the cycle continues, all through the night.

I am trying to write my sermon for Sunday. Normally I would have finished it by now. It is not that I cannot write the words; I cannot even get to the words, because I am bereft of ideas. All I can think of is jokes, and they are feeble and wildly inappropriate. Strange that I should think like that, when humour is the last thing on my mind, and these are not times for laughter.

It is no good, I can compose nothing of my sermon. I shall have to resume my walk, although I only have twenty minutes left. Then I must haul myself off to Mrs Roper, whose seven or is it eight children will set up a rattle in my fragile brain. I should pray, but I do not even feel like that. Some air may help. Richard, Richard, move yourself.

8th October 1915

I cannot recall the events of today with clarity, nor am I confident of their sequence. I know that I returned from a tiresome visit to Mrs Hawkes to find Adela alone in the house.

'Papa! Papa! They have taken Mama away.'

'Who, my darling? When?'

'The police, to Bridport. Tristram went with them. He told me to stay until you came back.' She started crying.

By the time I got outside, I was shaking so much that I had difficulty cranking the motor. Is there no end to all this? There may be, and it is too horrible to contemplate.

I walked into the police station, hardly knowing where I was, and was led to a small room. Tristram was sitting with Helga and a young man I did not know. A police officer whom I recognised was standing beside the table. Mr Oakley had gone away for the day, Tristram told me, so the stranger at the table was one of his assistants. Yes, that was it.

As Tristram had suspected, a letter has been intercepted, but it was not one written by Helga. It was a reply from her Uncle Gerd. The police were claiming that it contained incriminating evidence against Helga. Tristram held the original letter, while the policeman read out a version which had been translated into English. Or did he? No, I think that it may have been the young man later. One thing is certain. I have a transcript before me now, so I know exactly what it says.

"My Dear Helga,

Thank you for your beautiful letter with all its news. But first I must tell you something wonderful from here. Freda has come to Leipzig and is now living with me. She is much better, and she sends her heartfelt love. The growth on the leg is increasing more slowly than expected. She has been given pills which make her sleepy, but she feels only a little pain. When I read your letter to her, a slow smile spread across her face and she said, 'My darling girl' over and over again.

Thank you for the cuttings from the newspaper and for the picture postcard. It is interesting to see how much it is the same in England as in Germany. The soldiers here also look so young. It is good to see them smiling from their beds in the hospital, but I wonder whether they smile all the time. I think not. It must be very distressing for that boy on your farm who has lost his mind. Yes, the casualties of war mean more than dead bodies and missing limbs. Let us hope that it will end soon and that we may be reunited in a little time.

It is such wonderful news that Adela has been performing in public. I always knew, even from far away, that she had a great musicianship. I submit my greetings to her, to Tristram and to your husband, whose work and yours must be a great comfort to the bereaved and those whose loved ones are absent.

I only go out a little, for short walks in the park, and to the shops. I have not been to a concert for a long time.

I pray that we may all be together again. With great love from Freda and me,

Your affectionate uncle,

Gerd"

I am not sure what happened next, or where. Words were exchanged, but I was not listening. One moment we were at the police station, the next in the solicitors' office, but Mr Oakley was not there. I cannot recall the order in which events occurred. All I know is that I was shaking uncontrollably, and that Tristram was comforting me.

'Helga Anne Hall, you are charged with three offences under the Defence of the Realm Act 1914…' I had been only half listening, but now I jerked awake. 'One, of disclosing to a citizen of an enemy combatant nation information regarding war casualties beyond that which appears in the official casualty list. Two, of expressing an opinion as to the condition and morale of His Majesty's armed forces.

Three, of sending photographs to a citizen of an enemy combatant nation.'

Helga sat with a face of stone. Tristram seemed anxious to leave. I was surprised that Mr Oakley's assistant, who had said virtually nothing, did not want to contest any of this.

'Look here, this is ridiculous. I am sure that everything my wife has said can easily be explained.' And then I broke down. I could not continue. In her hour of need, I could not defend my beloved wife.

'Mr Hall,' said the young assistant. 'There is nothing to be gained by staying here. I will explain the situation to you if you will kindly come to my office with your wife and son.' He said something to the policeman, and I realised that he was completing the formalities of Helga's weekly registration as an enemy alien, this being a Friday. How utterly ridiculous, how absurdly petty.

When we were all seated in his office, he explained, 'In the absence of Mrs Hall's own letter, the evidence is all circumstantial. Although we cannot recommend that your wife should tell anything other than the truth, she acted correctly by refusing to disclose to the police the contents of her own letter which, in any case, it would be hard for her to recall in its precise words.'

'Refusing? The police?' I could not understand what was being said. 'But that will not look good,' I blurted out, my whole body shaking. '"Mrs Hall, when questioned, you refused to disclose what was in your letter." That will not sound good. No good at all.'

'The right to remain silent is enshrined in English Law, Sir.'

'How can I know?' I said, throwing up my hands in despair. 'What did you write, Helga?'

'Father,' said Tristram, 'I think that we should reflect on the situation, before we commit ourselves too deeply. Mr Oakley will be here on Monday.'

'Yes, yes, all right, Monday, then. When will she appear in Court?' I assumed that it would be weeks or even months away.

'During the course of next week,' replied the assistant.

'What? How can she prepare her case? What about her defence? What about the time for preparation?'

'All cases are heard in a Magistrate's Court first, Sir. The majority, in fact nearly all such cases, are decided then and there. The only cases which go on to the County Court, apart from appeals, are those where the charge is particularly serious, and then only if the defendant pleads Not Guilty.'

'Not Guilty? Of course she will plead Not Guilty. She *is* Not Guilty,' I roared. I had completely lost my temper with this inadequate young man.

Tristram moved in front of me. 'Father,' he said sternly, 'none of us should be hasty in our judgement. Let's wait until Mr Oakley can assess the position? Yes?'

I was led away, as though I were the criminal. I have still not prepared my sermon for Sunday. My God, my God, why hast Thou forsaken me?

10th October 1915

They are laughing at me in the pulpit, I know they are. Oh Richard, look at their faces, gaping up at you. They are mocking you, Parson, can't you tell? Do they think that a German has climbed up into the pulpit with a string of sausages over his shoulder?

I'm very worried about Papa. He's lost even more weight. Just now, he stumbled over words which he's uttered a thousand times. He said, 'Almighty God, unto whom all hearts be open, all desires known, and from whom all secrets are hid.' And then, 'Have mercy upon the whole Church, and so rule the heart of thy chosen servant Edward.' King George has been on the throne for the past five years. Just now he looked as though he was struggling to climb the stairs to the pulpit. Mrs Clucas's youngest little girl has started crying, poor thing.

'I have not chosen a text for today. I thought that it would be decent for all of us if we did not have one. We should remember our brave soldiers at the front, and on the high seas, sailors. There is a great new battle going on; where is it, now? In Belgium. Ypres, no, I do not think so. Loos, that is the place. Loos. Some of our men, your men, will be there, I expect, in the battle. What is wrong with that?'

This is terrible. Papa is rambling. It seems as though he hasn't prepared a sermon. Normally that would present no problem, as he can be quite brilliant when improvising, but not today. Mrs Clucas's youngest girl has started bawling.

'We must all die in the battle of life, as Our Lord Jesus taught us, who died for our sins. We salute those who have chosen, have shown us the way.'

The congregation is becoming restless. There are mutterings from the back, and uncomfortable glances. It's hard to hear what Papa's saying. He keeps pausing in his speech and staring at the child.

'But patience is a virtue, and impetuosity a sin. If we cannot stay the course, what then? We will all, we will all... Stop that child!'

Papa has roared so loudly that it seems his words are still hanging in the air. Now there is silence, broken only by the whimpering of the little girl. Slowly Mrs Clucas rises to her feet and leaves, carrying the baby, with the other two clutching at her sides. Her shoes clack slowly up the aisle. I look back at Papa. His shoulders are shaking. Some more members of the congregation get up and leave.

'Forgive me for that outburst; I am not feeling myself.' He climbs down from the pulpit, a bleak and haggard look on his face. Most of the congregation remains. Back before the altar, Papa pulls himself upright. 'Let us continue the service.' We launch into *Oh God our Help in Ages Past*, and the singing is strong. Papa is recovering and singing too. There are just the final responses and the Blessing to come. Please, Papa, keep going. There, another mistake, 'The Lord be with me' instead of 'The Lord be with you'.

Now it's over. Most of the congregation, many more than usual, have made off quickly through the lych-gate into the lane. A few loyal ones have remained. Molly Hearn, bless her for her humanity, clasps Papa by the hands and looks into his eyes, smiling. Eden Goode does the same.

Papa unexpectedly says, 'I am not a German.' These words seem so strange. No one can have been thinking even vaguely along those lines. Jack Hearn says soothingly, 'Of course you're not, Squarson.' And then everyone melts away.

I cannot stop weeping. *'And as Peter was beneath in the palace, there cometh one of the maids of the high priest. And when she saw Peter warming himself, she looked upon him, and said: And thou also was with Jesus of Nazareth. But he denied, saying, I know not, neither understand I what thou sayest. And he went out into the porch, and the cock crew. And a maid saw him again, and began to say to them that stood by, this is one of them. And he denied it again. And a little after, they that stood by said again to Peter, Surely thou art one of them: for thou art a Galilean, and thy speech agreeth thereto. But he began to curse and swear, saying, I know not this man of whom ye speak. And the second time the cock crew. And Peter called to mind the word that Jesus said unto him, Before the cock crow twice, thou shalt deny me thrice. And when he thought thereon, he wept.'* As I am weeping.

I am hearing Richard weeping in his study. I never go in there unless he is inviting me. But this terrible sound, and the memory from an hour ago, is giving me determination. I knock and open the door. 'My darling?'

He is looking at me with swollen lips, his eyes bloodshot, mucus collecting above his mouth. His eyes are horrible.

'I have denied you. Like St Peter, I have abandoned you, my love, my only love.' He hunches, still looking up at me out of the tops of his eyes.

I step towards him. Just as I put my hand out to him, he brings his head crashing down violently onto the desk. I kneel down by his side and fold my arms around him. We sob and shake together, sharing his pain.

11th October 1915

Father's in no condition to take a decision regarding his own affairs, let alone someone else's, yet today

Mother's fate is in his hands. He's insisted that he and he alone should accompany her to see Mr Oakley.

I hope Mr Oakley will decide for them. There's no direct evidence of what Mother wrote in her letter, only implications from Great Uncle Gerd's. On Friday, Father was insistent that she should plead Not Guilty. He may be right, but this morning, so far as he was expressing any opinion coherently, he seemed to be saying the opposite. She must tell the truth, he kept saying. When I started asking Mother to recall what she'd written in her letter, he snapped at me that I mustn't distress her. If she's to stay silent before the magistrates, as she did in front of the police, then it doesn't matter what she may have written. But if she decides to justify herself, then she'd better start preparing the ground now. And Father had better stop trying to prevent her.

I tried to get them to think of the effect which Mother's plea would have on her second appearance before the Advisory Committee on 15th November. Father wouldn't consider it. In his confused state, he doesn't seem to have begun to understand the significance. If Mother pleads Not Guilty, and then is found Guilty, the result may be fatal. She'll receive punishment from the magistrates and may still be deported. If she pleads Not Guilty and the magistrates find her Not Guilty, then she will have a strong hand to play before the Advisory Committee, and may escape repatriation. If she pleads Guilty, the process with the Court will be over quickly but, whatever her sentence, she'll have gained a criminal record on something directly pertinent to the case for her repatriation. But I couldn't get Father to see that. He can't see beyond Wednesday. Let's hope Mr Oakley can.

They've left for Bridport. I should have gone with them. I should be there.

They're back. Mother will appear in Court the day after tomorrow. She'll plead Guilty. She'll admit her guilt needlessly. They may fine her; they may imprison her. Father says her sentence will be light compared with a Not Guilty plea. That is muddled thinking. It assumes that her case is weak, but far, far more important is the fact that she'll have obtained a criminal record, and one that will - not might, will - count against her at the Advisory Committee hearing next month.

Unable to trust myself, I fled the house. I should have been stronger. I should have declared Father unfit to handle the situation and forced myself into a position of command. Even now it may not be too late. I'll go and see Mr Oakley myself tomorrow and find out what he advised.

12th October 1915

I've seen Mr Oakley. He received me politely and described the processes he'd been through with Father. He was too loyal to say who took the final decision, but he did hint that Mother was very reluctant to stay silent in Court, yet didn't want to disclose what she might have written in the letter.

So there it is: a joint decision, and a wrong one. I was going to go with them tomorrow. Now I'll stay here. I know what I must do. There is a lot I need to arrange on the farm in a very short space of time.

13th October 1915

They're back from Court. Mother's been fined £80, a huge sum, but at least it isn't a gaol sentence. Father seems delighted. It's the first time I've seen him smile for ages. He shouldn't be pleased. With just over a month to go before the Advisory Committee hearing, Mother's now got her criminal record. She herself is very quiet. Gone are the tears, alternating with defiance. Seeing what can only be described as Father's nervous breakdown, it's easy to forget the strain which she herself has been under since early summer. That seems a long time ago, when her nightmare started, following the sinking of the *Lusitania*. And then there's Adela. Mother's been so much at the centre of recent troubles that it's easy to forget how dangerously the threat of repatriation hangs over Adela too.

They all need me. I'll be no use to Mother if she is repatriated, nor to Adela. There's a chance, and it's a faint one, that I can save them. It's a chance I must take.

I've completed the outline of my plan. I'm

working on a full winter schedule for the farm. I've decided to recommend to Father that Franco Malpiero be made farm manager. His own work with horses has been scaled right down. As a leader of men he's barely adequate, and his knowledge of what goes on outside his own area of responsibility is sketchy. But when I look at the alternatives, he's the best choice.

After that, I'll begin to write my farewell notes. I'd almost decided to confide in Adela, but I don't want to upset her sooner than necessary. And I couldn't bear to leave her in tears, mine or hers. My greatest worry is Father. If Mother's repatriated, he'll go to pieces. If Adela goes too, it'll be better for Mother, but worse for Father. But if there's any possibility that I can save Mother, and Adela as well, I must try to do so. It's better this way.

In four days' time, early in the morning, I'll leave before dawn, my farewell messages in place. Duty calls. I've been sucked in. I'm off to join the war, so that when Mother and Adela stand before the Advisory Committee, they can say with pride that they have a son and a brother - well, sort of brother - who's willing to sacrifice himself for God, King and Country, and who recognises that we must all pull together. Some small-minded sergeant will bellow into my face, and I'll envy him that he cannot see the irony.

17th October 1915

It's a glorious Autumn day. The larches pour down the valley in a golden river. I'm taking a couple of hours off to be by myself here for one last time. I've walked down past Coney Piece and am sitting on my favourite log by Reed Pond. A picture of this old willow tree hangs in Father's study. It was painted long before I was born, and shows that it'd been snapped almost in two by some storm goodness knows how long before that. But it lived on. When I was a boy, I used to climb up its trunk to find beetles and spiders in the splintered wood. It's still alive, decades since its crown smashed to the ground. This log I'm sitting on is the remains of one of its branches.

When I die, my influence will be tiny, but it will be more than nothing. I'll be the new wall around the rickyard, the way Wester Ground is drained, *Schrebergarten*, the discovery of a tiny baby's tomb at Hilla, Walter's book, the rehabilitation of Ned with the help of motherly ewes. Don't dismiss these as trivial. I seek no other memorial, for it's futile to reach the end of one's days and wish that one could have done differently. If my bones shall do no more than nourish a tree, that alone is positive. The rottenness of Man is that he would deny such contributions, and would rather imagine that his "soul" went somewhere else; not to give, not to nurture, but to be received by the cosseted bosom of a cocooning god. "Better to give than to receive," they preach, yet all they dream of is the cultivation of their own souls. "Lord save me, Lord protect me, Lord deliver me." Deliver thyself, thou hypocrite.

A nine-year-old girl in Ireland claims she saw a tear rolling down the face of a statue of the Virgin Mary. Now others say they've seen it too. Thousands have flocked to the site. Views in the Catholic Church range from the sceptical to the cautious. The Church of England is scornful. But why? It is surely an act of faith. The Authorities question it, and in doing so use logic and common sense to doubt that it really happened. But faith, we're told, is beyond reason. They're hypocrites, these bossy archbishops. Their outrage stems from the fact that the miracle didn't originate from them; was not part of the official scriptures, nor part of their controlling plan.

Are these gullible people capable of asking themselves why these statues only shed a tiny bit of water or move a fraction of an inch? Do they wonder why the Virgin Mary doesn't arise from her plinth and walk down the aisle in full view of the congregation, bestowing blessings to left and right? Even the "miraculous" healings at Lourdes are within the statistical realms of chance. Have any of the tens of thousands of pilgrims who flock there asked why it is that all the claimed miracles are of illnesses from which the sufferers may occasionally be expected to recover in any case? What if a pilgrim suddenly regrew an amputated arm or leg? Do they ever wonder why this has never happened?

A planet made of blancmange, a tear rolling down a statue's face, a burning bush, the resurrection, feeding the five thousand: what's the difference? Believing in any of them requires an act of faith. They're all without foundation. They're all unlikely, and they all fly in the face of common sense. The only thing which distinguishes them is that some are blessed by Authority and some are not. And Authority, as we know from history, is rarely a force for truth or goodness. Hence this war. Authority depends upon people submitting to it. Hence this war. And now I too must submit. I must go to war to feed the authority of Authority. I must be another log in its consuming fire, so that it may burn the stronger and consume the more. It is my duty. When a stupid man is doing something he's ashamed of, wrote George Bernard Shaw, he always declares that it's his duty.

A cloud's shadow passes down the valley like a rippling cloak. But the sun's still warm on my arms.

If you say that faith is above or beyond reason, then you must ask yourself where it comes from. Most people say it comes from God. But in that case, and if there's only one God, there should only be one faith. Most religions claim that theirs is the One True Faith. Yet one all-powerful God would not allow such a conflicting divergence.

Epicurus put it so succinctly two thousand years ago. "Is God willing to prevent evil, but not able? Then he is not omnipotent. Is he able, but not willing? Then he is malevolent. Is God both able and willing? Then why is there evil in the world? Is he neither willing nor able? Then he shouldn't be called God." Ah, says the modern theologian, he is both willing and able, but gives us access to evil so that we may be tested. What a ridiculous notion. How could he set a test without informing his pupils that they're to be tested? It's like this war. Our leaders don't know why they're fighting – sorry, why they're making others do the fighting for them – so they use vague phrases like "for King and Country". This is an opiate to dumb the reason. The King didn't declare war. He's fighting his cousin, so why pretend that we're fighting for him? It's the same old problem: minds stuck in a traditional past through lack of free thinking. The mantras of the past are the best known, so the easiest to repeat. People think they're the safest. I say they're the deadliest.

So where does faith come from? Man! A Mohammedan is a Mohammedan because his parents and teachers taught him so; a Jew a Jew and a Christian a Christian for the same reason. This is demonstrably true, otherwise the statistics for inherited belief wouldn't be so stark. John Stuart Mill wrote, "He who lets the world choose his plan of life for him has no need of any other faculty than that of the ape-like one of imitation." And here I am, off tomorrow to join the other apes.

That reason is superior to faith is demonstrated to us by the hour. If I stand at the side of the road, reason will tell me when to cross, whereas faith will lead me under the wheels of the tram. Reason evolves inexorably. Sometimes, down the ages, our understanding of science has been wrong, and we've entered a cul-de-sac. But we've retraced our steps, and rediscovered the correct path. So why should anyone wish to put faith above reason? I don't know, but I can say why they shouldn't do so. There are many, many faiths in the world. Down the ages there have been many more. Gods have been created, worshipped, discredited and forgotten. As someone once said, if you have rejected all these gods of history, why can't you reject just one more?

Here's a modern parable. A hundred years ago, a lobster pot came adrift from its moorings. There was no longer a marker to show the fishermen where it was. After a few weeks, the lobsters and other fish in the pot died of starvation. Other lobsters and fish, attracted by the stink of rotting flesh, entered the pot to eat the corpses. Then they too died. The cycle was repeated. For week after week, month after month, year after year, decade after decade, fish and lobsters died without benefit to themselves, their fellow creatures or to man. Religion is like that. War is like that: a self-destructive cycle of following the ones who've gone before.

The Church has made a huge mistake by actively supporting the war. It's been lured into promoting the glorification of sacrifice and death by holding up the example of Jesus, forgetting that Tommy Atkins is not the Son of God. Tommy Atkins's widow, grieving at home and not having the privileges of the Virgin Mary and Mary Magdalene, and seeing no miracle of resurrection, feels betrayed, as well she might.

The late afternoon sun is flashing off the newly ploughed furrows of Turner's Piece, as if from a shattered mirror. Rooks are strutting between the serrated shards. In just a few hours from now, they'll be flying home to roost in the trees below Wester Ground. By the time they return in the morning, I'll have gone.

So, Tristram, it has come to this. Everything that

I've fought against, I must now fight for. All the lies which I've tried to expose, I must now proclaim. Forward, for God, King and Country. I'm off to meet the Germans again. I'll have to learn to hate them. How can I? Hate is a form of faith. In order to attain it, one has to assume a state of partial blindness, which in turn necessitates the ditching of one's reason. In order to kill, I must hate. In order to hate, I must expunge from my mind the possibility that Germans are in any way decent people. All the shades of grey, all the mitigating circumstances, all thoughts that I might be facing an innocent, terrified boy with a doting mother at home, or perhaps a man with a wife and children huddled in poverty and fear, must be driven out and replaced with a certain conviction that the person whom I must kill is a filthy Hun who bayonets babies and puts them into his sausages.

Not that the Germans do much to further their cause. They have just executed a British nurse called Edith Cavell. They say she was spying. Perhaps she was, but it's still a foolish thing to do. The propaganda gain for the Allies is enormous. Then there was the *Lusitania* medal. After the *Lusitania* was sunk, the Germans minted a special medallion to celebrate the event. What the British did next showed that they understood the situation far better than the Germans. Three hundred thousand replicas were minted in Britain with the message that people shouldn't destroy them, but should pass them on to their friends with the words "Another triumph for our Glorious Navy".

Now they've started to bomb London from their

Zeppelins. Their objective is to strike terror into the civilian population. But as with the naval bombardments of Scarborough, Hartlepool and Whitby, all the evidence points to a uniting of people and a strengthening of their resolve.

The afternoon is too beautiful for these dark thoughts, but what remains? It's time to think of my loved ones. Goodbye, Father. From you I learned to love people, to respect them and to enjoy their company. You taught me how to manage men, and to always think of their well-being. I inherited your love of the land, and nature, the joys of riding a horse, and such masculine pleasures as how to play a fish and navigate from a map. I loved your laughter and your jokes, though I could never think them up or tell them as well as you. When I'm far away, I'll recall your smell of leather and oil and soap, which will comfort me when my heart starts to fail. You're disappointed in me, I know you are, because I've turned my back on what you regarded as your greatest gift to me. At least be comforted that we achieved a mutual respect for each other's position, and know that I will be both surprised and delighted if I'm woken after death to find you were right all along.

Mother, I'm doing this for you, to absolve you from your crimes. And what were those crimes? Of being honest and true to yourself; of refusing to write a sycophantic letter to *The Times* proffering a false loyalty which you didn't feel it right to parade through crocodile tears; of providing comfort and a reminder of home to Josef Reker when others were putting urine and blood in his lunchbox; of writing words of love to your dying mother, and of sharing common problems with your Uncle Gerd, showing peace and understanding across the warring divide. I hope you'll use my departure to good effect on 15th November, and that you'll think kindly of your son, who loves you with all his heart.

Goodbye Elizabeth, my fascinating neighbour. With your stillness and your grace, you were the first to reveal to me the attraction of your sex. Fate might have brought us together for life. Would it have been better for either of us? I'll never forget those exchanges with your eyes, which left so many words unspoken between us. How do you view me now? I'll never know.

Walter, Fritz, I salute you. There were no barriers between us, only admiration and love of our work and each other. We were not the ones who stretched the barbed wire across, and at least we were able to hold on to our mutual respect from a distance. Now I must cross the line and march towards you, with mistrust in my eyes and aggression in my step. My brothers, I'm the one to commit the first act of betrayal. Forgive me, and try to understand my reasons.

Ingrid, our time was so brief, so precious, so lost. We were young, we were in love; I still am, my darling, but we were like flowers in the moonlight, petals floating down a river. You should have been my life. It didn't last, it couldn't last, the world of men is too cruel for that. Yes, I will remember the cedar at Latakia, I will always remember you there and what you gave me, when we were shown what bliss seemed to be available to us and which was not to be. Was that my life which flashed before me then? I pray, oh how I pray, that life will provide more than that for you, even if it's with someone else. That is my gift to you, Ingrid, proof of my love. Do not forget, but do not dwell on it forever.

Farewell, Adela, you who were once my sister. I realise now that our friendship has been the backbone of my life. Mother once told me that you worshipped me. Now I know that it is I who worship you. When I leave tomorrow, my heart will cry out that I should walk to the side of your bed and kiss you on the cheek. Dragging my feet away from you will be the hardest act of my life. I'm breaking my promise, Adela, that I would never fight your family. I long to talk to you, to tell you why I'm doing this, to make absolutely certain that you understand my reasons and accept that I do it out of love. Instead, you will see my cowardly note and wonder why I denied you one last opportunity to express your love for me.

No, I won't have it. I need to be with her now. There are only a few hours left, and she's up at the house. I want her here, now, to share the last of this glorious afternoon with me.

'Adela?'

'Yes?' I'm surprised. I've hardly ever known Tristram interrupt me when I'm playing the piano.

'Will you take a walk with me?' He looks at me with an intensity which is unnerving, yet exciting, as a lover might do.

I close the lid of the piano, intrigued. There's something about him which I can't ignore.

We walk out over the orchard and down the track past Coney Piece. It's a beautiful afternoon, with that musty, tobacco and fruit cake smell of autumn. When we reach Reed Pond, Tristram spreads the ground sheet he's brought with him over an old log. He takes my hand and asks me to sit. He lowers himself beside me. He turns towards me and then looks away.

'Do you remember when we came here once, and I caught a frog which stained your frock with yellow liquid?'

'And I had to pretend to Mama that it'd come from a bird in the sky, just to protect you?'

'And I gave you a present to show how grateful I was that you hadn't blamed me?'

'And that present was wild strawberries, which made an even worse stain on one of the armchair covers?'

'And so I cut my finger to make it look like blood?'

'What a naughty boy you were, and sometimes I think you still are.'

We watch a wren hopping amongst the undergrowth at the side of the pond.

'Adela?' He doesn't follow this up.

'Adela?'

'Yes?'

'When we're no longer…'

I look at his face. It's cracked with grief.

'Hush,' I say. 'It's all right. Whatever happens, it won't be for ever. If I'm sent to Germany alone, I'll come back when the war's over, I promise. If I'm sent with Mama, I'll look after her. And if she's repatriated, but not me, she'll be with Grandmama and Great Uncle Gerd, and you and I can look after Papa.'

I see that tears have formed in his eyes. One rolls slowly down his cheek. I place my hand in his. 'There, it will be all right.'

He looks away. He doesn't want me to see his tears. 'Will you come here sometimes?'

'With you? Of course, my darling.'

'Even if I'm not here?'

It's a strange question, but I reply, 'If you like. But what if I...' Now a tear is falling down my cheek too.

Tristram looks full into my face, no longer attempting to hide his tears. 'If we're not able to be together, you will understand?'

'Of course I will. Don't worry about me. Wherever I am, I won't forget.'

'Thank you.' He does little more than breathe the words, but even so I can tell that his voice is thick with emotion.

'Come on,' I say, rising to my feet. 'I'm not much of a composer, but I'll write a short piece for you at the piano. We can compose it together. We'll call it Tristram's song.'

We walk back up the hill, discussing the form of the music.

18th October 1915

I've moved around the house silently, gathering the few things I need for the journey. My little pile of farewell messages rests on the dining room table. I blow out the candle and unlatch the door. They're all asleep upstairs.

The air is cold and sharp and still. I can hear cattle snorting down in the yard. There are a few stars, but no sign of dawn yet. It's still an hour before the first men will start to assemble, stamping their feet and blowing on their hands.

I can just see the outline of the house, Mother and Father's room on the left, Adela's on the right. I must walk quickly away.

Goodbye. I may yet see you all again.

author's notes

Fiction from the Facts

Corncrakes, once the sound of summer in rural Britain, started to die out in the second half of the nineteenth century. By 1909 they had almost completely disappeared from the South of England. The reason was changing agricultural practices, as described in the early scenes of the novel. I used the title *The Corncrake* to represent Richard, a dying 'breed' who was resisting change and would become damaged by his refusal to adapt. I have heard corncrakes in Donegal. It's a monotonous sound, like a nail being drawn across a metal comb, on and on. But I was filled with wonderment.

Schrebergarten were real. They were invented by a man called Schreber in Leipzig exactly as Tristram described. I am not aware that they were ever used to solve the labour shortage in agriculture. Would Tristram's plan have succeeded had the war not intervened? We will never know.

Ethel Smyth, Thomas Beecham and all the other composers, conductors and music personalities in the novel were all real people, with the exception of Mr Fielder-Grilsen. I confess to presenting Ethel Smyth as something of a caricature. These days she would be described as bi-sexual rather than a lesbian. I wanted Tristram's emphasis on her attraction to women to be a goad for Richard's possessive protection of Adela.

There are several versions of the story of how *Silent Night* came to be composed. Helga's is probably incorrect, but it is rather sweet and, since she is a fictitious character, I have no problem with her embellishment of the story.

To query whether Tristram's objections to the Old Testament are based on fact is to ask the wrong question. The point is that they are all there in the Bible, whether fact or not: Moses ordered the stoning to death of a man for picking up sticks on the Sabbath (Numbers Chapter 15). He ordered genocide, rape and slavery against the Midianites on a massive scale (Numbers Chapter 31). Moses, commanded by God, destroyed "the remembrance" of the Amalekites (Exodus Chapter 17). He broke his own rules by marrying a woman from another tribe (Numbers Chapters 12 & 36). Worshiping other gods led to execution, not just of the person who committed the crime, but by eradication of all the people connected with that person (Deuteronomy Chapter 13). Whether these stories are true or not is not the issue. The point is that they are there in the foundations of two major religions propounding morality: Judaism and Christianity.

There are many instances in the Bible where child sacrifice is condemned, utterly. But there is also some evidence that child sacrifice to Yahweh took place in ancient times at the Tophet. This is a complex subject, and I am not qualified to give an opinion on it. All I wanted to show was that Tristram joined Walter Grattin and his team with an open mind as to what they might uncover.

The war of 1914-18 has suffered from having several titles: The Great War, the First World War, World War One and even WWI. For the sake of simplicity, I will simply refer to it here as the War. For obvious reasons, I only addressed the War on the western front, although I did mention the Dardanelles and Gallipoli briefly.

I am often astounded by the misconceptions regarding the War, yet perhaps I shouldn't be. The futility, waste and sheer horror of the great trench battles of 1915, 1916 and 1917, The Somme and Passchendaele in particular, dominate our impressions. What is forgotten, or perhaps inadequately understood, is that there were more casualties per day in the opening weeks of the War, and almost as many in the final year, than in the stalemate of the trenches. The bloodiest day of the War on the western front was 22nd August 1914, when 27,000 Frenchmen were killed in Alsace and Lorraine. (On the first day of the Battle of the Somme, 19,000 British were killed.)

Another misconception is that the War was static. From October 1914 to February 1918, it was, but in the early weeks and the final eight months, the armies were mostly on the move, and strategically that is when the most important battles were fought. The Battle of the Marne, little over a month after the War had started, is one of the most important battles in British history, and was even more crucial for the French. Why was it so strategically important? Because it prevented Germany from sweeping to a rapid victory, and once the Germans had dug in after their retreat from The Marne, the nature of the War changed utterly for the next three and a half years until March 1918. From The Marne onwards, we can now see with hindsight that Germany was on balance unlikely to win the War, even though the War had run less than five percent of its course. Yet on the centenary in 2014, the media hardly mentioned the Battle of the Marne.

Conscription became law in January 1916, shortly after Tristram left to join the army. Had he not gone in October 2015, he would have faced the decision a few months later as to whether to be conscripted or registered (and consequently jailed) as a conscientious objector.

All the battles and other incidents in the War happened as I have described them, and I have been faithful to the dates.

All of the newspaper extracts read by Tristram have been quoted verbatim, whether passed on by Mercury of the Tack Room or not. The posters referred to were also completely real. All the Acts of Parliament referred to by Tristram and Colonel Sawbridge were also fact.

Who was Mercury of the Tack Room? I haven't a clue! Some mysteries in real life are unsolved, and so

I believe some may reasonably be unsolved in fiction.

The origin of the myth of the Angel of Mons is interesting. A month after the battle, an author called Arthur Machen wrote a fable called *The Bowmen,* about some phantom archers who protected British soldiers. In spite of Machen's insistence that his story was fiction, it was seized upon and spread as fact.

I have followed the history of censorship during the War to the letter, and the hazardous way it could be got round, as attempted by Tristram and Helga.

Helga and Adela would have been classed as Enemy Aliens. Remarkably, women who were born in Germany really would have qualified potentially for repatriation, unless they had been resident in Britain for thirty-five years or more.

The Advisory Committee for Repatriation did exist, and its terms of reference were as I have stated. I have used the names of the actual members of the Committee. In practice, women of alien origin were usually not repatriated, although many were. I have presented many reasons why Helga's and consequently Adela's positions were precarious. Would they have been repatriated? It's more fun to let the reader decide.

I wanted to show how the War was prolonged by two forces not given the attention today that they deserve. One was the endorsement of the War by the Church of England, personified by Richard. The cry of 'For God, King and Country' may seem absurd to us today, but it was a strong motivator at the time. So was the mentality that the nation should keep fighting in order that those who had gone before should not have died in vain.

The second cause was the bile of hatred spewed forth by the worst of the press, in particular the publications of the Harmsworth brothers, Alfred, First Viscount Northcliffe, and Harold, First Viscount Rothermere. These men between them had immense political power, and controlled a majority of Britain's newspapers and news magazines. The rantings of the *Daily Mail* and in particular *John Bull*, the latter published by the MP Horatio Bottomley, are frequently quoted in *The Corncrake*. Their effect on those surrounding the Hall family was, of course, fictitious. But their poisoning of the mood of the country was not. There can be no doubt that the Germans committed serious atrocities against civilians, far greater than Tristram implied, particularly in Belgium. But the press's portrayal of the Hun who went around bayonetting babies created a mood which, I believe, did much to prolong the War. Even so, I find it fascinating that loathing of Germans was much stronger in the First World War than in the Second, even though the Germans were committing far worse atrocities in the latter.

I have drawn on two excellent books for much of my inspiration for *The Corncrake*. These are *The Enemy in our Midst: Germans in Britain during the First World War*, by Panikos Panayi (Berg Publishers Limited, 1991), and *Keep the Home Fires Burning: Propaganda in the First World War*, by Cate Haste (Penguin Books, 1977).

Finally, I should like to acknowledge that I have

used quotations from the writings of Nietzsche as translated and relayed by the great and ever-lucid H L Mencken. I refer the reader to the large number of books either written by Mencken on Nietzsche, or written by Nietzsche and translated by Mencken. They can be found by perusing the lists on Amazon and other book retailers.

readers review

I do hope that you've enjoyed *The Corncrake*. I'd be delighted if you would take the time to leave a review on Amazon. Reviews are so important to authors, and do not have to be too long or detailed. Just a word to say that you liked the book would be very much appreciated.

Charles Moberly

viewauthor.at/CharlesMoberly

also by charles moberly

The Scrotum Toad

Tangle is a tree-hugger who is often mistaken for a glamorous witch. She is proud of her organic smallholding in the heart of Africa.

When threatened by a bullying and corrupt businessman who starts trashing the environment and the local people, who can she turn to?

Surely not that foul-mouthed Aussie TV presenter, nor those famous and fabulously wealthy international holidaymakers who suddenly invade her precious patch. And how could an international food-eating competition, sponsored by the USA's tin-eared goodwill ambassador, solve her problems?

Surrounded by xenophobic bickering, Tangle struggles to assert her authority, aided by some unlikely admirers.

The Scrotum Toad is an outrageous comic novel which will have the easily offended spluttering over their lattes. Nationalities, cultures and occupations are satirised shamelessly.

You have been warned.

Available on Amazon in Paperback and Kindle

Coming soon...

Try the Leopard's Mouth

Briony and Tom, both in their twenties, are very different characters. But opposites attract, and in business and in love, they complement each other.

The onset of the Rhodesian – Zimbabwean War of Independence tears at the couple's relationship. Misunderstandings arise from their conflicting personalities and from external pressures. Events pull them apart, but also bind them together.

Try the Leopard's Mouth is a romantic thriller set in Africa. But it is also a historical novel, grounded in real events in the period 1970-80.

Printed in Great Britain
by Amazon

80506315R00233